SUNDERED REIGN

THE CHRONICLES OF FREYLAR

- VOLUME 4 -

by

Liam W H Young

First edition printing, 2019

ISBN 978-1-78972-459-2

Copyright © Liam William Hamilton Young 2019.

All characters appearing in this work are fictitious. Any resemblance to real persons, living or dead, is purely coincidental.

All rights reserved. No part of this book may be reproduced in any manner without written permission except in the case of brief quotations included in critical articles and reviews. For further information, please contact the author.

Cover Illustration Copyright © Liam William Hamilton Young 2019, moral rights reserved by Hardy Fowler.

A catalogue copy of this book is available from the British Library.

Printed and bound in the United Kingdom by Biddles.

www.thechroniclesoffreylar.com

ACKNOWLEDGEMENTS

Foremost, I would like to thank Hardy Fowler once again for the excellent cover art illustration for this book. Hardy is an absolute pleasure to work with, and really understands my vision for the world of Freylar.

Again, I would like to thank Matthew Webster for his enormous contribution to this book, and the series as a whole. Matt continues to be an amazing sounding board for this ongoing project, and I am extremely fortunate to have him along for the ride with his invaluable editing services.

Always, my thanks go to Kevin Forster for his experienced counsel regarding the correct use of medieval weaponry.

Lastly, thank you to Tibor Mórocz for proofreading this book. His keen perception continues to challenge me, giving me the impetus I need to complete my storytelling.

I dedicate this book to all those struggling authors working tirelessly to bring their stories to life. During my time spent working on The Chronicles of Freylar, I have learned so much about good writing and storytelling – the hard way – now fully appreciating just how difficult it is to create a complex written series. However, these invaluable lessons are just the beginning of an author's journey; the never-ending struggle to promote one's own work is an enormous challenge, sadly one that frequently claims the existence of many amazing stories, forever confining them to obscurity. I am fortunate that my written works are now creeping into the light, in part due to my own determination, but also because of you, the readers, the fans, to whom I am forever grateful for spreading word of my own work. Thank you all.

TABLE OF CONTENTS

ONE Confession

TWO Pyre

THREE Escape

FOUR Honesty

FIVE Loyalty

SIX Hunted

SEVEN Fulcrum

EIGHT Pawn

NINE Resolve

TEN Deception

ELEVEN Louperdu

TWELVE Consequences

THIRTEEN Revenant

though she does not wish to serve them. On this point, she and I have opposing views, and I need you to understand that fact.'

'I get it Nathaniel; my eyes are wide open now. She lives alone in her self-indulgent tower. Surrounded by aides and house guards, who continue to serve her in fear of her silent wrath.'

'Until recently, Mirielle's rule was administered more subtly, guided carefully by Aleska's counsel. But our queen stands alone now, her only crutch being Marcus. The Blade Lord serves Mirielle obediently, through a strong sense of loyalty, and, dare I say, love…'

'You believe Marcus has feelings for Mirielle?'

'For someone who is generally quite perceptive, Rayna, where matters of the heart are concerned, you frequently lack awareness. But, I will give you a pass on this occasion; it cannot be easy for you, living in a female body.'

'It was a struggle when I first acquired Alarielle's body. However, things are different now; your daughter has aided me with the transition, in addition to Kirika's own, less subtle, efforts.' replied Rayna, gesturing towards her fitted attire.

He laughed softly. The sound of his voice echoed around the chamber where The Guardian had first woken into Freylar. He watched as the warm moisture from his breath lingered in the air; the normally cool cavern was now bitterly cold due to winter's caress, which had come early to the vale. The ground was hard under foot, and the typically verdant landscape now looked barren and naked – where it protruded through the snow at all – save for the evergreens, still clinging to their beauty, unlike their deciduous kin.

FOURTEEN Misdirection

FIFTEEN Fallen

SIXTEEN Arbiter

SEVENTEEN Insurrection

EIGHTEEN Cordon

NINETEEN Trial

TWENTY Nemesis

TWENTY ONE Genesis

EPILOGUE

DRAMATIS PERSONAE

ONE
Confession

'We need to talk.'

'Yes...we do. But why here Nathaniel?' asked R[a] inquisitively. 'If it's privacy you're after, we would h[ave] had that back at our tree. Was it necessary for me to m[eet] you here, of all places?'

The Cave of Wellbeing was like a second home [to] him, given his rank amongst the renewalists, though h[e] failed to appreciate the location's meaning to his surr[ogate] daughter. For Rayna, the site represented her genesis [as] Freylar, and for her growing number of followers, the renewalists' private sanctuary was fast becoming a pl[ace of] reverence as birthplace to The Guardian. It was comm[on] knowledge that Rayna loathed the title of Guardian, b[ut the] light bringer had done nothing to dispel the label ped[dled] predominantly by others.

'Privacy was not my only reason, but all will bec[ome] clear after I explain the situation.'

'You mean the growing civil unrest throughout t[he] vale?'

'In part.' he said, releasing a heavy sigh. 'Rayn[a, I am] not an honourable Freylarkin. I have done – and wil[l] continue to do – many questionable things. My actio[ns,] of which I have executed in the shadows, have shape[d] Freylarian society.'

'For the better, I hope.'

'I sincerely believe so. My actions protect the [people] and have never been motivated by self-interest or pe[rsonal] gain. That is where – I believe at least – I differ fro[m the] queen. In her heart, Mirielle wants to help the peop[le]

'At any rate, Mirielle's judgement is impaired, and her rule is waning. She loses support with each passing cycle, giving rise to the increased civil unrest that you mentioned.'

'What's your point, Nathaniel? Need I remind you that it's freezing in here?'

He laughed once more. Rayna possessed the knack of finding a way to cut to the heart of any matter, dealing with awkward situations head on, in a jovial manner, using humour and banter to achieve her goals without damaging her relationships with others. He found Rayna's approach refreshing. He admired her inoffensive straight talking and ability to get the job done, as did many others. The Guardian had been instrumental in repelling two invasions since her arrival in Freylar. Furthermore, her descent from the realm of the Sky-Walkers, and her ability to defy the Narlakai's attempts to consume her soul, had given rise to her demi-god status. Rayna had won the adoration of the forest dwellers, earned the favour of the civilian Freylarkai living in and around the Tri-Spires, and now she had the respect of The Blades. In addition, there were those who actively revered The Guardian; previously, this type of behaviour had been limited to The Vengeful Tears, but now scenes of worship were becoming more commonplace. For the Freylarkai, Rayna had become both a symbol of hope and a herald of change.

'My point is this: I am about to tug on some old strings, for a second time, the results of which could lead to further release.' he said, holding Rayna's stare. 'But regardless of my intentions, I *need* you to understand my motives.'

'And these intended actions, are they a result of the public sentencing tomorrow?'

'The Queen's recent actions are symptomatic of her growing insecurities, of which I have been aware for some time now. Freylar is still relatively new to you Rayna, as such there are a great many things that you are blissfully unaware of.'

'Then perhaps you could fill me in, starting with Caleth?'

He sighed heavily again, before gesturing towards the stone plinth where his daughter's body had lain when first inhabited by Rayna. The light bringer had a concerned look about her, perhaps because his choice of perch had a sense of finality about it. It was then that he realised the insensitivity of his request.

'I am sorry. Would you prefer to sit elsewhere? I realise that this place may be uncomfortable for you.' he said, cursing himself for his insensitivity.

'I appreciate your acceptance Nathaniel – having robbed Alarielle of her body – but I am finding it difficult to shake the notion of theft.'

'My daughter's soul had already departed from that body, so the only consent you required was mine, as her father, which you have. But if you like, we can descend to one of the lower caverns?'

'No, this will be fine; I have exorcised the demons from my former life, and now I must do the same for this life.'

'Then let us sit closely together and share each other's warmth. I will do my best to explain objectively how we came to this point.'

Rayna nodded, after which they sat down next to each other on the cold hard floor, their backs pressed firmly against the stone plinth.

'I remember when Kirika found me here, shortly before your arrival. I was a mess, but she pulled me back from the depths of my despair, giving me the kick I needed to go on. I was ready to end it all here; in my heart, I knew that Alarielle would not be returning to me, but my mind could not accept the fact. Together, you have saved me, and I am indebted to you both. My priority is the future of the Freylarkai, but I will do anything I can for the two of you. Now, Kirika needs help, and I intend to save her. I would like you to join me in this, Rayna, since you have a significant role to play. However, I cannot ask this of you without being completely transparent.'

'What do you mean exactly?'

'You need to be aware of my agenda, and the deeds I have undertaken in pursuing it. As I said to you earlier, I am not an honourable Freylarkin. Now you will learn why...'

'We need to talk.'

'Yes...we do. But why here Nathaniel?' asked Heldran plainly.

'Because if word of my colluding with you gets back to The Blades, there is every chance that I will be expelled from the Order, irrespective of Korlith's reaction to your own presence here.'

'How did it get to this?' asked Heldran wearily. 'Such loathing between our Orders.'

'Because we tolerate it!' he said bluntly. 'For too long now we have sat back and allowed Caleth to drive an ever-widening wedge between our Orders. His paranoia is without limit, and your Order's elusive behaviour has placed further strain on the turbulent relationship that exists between our commanders. Despite my teachings, I alone cannot expunge the poison Caleth has been spreading throughout The Blades for tens of passes. Caleth's distrust of the Knights Thranis is now innate; there can be no arbitration between The Blade Lord and Korlith at this juncture – we are well past that now.'

'I understand what you say, but I cannot move against Korlith, despite his failings.' replied Heldran in his deep imposing voice.

'And that is not what I ask of you; I appreciate that loyalty is the foundation upon which your Order is built. Besides, Korlith is not the problem, despite his secretive ways. You now command the unwavering respect of the knights; you will be the next Knight Lord – we both know this.'

'He still has a great many passes left in him, and the damage wrought by Caleth is deep-seated within our Orders; it cannot be purged, at least not in a single generation. I myself have been polluted by its ongoing affects and can no longer discern truth amidst all the lies.' explained Heldran. 'Of The Blades, I choose to believe your tongue alone, Nathaniel – despite your agendas.'

'Thank you, old friend.' he said with a warm smile. 'I agree with your grim assessment, however, we can stem the flow and give future generations a reprieve. They will be the ones to form a new trust. We can at least try to facilitate future change in direction by altering the present.'

'And what would that alteration look like?'

'It is simple; we release Caleth!'

There was no discernible reaction from Heldran following his blunt proposal, yet the knight's lack of visible emotion was not unexpected. They had faced many challenges together in the past, all of which had added to the weight of the knight's burden over the passes, ergo Heldran was no longer fazed by the notion of release. After a quiet moment of contemplation, the knight looked at him sternly.

'You are seriously suggesting that we do away with The Blade Lord? Nathaniel, you are mad to consider such action.'

'I would rather choose madness than cling to the foolish hope that Caleth's paranoia will not destroy us from within. If we do not act now, distrust between our Orders will be the least of our concerns.'

'You imply open war between us.'

'Yes, I believe that is a likely outcome.' he replied flatly. 'Caleth's paranoia stems from his insecurities, and the Knights Thranis are a threat to his command.'

'We have no desire to instigate an insurrection.'

'*I* know that, but *he* will not believe it.'

'But release…Nathaniel, you risk too much. Think of the political fallout if you or I were caught. Would it not add more fuel to the fire? Regardless, where are the ethics in all of this? And there is your daughter to consider. What does Alarielle's future look like if you, in particular, are caught?' Heldran paused for a moment to consider the strength of their relationship, before pressing the point further by citing a matter that was still raw for him. 'You are a single parent now Nathaniel. Much has been taken from you already – can your soul endure further loss?'

'I understand the risks, Heldran, but doing nothing courts further danger. We need to rid ourselves of this contagion to prevent further infection of our ranks. Already, the poison has spread to my own abode; Alarielle herself distrusts you – I see it in her eyes. If we do nothing, you and I will be forced to stand opposite one another, upon the precipice of war, from which one of us *will* fall.'

'You are over-dramatizing the current state of affairs.'

'Am I? Those Blades who have openly challenged Caleth's will have all been sent on senseless sorties to the borderlands – none of whom have returned.' he said pointedly, seeking to convey the gravity of the situation.

Heldran did not reply immediately. Instead, the knight considered his words carefully before finally choosing to respond. The knight's giant physique and battle-tested countenance veiled his pragmatic approach to decision making. Heldran was a master of illusion, a trait that he greatly admired.

'You are certain of this?' asked Heldran in a foreboding tone.

'I would not claim it to be so, otherwise.'

'Then this is indeed a problem. Freylar has enough enemies eroding its ranks already, it can ill afford to feed on itself.'

'Then you agree that this needs to be done?'

'Reluctantly…yes.'

'I did not want to ask this of you Heldran, but there are so few that I can trust, and I cannot do this alone. I need someone I can rely on to watch my back.'

'And you shall have it. I give you my word.'

'Thank you.'

'Consider it a debt repaid.'

'You owe me nothing.'

'Do not lie to me Nathaniel – I am not blind to your machinations.'

He chose not to give credence to the knight's suspicions. The last thing he wanted to do was to saddle the knight with further secrets. Over the passes, Heldran had built up an extensive network of contacts and informants, meaning that information flowed readily to the experienced knight, who was a master of information gathering. It was surprising, therefore, that Heldran had not learnt of The Blades' ill-fated sorties to the borderlands. It was possible that he had overestimated the reach of Heldran's information network, or perhaps Caleth had simply outmanoeuvred the Knights Thranis, he mused. Given the risks at stake, he chose to believe the latter.

'So, where do we start?'

'I believe it is imperative that we do not underestimate The Blade Lord.'

'Meaning what, exactly?'

'First, we need the right tools for the job. Then we eliminate his support network, before finally making our move.'

'I see.' said Heldran curiously, 'And where do you propose that we procure these *tools*?'

'I know someone; his methods are unorthodox, but he gets results.'

'Do you trust him?'

'No, not at all, but it is only his talent that I am interested in. He does not need to know about any of this.'

'Fair enough. And what is his name?'

'His name is Krashnar.'

'You're leaving?'

'Yes.' replied the knight flatly. 'I have overstayed my welcome, plus I must lead The Vengeful Tears to the Ardent Gate where they can begin their training.'

'Vorian, you are always welcome here.'

'In your company, yes, but others are wary of my presence in the vale.'

'You mean Queen Mirielle – despite saving her from that wretched abomination.'

'The Queen, The Blade Lord, others... Rayna, this place is fractured. Someone needs to find a way to mend its wounds, before they become untreatable. My presence here irritates that wound.'

'I take it that you plan to leave on foot?'

'Yes. It will be some time before The Vengeful Tears become privy to our secrets.'

'Makes sense.'

She was sad to learn of the knight's departure, though she was not the least bit surprised to learn of the news. Vorian had completed his mission – alerting the vale to Krashnar's presence – and now intended to shepherd The Vengeful Tears back to the Ardent Gate. There, the once disillusioned Blades would begin new lives, where they would integrate with the Knights Thranis by training to become knights themselves. Part of her was jealous of Dumar and the others, and of the adventures they would undertake as members of the knights' Order. The knights lead uncomplicated lives along Freylar's southern lands; theirs was a simple and honest existence, which she greatly admired, and missed. Quite the opposite of life in the vale, which was fast becoming mired in politics since her return.

'Will you at least stay for Ragnar's pyre?'

'Of course.' Vorian replied. 'Though I did not have the honour of fighting alongside Ragnar in battle, nonetheless, I would very much like to honour his passing. But Rayna, are you sure my presence is wise?'

'Ragnar was a warrior. He was not the administrative type, and was unwilling to be shackled to a bench. He knew the risks – as do we all – and he chose to sacrifice himself defending what he believed in. He would have wanted a send-off befitting a warrior. You helped us, and you helped the Captain, to defend the vale, as did The Vengeful Tears. You have all earned the right to attend the ceremony. As a fellow warrior, Ragnar would have welcomed your presence.'

'Very well.' replied the knight. 'We shall attend and honour his passing.'

'Good. However, in the interests of politics, it might be prudent for you to stand near to me.'

'In *your* company.' said Vorian, followed by a wry grin.

'Baby steps, Vor.'

The knight laughed heartily before extending his right hand. She clasped his hand firmly, after which they pulled each other close, giving one other a firm pat across the back. She had welcomed Vorian's aid during the recent invasion, and enjoyed seeing the knight's confidence grow during his brief stay in the vale. There was little doubt in her mind that the knight would develop into a sound commander, provided he continued to push himself and welcome new experiences. Although reserved at times – due to his insecurities – she saw the same potential in the knight that Heldran surely recognised. She was convinced that the Knight Lord had deliberately sent Vorian to the vale to help develop his confidence.

'Think of the vale as a rough stone; in time we will erode it, thus fashioning it into a smooth pebble.'

'I have little doubt that your charisma will achieve such, but you must ensure that you surround yourself with those whom you trust. They will guard your back, which you alone cannot do. The physical battle may be over, but now you face dangers far worse – those that you cannot see! As I understand it from the others, you have done well to win the support of the vale during your short time in Freylar, but your actions will have incurred the ire of others. Their backs are to the wall now, Rayna, and that is when they will fight at their fiercest. Just be careful, and do not allow yourself to become a scapegoat – a malicious tongue can undo the greatest of heroes.'

'Thank you, Vor. I appreciate your counsel, as well as the protection that you and the Vengeful Tears provided for our queen. Although Mirielle did not thank you in person, I do so now on her behalf. Please extend my thanks to the others.'

'You are welcome, Honorary Knight Rayna. We each swore an oath to aid you in light of what you did for our Order. Each of us will honour that oath. Besides, you are family now, despite the distance that separates us.'

She nodded respectfully, accepting the knight's oath as fulfilled. Saving Knight Restorant Loredan, Knight Captain Gedrick, and the others, meant a great deal to the Knights Thranis. Without her aid, it was likely that the Order would have received a hammer blow from which it may not have recovered.

'Also, please inform Heldran of my appreciation. Without your intervention, it is likely that we would not have been able to convince certain individuals to heed Darlia's warning of a renewed invasion. Moreover, Queen Mirielle would have been released.'

'I shall indeed, although I suspect that latter part may in fact not have been overly helpful, judging by her reaction to Darlia's words in the arena.'

'Mirielle's release would have riled the Freylarkai, possibly even compelling them to act without thought. The way I see it, the Queen's changed disposition is becoming a problem, but the issue needs to be dealt with delicately – martyrdom creates other issues.'

'I understand.'

'Well then, the ceremony is this evening. They are already building the pyres in the arena.'

'There were others whose bodies were brought back?' asked the knight with a surprised look.

'Yes. Most of the released were desiccated by the Narlakai, who – as you know – leave nothing besides empty husks that have since been scattered to the wind. However, Lileah's pet chimera was another matter entirely; the beast left a trail of broken bodies in its wake before the Captain was able to bring it down.'

'What of the renewalists?'

Secretly she hoped that Vorian would not press his enquiry, but the knight was nothing if not thorough.

'Most were unable to tend to the casualties in time, largely due to my own actions. Apparently, blindness is not conducive to helping the wounded.' she said, sarcastically rebuking herself.

'Do not be so hard on yourself. As I understand it, if you had not done that which you did, the remaining Blades would have been overrun, leading to slaughter in the vale. This was a victory for the Freylarkai.'

'The end justifies the means?'

'Rayna, war is ugly.'

'I know. Nonetheless, this victory feels hollow.' she said, trying not to sound dejected. 'The attack on Scrier's Post rocked The Blades, but this latest encounter has devastated our ranks. Lileah's failed invasion has also damaged relations between key individuals.'

'You are resourceful – you *will* find a way – and from the ashes of this unfortunate situation will rise something much stronger, tempered by strife and loss.'

'I sincerely hope that you are right, Vor. In any event, I suggest that we go round up Dumar and the others. The politics can wait. This evening, we pay our respects to the fallen Captain.'

TWO
Pyre

'Ready the torches!'

His words echoed across the arena, despite the impressive number of Freylarkai present, all of whom had turned up to honour the released. Aside from the crackle and fizz of a single lit brazier, his voice alone made the only sound; not a single murmur passed the lips of those present, all of whom stood perfectly still – despite the cold bite of winter – out of respect for the fallen. At Kirika's request, six pyres had been constructed in the arena by civilian telepaths. Five of these were erected in positions that formed a large circle, with the sixth at its centre. The wooden pyres had been stacked incredibly high, and upon each lay the broken bodies of those who had fought valiantly in battle. He rebuked himself for not knowing all of the fallen as well as they had each deserved, but such was the nature of command and his rank of Blade Lord. It was impossible to know the lives of all those under his command who he committed to battle, although in light of the Order's recent substantial losses, perhaps that would change going forward, he mused. Regardless, he knew the impressively built red-haired Freylarkin atop of the central pyre all too well: Ragnar, Captain of The Blades, and life-long close friend. He reminded himself that service to The Blades courted release with each passing cycle, nevertheless, the cold reality of loss weighed heavily on his soul. Despite the Captain's gruff and ill-mannered nature, Ragnar had been a true friend over the countless passes they had fought together. They had saved each other from release on many occasions, although Ragnar's last act of salvation had come with a heavy price; the Captain had selflessly sacrificed his life to save them all from certain release, following a brutal onslaught from Lileah's ferocious chimera. The savage creature had unexpectedly – after flanking their force with its preternatural speed – devastated their ranks. The beast's colossal bulk had battered The Blade's archers, scattering and trampling their bodies underfoot in its horrendous charge. Although he had been the one to end the creature's unrelenting rampage, ultimately he had been unable to bring the beast down during the violent encounter. That task had fallen to the Captain, who had bravely received the creature's renewed charge in order to finish the job that he had started. He cursed himself for failing to take down the chimera alone. Had he done so, there would be one less corpse atop the pyres standing before them now.

One-by-one, the Freylarkai entrusted to light the bonfires lit their torches, before gathering around the six pyres ready to reduce the bodies of the fallen to ash.

'Is there anyone here who wishes to speak for the released, before we cast their ashes to the wind?'

Though he was accustomed to public speaking, he had always relied on Ragnar to rally The Blades. As a public figure, he was inspirational – he was keenly aware of the fact – and he could charm almost any individual. Yet he lacked the grit and passion necessary to embolden the mob; Ragnar had always been the one to ignite the fire within their hearts.

'I will speak for the released.'

The solitary voice was immediately recognizable. He turned his head towards Rayna, now habitually referred to by The Blades as The Guardian. Kirika and her elder sister

Darlia, whose presence was taboo, flanked the demi-god light bringer. Vorian of the Knights Thranis stood close by too, accompanied by his newly adopted Vengeful Tears. Both Nathanar and Natalya were also part of the formidable group. The allegiance – now on public display – between Rayna and the scrying sisters made him feel uneasy. Together they represented a powerful triad, rooted in solid foundations. Kirika – much like Rayna – commanded the respect of the people, and her recent actions during the battle for Bleak Moor had put her in good standing with her fellow Blades, bringing her back into the fold. This rise in popularity and her position on the ruling council, in addition to her political prowess, placed her at the fore of Freylar's direction. However, it was her sister, Darlia, who represented the greater concern. The once-notorious scrier had earned a measure of respect from the people in light of her public address to the Freylarkai, warning them of Lileah's invasion. The Freylarkai's short memories had seemingly forgotten – or perhaps they had conveniently chosen to forget – Darlia's past transgressions. The infamous scrier's return to Freylar represented an open challenge to Mirielle's rule, given Darlia's public exile by the Queen for pushing the boundaries of her ability. Darlia's return was a problem that needed handling carefully. Then there was Rayna herself, more commonly referred to as The Guardian due to her unique arrival in Freylar, and her instrumental role in thwarting two invasions of their domain. Rayna's popularity grew with each passing cycle, and there were those who actively revered the light bringer due to her demi-god status. In addition, Rayna had earned the respect and loyalty of The Knights Thranis, as well as that of the surviving Blades, including Nathanar and Natalya. He could feel the reigns of command slipping between his fingers as fresh pieces moved across the board, encroaching on his position. Though he harboured no animosity to any of his peers – Darlia being the possible exception – he was not blind to the shifting mood of the people and the desire for change. Once more, The Guardian had the opportunity to address the mob – he was powerless to stop it – which would no doubt bolster the public's perception of her. He considered the possibility that Rayna failed to fully realise the consequences of her actions, and that it was simply her way, having allegedly squandered her previous life amongst the Sky-Walkers before arriving in Freylar. However, there was nothing conventional about Rayna. The Guardian had repeatedly tackled difficult situations in an unexpected manner, catching opponents off guard, including Lothnar. He wondered how he would fare if an unfortunate situation arose pitting them against one another, and hoped dearly that such a scenario would never play out. However, he was not blind to the fact that Rayna's actions now irritated Mirielle, at a time when Freylar's queen was almost certainly at her most insecure. With Aleska gone – away on other business – he was the only one who could hope to manage Mirielle's increasingly capricious behaviour. He could feel the burden he shouldered increasing. Managing The Blades' battered morale, Mirielle's changed disposition, and the continued defence of Freylar weighed heavily upon him, and now he had lost a good friend, one who had provided a much-needed sounding board over the passes.

'As you wish.' he replied, offering Rayna an accepting nod.

He wondered where Thandor, Lothnar and Nathaniel stood amidst the sea of change, and whether they too would succumb to the allure of something different. Thandor took an informed view of all things, and always kept the bigger picture in mind. If not for his aloof nature, the veteran Paladin would have been suitable for the role of Blade Lord. Lothnar, by contrast, was an uncomplicated Freylarkin, frequently driven by predictable emotions. Lothnar distrusted scriers and was wary of The Guardian. He had also shunned Nathaniel's teachings and had enjoyed a close friendship with the released Captain, who had openly loathed scriers. It was difficult, therefore, to imagine the nomadic Paladin aligning himself with the once-divergent sisters. However, for the first time in as long as he could remember, he could sense the Paladin holding something back, like a key piece missing from a puzzle. Finally, there was The Teacher to consider – probably the most complicated of the three. Nathaniel had been his biggest supporter during his ascension to the role of Blade Lord. Over the passes, the much-respected Freylarkin had endorsed his command tirelessly, thus creating a strong bond between them. However, the sudden loss of Nathaniel's daughter, Alarielle, had understandably disrupted The Teacher's focus, which had previously been resolute. Nathaniel's world was subsequently tipped upside-down by the arrival of Rayna, who now inhabited the restored body of his released daughter. Yet despite the unforeseen turmoil, Nathaniel was loyal to The Blades and saw himself as a father figure to their Order. Given the hammer blow they had suffered in the wake of Lileah's invasion, The Teacher would likely have his hands full strengthening the Order at the grass roots. However, despite his favourable analysis, Nathaniel's close proximity to Rayna made him uneasy. When first Rayna had made a name for herself at Scrier's Post, he had supported her subsequent development, though he had not foreseen her alarming exponential rise in popularity. It was now impossible to wander the alleys surrounding the arena without overhearing enthusiastic talk of the renowned light bringer.

'I will miss Ragnar dearly.' said Rayna emphatically.

The Guardian remained where she stood, although she turned to face the bulk of the gathered crowd in the tiered stone seating.

'He could be gruff and unfriendly at times, plus he drove me mad with his incessant rambling at Bleak Moor on the eve of battle.' continued The Guardian, whose words prompted hearty laughter from the audience. 'Nevertheless, he was an inspiration to me – if not to all of us – and his release has left a gaping hole in our lives, largely due to his immense size.'

Once more, the crowd found the humour in the light bringer's words. Rayna deliberately tugged at their nostalgia in her habitual light-hearted manner, in a bid to win their favour.

'His memory, and those of the others who we honour this cycle, will live on in us all. Tales will be told of the Captain's annoying habits, but more importantly of the fact that he, and the others, gave *everything* to save our people. To forget their deeds, or worse, to forget *them*, is to dishonour them. I ask that we each remember those who have sacrificed themselves so that we can go on. Let us remember the released.'

Following her speech, The Guardian raised her left hand, deliberately displaying the scar that ran across her palm. Lothnar had caused the wound during her duel with the Paladin at the Trials. Since her unexpected victory in the arena that cycle, the unorthodox symbol had been used with great effect on multiple occasions, to rally The Blades behind the light bringer. The vivid scar – which Rayna deliberately refused to have healed – represented the light bringer's unwavering determination; it epitomised her resolve and the strength of mind, required to get the job done despite overwhelming odds. Ironically, it was the Order's most compliant Blade, Nathanar, who had first leveraged the symbol's power, with Natalya and Kirika following suit. Now, The Guardian used it herself to rally the gathered Freylarkai, each raising their left hand in response, thus giving further credence to her words. Rayna was a quick study, and with The Teacher's tutelage she had quickly learned how to handle herself in a fight. However, Nathaniel was not her only mentor; Kirika too played a role in her development. In addition to the martial arts imparted by Nathaniel, Rayna was now beginning to handle herself politically, by learning how to wield the invisible weapons of statecraft. If not correctly managed, The Guardian had the potential to become a formidable opponent, rather than a useful ally.

'Light them!' he said loudly, ending Rayna's sermon and giving the torchbearers the signal to set the pyres ablaze.

The thrown torches flew through the air before igniting their targets. Despite the cold damp touch of winter, the kindling performed its job admirably, immediately catching fire upon contact with the flaming projectiles. Within moments, the pyres were alight. The flames spread quickly, giving rise to impressive conflagrations each of which rapidly consumed their prey. The bodies of the fallen crackled and fizzed as the flames greedily devoured them. The audience looked on in silence. Aside from the fires burning furiously, there was no sound in the arena whilst those gathered quietly paid their respects. No tears were shed for the released; instead, a quiet moment was shared by those present in honour of The Blades who had fallen in battle. Ultimately, it was Rayna who was first to break the quiet solace.

'I remember Kryshar.' she said as they each watched the mesmerising flames consume their fallen comrades.

'I remember Katrin.' said Vorian unexpectedly, followed by Nathaniel, whose voice was full of emotion, 'I remember my wife and daughter.'

Across the arena, all those gathered announced in turn the names of loved ones who had since journeyed to the Everlife following release. It was a powerful public display of emotion, which he had never before witnessed in his time, spurred on by Freylar's habitual catalyst.

'What am I going to do with you?' he whispered quietly to himself, musing over what the future might hold for the pieces assembled before him.

She cried out in pain once more.

'My queen, with respect, you must remain still.' said the renewalist who had been diligently tending to her wounds since the attack.

'Can I be of assistance?' asked one of Kirika's aides.

The Freylarkin's feigned sincerity irked her, their presence likely serving the sole function of keeping the Fate

Weaver informed of her slow recovery. Two cycles had passed since the exiled shaper's attack. Krashnar's attempt to violate her – in her personal quarters no less – had been only partially successful, though she refused to acknowledge the fact publicly. She could still feel the sickening touch of his vile tongue sliding across her skin. In addition to the mental anguish she had suffered, her body had been ravaged by the shaper's perverse ability; Krashnar took great pleasure from shaping flesh, and had succeeded in deforming hers. Since the attack, her wounds had been expertly healed, courtesy of the renewalist loitering beside her bed, however, the mutilation of her body had been more problematic. By her decree, it was forbidden to work the flesh of another in Freylar, as such there were few with the ability to aid her. Therefore, as Freylar's most powerful shaper, she needed to help herself. Her attempts to correct her limbs – which had been grotesquely twisted – had been hit and miss. For each success, there had also been failure, followed by pain and the humiliation of the renewalist's necessary assistance. Working together, they had been able to undo most of the damage caused by the exile, though her left arm remained locked, unable to bend at the elbow that – her unique sight informed her – no longer existed. With the joint entirely gone, it fell to her to fashion a new one. Unfortunately, she lacked the experience working with flesh and bone necessary to do so.

'Leave me!' she barked angrily, causing the frightened aide to recoil before scurrying away. 'That goes for you as well!' she continued, now directing her venomous gaze towards the house guards, who loitered by the chamber's broken door.

'As you wish.' replied the guards in unison, before taking their leave.

She recognised one of the guards from the arena – Ralnor – who had previously disobeyed her order to apprehend Darlia during the scrier's commotion at the Trials.

'Not you! You will remain here.'

She decided then that she would take a personal interest in the house guard's future development in order to curtail any further disobedience. She commenced by picking him up on his previous oversight.

'You alone will guard me. Note that I expect you to carry out my orders this time.'

'Yes, my queen.' replied Ralnor nervously.

The lone guard quickly returned to his post by the battered door, which Vorian and The Vengeful Tears had ruined prior to driving Krashnar away. She supposed that Krasus would be the one to carry out repairs, given her weakened state; she made a mental note to summon the over-confident shaper to her chamber once she had finished tending to her injuries. Krashnar – who had made good his escape – had ambushed her in her quarters after stealing Hanarah's identity, using the Freylarkin's likeness to infiltrate the Tri-Spires. Security that cycle had been stretched thin due to the Trials, therefore she had refrained from reprimanding The Blade Lord for allowing Krashnar to be so bold. Besides, she could feel the walls closing in around her, thus she needed her allies – now was not the time to push them away. Marcus was loyal to her. The Blade Lord was one of the few Freylarkai whom she could trust implicitly, aside from Aleska. Since the venerable scrier's necessary departure, holes had begun to appear in her rule. Though she valued Marcus' counsel, he was a military Freylarkin at heart, and with the invasion over, she required a different type of cunning to manage the domain in the wake of Lileah's invasion.

'Ralnor, get me a Sky-Skitter. Ensure that it is one of our most reliable.'

'As you wish, my queen.'

The nervous house guard immediately turned and left the chamber, leaving her with the fastidious renewalist, who continued to loom over her bed.

'You need not remain here.'

'I will remain until your wounds are healed.'

'This is not a wound that you can heal.' she snapped, 'The joint no longer exists, ergo it cannot be healed by your ability.'

'You will create a new one.'

'Perhaps, but it will not be this cycle.' she said with growing frustration. 'If you want to help, go and find me something that I can practice on. Maybe that dire wolf that keeps loitering around here.'

She immediately regretted her choice of words, though she could no longer hold her anger in check. Krashnar had invaded her private space, violated her, and now she would be subject to ridicule due to her lame arm. Furthermore, her rule was being scrutinised and challenged by those who served her. In addition, there were exiles running around in Freylar, completely unchecked. She could feel the threads of her rule unwinding, prompted by the actions of a few – a state of affairs that she would quickly change, once back on her feet.

'I am sincerely sorry for your loss.' she said, turning to face her sister, whose pale cheeks glistened with tears.

They stood beside one another next to an unmarked grave near the base of the Eternal Falls. Natalya had helped them to move Lileah's body close to the site – minus her head, which had been pulped by Darlia's ornate mechanical claw. They had insisted on carrying Lileah's body between them, in private, to its final resting place. It was during this time that she appreciated the horrors inflicted on the released telepath's body. Digging Lileah's grave, in addition to carrying the increased weight of the Freylarkin's flesh-metal corpse, had taken its toll; she felt physically exhausted and her back ached.

'She chose to follow this path, though I must shoulder much of the blame for setting her upon it.'

'We each deserve a second chance.' she said sincerely.

'Hundreds have been released due to my actions.'

'Yes, but you saved thousands more by warning us of Lileah's invasion. Besides, you will spend the rest of your cycles helping the families of those victims of the Narlakai by giving them the closure they seek. After your encounter with their freed souls, you alone can do this.'

'That knowledge, which I shared with you in confidence, does not ease my burden, Kirika.'

'Nor should it. We are each defined by our actions. The important thing is that we learn from them.'

'Agreed, however, we are also responsible for them.'

'Indeed. When you and I return to the others, we will both face the consequences of our actions.'

'I am sorry for your poor standing with the Queen.'

'It was my choice, and a necessary one. Besides, Mirielle and I were on an inevitable collision course.'

'Have you scried the outcome?'

'Yes, but there are too many paths to trace, and Rayna intersects all of them.'

'The Guardian is your strongest ally, but also your greatest weakness.'

'Rayna blinds our second sight; nonetheless, it is a handicap of my own choosing.'

'You need to be careful and ensure that Mirielle does not find a way to discredit the light bringer – symbols can be tarnished, or worse, corrupted.'

'Your counsel is wise, and the thought had crossed my mind. With the exception of a few, allegiances are clear. Mirielle is not the type to divide and conquer – that is Aleska's forte. Mirielle lacks patience and the disposition for drawn out campaigns. She will look to deal our movement a critical blow using blunt instruments. For this reason, you must go into hiding.'

'But where would you have me go, sister? Who – beyond those in the Queen's line of fire – would dare offer me sanctuary? If I return to the borderlands, I cannot lend you my support.'

'Darlia, you do not need to flee the vale. You can hide amongst the very people over whom she rules.'

'Forgive me sister, but I lack your confidence.' replied Darlia, raising her conspicuous mechanical claw.

'That does not matter. The people will conceal you in their homes. Ordering the house guards to search the dwellings will harm Mirielle's standing with the people – she *will* realise this. Besides, the Queen cannot realistically search every home, and you will be on the move.'

'Kirika, I do not understand. Why would the Freylarkai take me in after everything I have done?'

'The people only know what Mirielle tells them, but what is more important to them is family. Tell them I have sent you. When you bring word to them of their loved ones who have journeyed to the Everlife, they will welcome you with open arms – the people *will* protect you.'

Darlia considered her words carefully, before wiping the tears from her face with her good hand. It pained her to see her sister so heartbroken. Despite everything her former lover had done, Darlia loved Lileah, even in release. It saddened her that Lileah's body needed to be buried in secret, away from prying eyes, but if the Freylarkai or Mirielle learned of its location, there was every chance the remains would be exhumed and put on public display.

'So be it. I will operate in the shadows, playing the role of the agitator by seeking to strengthen your name.'

'That is a bold move sister, and by no means without its share of danger. You will be on your own, you understand.'

Darlia smiled.

'Forgive me sister, but in this you are wrong. I will not be alone. I will have the people, and they *will* protect me.'

THREE
Escape

'Let us out of here!' she cried angrily once more.

For three cycles – by her count at least – they had been ensconced in the chamber, unable to leave. Their only visitors had been Mirielle's house guards, tasked with watching over them – for their own protection, or so they had been informed. The guards unlocked the chamber's heavy wooden door several times each cycle, primarily to offer them food and empty the toilet bucket provided for them. Although they had been treated well neither of them was allowed to leave the room, as decreed by the Queen. According to the guards, The Blades had yet to apprehend the rogue shaper Krashnar, the returned exile responsible for the release of Ricknar and the heinous mutilation of both Cora and her released mother, Hanarah. To sate his twisted need for amusement, Krashnar had fused Hanarah's torso to her daughter's back, turning both mother and daughter into some kind of hideous arachnoid construct. Shaping the flesh was prohibited throughout the domain. As a result, the Freylarkai – with the exception of Krashnar himself – did not possess the skill required to aid Hanarah and her daughter in their time of need. Even Mirielle – Freylar's most powerful shaper – lacked the specific skillset and experience necessary to undo Krashnar's abhorrent work. Therefore, she had little choice but to coerce their queen into assisting with the ugly process of separating the victims, despite Mirielle's reluctance to lend aid. Regrettably, however, Mirielle's lack of familiarity with Krashnar's niche work meant that only one could survive the ordeal. Hanarah selflessly sacrificed her own life to save her daughter's, but it had fallen to herself to ensure that Mirielle completed the awful separation process. Hanarah's grizzly release had affected them all, though none more so than Cora. The young Freylarkin was now completely withdrawn and refused to talk. Cora sat in a corner of the chamber with her head buried firmly between her knees. The downcast Freylarkin tried desperately to block out the world around her, unable to cope with the miserable hand life had dealt her. Despite trying repeatedly to comfort Hanarah's daughter, each attempt to do so had been met with fierce resistance – Cora had physically pushed her away – followed by a torrent of tears. Cora's reaction to her presence was understandable given her role in the macabre events leading up to her mother's release. Yet whatever ill will Cora harboured towards her surely paled in comparison to her own self-loathing. She hated the awful feelings of guilt and shame that clung to her like a foul stench refusing to dissipate. She had reminded herself repeatedly during their confinement that she had simply carried out Hanarah's final wish. Nevertheless, her actions left a bitter taste in her mouth – she felt like a criminal, despite her honourable intentions.

'I demand that you release us!' she cried again, hoping that someone – aside from the house guards – would hear her desperate plea for help.

Freylar's queen had said very little after the incident. At the time, she had thought little of it, distracted as she was by the distasteful event's shocking climax. After they had returned to the Tri-Spires with Hanarah's ruined body, she had subconsciously attributed Mirielle's quiet demeanour to shock. However, having since reviewed the incident objectively, it was likely – evidenced by their prolonged detention – that Mirielle in fact had an alternate agenda. There was no reason to believe that Krashnar would attack *them* again, and besides, what would be the point, she mused. Krashnar had already succeeded in spreading fear and terror amongst the Freylarkai, using Riknar, Hanarah and Cora to do so. Even if the vile shaper harboured designs for a prolonged war of terror against their kin, surely he would not seek to target Cora for a second time. It was clear to her now that their confinement was in fact imprisonment. Either Mirielle wanted to punish her for forcing her hand, or Freylar's queen wanted the incident kept quiet.

'You cannot keep us locked up in here forever!'

Despite her outbursts, Cora continued to remain silent, with her head still buried firmly between her legs. She did not know what was worse: their ongoing incarceration, or bearing witness to Cora's melancholy state of depression. Her reputation as Freylar's most skilled dressmaker was the cornerstone of her livelihood, and one that she worked hard to maintain.

'Go and see Larissa, she will fix you up.' or 'Larissa will sort you out.' they would say.

She had earned the respect of the Freylarkai due to her skill as a seamstress – she had even served the Queen on occasion. She was accustomed to frequent contact with the people and busying herself with her work. Now she had neither as a result of being hidden away like some kind of dirty secret, which would no doubt harm her reputation. The thought of it infuriated her.

'Let us out of this prison!' she screamed, this time banging her fist against the chamber's thick wooden door.

Perhaps saying the words aloud would provoke some kind of response from their captors, she hoped, but once again, there was no answer. Those who knew her well, including longstanding clients and respected council member Kirika, would often praise her for her confidence. She was outspoken, often wilful, and had a fearless attitude towards the world. But something was different now; the world around her had changed. Everything seemed wrong, and for the first time, in a long time, she actually felt afraid.

It was getting late. Her students were inside the main sanctuary conversing enthusiastically with one another whilst she remained alone outside, in the courtyard, staring vacantly at the memorial erected by Krasus. Nathaniel had requested its construction, immediately after their bitter disagreement over her work at the sanctuary. The handsome Freylarkin had made the unexpected request the moment it had become clear that they would not see eye to eye on the issue of scrying. The memorial stood at the far end of the courtyard; a reminder of those Blade Aspirants released during the attack on Scrier's Post. However, to her it was more than a place of remembrance for those who had sacrificed their lives to defend the vale. The memorial represented the loss of a much-cherished friendship, and a growing division between their kin. Nathaniel was unable to embrace the change her training would bring to those with her ability. With her guidance, the act of scrying would no longer be taboo or subject to complex sanctions. Scriers would be free to use their ability for the betterment of the Freylarkai, supported by the knowledge of her teachings to ensure that they remained on the right path, therefore avoiding a repeat of Darlia's insatiable thirst for knowledge. Nathaniel was unable to comprehend the vision that both she and Mirielle shared, and there would be other doubters – of that she was certain, courtesy of her waning second sight. Nathaniel did not intend to let the matter drop. The much-respected Freylarkin, often referred to as The Teacher, would rally others to his side, including those of influential stature. Since his departure from Scrier's Post, she had worked tirelessly to foresee Nathaniel's next move, examining the many strands of fate woven together to create his destiny. Yet many of those strands were unconnected loose ends, clouding Nathaniel's path with uncertainty. It was a strange phenomenon that she had not previously encountered, causing her to wonder if age was playing its tricks on her again. Yet perhaps something else thwarted her second sight, she mused.

'Aleska, will you not come inside and join us?' asked a familiar voice from behind her.

She turned and saw Keshar. The eager young scrier appeared concerned for her wellbeing, no doubt due to the encroaching winter's bitter caress.

'You should not be out here; you will catch a cold. Come and sit with us.'

'Thank you. I will be in shortly. Though I may just turn in for the evening and leave you youngsters to it.'

'You are always welcome to join us.'

'I know.' she said, offering her student a warm smile.

In truth she found it awkward conversing with Keshar since the arrival of the others. Their presence made her *feel* old, something that her body had been quietly telling her for the last few passes. With Kirika, things had been different. Although still blessed with the vigour of youth – relatively speaking – the gifted scrier possessed a respectable level of maturity. As such, she had felt comfortable discussing matters with her former student. Keshar, however, was too young, and the presence of the others only widened the age gap between them. Secretly, she had hoped to receive more mature students to the sanctuary by now. However, the young were typically fearless and impulsive; it was no surprise, therefore, that *they* would be the first to seek out the rejuvenated sanctuary. In time, older generations of scriers would make their pilgrimage to the sanctuary, once word spread of its reimaging. In the meantime, meaningful conversation would be in short supply.

'May I ask what you are doing out here?'

'I am collecting my thoughts, trying to make sense of our domain. I find that it helps to calm my mind, and thus helps me to see more clearly.'

'I see. So it is another form of meditation?'

'Something like that.'

Before the eager young scrier could assault her with further questions, a Sky-Skitter flew in low across the perimeter wall of the courtyard. The sleek corvid circled the sanctuary several times, announcing its presence with its distinctive shrieking cries. She raised her right hand above her head, bending it at the wrist, offering the Sky-Skitter a place upon which to perch. The trained courier expertly landed on the back of her hand, where it spread its impressive black wings before settling down. Attached to its right leg was a tiny message scroll – the purpose of its arrival – which she quickly detached before coaxing the Sky-Skitter onto the memorial.

'Another message from the vale?' asked Keshar inquisitively.

'Possibly.' she said, giving nothing away.

She quickly decoded the scroll's message using a private cipher, used only by herself and Mirielle.

'Dear Aleska, I need you! Much has happened these last few cycles, which I can only summarise here. Marcus has repelled a fresh Narlakai invasion, Darlia has returned to the vale and Krashnar has attacked us – me especially. Furthermore, Kirika has openly defied my rule, and others have shown equal disobedience. Everything feels like it is coming undone. Events are spiralling out of control and I am absent my keystone – I need you back. Mirielle.'

'What does it say?' asked Keshar impatiently.

Taken aback by the pointed communication, she omitted to respond to the young scrier's question. No doubt Keshar had gleaned the disturbing nature of the grim message from her startled expression.

'Aleska…are you OK?'

'It is nothing child. You need not concern yourself. However, there is a matter of state that I must attend to. The Queen requires my urgent counsel – that is all.'

'I understand.' replied Keshar in an unconvincing tone.

Her student clearly had more questions, however, the eager scrier knew – by now – the futility of pressing such matters with her.

'When do you intend to depart?'

'I will leave at first light.'

'So soon?'

'This cannot wait.'

'Then I will come with you.'

'No.' she said pointedly. 'I need you to remain here and continue your studies with the others.'

'Aleska, you cannot travel alone.'

'I will be fine, my child. Besides, I need you here to guide the others in my absence.'

'How long will you be gone?'

'I do not know; however, I will not jeopardise everything that we have worked hard to create here. I will ensure that I maintain regular communication with you during my absence.'

She could see the look of concern etched on Keshar's face, but despite not wishing to leave the sanctuary, she could not ignore their queen's plea for assistance. Mirielle needed her support, and she would not abandon her closest friend to navigate the turbulent events unfolding alone. Mirielle would need her keen mind and political prowess, in addition to her second sight, to ward off the challenges to her rule.

'I will miss your teachings.'

'And I will miss giving them. However, this is only a temporary setback to our schedule.'

'Aleska, will you do me a favour when you return to the vale?' asked the young scrier expectantly.

'Of course, what is it?'

'Will you stop by my family and let them know that I am OK? In particular Riknar, my brother.'

He groaned in discomfort due to the pain in his right thigh. The irksome knife had buried itself deep into his leg, but the darkness inside him had absorbed most of the damage, mitigating the worst of its effects. Even so, it ached. Without the unnatural strength of his symbiotic dark companion, he would not have been able to escape his attackers, who had quickly surrounded him following the command of their curious leader.

'Why were the Knights Thranis present?' he mused aloud, struggling to understand their involvement.

Subconsciously, he expected the parasite inside him to provide the answer, but it was not interested in politics or reason; the only thing it desired were fresh sensations, specifically the pleasures it derived from inflicting its sadistic torments on others – actions which were fast becoming commonplace. In any event, he had failed. Though her own wounds had been far worse, he had no doubt that Mirielle would recover from her injuries with the aid of Freylar's renewalists. She would continue to rule over the vale, her arrogance unchallenged, whilst he licked his own wounds in humiliation after being forced to retreat. Now, Mirielle's guard would be up, making it almost impossible to infiltrate the Queen's ranks for a second time. He cursed the lone knight for interfering, denying him the pleasure of Mirielle's flesh, which had been long overdue. Still, he had at least whet his appetite, enough to sate the hungering darkness inside him – for now at least – although it would not remain contented for long. Soon the parasite would compel his actions once more, coercing him to perform acts far darker than those he had already committed. He dragged his long rough tongue along his bottom lip, causing it to sting as fresh saliva permeated its dry cracked surface.

'Who are you?' he questioned, musing aloud to no one in particular, frustrated by the recent events that had scuppered his plans.

He sat firmly on his backside in a wood to the north of the vale and glanced down at his ruined attire. The tattered female garment, which he had stolen from his last victim, barely clung to him. What was once a dress now resembled little more than torn pieces of fabric struggling to cover his ugly modesty. He laughed heartily at his own humorous visage in a cracked hoarse tone, finding strange amusement at the state he had been left in by his thwarted attempt to defile Freylar's queen. His thoughts turned to Lileah, wondering if the bitter Freylarkin, motivated solely by anger and the need for revenge, had succeeded where he had not. Assuming the vengeful little waif had made good on her plans to invade Freylar and defeat The Blades, it would not be long before his path once again crossed Mirielle's. With The Guardian incapacitated – maybe even released – there would have been little to prevent Lileah's wrath from ravaging the land. It was strange, therefore, that he had not seen or heard anything on the subject whilst skulking around the leafless wood, looking for fresh water and whatever food he could scavenge from the land. His changed body needed very little to sustain it, instead drawing energy from the darkness inside him. Nonetheless, his pitted potbelly groaned despite his altered metabolism, reminding him that he still required *some* nourishment. Nuts and winterberries had begun to adorn Freylar's woodland, enough for him to forgo the irksome prospect of hunting game at least. Although his dark companion had granted him significantly increased strength and speed, the tiresome thought of running around the woodland chasing game did not appeal to him.

    He scratched his one good ear, irritated by an insect crawling across its upper cartilage, which he snatched up using his long bony fingers. He studied the pest for a brief moment, analysing its movement, in particular the way in which its tiny little legs turned mechanically, tirelessly attempting to drive it forwards despite his vice-like grip.

His belly groaned once more. Without further thought, he pushed the hapless insect between his cracked lips before crunching the creature into an unsatisfying paste. After a few attempts, ultimately succeeding, to swallow the impromptu meal, he pushed himself upright and resumed skulking around the wood. Passing between the leafless trees, he remained ever mindful of the placement of his grubby feet, carefully dodging the organic detritus shed by the woodland to avoid inadvertently snapping any fallen twigs, thus potentially drawing attention to his presence.

'Where is a good fisherman when you need one?' he said sardonically.

Although he had maintained a low profile since fleeing the Tri-Spires, nonetheless, he had expected to meet at least one Freylarkin with the misfortune to cross his path. Instead, there had been no one. No sight of a victorious army returning to celebrate an unlikely victory, and certainly no glimpses of Lileah's dark host pouring into the vale. Perhaps in his haste to flee his attackers he had drifted further north-east than he would have liked, inadvertently straying towards paths less travelled. In his defence, he had little experience of flying. Rarely had he the need to use his wraith wings, and the large flesh wings that he had shaped to make good his escape had been little more than slaves to the wind that had largely directed his course. The fleshy sails had served him well, saving him from an untimely release. Regardless of their virtues, however, they had since become an annoyance. Without a sufficient flesh sacrifice to offset the oversized appendages, his newly acquired wings had only been temporary additions. However, their abrupt genesis had left massive scarring across his back. Even now, after they had subsequently abandoned him, he could still feel the lumpy scars with the remains of his callused fingers, a reminder of the power Mirielle commanded even in her weakened state.

'Pissing Knights.' he said, cursing the estranged Order. 'Why defend *her* of all people?'

'Krashnar, I know you are in there.'

'I am busy. Go away!' came a distant voice from behind the door.

The shaper's abode lay to the west of the ancient bridge that spanned the wide river cutting through the vale. The wooden bridge acted as a conduit, linking the inhabitants from either side, joining the lives of the forest dwellers to those living in and around the Tri-Spires. Occasionally Freylarkai would choose to fly across the river, though most used the bridge, which acted as a hub for Freylarian society. The Freylarkai loved to gossip, and the hallowed crossing provided an ideal platform for their habitual chatter.

'I thought you said that you knew this Freylarkin?' asked Heldran with a puzzled look on his face.

'He is…less than hospitable.' he replied, failing to mask his obvious frustration. 'The antisocial git will require an incentive to open up.'

'I can think of an incentive.' replied Heldran, straightening his back and raising himself to his full height.

'That will not be necessary. Besides, one swipe from the back of *your* hand and there will be no shaper left.'

'I was thinking more the door. Then perhaps scare him a little.'

They grinned mischievously at one another like adolescent males, relishing the fanciful thought of putting the frighteners on the irksome shaper. The reality, however, was very different; they could ill afford any unwanted attention. The remote nature of Krashnar's abode, a large isolated shack against the trees alongside the river, was in their favour. However, Caleth had spies everywhere due to the nature of his deep-seated paranoia; it was possible that The Blade Lord's agents spied upon their every move. The smarter approach would be to convince the aloof shaper to invite them in willingly, thereby avoiding a potential public spectacle.

'As much as I would like to see you tear down this hovel and scare its inhabitant, I have an idea which will – assuming it works – attract far less attention.'

'You never said that this joint venture of ours would be boring, Nathaniel. Do I need to reconsider my lot?'

He gave Heldran a wry smile, then proceeded to bang once more on the rickety door to Krashnar's hovel.

'Go away!' rasped the irritable voice.

'Do you not wish to hear what I have to say?'

'No, I do not!'

'I have a need for your unique…talent.'

There was no response from the obstinate shaper, though his keen hearing detected the sound of shuffling from behind the door. Peering between the tiny gaps in the poorly constructed barricade, he spied movement suggesting that he had piqued the shaper's interest.

'There are some items I need you to fashion for me.'

'Bah. If you seek trinkets go someplace else; there are others who indulge in the shaping of such mundane effects.'

'My desires are anything but mundane.'

'I will be the judge of that!'

He smiled at Heldran who acknowledged his ploy with a subtle nod of his large head. Even if he succeeded in convincing Krashnar to open the door, he was unconvinced that the Knight would actually fit through it, such was Heldran's impressive size. Rather than spoon-feed their uncooperative audience member, he chose instead to remain silent, therefore garnering more of the shaper's attention.

'So...what is it? I do not have all cycle!'

'I would rather not discuss the matter out here. I understand that the shaping of flesh is taboo.' he replied, knowing that the irksome shaper would readily take the bait.

The door to the hovel juddered violently as it scraped against the forest floor, its direction of travel impeded by woodland detritus littering the ground. Aiding the shaper, Heldran grabbed the top of the partially open door with his left hand, wrenching it open fully with minimal effort, thus exposing their quarry.

'This better be worth it, else you can both sling your hook.'

'May we come in?' he asked politely, biting his tongue.'

The shaper said nothing and instead disappeared into the gloom, leaving the door wide open. He gave Heldran a quick wink then followed Krashnar into the dirty smelly abode, rank with filth and grime. After no small amount of effort, they both managed to navigate their way into a cramped room that had a single wooden stool. Their unwelcoming host sat down, forcing them to stand – unless they chose to sit amidst the things wriggling across the grubby floor.

'I like what you have done with the place.' said Heldran sardonically.

'Bugger off!' replied the shaper tersely. 'Now what is it you propose?'

Krashnar was an unconventional Freylarkin – to say the least – who chose to keep to himself for the most part. Occasionally one would see the wretch skulking around the vale, his face largely covered by his long brown unkempt hair that twitched with a life of its own; presumably, the things living on the floor had also sought refuge in the shaper's matted hair. The shaper exhibited terrible hygiene, yet despite this, he continued to endure on the fringes of society without the aid of others or the comforts of modern living.

'I need you to construct two blades for me.'

Krashnar's face contorted and a wave of anger washed over the shaper's grubby features.

'These blades will be unique.' he continued promptly, not wishing to fan Krashnar's obvious ire.

'How?'

'I require two extremely terrible weapons.' he said fixing the shaper with a cold stare. 'The first must be capable of releasing an opponent whilst leaving *no remains*.'

The shaper stared at him mutely with a stern look, his anger replaced by obvious interest. The bizarre nature of his request had clearly struck a chord with the irritable shaper.

'The second must permit its wielder *quiet* access to secured areas.'

'What does that even mean?' replied Krashnar with a sudden look of confusion.

'It means that its wielder must be able to advance quietly, circumvent locked doors, navigate blind corners – would you like me to write this down for you?' he replied sarcastically.

'And just how am I supposed to craft a weapon like that? I would need…a Waystone, or something of that ilk.'

'I can source you one.' replied Heldran unexpectedly.

'Nonsense. Caleth's armoured puppets guard the only known Waystones. He watches the ancient stones closely, secured by his lock and key – you know this! You would need these fanciful weapons of which you speak in order to first acquire the raw materials necessary to even attempt their shaping.'

'I can source you one.' said Heldran firmly once more. 'Can you build the weapon or not, shaper?'

He raised his eyebrows at Heldran's direct approach. Krashnar recoiled following the Knight's stern proclamation, abandoning his stool to move towards the far corner of the room. Once there he seemed to fade from sight, melting effortlessly into shadows as though one of their kin.

'Of course I can!' rasped the shaper's voice from the dark. 'But I will need *two* Waystones, each attuned to the other, you understand! Also, this other weapon you mentioned will pose a greater challenge.'

'How so?' he asked, curious as to why the notorious shaper would find the proposed task troublesome. 'Is such a weapon beyond your warped talent?'

'Do not be so ridiculous! Its construction is not in doubt, only *your* ability to acquire the material necessary for me to shape it. Besides, why is it that you need these weapons? It sounds a lot to me like you are planning an assassination.'

'That it none of your concern.' he replied flatly.

'This material – what is it that you need exactly?' asked Heldran, clearly looking to steer their conversation back on track.

'I need you both to go to the borderlands.'

'Why?' he asked, eager to understand the reason for the shaper's unexpected request.

'To capture a Narlakin.'

FOUR
Honesty

'How are you feeling?'

She could sense that Marcus wanted to look towards her arm, but instead he held her gaze out of respect. She clutched her fused joint with her right hand, trying to offer some semblance of a natural pose, though it had thus far failed to convince any of her subjects, as evidenced by their wagging tongues.

'I will get over it.'

'Mirielle, there *is* no getting over it.' replied Marcus, who stepped closer to offer her comfort.

She flinched as he approached, unsure whether her reaction was a result of her shame or his proximity. She felt embarrassed by her disability. Furthermore, she felt a sense of dread whenever others approached her, as though she believed that they too intended to cause her harm – which she knew was not the case. The abhorrent shaper had left his ugly mark on her soul, as well as on her body.

'He violated you!' Marcus continued. 'You cannot ignore this, pretending like it never happened. Mirielle, talk to me, please.'

'Marcus, it is irrelevant.' she replied, turning towards the wooden workbench in her chamber. 'I need you to do something for me.'

'What do you need?'

'Certain recent events have undermined my authority, making me look weak in front of the people. There can be no doubt over my authority; therefore, these actions cannot be allowed to fade quietly into the background.'

She glanced over her left shoulder and caught a glimpse of The Blade Lord's knitted brow. She knew that her words would weigh heavily on Marcus, but she needed to weed out those who would challenge her rule in order to strengthen her leadership. To achieve such an end efficiently, she required *something* that would draw the attention of the Freylarkai and bring them together, whilst also enabling her to bind them to her will of their own volition. The means of facilitating her ambition needed to be fair – or at least perceived as such. Forcing the Freylarkai to unite behind her would ultimately fail, ergo she required them to fall in line behind her willingly – she needed a villain.

'There is going to be a public trial.'

'What?'

'I would like you to apprehend the exile Darlia…and her sister. Both are to be taken into custody and brought back to the Tri-Spires where they will both await trial. In the meantime, a jury will be appointed to--'

'Mirielle, do not do this, please.'

'Marcus, their actions cannot go unanswered. Darlia shunned her exile and Kirika deviously engineered a means of circumventing the ruling council's judgement.'

'Their actions were in the best interests of the people.' replied Marcus earnestly.

'The ends cannot justify the means if there is to be order amongst us.'

'Order is a noble ideal, but sometimes we need to be managed instead.'

'Then you agree with their actions?' she replied, turning to face him once more.

'I do not agree with their chosen method of execution, but there *were* extenuating circumstances.'

She turned to her workbench once more and absentmindedly cast her gaze over the intricate objects strewn across its surface whilst trying to keep her emotions in check. The last thing she wanted was to fracture her close relationship with Marcus, but she could not afford to look weak in the eyes of the people. Despite her decision, she knew that The Blade Lord would execute her orders – Darlia's mechanical claw was testament to the fact.

'I want them brought back here. As of this moment, Kirika is no longer a member of the ruling council. Do you disagree?'

'It is possible that Darlia will accept your judgement due to a sense of guilt and a need to atone.'

'*Our* judgement.' she said, interrupting The Blade Lord. 'This is the will of the ruling council.'

'However,' Marcus continued, unfazed by her remark, 'Kirika will not come willingly. Be forewarned, there *will* be repercussions.' replied Marcus flatly. 'Kirika is not to be taken lightly, and we do not yet fully understand the extent of her support. Furthermore, what is the charge for her arrest?'

'Is it not obvious?' she said, genuinely surprised that Marcus required clarification on the matter. 'The charge is treason.'

She looked over her shoulder and saw Marcus glaring at her with a stony expression. She had seen the look before, though never directed towards herself. The Blade Lord was clearly conflicted on the matter. Nonetheless, he was duty-bound to execute her orders. As her right-hand and charged with responsibility for the defence of Freylar,

Marcus would never go against her will, regardless of the consequences of such action.

'You risk civil war.'

'*She* has already started one!'

'We cannot manage a potential insurrection – not in our weakened state. If this is truly your will, you will need more allies.' Marcus proclaimed. 'I can enforce your will, but you need Aleska's counsel to make this play out according to your design.'

'I have already recalled her to the Tri-Spires. She will be with us shortly.'

Marcus twitched his eyebrows, unable to mask his surprise. Regardless of his subtle change in body language, her unique vision allowed her to discern his true feelings with ease, despite the visual cues one typically relied upon.

'I see. You will also need compelling leverage over Kirika if this is to end quietly. A messy public trial will not help matters.' The Blade Lord continued.

'Agreed. I already possess the means required to coerce the Fate Weaver's cooperation.'

'And what is that?' asked Marcus who continued to regard her stoically.

'Do not burden yourself with such troubles. I have the matter in hand.' she replied. 'If Kirika refuses to adhere to my terms there will be an additional trial, and she will not like my choice of defendant.'

Despite the anxiety that had swept through the vale in the wake of the Lileah's second invasion, she felt at ease in Kirika's company. It had been a while since they had spent time together, and so Kirika's presence was most welcome, reminding her of the time they had spent together when she had first arrived in Freylar. Nathaniel too had benefited from having the renowned scrier lodge with them. Despite the grim expression that now seemed permanently etched on his face, there was a noticeable spring in the master renewalist's step. Throughout Kirika's stay, there had been numerous discussions between them, also involving Darlia and Lothnar, who had both since left Nathaniel's tree. The running theme had been the management of Freylar going forwards and how best to deal with Mirielle's waning rule. Although she had been privy to the majority of the discussions, in truth she had not fully engaged with them, preferring instead to allow others to lead on politics and matters of state, in particular Kirika and Nathaniel. It was clear to her now that her role in Freylar was to harness the mood of the people and to give them something behind which they could rally. However, she would not be the one to lead them. That burden lay with others who could foresee the future more clearly. Taking a step back in their meetings had allowed her to better observe the relationships between all those present. In particular, it had been interesting to see how Nathaniel interacted with others when not in the arena instructing his students. When engaged in his sermons, Nathaniel employed a simple and direct approach, however, watching him work everyone gathered around the old wooden table in his cramped living space revealed a very different management style. She quickly discovered that the master renewalist was adept at planting thoughts in the minds of others and, more importantly, making them stick. It was clear to her now that Nathaniel had a ubiquitous influence in Freylar's development, and had likely tugged on the strings of its inhabitants for quite some time given the ease with which he operated.

'You should try and get some sleep Rayna.'

She turned her head towards Kirika, who lay beside her. Due to the modest living space in Nathaniel's tree, her Blade sister habitually shared her bed during her stay. Kirika lay on her side, casually regarding her with languorous eyes.

'There's something I need to tell you – in the strictest confidence, you understand.' she said, rolling onto her side to face Kirika.

'You are not normally this troubled. What is it?'

'It's about Alarielle.'

'What about her?'

'You may think I'm a coward…but, I just don't have the heart to tell him. Especially now, given everything that is going on.'

'Are you referring to Nathaniel?' asked Kirika, pushing herself up onto her left elbow.

'Yes.'

'What is it? What has happened?'

'When I fought that immense Narlakin during the battle for Bleak Moor, it had me beaten.'

'Yes, we all saw it. We thought it had taken your soul, yet you rose to your feet and destroyed not only it, but Lileah's entire dark host.'

'True. But it *would* have taken my soul, if not for her…'

'If not for who? What are you saying Rayna?' asked Kirika, her eyes now wide open.

'Alarielle offered her soul instead – against my will – thereby deceiving the Narlakin into thinking that it had defeated me.'

'So you are telling me that Alarielle willingly sacrificed her soul?'

'Yes, so that I would survive. One of those horrors trapped her soul, again, and it was *my* fault. I was responsible for her demise – my reckless abandon made it so.'

'She *chose* to sacrifice herself – that is not your fault! Nathaniel will come around – assuming you tell him, that is.'

'In this, I do not readily share your optimism. You have to understand that in that moment I allowed my rage to consume me entirely. I hated myself for prompting what happened. I was so angry that I poured my vengeance and hatred into my inner light, which I recklessly unleashed indiscriminately.'

'The fact that you did so turned the battle in our favour!'

'Perhaps, but it was careless. In my desperation to release Alarielle's newest captor, I also hurt our people.'

'Yes, you did. Nonetheless, it was a price worth paying.'

'Was it?'

'What do you mean?' asked Kirika curiously.

'The attack obliterated the Narlakai, but…once free of her captor, Alarielle had a choice. She could have returned to me, but instead she chose to journey to that *thing* which ensnares us.'

'You mean the sphere of light which brought you to Freylar?' asked Kirika with keen interest.

'Yes. The Freylarkai ignorantly refer to that which lies beyond the boundaries of the living as the Everlife, but release is not the hallowed pilgrimage they believe it to be.'

'What are you saying Rayna?'

'I'm saying that release is just another word for feeding. That *thing* feeds on our souls when we cease to exist in the physical world. It is a predator, patiently waiting for the release of our souls so that it can harvest them – it is the true soul stealer. The Narlakai are not our enemy, they are our salvation. They protect us from the true enemy. *They* are the Everlife!'

'But it saved you before. It – whatever it is – brought you here.' said Kirika with a grave expression, made all the grimmer by the shadows spilling across her elfin features. 'Why bestow an act of benevolence upon you if – like you say – our sole purpose is to provide it with nourishment?'

'Because of the Narlakai; they live far longer than we do. In fact, do they experience release, naturally that is? Tell me, has anyone ever seen an *old* Narlakin?'

'Rayna, I am having a tough time accepting this.'

'Understandably so. You were raised to believe that the Narlakai are the enemy. However, I am not certain that is in fact the case. What if the Narlakai are simply new vessels for our released souls, and that the entity that brought me to Freylar did so in the hope that I would destroy those who deny it sustenance.' she said, vehemently. 'Consider these facts. The Narlakai do not attack the Freylarkai, unless provoked. Furthermore, the only Freylarkai capable of destroying the Narlakai are light bringers. *It* placed my soul into the body of a light bringer. It empowered me – I now believe – in order to use the anger and resentment that I harbour to satisfy its own agenda.'

Kirika said nothing. The renowned scrier stared at her wide-eyed in bewilderment, clearly struggling to make sense of the heavy payload she had just delivered.

'But if that *were* true, why would the Narlakai seek to deny their host its source of nourishment, and why would we want to avert such an end? If we are all part of this entity, why would we wish to disrupt this wheel of fate, or whatever it is?'

'I do not know, at least not yet. I have minimal contact with the entity, and when it does deign to communicate with me, dialogue is brief and one-sided.'

'Rayna, you have already defied our beliefs simply by being here. If you decide once more to challenge our preconceptions, you must tread carefully. Religion can be a powerful tool, and if used as such it must be wielded carefully.'

'I know, and I will proceed with caution. It's just that my perception of these things is very different to your own in light of my unique experiences.'

'Things have certainly changed for you since your rebirth in Freylar.'

'More than you know.' she said, rolling onto her back and turning her head towards the wooden ceiling.

'What do you mean?' asked Kirika with obvious interest.

'It's nothing.'

'You cannot bait me like that, only to then deny me my prize – out with it Rayna!'

'You'll think I'm being stupid.'

'No, I will not. I have never judged you, nor do I intend to do so.' Kirika replied earnestly. 'We are each defined by our experiences, and despite your relatively short existence, you have experienced a lot. You have endured and seen things that I never will – who am I to judge?'

There was a lull in their conversation whilst she considered Kirika's words. The young scrier was wise beyond her years and had significantly grown in confidence since her secondment to the Knights Thranis with Heldran and the others. Despite her own relentless determination, she now faced a challenge that she could not get to grips with. Perhaps canvasing Kirika's thoughts would provide a fresh perspective on the issue that she was otherwise failing to understand.

'It's something Alarielle has done.'

'Are you referring to her decision not to return?'

'No, it's not that.'

'Then what is it?' asked Kirika who leaned in closer.

'During our time together, she discovered a way to instil her experiences upon me – these experiences enabled me to defeat Lothnar in the arena.'

'What do you mean by instil?'

'It's hard for me to explain, but it's like she found a way to forcibly communicate with me at an alarming rate. She was able to pass on experience, knowledge and feelings in an instant, and without my consent.'

'So, she could control you?'

'Not directly, but she was able to alter my own perception relative to her own.'

'That does not sound like a pleasurable experience.' replied Kirika. 'Surely her actions were a violation?'

'For the most part I consented to this practice.'

'But not always?'

'No.' she replied absentmindedly, recalling the moment when her opponent had tried to devour her soul. 'During the moment prior to her release – for the second time – Alarielle left me what she called "a parting gift".'

'What was it?'

She hesitated unexpectedly, unsure how to articulate the gift she had received. In truth, she was embarrassed by the subject matter and so she found it difficult to discuss.

'Rayna, what was the gift?' Kirika asked again gently.

'I suppose you would call it…lust.'

'Go on.' Kirika prompted, her pupils now fully dilated, having adjusted to the gloom.

'It's hard for me to explain.'

'Try…'

'You and I have shared a bed together previously, and during those times my feelings towards you were mixed. My mind's desire was completely at odds with that of my body.'

Kirika gave her a wide grin, akin to that of a little girl teasing another over matters of the heart.

'I knew you would react like this!'

'Oh come on sister. Indulge me in my moment of amusement at your expense.'

'I think there has been enough laughter at my expense since my arrival here.'

'It is refreshing. Your honesty and, sometimes, childlike wonderment in awe of that which is new, is infectious. You make others smile when you react in such a way.' explained Kirika warmly in an attempt to ease her embarrassment. 'You found me attractive – I get it. You were born a male; you cannot simply switch off certain desires, even if your body no longer craves them.'

'But that's the thing. Alarielle's gift flicked that switch!'

'Oh…I see.'

There was another pause in their conversation whilst Kirika digested all the facts, trying to make sense of them.

'So you are now attracted to males?'

'Well…yes, I believe so.' she replied awkwardly. 'This is all Alarielle's doing – I did not agree to this.'

'So you are confused?'

'Absolutely, and it gets worse!'

'How could this be any more confusing?' asked Kirika, who was now fully invested in their conversation.

'Because I keep thinking about *him*.'

'Rayna, who are you referring to?'

'Lothnar!'

She struggled to recall the last time she had heard the sounds of the forest at night. In the borderlands, everything was quiet and still, but in the heart of the vale, quite the opposite was true. Everything moved. When the sun dropped below the western horizon, all of the night creatures busied themselves, evidenced by the incessant noise of their constant shuffling amongst the winter bracken. The ground beneath her feet had hardened due to the frost, but despite the drop in temperature, the surrounding woodland was far more hospitable than the arid waste of the borderlands. The autumnal tree cover provided a most welcome respite from the callous wind; no longer did it cut to the bone, numbing her senses.

After picking her way through the golden forest, the landscape opened up, giving way to expansive farmland, nestled amongst which was a small farmstead community that she picked out of the gloom with her keen vision. Kirika's directions had served her well, though she would need to complete the remainder of her pilgrimage on her own, relying on her own wits and ability to win over her audience. The list of names that she had constructed following her contact with the departing souls at Bleak Moor was alien to her. However, she was fortunate in that her sister knew of the community due to her role, and was therefore able to point her in the right direction. Now, though, she would be reliant on the aid of the people to guide her next move. The success of her initial contact with the farmstead would be critical. Mindful that she might be perceived as infiltrating the community – having already scried that unsuccessful outcome – by those working the late watch, she decided instead to take a well-used path leading to the small group of dwellings ahead. As she had foreseen, her calm measured approach reassured those who spied upon her every move, seeking to understand her intent. Eventually, not more than fifty paces from one of the outlying dwellings, one of her keen observers broke cover and approached her cautiously.

'Your name please.' came a terse male voice from the shadows.

'My name is Darlia.' she said warmly.

Realising the need for complete transparency, she raised her ornate bronze mechanical claw, allowing her unidentified assessor to gain her true measure.

'You are the exile everyone has been talking about.'

'That is news to me.' she said, surprised by the comment. 'Clearly I have failed to appreciate the extent of my notoriety.'

'Both you and your sister saved the vale; that is hardly cause for infamy.'

'Our queen takes a different view.'

'Mirielle does not speak for the people. We are of no concern to her; she has detached herself from us completely, choosing instead to while away her cycles in that tower of hers.'

Taken aback by the obvious disdain in the Freylarkin's contemptuous words, she decided to probe the matter further in order to better understand the political landscape that lay ahead of her.

'Who else amongst you shares your view?' she asked, curious as to the extent of the animosity harboured by the wayward community.

'Each of us believes this. Not once, since erecting that tower of hers, has she deigned to visit us. We are of no concern to her, despite the key role we play in the survival of our people.'

'Forgive me, for I intend no offence, but I find it hard to believe that she has never inspected your produce. A queen should take a more active role in the development of her community and the people who sustain in.'

'Mirielle has no interest in our troubles, nor does she send a representative on her behalf. Even now, we are struggling to meet our quotas due to the wolves who hunt our herds. At any rate, what hope is there when she cannot even defend those living in and around the Tri-Spires. She allowed that evil shaper to terrorise us, so that she could host her precious games, despite your sister's counsel. Mirielle put the safety of our kin at risk so that she could stroke her own ego and lord her status over us.'

The Freylarkin's brutal words shocked her into silence, causing a brief lapse in the conversation between them.

'You are well informed.' she said, eventually recovering from the scornful verbal barrage.

'The people talk – a lot.'

'Yes, we do love to gossip. However, I hear the truth in your words, and I appreciate your plight. I, more than most, know what it is like to be eschewed by Mirielle's cold heart.'

'It grows colder with every pass. I fear that once it has frozen, the future that was once bright for our people will diminish along with it. Please understand that we harbour no ill will towards our queen, despite her growing questionable judgement and recent transgressions. Irrespective of the doomed path she now treads upon, each of us recalls the good she has done for our kin. However, her time has now passed and we require fresh leadership. It is regrettable that our queen does not recognise the need for change. Indeed, there are those that cling to her changed principles, but they are not *our* principles – we will not adhere to them.'

She had travelled to the farmstead seeking to provide closure for those families in desperate need, who had lost loved ones during the battle for Scrier's Post. In doing so, she had hoped to win their favour and garner support for her sister's campaign. Yet without any real effort on her part, she now stood upon the fulcrum of something even greater. If the community's alleged disposition was indeed as had been portrayed to her, there would be no need to sell Kirika's ideals to them – all they required was a shepherd. Realising that the wayward community would not respond well to direction, she would instead lay the foundations for an unshakable trust and convince them to draw others towards the light. Kirika already had a strong following throughout the vale, bolstered by Nathaniel's clever ministrations. If she could cajole the outlying communities into backing her sister, their vision of a smooth transition of power would likely become feasible. With overwhelming support throughout the vale, Mirielle's rule would fast unravel, ultimately becoming untenable.

'May I ask your name?' she said, taking her first step towards building a trust with the farmstead community.

'You may. My name is Gaelin.'

'Well met Gaelin.' she said, smiling warmly. 'I know that you have families living here who mourn the loss of loved ones at Scriers Post. Furthermore, you have just informed me of your wolf problem. I would like to help on both accounts, provided you will let me.'

FIVE
Loyalty

'Nathaniel, please open the door.' said Marcus firmly once more.

A sense of dread crept over him. For countless passes both he and Marcus had worked towards the same end, their agendas aligned. However, in his heart he knew there would come a time when their paths would diverge, forced by the actions of another. That moment, which he had feared for so long, was now finally upon them.

'Are you sure this is what you want?' he said, turning to Kirika, who tried her utmost to remain calm.

'This needs to happen. Neither you nor I can stop it, so let it happen on our terms.'

'But what if you are wrong? We will have lost one of our main pieces.'

'Trust me Nathaniel.'

'I do. Nevertheless, you cannot scry the outcome given Rayna's involvement in all this.'

'You know as well as I that we need to build on the people's growing disdain for Mirielle's rule. This course of action will facilitate that.' replied Kirka earnestly. 'I realise that this is hard for you Nathaniel. Time and again, loved ones have been cruelly snatched from you. Each time I have watched your soul diminish, akin to a fire starved of fuel. I do not *want* this, and I certainly do not wish to hurt you. However, you and I have discussed this matter at length. This needs to happen – you know this.'

He sighed, acknowledging the truth of Kirika's words, but the sober realisation did nothing to make the situation any more palatable.

'Open the door Nathaniel!' boomed the muffled voice of The Blade Lord, whose patience was now wearing thin.

He turned to Rayna, who looked bleary-eyed following a troubled night's sleep, the reason for which she had remained strangely tight-lipped about all morning.

'Kirika is no longer your student Nathaniel.' said Rayna, offering him a hard stare. 'She knows what she's doing. Have faith in her judgement.'

'Fine, so be it.' he said, realising the futility of rebelling against their combined will.

Without further delay, he opened the door to his tree and boldly stepped through, pushing aside the house guards flanking The Blade Lord who stood before him now with a stern look etched upon his face.

'What is the meaning of this intrusion Marcus?'

'Are they with you?'

'What, no morning pleasantries, after you come banging on *my* door?'

'Are Darlia and Kirika with you or not?'

'I am here.' said Kirika, who passed through the door behind him, shortly followed by Rayna. 'However, my sister is not.'

'Where is she?' asked Marcus sternly.

'I do not know.'

'I will ask you again. Where is she?'

'You were given an answer. Now leave us.' he interjected angrily.

'I am afraid that I cannot do that, old friend.' replied Marcus, who turned his full attention to the renowned scrier. 'Kirika, by order of the Queen, you will accompany me back to the Tri-Spires, where you will be tried for your crimes against the domain.'

'What crimes?' asked Rayna, who continued to rub her tired eyes.

'The charge is treason.'

'That is nonsense!' he said tersely.

'Your objection is noted; however, a jury will be appointed to deliberate over the matter.'

'Marcus, you cannot be serious!' he said furiously.

'You mean a jury of *her* choosing?' asked Kirika pointedly.

'I cannot discuss the format of the trial at this time, as well you know. My orders are to bring you back to the Tri-Spires safely.'

'I will not allow it!' he said, giving Marcus a venomous glare.

'Stand down old friend!' replied The Blade Lord sternly. 'Kirika knew that her actions in the arena would provoke a response – this is it.'

'And you are on board with this?' he replied angrily.

'What choice do I have? I will not go against the orders of *our* queen, to whom I have sworn fealty.'

'You also swore an oath to protect the domain.'

'Which I am doing!' replied Marcus tersely.

'I did not train you to blindly follow the orders of another.'

'I owe you much, but do not test me Nathaniel!' snapped Marcus, giving him an uncharacteristic fiery glare.

'This doesn't have to happen--' he began to reply.

The house guards drew their falchions abruptly, rudely cutting him short, prompting him to take a purposeful step towards Marcus – the time for words had clearly ended. The Blade Lord's compass had been set and there would be no altering its direction through carefully constructed dialogue. Marcus was loyal to a fault, the result of which was about to play out before them.

'Sheath your weapons!' cried Marcus loudly. 'Restrain them, and detain Kirika.'

The guard on his right moved towards him, grabbing his right forearm viciously. Instinctively, he placed his left hand over the guard's own, clamping it in place, then twisted his right hand round and gripped his opponent's exposed wrist. With no regard for the guard's welfare he stepped back and down, viciously dragging his opponent to the ground. The guard cried out in pain whilst he deftly removed his opponent's falchion, claiming it as his own. His victory was short-lived, however, as two more guards quickly set upon him, angered by the ease with which one of their own had been taken down and promptly disarmed.

'Your mistake!' he said angrily, wielding his new weapon with unerring alacrity.

The guards rushed him with their falchions drawn, desperate to land the first cut, but in their haste they failed to guard their bodies adequately, leaving them vulnerable. He moved forwards and to the right, slicing his blade across the armour of the nearest guard whilst evading a cut to his head. His blade glanced off his opponent's armour, but the point had been made, causing the guard to hesitate given the ease with which he had landed his blow. Taking advantage of the guard's lapse in concentration, he swapped the stolen falchion into his left hand and drove its pommel hard into the side of the guard's head. His stunned opponent stumbled sideways blindly, before collapsing awkwardly to the ground, dragging the other guard down with him. On his left, a controlled burst of light exploded outwards, bathing the woodland in brilliant white light. In that brief moment, the exposed leafless trees looked like eerie silver statues against their over-defined shadows. As the light increased in intensity, the trees seemed to grow enormously in length, before abruptly returning to their original height. The handful of guards caught in the wake of Rayna's attack dropped to their knees clutching their eyes, abandoning their weapons. He knew first-hand how debilitating the attack was, but before he could sympathise with their plight, he felt the invisible force of Marcus' unfettered telekinesis. It brutally smashed into him, lifting him clean off the ground. He felt his body travel through the air prior to landing violently on his back, where he lay for a moment, dazed by the sudden attack, before instinctively scrambling to his feet. After righting himself, he became acutely aware of his unsteadiness; the jarring attack had left him completely disorientated, robbing him of his sense of balance.

'I warned you *not* to test me, Nathaniel!'

Marcus' terse words caused his vision to snap back into focus. Rayna too had been laid low by the raw power of The Blade Lord's mind, and was only now regaining her feet.

'Do not test me again, either of you!'

'Marcus, you do not understand.' he said, trying to regain his composure.

'I understand well enough that you are actively defying the will of our queen.'

'With good reason!'

'Nathaniel, let it go – fight another cycle.' said Kirika, who moved to stand between him and The Blade Lord.

'Kirika, come with me now, please.' said Marcus flatly.

'Marcus, Mirielle's judgement is impaired – you know this!'

'Nathaniel, you are not aware of all the facts. This is the Queen's command and I *will* execute her orders.'

'Has she told you about Scrier's Post?' he said ardently, desperately hoping to find a chink in The Blade Lord's resolve.

'What of it?' asked Marcus impatiently.

'Aleska has rejuvenated the practice of scrying at Scrier's Post. She had Krasus restore the ill-fated site and is now training those with the ability at the sanctuary.'

Marcus said nothing, though his expression hardened upon hearing the news.

'Aleska is actively practicing scrying with a new generation of students.'

'Why?' asked Marcus flatly.

'Because they believe that the answer to all this is to control the ability, rather than restrain it.'

'Who are *they*?'

'Marcus, Mirielle sanctioned this!' he said bitterly, throwing the falchion on the ground before him.

There was a lull in their heated exchange, during which Rayna and the house guards regained their feet and stood opposite one another glaring angrily.

'Kirika, please come with me.'

'Marcus!' he said angrily.

'I will discuss this with the Queen. Nevertheless, her orders stand and you *will* desist with this insurrection before it goes any further. This ends here, before it goes beyond my control. Is that understood?'

Kirika turned towards him, offering him a look that he knew all too well. She was right of course, but he abhorred the notion of lying to The Blade Lord. Despite his loyalty to Mirielle and staunch adherence to Freylarian law, Marcus was a good friend, one that he wished to retain. He knew deep down that there would be many casualties on the road to ending Mirielle's reign, though he dearly hoped that his friendship with Marcus would not count amongst them. History had taught him well that there was a time and place for scruples – this was not it. Swallowing his pride, he took a step back, before uttering the words that he knew would leave a bitter taste in his mouth.

'Understood. However, know this Marcus: if you do not ensure that the jury is fair, and not of *her* choosing, there will be a reckoning.'

The Blade Lord gave him a hard stare before ushering Kirika away from the scene, flanked by the house guards, many of whom gave him sidelong smirks as they escorted the renowned scrier away. After the group left, he turned to Rayna whose face was loaded with anger.

'No! Not this time.' he said, holding Rayna's stare. 'This is not an enemy you can easily trick, or bludgeon with a crude weapon. This is a game of subterfuge.'

'Then why inform him of Scrier's Post?'

'That was an appetiser, designed to distract and muddy his relationship with Mirielle. The real move is the one that you do not see.'

'Then tell me what it is. Tell me how I can help.'

'It is simple: you can help, by not helping at all.'

There was something comforting about hearing the sound of the water crashing into the pool below. Listening to the venerable waterfall always seemed to put his mind at ease, allowing him to focus more clearly. He had spent a lot of time by the Eternal Falls after the release of his wife, sitting in solitude trying to make sense of his loss. During that time, he leant heavily on others to help care for Alarielle whilst he grieved in isolation, unable to cope with the incessant cries of his new-born daughter. He remembered the shame he felt abandoning the wellbeing of his daughter to the care of others, though in time he learned to forgive himself, eventually reintegrating with the world and even bringing Alarielle to the falls with him. Together they would sit by the waterfall listening to its soothing crescendo. He stared fondly at the tree against which he had habitually sat, whilst his infant daughter slept peacefully in his arms. As Alarielle grew older, they continued to visit the Eternal Falls together. There were times when he would make the familiar climb to the top of the falls with Alarielle heavily strapped to his back, cocooned in blankets to shelter her from the spray. After learning to read and write, Alarielle learned how to climb to the top of the falls herself, unaided. Once she had conquered the Eternal Falls, he introduced his daughter to the falchion and began instructing her in its correct use. Alarielle had a natural talent for wielding the blade and it was not long before she became a proficient sparring partner in the arena. Bringing a smile to his face, he fondly recalled the time his eager young daughter won her first competitive sword fight in the arena.

'Caught you reminiscing eh?' came the familiar deep voice of Heldran.

The abnormally large Freylarkin combed his large fingers through his long dark brown hair that flitted around in the warm breeze.

'How is it that a Freylarkin of your stature does not have children? Surely you have caught the eye of many a female in your time.'

'I do not recall you getting this deep on me before undertaking a mission. Has parenthood altered your perception of such things?'

'Maybe.'

'It just never suited me.'

'What, parenthood?'

'No, being here…this place.'

'You mean the vale?'

Heldran nodded slowly before sitting down next to him. Even when seated, Heldran was an imposing Freylarkin due to his impressive build.

'Why?' he asked curiously.

'This place is too dishonest for me. The people here focus too heavily on the betterment of themselves. In other words, the vale is too civilised for my ilk.'

He laughed, which in turn prompted a smile to form on Heldran's weathered face.

'You prefer the raw way of life the Ardent Gate offers.'

'Yes. Life there is both simple and honest. Plus, we are family – all of us.'

'I think I understand now.' he said, sympathising with Heldran's candid response.

'Yes, I believe that you do. You know what it is like to lose family. Hence, you understand why it is that I choose not to return. Besides, politicking never really suited me.'

'And it does me?' he asked, raising an eyebrow.

'You are certainly better at it than I. Case in point: right now you are quietly operating in the shadows, working on a way to prevent the poison that has contaminated your ranks from spreading any further.'

'Some would call my actions treasonous.'

'You are betraying one Freylarkin – not the domain. Besides, how can they label an action if they are unaware of it?'

'Ah, I forgot that secrecy is one of your skillsets.'

'Freylarkai talk a lot. We merely protect ourselves against the threat of wagging tongues.'

He laughed once more. Given Heldran's impressive size, he could not imagine the Freylarkin requiring any protection from his enemies.

'I see that you have brought the item I requested.'

'Yes, although I had a tough time finding one this large. In any event, perhaps now you will tell me what you intend to use it for?' asked Heldran who unravelled a roll of thick fabric on the ground revealing the sack's true size.

'Excellent, this will do.'

'For what?' asked Heldran irritably. 'I am still in the dark here.'

'We are going to use this as a net.'

'What? You seriously mean to capture a Narlakin with this – have you taken a knock to the head?'

'Many, you know that.' he replied with a wry grin.

'I am being serious. No one has ever captured a Narlakin before, yet you propose that we simply *net* our prize.'

'Strictly speaking it is not a net.'

'I *know* – get to the point.'

'One of us will distract our prey, whilst the other flanks the horror and severs its appendages. Once we have immobilised the soul stealer, we will net it with this sack.'

Heldran stared at him mutely – in truth he had hoped for a more positive response.

'You are joking, right?'

'You could be more supportive.'

'Oh my, you are being serious.'

'If we dismember the *thing* it will be far easier to capture.'

'Have you done this before?' asked Heldran, with a concerned look.

'No, never.'

'How do we know that this sack will even contain it?'

'We do not. There is no precedent for capturing such an adversary.'

'Of course we are assuming that we can even locate one on its own.'

'It is possible that we will need to fight a few.' he replied, offering his good friend a mischievous grin.

'You really have not thought this through, have you?'

'I need you Heldran. I cannot do this alone. Besides, it must get pretty dull fighting the Ravnarkai all the time.' he said followed by a smile.

'The Ravnarkai know how to bleed, and they do not try to wrench souls from the bodies of others! What you propose is madness.'

'Maybe, but it will be fun.'

Heldran wrestled with his common sense, trying hard to dissuade himself from accompanying him on his reckless mission. Heldran's concerns were valid; there were no guarantees that his proposed scheme would bear any fruit. If his plan failed, there was a good chance that neither he nor Heldran would return from the borderlands. The Narlakai were best left alone, they were not to be trifled with. Caleth actively sent Blades – specifically, those who opposed him – to the borderlands, with orders to thin the Narlakai ranks. Ultimately, this strategy was a means of disappearing those who challenged his rule, yet in a strange twist of events, he now proposed the same risk-inherent sortie. Ironically, the more he thought about his own proposal, the more he convinced himself that it was in fact a bad idea. However, despite his own growing reservations, something had struck a chord with Heldran, who now bore an ever-widening smile.

'Go on then – count me in!'

'You finally picked a side then.'

She stared coldly at The Blade Lord who stood opposite her, blocking the only exit to her dimly lit cell.

'What did you expect, Kirika?'

'You know how The Guardian's presence interferes with our scrying.'

'I have read your security reports. Even so, intuition or precedence must have led you to this conclusion. Ergo, you have prepared for this eventuality. Do not think for one moment that I was fooled by that show you had Nathaniel put on for me. Indeed, it saddens me that the pair of you deigned to insult my intelligence.'

'Rayna too was present.'

'Yes, and it angers me that you have involved her in this mess!'

'How could I not; you understand the power she wields.'

'Of course I do. She now controls the mob! That much was clear after her little stunt at Bleak Moor.'

'Then let me out of this cell Marcus!'

'You know that I cannot do that. You are not above Freylarian law, Kirika, nor is your sister!'

'The law is a self-serving one, designed to maintain *her* rule.'

'Both you and your sister – once she has been remanded – will be tried in accordance with the law, which you clearly no longer hold any regard for.'

'You cannot be this blind, Marcus. These are not your words. Mirielle's judgement is impaired, yet here you stand playing the role of her mouthpiece. She is no longer fit to lead the people – you know this. Her rule is coming to an end and it is time now that we look towards successorship.'

'You do not understand the burden she shoulders and the impact it has on her soul. She has sacrificed her own happiness to lead the people through numerous troubled times.'

'Marcus, you are right.' she replied softly, trying to empathise with his words. 'Nonetheless, where is that leadership now? It is spent, as well you know. Yes, Mirielle has seen us through hard times, and yes, she bears a phenomenal burden that none of us can fully understand. However, the old cannot endure forever; it must eventually make way for the new – that is the way of it.'

'Kirika, listen to me very carefully.' replied Marcus calmly, taking several ominous steps towards her. 'I *will* not involve myself in a coup to oust our queen, nor will I tolerate any attempts to do so by others. I have listened to your words, and I accept your position on the matter. However, I do not believe that the time of which you speak is upon us. Furthermore, your attempt to force an evolutionary step in our hierarchical structure is poorly timed; Freylar is vulnerable right now, and your political unrest weakens its foothold. Promise me that you will stop this now, whilst there is still a chance for me to salvage the situation. This folly of yours has already cost you your position on the ruling council – please do not compound your error in judgement.'

'*My* error!' she snapped back, deliberately moving to stand within a pace of The Blade Lord, her steely eyes locked intently on his own. 'She is rescinding the sanctions on scrying, now, without our consent!'

'So all of this is because your pride had been wounded?'

'Do not be so facetious Marcus – it does not suit you.' she fired back angrily, irritated by his flippant remark. 'The council exists, or rather existed, to ensure that Freylar's wellbeing is not subject to the whims of one individual. You have both lost sight of that ethos, yet you stand here, talking of *my* ego.'

'I recall informing both you and Nathaniel that I will speak with Mirielle about the issue.'

'Then bring her down here now and let us discuss the matter openly.'

'As I said, you are no longer on the ruling council.'

'Marcus, what council? She decrees and you obey, due to your staunch loyalty, or – as I suspect – out of misguided love for her; she does not feel the same way as you do Marcus, because she does not know how to!'

'Enough!'

'I was merely a spectator, as well you know, brought in to make up numbers and to provide the illusion of democracy.'

'I said enough!' Marcus snapped back, in a manner that she had not seen before.

Clearly, she had touched a nerve. For some time she had suspected that Marcus had feelings for Mirielle, but until now she had never questioned him on the matter, nor had she violated his privacy using her ability in order to learn more. She respected The Blade Lord's private life. However, his apparent feelings for Freylar's queen posed a problem.

'You will remain here in custody until your trial.' said Marcus firmly, before turning his back on her to leave the cell.

'The old must make way for the new, Marcus.' she said, repeating her earlier words.

The Blade Lord glanced over his left shoulder, offering her one final look of disapproval before closing the cell door with the power of his mind. The sound of the thick wooden door thumping against its stone archway echoed around the room, marking the end of their conversation.

'Let the people decide!' she cried out, hoping to lure Marcus back to her cell. Instead, there was nothing – she was alone.

SIX
Hunted

Her journey south to the vale had been slow, and she had underestimated the toll the increasingly cold weather would exact from her tired body. She loathed the passage of time; each passing cycle brought with it fresh torment, which, for the most part, targeted her aging joints. In her youth, a pilgrimage to Scrier's Post would have taken half the time it now did, but those cycles were little more than faint memories, growing ever dimmer. She picked her way unsteadily through the wood, finding it difficult to navigate the uneven ground. Although she was still capable of seeing through the night's gloom, her vision no longer provided the clarity it once did. She was, however, keenly aware of the excessive noise that she made as fallen detritus crunched and snapped under her slow advance, garnering the attention of the nocturnal audience watching her clumsy movements. Woodland creatures scurried through the bracken, quick to avoid the tread of her ponderous approach. In addition to the incessant rustling of nightlife all around her, she heard the occasional sound of loud cracks; the woodland it seemed was determined to make her jump. Following each loud noise, she stared into the void, trying to convince herself that no one followed her. Light from the moon spilled down through the leafless trees casting shadows that appeared to dance amidst the sparse foliage. Moving deeper into the woods, her increasing anxiety started to get the better of her, and in turn affected her breathing, which now sounded laboured. She tried to engage her venerable second sight, though with her mind jumping at shadows, establishing the focus required to engage her fickle ability became impossible. She had made a mistake travelling alone; now her frayed nerves tormented her wounded pride. She felt afraid of the surrounding woodland that she once knew so well. It haunted her every step, preying on her aging vulnerabilities, determined to thwart her clumsy passage by relentlessly assaulting her mind.

'Who is there?' she said, finally succumbing to her growing anxiety.

There was no answer. Instead, she heard the sound of another ominous crack in the distance that echoed around the cold woodland.

'Who is it?' she said, this time with a hint of panic in her voice.

Again, there was no answer. More rustling emanated from the winter bracken prompting her to quicken her pace in a bid to put the eerie terrain behind her. She pulled up her thick robe, trying hard to prevent it from snagging on fallen branches and other detritus littering the ground. Despite her best efforts, the dark purple garment fought tirelessly against her, its train eventually entangling itself on a rotten tree stump. She tugged at the thick material hoping to free it, but her winter attire remained entangled. Another crack echoed around the woodland causing her anxiety to increase sharply. Fear clouded her judgement now, causing her to tug repeatedly at her garment, desperately hoping that force alone would lead to her salvation. She heard the sound of fabric tearing as she continued to tug irrationally at her robe until eventually the defiant stump released her from its grasp. The momentum from her violent wrenching sent her careering towards the hard, unforgiving ground. She fell awkwardly, half landing on her back. Her right elbow took a heavy knock where she tried to twist her body to cushion her fall. Yet despite the bad landing, she quickly picked herself up, cursing her creaking joints whilst checking her injury. She brushed away the dirt from her elbow. The cold air stung her wound, which started to bleed. In her youth, such falls would have meant nothing, but now her paper-thin skin felt the brunt of every impact.

'Clumsy old fool!' she said, scolding herself for her error.

'Indeed.' rasped a horrid voice, carried by a foul breath that tickled her right cheek.

She turned her head. A calloused hand immediately wrapped itself around her mouth, muffling her screams, which became little more than a weak cry. The fingers and thumb of her attacker pressed firmly against the side of her face, just below the cheekbones, locking her head in a powerful vice-like grip. Two small black circles emerged from the gloom, staring intently at her. The obsidian orbs seemed to draw in what little light existed, like gateways to another realm intent on stealing the moonlight. She tried desperately to escape her attacker's grasp, clawing frantically at the rough hand clamped around her jaw. Despite her frantic attempts to free herself, the powerful hand fixed her in place, denying her any chance of escape.

'You remember me.' the voice rasped again. 'Of course you do…you were that bitch's scheming right hand. No doubt you had a part to play in my exile.'

The orbs grew larger as her attacker closed in. She could smell his rancid breath once more, made all the more prominent by the crisp cold air.

'Funny how things work out – do you not think?'

She tried to scream again, but only succeeded in muffled whining. Given the futility of her pathetic cries for help, she used what little strength she had left to kick at her assailant, managing to land several well-placed blows to his shins. Her attacker grunted, before placing his other hand around her throat and forcing her backwards until her head crashed against a large tree. The force of the impact jarred her entire body. Her vision blurred and she could feel warmth spreading from the back of her head. She felt her feet rise off the ground; her legs hung limply from her body as her attacker pushed her slowly upwards, grating her back against the cold bark of the tree. The pressure against her throat was immense, cutting off her ability to breathe. Her neck stretched and her head titled backwards causing her to cough and splutter. She felt lightheaded and the stars above began to spin. Snowflakes fell from the clear night sky, some of which came to rest on her forehead. Winter, it seemed, had come early to the domain. They were often harsh in Freylar, and it now seemed likely that this one would be her last.

'Now then,' rasped the voice close to her right ear, 'Tell me everything, and perhaps you will leave this place with all four limbs still attached, as nature intended.

'Forgive my interruption, but the other visitors have arrived.'

'What, so soon?' replied Gaelin with a genuine look of astonishment.

'Yes. Both he and his companion just appeared within the farmstead.'

'You mean to say that we did not see them coming?'

'That is correct.' replied the female Freylarkin sheepishly.

'I see.' said Gaelin with a concerned look. 'Well then...please invite them in.'

Gaelin turned towards her as the messenger quickly wandered off to escort their guests. The farmstead leader was tall and slender, and clearly looked uncomfortable playing the role the people had pressured him into accepting. Gaelin came from hard working stock, thus he had little ambition beyond working the surrounding fields. In all likelihood, the community chose Gaelin to lead their wayward operations because of his impressive height, and little else, believing that his physical stature would be enough to validate his command. Though perhaps her low assessment of Gaelin did the Freylarkin a disservice, she mused. After all, she had not met any others capable of leading them during her brief stay with the outlying community. Indeed, she had come to know them rather well in the short time spent amongst them, during which she had enlightened several families regarding the fate of their loved ones previously thought forever lost to the Narlakai.

'How did he slip past the sentries unseen?'

'He is a Paladin.'

'What!' replied Gaelin sharply, 'When you asked for a Sky-Skitter we trusted you Darlia, yet you have brought a Paladin here!'

'It is not what you think.'

'He is a Blade; they serve Mirielle!'

'Not all of them. In fact, I think you will find that quite the opposite is now true.'

'I do not understand.'

'Trust me Gaelin, he is here to help. Let me have a moment to explain.'

Before Gaelin could respond, Lothnar pushed aside the heavy drape covering the entrance to the dwelling and strode confidently in, flanked by Krisis. The panicked farmstead leader rose from his stool and took a few steps backwards at the sight of the pair, especially Krisis, whose yellow eyes reflected brightly in the gloom.

'There is no need to be concerned.' she said, trying to allay growing tensions. 'Lothnar is here to help, as is Krisis.' she said, extending her good hand towards the dire wolf, who sniffed repeatedly at his new surroundings.

Krisis plodded slowly towards her whilst continuing to sniff at the stale air, before finally sitting down on his hind legs beside her, ready for her to lavish affection upon him – which she did. The display of affection between her and the dire wolf seemed to put Gaelin at ease. The wary Freylarkin slowly approached her, grabbed his stool and finally sat back down, albeit a few paces further back from his original position. Krisis seemed unperturbed by Gaelin's cautious demeanour, paying him little or no attention, instead enjoying the affections she administered.

'Please, take a seat Lothnar.' she said, trying to soften the Paladin's roguish appearance.

'I prefer to stand.' replied Lothnar, who leaned against the wooden column supporting the roof of Gaelin's modest abode.

'*You better be right about this Darlia.*' communicated the Paladin privately, planting the terse words directly into her mind.

'Thank you for attending at such short notice, and for coming so quickly. I will get straight to the point.' she said, sensing that it would be unwise to keep the Paladin waiting any longer than necessary. 'Gaelin, who leads the community here, informs me that they are beset by wolves who plunder their herds at night. This has been going on for some time now. Mirielle is doing nothing to aid the people who are now struggling to meet the vale's demands. Word has reached Gaelin's ear from other farmstead communities reporting the same problem. In light of your ability to communicate with the children of the moon, I thought that perhaps you could assist the people here?'

Lothnar turned his head towards Gaelin and gave the Freylarkin a hard stare. The reluctant leader seemed to lose some of his stature under the Paladin's glaring scrutiny.

'You speak for the people here?' asked Lothnar plainly.

'Yes.' replied Gaelin promptly.

'And the people here…they have no love for our queen?'

Gaelin looked nervously at her, unsure whether or not to trust Lothnar, whose demeanour was anything but hospitable. She nodded to Gaelin, offering the Freylarkin a reassuring smile – or at least she tried; smiling was no longer an action she was comfortable with.

'You can trust him.' she said, knowing that she would ultimately convince him, having already scried the events unfolding before her.

After a moment's pause, Gaelin turned his attention back to the stoic Paladin.

'Mirielle does nothing to aid us. She hides in her tower and cares naught for the troubles of the people, yet she expects us to serve her without hesitation or question. Darlia says that there are Blades who share our desire to see change – is this true?'

For a long time Lothnar said nothing. The nomadic Paladin remained steadfast, content to continue his visual analysis of Gaelin, who became increasingly uncomfortable and agitated by Lothnar's lack of response. Although her second sight had always served her well, she began to wonder if her concentration had been impaired when scrying the outcome of their meeting.

'Darlia speaks the truth. Many of us wish to see change. The ruling council no longer functions. Case in point, Mirielle has recently taken Kirika into custody and intends to hold her accountable for her actions at the Trials.'

'What! When did this happen?' she asked, ceasing Krisis' affections, much to the dire wolf's displeasure.

Although her second sight allowed her to *see* events yet to unfold, the lack of sound afforded by the ability was maddening to many a scrier. Some tried admirably to read the words upon the lips of those whom they scried, but the process was difficult and error prone. As such, scriers frequently paid close attention to body language, using tell-tail signs to understand reaction and mood. However, such expressions were frequently discerned out of context, thus distorting their meaning.

'A couple of cycles past. We have not heard from your sister since. Mirielle has her under house arrest in the Tri-Spires pending trial.'

'We *must* free my sister! Lothnar, we need to go to the Tri-Spires *now*.'

'No…what we *need* to do is play her game – our way. Right now, we are on the back foot, but we have time before the trial takes place, giving us the chance to formulate a strategy.'

The Paladin's considered response surprised her. Lothnar had a reputation for allowing his emotions to get the better of him, however, Lothnar was thinking clearly now, evidenced by the logic underpinning his assessment.

'Since when did you become the voice of reason?' she asked sincerely.

'It took me a while, but I finally learned, through my own failings, that rushing into situations unprepared does not end well – a lesson *you* and others taught me well. Mirielle holds the seat of power in the vale. If we are to supplant her, we need to harness a level of power greater than her own.'

'Irrespective of Rayna's influence over them, The Blades are virtually spent. Between them, Kirika and Rayna hold sway over the forest dwellers and some of the Tri-Spires' inhabitants, but Mirielle controls the remainder, in addition to the house guards. She has Kirika, is doing her best to vilify you, and there is Marcus to consider. We need more support Darlia. Aside from your need to atone, you came here to sow doubt amongst the people, with a view to further undermining Mirielle's rule. Doubt is no longer adequate – you need to push them off the fence. If I can assist towards that end, I will.'

'You are right.' she said promptly, keenly aware of the lengthy silence between them whilst Lothnar communicated with her privately. 'Besides, my sister is not the priority here – Gaelin's people are. Lothnar, will you assist me in helping them?'

Lothnar nodded slowly before turning his attention back to Gaelin who seemed visibly more at ease now, albeit he did until Krisis decided to relocate. Having lost his source of affection, the black dire wolf began pacing slowly around the room, stopping occasionally to sniff at the floor. She watched with amusement as Gaelin's worried eyes tracked the animal's ponderous movement.

'Gaelin,' barked Lothnar, quickly regaining the attention of the farmstead leader, 'Gather your best fighters – and a renewalist, if you have one. I intend to give the pack something to think about.'

'You mean to attack them, head on?' asked Gaelin with a look of grave concern.

'A wolf pack is not going to respond to pleasantries. It is time to get your hands dirty with the rest of us.'

'But I have never fought wolves!' blurted the farmstead leader.

'That will change soon enough.'

She enjoyed The Blade Lord's company, although she was keenly aware that she struggled to show it. Meddling with her vision had enabled her to see sights previously hidden from her, however, over the passes her new perspective had become more of a curse than a blessing. Now, she habitually questioned her decision, all those passes ago, specifically the sacrifice she had made in order to acquire the vexatious ability. She turned her attention from the vale back to Marcus; The Blade Lord leant casually against the arched window in his chamber.

'Does it scare you?' he asked, staring vacantly through the opening.

'You mean the vale?'

'No, I meant the window. Although, it is interesting that you mention the vale in such context.'

'I suppose that I am more wary of it now, having fallen through it once already. Though I feel safe knowing that you are here.' she said, confident that The Blade Lord would catch her again, if needed.

'You are wary of exiles too.'

'Naturally – they are a threat. They cannot be trusted not to endanger the domain.'

'Even if they seek to atone for their past wrongdoing?'

'They *cannot* be trusted Marcus.' she replied, irritated by The Blade Lord's display of compassion for Freylar's enemies. 'Why do you question me on this? You know my view on the matter.'

'What about your view on scrying? Specifically, how it aligns – or not as the case may be – with the ruling council's own view on the practice.'

She gave The Blade Lord a hard stare. It was rare that Marcus called her to account for her actions, yet that was exactly what he was doing. Clearly, he had learned of Aleska's work at Scrier's Post, but how, she mused. There was no possibility of the venerable scrier disclosing the matter to others. Furthermore, she had told Krasus, the arrogant shaper who had assisted with the site's redevelopment, in no uncertain terms, to remain tight-lipped on the subject.

'You are referring to Aleska's work at Scrier's Post I presume?'

'Indeed I am.'

'Who informed you?'

'Does it matter?'

'It matters to me!' she replied, aware that her tone of voice implied paranoia on her part.

Silence passed between them. Ordinarily, such moments were comfortable, but now all she felt was his disapproval, despite his stoic appearance. She dipped her head, allowing her hair to obscure The Blade Lord from sight, hoping that doing so would alleviate the guilt she felt from excluding him from their agenda – which it did not.

'I am sorry for not including you in this.'

'Did Aleska insist on the clandestine nature of your actions?' asked Marcus plainly, doing his best to preclude any emotion from his enquiries.

'No, it was not that. You had enough on your plate following the loss of the Blade Aspirants at Scrier's Post. I had no desire to burden you with this issue.'

'The security of the domain *is* my burden – you appointed me to shoulder it for you.'

'Scrying is not a matter of security, Marcus. This is about leading our people into the future, armed with the information needed so that we can travel the correct path, thus avoiding such incidents from ever transpiring again.'

'But we discussed this at length. Both the ruling council and other respected members of the community agreed that the ability needs heavy sanctions. Even Darlia herself now recognises a need to reign in the ability.'

'And look where that got us!' she shot back, fixing her unflinching gaze on The Blade Lord.

'Those tragic events manifested because of her exile; we took her sister away from her.'

'There is more to it than that – you forget Lileah's role in all this.'

'If that is the case, I need full disclosure Mirielle, so that I can properly assess the threat to our domain.'

'Marcus, I do not want you involved in this. The people respect you. I do not want your clean image tarnished with this grubby affair. Aleska has spent her cycles managing unsavoury events, I am confident that she will deal with this latest incident when she returns to the vale.'

There was another lull in their conversation as Marcus considered her response. She admired The Blade Lord's ability to keep his emotions in check, focusing on what really mattered. Even though her actions had clearly wounded his pride, Marcus did his utmost not to show it, though her unique vision revealed everything to her.

'When I saved you, after you fell through this very window, do you recall the conversation you and I had subsequently?'

In truth, she did not remember his words verbatim, although she still recalled the subject of their conversation. Their private discussion had largely focused on her own doubt and ability to lead, moreover in light of her self-perceived lack of understanding of the world around them, in particular the *thing* in the sky. She looked up once more at the moving giant lattice layers still criss-crossing the horizon, a permanent reminder that none of them would ever truly be free, that they were all part of a grander mechanism. Like leaves, swirling on the ground in a turbulent breeze, none of them would ever truly be in control of their own destiny given the invisible cage in which they lived. The sphere of light – as The Guardian referred to it – owned their destinies. The Freylarkai led long lives, perhaps with scrying to aid them they could starve their captor of the souls it craved and outlast their hidden jailor. Such wildly speculative thoughts regularly assaulted her mind, torturing her during her every waking cycle. There were times when she wanted nothing more than to claw out her eyes and erase her memories, anything to return to the ignorant state from which she had evolved.

'I informed you, very clearly, that I have faith in your ability to lead us into the future. However, isolating yourself in this tower is not healthy for your soul. You need to re-engage with the people and assess their changing mood for they no longer see your vision clearly. You need to show them what I, and your other loyal followers, see in you. I said that I would always be here for you Mirielle – nothing has changed in that respect.'

'But you no longer agree with my direction, is that it?' she said, sensing that he had more to say.

'You cannot control all of the events that transpire in our domain. Watering down threats on the public stage, relentless scrying of the future and Aleska's collusions will not deter our attackers. Freylar has enemies, and it always will, but we become stronger by overcoming adversity together. The issue of scrying is divisive, but together we managed to overcome that hurdle and moved on. Clearly, I am not naïve enough to believe that everyone was happy with the outcome. Nonetheless, a collective decision *was* made. The dust has begun to settle, but reneging on this policy will upset the fragile balance that we have worked so hard to achieve.'

'I cannot lead the people if I am blind to the pitfalls that lay ahead of us Marcus. The Blades are depleted and the house guards will not offer much resistance to our enemies should they decide to attack us again.'

'The domain's military strength is *my* concern. We have begun forming a new trust with the Knights Thranis and we *will* rebuild our own Order. However, if we allow ourselves to be distracted by internal squabbles, or worse still, to become fractured, the domain's security will be further compromised.'

'I admire your optimism Marcus, but regrettably, I do not *see* it. Rayna is our only tie to the Knights Thranis, and I am not convinced that we can adequately control her. Furthermore, recruitment since the events at Scrier's Post has been lacklustre. The recent blow dealt to the Order will have worsened the situation.'

'Mirielle, have faith in the people.'

'I am sorry Marcus, but I need reassurances – scrying will provide me with that. Can I count on your support?'

Once again, The Blade Lord gave nothing away to the untrained eye. If he was feeling any anger or resentment towards her, he did not readily show it. Instead, he took her right hand and pressed it softly between his own, before leaning in to kiss her gently on the cheek.

'As I said before – nothing has changed.'

SEVEN
Fulcrum

He loathed the borderlands. Everything around them was dusty and dry. Rain appeared to have no effect on the parched landscape that seemed forever starved of water. When it did rain, moisture splattered across the arid landscape was absorbed almost as quickly as it fell, drawn down into the network of old tunnels and caverns hidden beneath the barren surface.

'How does anything survive here?' he said, as they flew low across the cracked relief.

'No idea, but if we do not stop for a break soon, *I* will not survive.'

He laughed to himself, amused by Heldran's troubles. Due to the Freylarkin's size, Heldran's wraith wings needed to work much harder, therefore he was unable to sustain flight for any real length of time. Had the Knight been wearing his armour, their progress would have been entirely on foot. However, both had agreed that agility and stealth were needed against the Narlakai.

'Perhaps I should have sat this one out.' grumbled Heldran who was clearly struggling.

'But then who would have provided my in-flight entertainment?'

'That is it – I am done!'

Heldran immediately decelerated and dropped to the ground, prompting him to do the same. As he skidded across the barren surface of the borderlands, dust and grit kicked up from the ground, forcing him to cover his eyes until eventually it dispersed. He turned around to face Heldran who was still recovering from his ordeal.

'I am surprised to see you struggling old friend. Would you like me to fetch you a chair?'

'Will you be able to make good on that offer after I am done batting you into Narlak with the flat of my ardent sword?'

Both laughed heartily, enjoying the banter that flowed effortlessly between then. If only their respective Orders shared their camaraderie, he mused. However, the actions of a few precluded such relationships. Both The Blades and the Knights Thranis distrusted one another, a debilitating mind-set cultivated by their leaders, Caleth in particular.

'Tell me again why we are here, poking around in a land which clearly does not want us in it?' said Heldran, who leant backwards, stretching his back and neck muscles. 'Can we really trust that wretched shaper to fashion what we need?'

'Nothing is certain, at least not without the aid of a scrier to assist us. Regardless, we need to try; for the sake of both Orders, Caleth needs to disappear, quietly.'

'Is that a story you can ultimately sell?'

'Although they choose to do nothing about it, nonetheless, The Blades recognise Caleth's paranoia well. It would not be a stretch if The Blade Lord were to disappear for matters of security. A period of uncertainty and confusion would no doubt ensue, but that can be managed and would ultimately pave the way for someone better to step in.'

'Would that person be you?' asked Heldran with a raised eyebrow.

'No, definitely not! I have no desire to stand on the grand stage. Besides, I will have too much dirt on my hands to assume such a role.'

'I see – you want an icon.'

'Yes!'

'And do you have one in mind?'

'There is one option, although I have concerns over the individual's suitability.'

'How so?' asked Heldran with obvious interest.

'I did not think that you would be interested in the politics of it all.'

'Ordinarily not, but if we are to go through with this mad plan of yours, I need to ensure that Caleth's successor is suitable for the role. This decision will affect both Orders. I see little point in trading one flawed individual for another, especially considering the underhand means required to facilitate the process.'

In truth, he would have preferred Heldran not to concern himself with future events resulting from their intended action. However, Heldran was highly skilled at information gathering; his request, therefore, was inevitable.

'A candid response, which deserves an equally candid answer.' he said, steeling himself for the Knight's inevitable scrutiny. 'As you know, it will be nearly impossible to undo the damage Caleth has wrought in a single generation. For this reason, I have an individual in mind who, first and foremost, will be able to unite our Order and quell internal disputes.'

'Admirable, but I fail to see how this will repair the damage between our Orders.'

'It will not, but I cannot broker a new trust between our Orders until we get our own house in check.'

Heldran raised an eyebrow once more.

'As you stated previously, our goal cannot be achieved in a single generation.'

'What are you not telling me about this individual?' asked Heldran flatly.

'The candidate I have in mind is well-suited to addressing the Order's immediate concerns; they will heal the fractures that run through the Order and rally The Blades. However, I am uncertain about their long-term suitability for the role.'

Heldran said nothing. The impressively built Knight gave him a hard stare, waiting patiently for him to elaborate on the facts that he had yet to disclose. He trusted Heldran implicitly, and had no qualms sharing his innermost thoughts with the Knight. However, he was unsure of Heldran's appetite for patience, specifically whether the Knight had the endurance to tread the long path ahead.

'I see. So, this current venture is purely aimed at putting a stopgap in place?'

'In all likelihood, yes.'

'It troubles me that you have not been able to find someone capable of fulfilling *all* of the necessary criteria.'

'I appreciate your concerns.' he replied, turning his gaze north towards the bleak horizon. 'It concerns me too – I do not like dealing with uncertainty. Regrettably, the once positive mind-set of The Blades has been undone, by The Blade Lord's questionable actions and ongoing paranoia. There is little trust within The Blades, let alone between our Orders. I have been hard-pressed to find a suitable candidate who can bring renewed direction to our Order.'

'This individual you have in mind, what is it they lack?' asked Heldran bluntly, cutting straight to the heart of the matter.

'The problem is not a lack of skill or presence, but instead something he possesses: a personality trait that will likely never wash out.'

'I see. So which one is it?' asked Heldran curiously. 'Righteousness, morality, stubbornness…compassion?'

'No, it is worse than that old friend. Those traits can be managed, through intervention or by altering one's perception of events.'

'Ah…' said Heldran wearily, 'It is *that* one.'

'Yes, the worst one of them all – devotion.'

'Forgive me Nathaniel, but when you said to me that you *needed* my help, your request implied that you actually *needed* my help.'

'You *are* helping.' he replied, glancing at Rayna, giving her one of his wry grins.

'How, by just sitting here?'

'Please be patient.'

'Who are you writing to anyway?'

He looked up once more from the tiny message scroll spread out before him, irked by the light bringer's incessant questions. Prior to Rayna entering his life, he had never known anyone with such an inquisitive disposition. Rayna was like a child, eager to learn new things, though at times her constant curiosity could be wearing.

'Does your curiosity know no bounds?' he said, realising at last the futility of his actions.

'I wouldn't want to disappoint you.'

'Clearly…' he replied, finally giving up on finishing the message in order to try sating Rayna's current interest – if that was even possible.

'Do you intend to get a message to Kirika?' asked Rayna, whose eyes widened at the prospect.

'No, she is on her own, for the time being at least. Without the aid of a telepath, particularly one whom we can trust, we have no means of contacting her.'

'Then why did you allow Lothnar to leave?'

'Allow? Ha!' he replied amusedly, 'You are mistaken if you believe that I have any control over that Freylarkin's actions – ultimately, he follows his own path.'

'You're evading the question.'

'But you have so many!'

'You know, there is a little of Heldran in you – the secretive bit that is.'

He smiled, acknowledging the truth of her words, whilst absentmindedly scratching one of the many scars on his left arm. His smile quickly faded as he fondly remembered those who had put them there, most of whom had left their world and had since passed into the Everlife.

'You will soon learn about my relationship with Heldran – there is much that I need to tell you.'

'Yes, including why Lothnar left.'

'He has gone to assist Darlia.'

'But he loathes her.'

'True, but a common cause makes for strange bedfellows. They are both committed, as are we, to bringing an end to Mirielle's rule.'

There was a strange lull in their conversation following his words, as they each quietly acknowledged the gravity of the situation. If somehow they managed to succeed, their actions would have profound repercussions, in all likelihood ushering in change to Freylarian law. The enormity of the challenge ahead weighed heavily on his soul. He had already succeeded in deposing one powerful individual, and now he intended to further extend his reach, to Freylar's queen no less. Previously, he had operated in almost complete secrecy, sharing his ambition solely with one other. This time, however, things were very different; both sides were aware of the other's intent, and division between the people was growing with each passing cycle. Word of Kirika's custody and impending trial had already begun to spread, prompting passionate open debate on the subject. With each passing cycle since her remand, more and more Freylarkai gathered by the old bridge to discuss Kirika's trial. Support for the former council member was strong, but there were those who frowned upon Kirika's actions, choosing instead to side with Freylar's queen on the matter. The reason for the latter seemed to be twofold: her blood ties with Darlia, and the way in which she had undermined the Queen's authority. In any event, Mirielle's supporters lived in the Tri-Spires on the well-to-do side of the river running through the vale. It was unclear whether they genuinely shared Mirielle's views, or instead, feared her silent judgement.

'At any rate, I am aware that we have strayed from answering my original question: to whom are you writing?' asked Rayna, trying to steer their conversation back on track.

'The things we are doing now,' he replied, deliberately seeking to derail Rayna's line of enquiry once more, 'How do they compare to your own actions during your previous life?'

He could tell by her expression that Rayna had not previously considered the parallels between the events unfolding in her new life and those from her past. Rayna largely kept the details of her former life to herself, although she had shared numerous stories with him in confidence, including the events surrounding a Kaitlin Delarouse, Austin – more commonly known as Trix – and a Mr L. Cameron, whom she had unwittingly murdered. These traumatic events had haunted Rayna, so much so that her mind had buried all recollection of them in an attempt to shield itself. It was only after her arrival in Freylar that her mind began to unravel, revealing the past atrocities and her role in the dreadful affairs. Yet there was a strange logic to her mind's self-inflicted torment. Rayna's conscious had instinctively dismantled its own protective barriers when her soul was most in need of the caged wrath inside of her. When Freylar's light was at its dimmest, Rayna was able to tap into these anger reservoirs and unleash her pent-up fury, manifested through the full extent of her ability to manipulate light. Her unrestrained fury dealt a devastating blow to their enemies time and again, and in doing so earned Rayna the respect of the people and gave credence to her namesake: The Guardian.

'When I lived in the Metropolis, I was nothing. Those sharing my social status were treated like vermin, or worse, something that needed to be scraped from the bottom of one's boot. Atrocities were commonplace. An uncaring government, eager to bury its problems, sanctioned each heinous act. I was powerless to fight back against a system that saw my kin as a blight on society, in need of disposal like unsightly waste. Trix chose to challenge that system, but his methods were too garish for me to follow him; he saw the world in black and white, as opposed to the shades of grey which I saw.'

'And that is how I see things.' he replied, resonating with Rayna's words. 'Despite her enhanced sight, Mirielle too now sees the world in pure contrast. Her tolerance for the subtle hues that make up our society has waned over the passes; she is no longer able to manage these subtleties. As a result, her stance has hardened due to her bullish actions. Clearly, she is not directly responsible for the atrocities that have befallen us. With that said, her recent poor judgement and questionable actions have steered us down a path to ruin.'

Rayna nodded slowly in agreement, reaffirming her alignment with his views.

'Regrettably, I was unable to help the Shadow Class. But things are different now; your training and Alarielle's ability have empowered me to fight back – I can help the Freylarkai.'

'Yes, you can, indeed you already have. However, your ability to manipulate light and your skill with a blade are not your greatest weapons. It is your honesty, determination and your leadership that the people value above all else.' he replied, before taking a moment to consider his following words. 'In the event that Mirielle does step aside, a power vacuum will emerge that will need filling rapidly.'

'And whom do you envisage filling that leadership void?'

'The obvious candidate is likely sat in a cell, on the other side of the river. She will need our help if she is to succeed.' he replied whilst easing into his rocking chair. 'This is a dangerous time for all of us. Battle lines are beginning to form, but it is not the enemy who we must face; a division is forming between our kin, testing friendships and shaping strange new allegiances. Kirika needs all the support we can muster. That is why Darlia and Lothnar have left, and why I write this message.'

'But who is the message for?'

'During your secondment to the Knights Thranis, I lost someone, to events that I did not foresee unfolding. This individual has potential – Kirika saw it first – and I write to them now, with new information, hoping that I can bring them back to us.'

'Who is this individual?' asked Rayna with keen interest.

'I cannot tell you. Understand that you have my utmost level of trust Rayna, but there are those who might seek to pry the information from your mind. For this reason, it is best that my intentions are not disclosed – that is why you are here.'

'I'm confused.' replied Rayna with puzzled look.

'Have you not been paying attention?' he said in a scolding tone, as though disciplining one of his students in the arena. '*Your* presence disrupts scrying, giving us a valuable edge.'

'I understand that, but what about Darlia and Lothnar – I am not with them. Surely, by your own logic, they are vulnerable to the second sight. Should I not be with them? After all, the needs of the many outweigh the needs of the few, or in this case, the individual.'

'Indeed, it is possible that their actions could be discovered.'

'But if you are aware of this, why…' Rayna began to reply, before the glaring truth suddenly dawned on her. 'You're using them as a decoy!'

'Rayna, it is imperative that Mirielle does not know what we are doing here.'

'But what *are* we doing?'

'Discrediting one of the Queen's closest allies!'

She had already postponed her visit to Kirika's cell long enough. Further delay of the inevitable confrontation with the young scrier would likely weaken her position, in particular, if Kirika sought to challenge the length of her detention. Unlike the custody of Cora and Larissa, she could not argue detaining the scrier on the grounds of personal safety, and an accusation of treason required a swift response. Despite her rhetoric, Krashnar's whereabouts was still unknown, and the vile shaper had already attacked Hanarah's daughter once, giving her the excuse she needed to detain the pair pending her discussion with Kirika – their destiny was now tied to the Fate Weaver's own. If Kirika chose to cooperate, there would be no need to take any further action; all would be free to leave and go about their business as free citizens. However, if Kirika decided to make things difficult, by continuing to oppose her rule, her hands would be tired, thus forcing her to resort to public sentencing. She hoped dearly that Fate Weaver would see reason in light of the undesirable alternative, but without the ability to scry, she had no idea as to the outcome of her meeting with the insurgent Freylarkin. On several occasions, she had considered consulting a scrier of her own, but that would mean making others aware of her agenda. Although, in theory, it was possible for any Freylarkin with the second sight to discern her future intent, despite the sanctions previously imposed by the ruling council, detection, in reality, was unlikely.

Unless she actively drew attention to her movements, no able scrier would have a need to pry into her future. Even so, she had taken great care to limit her contact with others. It was possible that Kirika could discern her agenda by piecing together information gleaned from scrying the futures of those whom she would meet. For this reason, she was forced to exclude The Blade Lord from certain decision-making, knowing that he would inevitably meet with Kirika. She hated keeping Marcus on the outside, and her feeble excuses would not wash with him forever, though until she had the issue of scrying firmly under her control, she would continue to play her cards close to her chest. There had been numerous times when she had wanted to explain this reasoning to Marcus, hoping that his tactical thinking would appreciate the merit of her approach. However, she was also keenly aware of his affections towards her – despite her inability to reciprocate. In all likelihood, the knowledge of her reasoning would be poorly received. If Marcus ever learned the truth of it, the trust relationship that existed between them would likely be broken.

Her heart began to beat faster as she approached the door to Kirika's cell whilst mindful of her cumbersome lame arm, which seemed determined to make any form of movement awkward. She hated confrontation; she was forever conscious about appearing nervous or forgetting her train of thought when under pressure. It was expected of her, as Freylar's queen, to manage stress with ease – most believed their leaders to be emotionally impervious to challenges against their authority. With that said, she always found conflict awkward, choosing instead to employ Marcus for such work. Yet on this particular occasion, she could not turn to The Blade Lord for assistance. Fate Weaver was one of the domain's most powerful scriers, who no longer required physical contact in order to scry one's future or past; line of sight over short distances alone was sufficient for Kirika to engage with a person or object. Therefore, she needed to take steps to ensure that her secrets remained exactly that. Although she acknowledged that she could not shield herself from Kirika's second sight indefinitely, for the time being at least she needed to maintain her anonymity.

There were no house guards stationed outside of Kirika's cell. In light of the scrier's impressive ability, she had deliberately ordered the guards to avoid Kirika's cell at all times. After checking the corridor to ensure that no one else was present, she approached the cell door, before pressing her back firmly against the granite wall adjacent. Satisfied that that there was no way that Kirika could see her through the narrow slit cut into the thick door, she called out to the scrier, seeking to gain Fate Weaver's attention.

'Kirika.' she said, quietly at first, careful not to arouse any undue attention.

She waited quietly for a response. Given that there was no natural light in Kirika's cell, it was possible that the scrier had chosen to pass the time by sleeping. Regardless, she continued to wait, but still there was no response.

'Kirika!' she said once more, this time in a more forceful tone.

Again, she waited patiently, until eventually, a groggy voice replied.

'Who is there?' asked the voice, followed by the sound of approaching footsteps from the other side of the cell door.

'Your queen.'

There was no reply. An uneasy silence passed between them, since neither was prepared to make the first move. It had taken her time to build up the courage necessary to voice her convictions, yet now she faltered, thwarted by the scrier's silent judgement. She tried several times to voice her proposition, but with each attempt, the words seemed to die in her throat.

'Say what you have come to say and be done with it.' said Kirika tersely, breaking their long silence.

'Very well.' she said, at last finding the confidence to speak. 'I want you to leave the vale.'

'Have you learned nothing?' replied Kirika sharply. 'You want me to accept exile?'

'It would not be exile.' she said, hoping to elaborate on her hasty words. 'Find a quiet place on the outer fringes, perhaps with one of the farmstead communities, well away from the Tri-Spires and the heart of the vale. Take your sister if you wish...'

'So that is it then: you want us to disappear?'

'I want you both gone, away from the public spot light.'

'Ah, so that neither of us can influence public opinion.'

'I need to surround myself with allies, not those who would challenge me at every turn.'

'You are afraid of us speaking openly, giving voice to the thoughts of others.'

'Call it what you like.' she replied tersely, 'Do we have an agreement or not?'

'No, we do not!'

She sighed loudly, frustrated by the scrier's stubbornness. Kirika's inability to walk away was not unexpected, though she had hoped for a better outcome.

'Put all of this behind you. Find some place remote where you can be with your sister, in peace, and remove yourself from the centre stage, quietly – that is my offer.'

'My answer remains the same.'

She could feel her anger rising inside. Deep down, she knew that Kirika would oppose her offer, forcing her to adopt a more heavy-handed approach. Accordingly, she had prepared for such a conclusion, though her soul was at odds with her planned means of coercion.

'Whilst you were busy with The Blades, engaged with the Narlakai at Bleak Moor, we had an incident involving a local dressmaker. Her name is Larissa. I believe the two of you know one another.'

'What incident?' asked Kirika sharply.

'An unfortunate one. I *had* hoped to keep the matter confidential, however, your lack of cooperation makes that very difficult.'

'What happened?'

'Larissa will be formally accused of the release of another.'

'Release! Who?'

'Hanarah, a local store proprietor and mother to one whom is currently in my care.'

'You expect me to believe that a famed dressmaker released Hanarah, leaving her daughter to survive in your care?'

'There were extenuating circumstances, but yes, that is the truth of it.'

'You are lying!'

'We have a witness – two in fact.'

'Who?'

'The daughter, Cora, and myself.'

'You were there when it allegedly happened?'

'Yes – I saw it with my own eyes.'

'Then your eyes deceive you. Not only is your judgement impaired, in addition, your self-meddling has affected your vision. You are no longer seeing clearly, both physically and figuratively speaking. Larissa would *never* have committed such a crime.'

'You think that you know her so well…why, because you purchased a few garments from her, is that it? If that is the sum total of your character reference for her, I fear for Larissa's future after her trial.'

'This is ridiculous – you must stop this Mirielle!'

'Why should I court risk by interfering with justice on *your* behalf, when your current raison d'être is to be a thorn in my side?'

'This is not justice!'

'Then help me find it!'

'No! I will not be coerced like this! Your actions only strengthen my resolve. You have lost your way Mirielle. You can feel your grip on Freylar loosening, to which your desperate response is this madness.'

'If you will not see reason, there is nothing further I can do to help your friend. Larissa will stand trial, in the arena, immediately before you do, where she will answer for her crimes.'

'What are you saying?'

'You know as well as I that the punishment for release is release itself.'

'Mirielle, *stop* this!'

'You have my terms.' she said, eager to end their heated conversation. 'I will give you the courtesy of two cycles, during which you can think over my proposal. Ask for me, should you decide to *soften* your resolve.'

'And what if I do not?'

'Then there is nothing further to discuss.' she said coldly. 'I will visit Larissa's cell, two cycles from now, and break the unfortunate news to her. In the meantime, I will continue to care for Hanarah's daughter – take comfort in that fact.'

'You heartless bitch!'

If spoken more than a pass ago, Kirika's words would have likely stung. Instead, hearing them now from her quarry, she felt nothing. In light of her anger towards the scrier, Kirika's venomous tongue had no effect. She briefly considered a departing remark, but ultimately decided against it; sometimes a lack words was more powerful than words themselves. Instead, she turned her back on the hysterical scrier and quietly walked away, leaving Kirika to scream alone in her cell.

EIGHT
Pawn

'I do not like it.' said Heldran sternly, whose voice reminded him of distant thunder rumbling across the horizon.

'Neither do I, but what choice do we have?'

They peered gingerly over the edge of a giant crack in the broken landscape, their bodies pressed flat against the dusty ground. Silently, they watched as their prey loitered beneath them in the shadow of the precipice, unsure as to whether or not the seemingly oblivious soul stealer was aware of their presence.

'We do not know how many more of those things are down there.' said Heldran in a low voice, after withdrawing slowly from the precipice.

'It is alone – we may never get another shot at this.' he replied passionately, whilst he too withdrew from the edge of the broken landscape.

'If we go down there, we could end up facing hundreds of the things whilst trying to get back out through those caverns.' explained Heldran calmly. 'Besides, there is little space to manoeuvre down there – we would not be able to flank it.'

'Perhaps you should have brought a smaller blade?'

Heldran regarded him with an uncharacteristic sidelong glance, suggesting that perhaps he was pushing his luck with the Knight due to his poorly timed quip.

'We *can* do this.' he said fervently, seeking to get Heldran back on side. 'I suggest that we drop down either side of it to gain the tactical advantage.'

'That would put the enemy between us.'

'Exactly!' he replied enthusiastically. 'If you descend first and bait it, I will then engage the soul stealer from the rear and sever its appendages, after which you will be able to net it.'

'But if we do not sack it in a timely manner, we could end up being outflanked ourselves – who knows what is lurking in those caverns adjacent.'

'When did you start to worry so much?'

'Since you started losing your mind.' replied Heldran gruffly.

He smiled at the Knight's quip. He understood Heldran's reluctance, but time was against them. For two cycles they had scouted the borderlands, with only the present opportunity to show for their efforts. Further absence from the vale would only arouse suspicion, and venturing into Narlak itself would be a fool's errand. Whilst there was every chance that they could move on and find another opportunity, it was equally likely that they would be forced to return to the vale empty-handed. In light of their absence and having already coerced Krashnar into aiding them, they were committed. They could ill afford to dawdle any longer in the desolate waste.

'Ignore me.' replied Heldran wearily. 'I have been spending too much time in the company of Morin.'

'With the greatest respect, our search is hindered by your bulk and poor night vision – time is not our friend.'

Heldran sighed whilst nodding his head in acknowledgement. Scratching around in the borderlands while it was light had been fruitless, as well the Knight knew. Yet despite concentrating their hunt at dusk and dawn, the Narlakai had remained elusive, thwarting their attempts to harvest the raw material Krashnar required.

'I have no desire to coerce you my friend, but are we doing this or not?' he said, hoping to spur the Knight into action.

Heldran sighed once more, before reaching for the sack wrapped tightly around his ardent sword.

'Fine, let us get it done.' said Heldran reluctantly. 'But if you lose your soul to one of those bastards, do not expect me to double back, just so that you can be on your merry way to the Everlife.'

The colossal Knight crouched on his knees, trying unsuccessfully to remain low as he retraced his path back towards the precipice.

'And, do not expect me to explain your folly to your daughter, *if* you fail to return.'

The mention of his daughter crystallised in his mind the risk they were about to take. Whilst they had been preoccupied searching the borderlands, he had selfishly neglected Alarielle, who was no doubt worrying about his prolonged absence. Although he had been known to wander off from time to time, it was rare that he remained absent for so long. In addition, there was still the time it would take them to journey back to the vale to consider. He had been away from their home for far too long. Growing suspicions aside, he needed to get back for his daughter's sake. In a strange way, he had enjoyed his time gallivanting around the dusty borderlands, spending time with Heldran, but ultimately they had a job to do. The time had come to complete their mission and return to the vale with the macabre trophy requested by Krashnar, necessary for the twisted shaper to complete his unorthodox work. He did not truly understand the nature of the sinister weapons Krashnar intended to fashion, though he expected the worst.

Whatever it was the aloof shaper had in mind, there was every chance that the disturbing blades would exact a heavy toll from those choosing to wield them.

'Mark my words old friend: I *will* be returning to the vale; I have a daughter to get back to, as you rightly pointed out. I did not intend to be absent for this long. Go now, and let us get this done.' he said to Heldran who nodded in agreement.

Like a pair of assassins in perfect synchronisation, they extended their wraith wings before launching themselves over the edge of the precipice.

She woke abruptly. Her breathing was shallow and rapid, and her skin felt damp and sticky. She glanced at her bed sheet, now soaked with sweat, further proof that she had in no way imagined the conversation responsible for her restless night.

"You heartless bitch!"

The words repeated themselves relentlessly in her mind, denying her any respite from the worry they carried with them. She pushed back the damp bed sheet and quickly stood upright, her feet flat against the cold hard floor. Living in the Tri-Spires had its benefits, chief among them shelter from the biting wind. However, during winter its inhabitants habitually felt the cold. Heating the entire structure was an impossible task, therefore an attempt was only made to keep the communal areas warm, in addition to the Queen's private chamber. She quickly put on a thick navy-blue dress and draped a heavy shawl over her head and shoulders, hoping to keep the worst of the cold at bay. Pacing aimlessly around her room, she tried desperately to make sense of it all. Like many who worked closely with the Queen, she had seen first-hand the changes in Mirielle's disposition since the invasion at Scrier's Post. Thinking back now, Mirielle's mood had started to change well before the Narlakai had attacked the sanctuary, but recent events since summer had noticeably accelerated her changed mind-set. Mirielle was no longer the understanding and kind ruler she once knew, instead, something much sharper had taken hold of their once benevolent leader. As she replayed the conversation back in her mind, she struggled to understand the motivation behind the Queen's ultimatum. Kirika was a good person, who always put the welfare of the Freylarkai before her own – demonstrated recently at the battle for Bleak Moor. Unsurprisingly, she struggled to comprehend why Mirielle harboured such resentment towards the famed scrier.

'Come on Kayla, think!' she said, chiding herself for failing to understand the politics behind it all.

She enjoyed a close working relationship with Kirika, to whom she was utterly loyal. That loyalty had led her to her former employer's cell, where she had inadvertently overheard the hushed conversation whilst loitering in the adjoining corridor. It had been difficult to understand their words at first, but as their choler rose, the appalling truth made itself known to her. She recalled the shocking moment when Mirielle delivered her ultimatum, using Larissa as a means to coerce Kirika into compliance. Knowing that such underhanded tactics were being used to maintain Mirielle's rule sickened her, though perhaps such behaviour was nothing knew, she mused. Maybe her eyes were simply open now; perhaps the distasteful event she had witnessed was normal practice behind closed doors. Regardless of her personal feelings, she wanted desperately to inform others of her inadvertent discovery. However, if nothing else, the passes spent working alongside the famed scrier had taught her one thing: knowledge was power, and needed guarding well. Nevertheless, she lacked the experience to act on the information alone. She needed someone trustworthy, able to divine the way forward for her. She knew of no one suitable within the Tri-Spires, aside from those already in custody. Furthermore, her proximity to Kirika made her a potential target for exploitation; she had no desire to assume Larissa's role, therefore she needed to get out of the Tri- Spires, and fast. Grabbing what personal effects she could carry, she quickly packed a small shoulder bag, not knowing if she would be returning to her chamber anytime soon – if at all. Fearing the worst, and with no place to go, she chose a second shawl, wrapping it tightly around her neck hoping to better her protection against the winter cold. There were reports of snow falling during the encroaching winter nights; it would not be long before the temperature dropped sufficiently to allow it to settle, covering the vale in a blanket of snow. The Freylarkai were no strangers to harsh winters and had grown accustomed to weathering the elements. Even so, she had no desire to endure the bitter cold any longer than was necessary.

After grabbing what she needed, she swiftly made her way along the warren of passageways connecting the myriad of chambers that made up the base of the Tri-Spires. A surprising number of Freylarkai had already risen and were eagerly going about their business. She envied their ignorance, oblivious to the politics surrounding them. Pressing on, she nodded politely to friends and acquaintances whom she passed, keen to avoid engaging them in conversation whilst maintaining the semblance of calm as she sought to exit the Tri-Spires in the most efficient manner possible. When finally nearing its exit, a voice unexpectedly called out to her, sending a chill down her back.

'Kayla!'

Startled by the sound of her name, she hesitated briefly before quickening her pace, desperate to flee the structure, completely disregarding the summons.

'Kayla, the Queen wishes to speak with you.' the voice cried loudly, warranting the attention of those around her, each now casting their gaze in her direction.

She immediately panicked. With her mind struggling to coordinate her movements under the pressure, she meandered into the path of another, inadvertently knocking a young female to the ground, garnering further attention. Adrenaline coursed through her body and she could feel her heart thumping in her chest.

'I am so sorry!' she said absentmindedly whilst frantically turning her head towards the menacing voice.

She stared wide-eyed at a house guard approaching her at speed from the end of an adjoining passageway. The same fear she experienced at Bleak Moor assaulted her once more, but without Kirika to guide her she could feel herself falling to pieces inside as her anxiety increased exponentially. Her mind began to fog up and the chamber around her started to spin, making her feel giddy. A hand suddenly grabbed her shoulder bag, tugging at it violently, pulling her face-to-face with a familiar acquaintance.

'Force me back then head to the exit.' whispered Ralnor quickly, who clenched the end of her bag with his balled left hand. 'Go, now!'

Reacting instinctively, she punched Ralnor violently in the face with her free hand, allowing the bag to slip from her right shoulder. A loud gasp rose from the onlookers as Ralnor fell backwards into the gathering crowd with his arms splayed, knocking those immediately behind him to the ground. Her audience withdrew from her in shock, causing a bottleneck to form around the end of the adjacent passageway.

'Kayla, stay where you are!' cried the other guard, now struggling to pick his way through the turmoil forming between them.

She glanced at Ralnor; a young male standing behind him held the guard upright in a tight grasp. Ralnor's lips bled furiously where she had caught him flush along the bottom of his nose, possibly fracturing it. Yet despite her vicious attack, the fallen guard winked at her. Ralnor bent his left wrist back, then slowly and deliberately splayed his fingers in a manner she instantly recognised. She gave the injured guard a discrete nod then turned and fled towards the exit. Once clear of the dumbfounded spectators she increased her speed, quickly fleeing the structure. Running now, desperate to put some distance between her and the Tri-Spires, she could feel the crisp air stinging her inside as she breathed deeply. Within moments, she was out of breath, entirely due to her poor fitness. Her legs were also beginning to tire, albeit because of her inappropriate attire as opposed to a lack of stamina. Quickly realising that running was not her best means of escape, she extended her wraith wings and sped off towards the river, hoping that she possessed the stamina necessary to make the required flight distance. Despite the cold wind buffeting her ears, she could hear shouting in the distance. The muffled words increased her anxiety, giving her the impetus she needed to press on. It was only after crossing the river that she finally relented, setting down clumsily on the opposite bank before recalling her tired ethereal wings. It was rare that she flew, evidenced by her lacklustre endurance, though despite her poor fitness, she held the advantage over her pursuers; the house guards were unable to sustain flight whilst wearing their armour, thus allowing her to make good her escape. Had Lothnar's scouts been pursuing her, things would have ended very differently. Instead, she slipped into the forest, quickly disappearing amongst the welcoming trees offering her refuge.

'What are you doing?'

She stared blankly at him, carrying the expression well. Others may have been fooled by her pretence, but not him; he knew The Guardian well enough to see past the façade that she now offered him.

'I don't understand your question.'

He sighed, failing to mask his disappointment. Of those around him, Rayna was the last person he expected to play such games. Since her arrival in Freylar, the fledgling light bringer had habitually demonstrated openness and a refreshing level of honesty. However, it appeared that Rayna had since familiarised herself with the art of deception; given her antics at the Trials during her duel with Lothnar, he supposed that such political tactics were inevitable. Still, it had been a mistake to allow Kirika a hand in Rayna's personal development. Now, he had to contend with the fallout of Mirielle's benevolent decision.

'She is a bad influence on you.'

'Who is?'

'Do not play games with me Rayna – it does not suit you.'

'You're referring to Kirika then.'

'Correct.'

'I did not come here to incur your ire Marcus, nor do I take you for a fool.'

'You came here because I summoned you.' he said, fixing her with his unflinching gaze.

After the events at Scrier's Post, Rayna had shown considerable promise. Indeed, she had managed to earn the favour of the Knights Thranis – something that he himself had been unable to achieve. Later, during the battle for Bleak Moor, The Guardian had earnt her namesake again by rising to the challenge and turning the tide of the battle in their favour. Regrettably, however, Rayna's accolades, coupled with her rapid ascension through the Order, had made her a political pawn. Rayna's increasing popularity, and the following that came with it, was undeniable – Kirika knew this fact well, and had steered The Guardian down a path that best served her own ambition. And then, there was Nathaniel; The Teacher's close proximity and strange blood ties to Rayna had no doubt coloured her view of events.

'Do you understand the precarious nature of the path upon which you tread?'

'Marcus, you and I are both victims of circumstance.'

'Ha, now that is the honesty I have come to expect from you.' he said as he moved away from her, perching himself on the stone window sill in his chamber, as was his way.

The tension in the room eased a little, prompting Rayna to relax; the famed light bringer sat on the edge of the writer's bench against the wall opposite his bed.

'Thank you for coming,' he said absentmindedly whilst casting his gaze across the vale, 'I was unsure if you would meet with me given the circumstances.'

Winter's touch had stripped the colour from the land, giving it a bare and uninviting feel. Washed-out bracken now dotted the vale, previously covered in verdant foliage and flora, and leafless trees stood motionless, withered testaments to their former splendour, now marring the view like a child's scribblings upon a once glorious canvas. Looking down upon the bleak landscape drained his motivation. During the many long passes since his appointment as Blade Lord, he had worked tirelessly to unite the Order and exorcise the demons ushered in by his predecessor. The job had largely been a thankless one, nevertheless, he had earned the respect of The Blades for his efforts, which – in his mind at least – was thanks in itself. Though despite his indefatigable attitude, he had failed to achieve the lofty mark set by himself – like most artists, he was his own worst critic. Regrettably, the last pass had seen nearly everything he had worked towards slip from his grasp. Dissention had grown between the Paladins and Valkyries, two invasions had savaged their ranks, they had lost a well-respected Captain and now a gulf was forming between those he previously called allies. The stresses and strains on the Order had reached breaking point, and without Ragnar by his side, he could no longer hold The Blades together. Irrespective of their opposed views on Kirika's custody, he needed Rayna by his side to stand any chance of healing the Order's wounds. Her enthusiasm and determination were infectious; both were tools that he desperately needed to embolden The Blade's waning resolve.

'Marcus, you are The Blade Lord – I swore allegiance to the Order, and therefore you, as its leader.'

'Yes, but you are also loyal to others, for reasons that I fully appreciate.'

Rayna chose not to respond to his statement. She knew that his assessment was correct, and that there would be no easy choice for what was ultimately to come.

'You need to choose a side in all of this.' he said whilst continuing to survey the vale below.

'I have no desire to oppose you Marcus.'

'Understood. However, we have both unwittingly become pawns in a game played by others; it is those individuals who would see you and me standing opposite one another.'

'I presume that you are referring to Mirielle and Kirika.'

'No,' he replied, failing to contain his laughter, 'I refer to Mirielle and Nathaniel!'

He turned his head towards Rayna who now wore an overcast expression. It was difficult to know whether he had confirmed Rayna's own suspicions, or whether he had revealed a truth previously unknown to her. He tried to recall the anger he had felt when Nathaniel broke the news of Mirielle's secret agenda. Hearing the words from another had wounded his pride – even now, he felt their keen sting.

'You must realise by now, Rayna, that *he* is the invisible hand that guides our actions. Nathaniel has been quietly grooming Kirika for this moment, as was the case for me, when I ascended to my current role.'

'What do you mean?' asked Rayna, whose grim expression intensified.

'The Queen – as I am sure you are aware by now – withheld certain knowledge from me, in particular her changed stance on scrying. Yet he is guilty of the same crime. There are truths that – I believe at least – Nathaniel has deliberately withheld from you, to avoid marring your opinion of him.'

'Heldran informed me of his questionable past, though I have yet to confront him on the matter.'

'Then you should do so. And once it is done, I need you to do me a favour: talk to him, for me, for his own sake. Get him to stop this, before it goes any further.'

'But what if his conviction is enough to convince me that his past crimes were justified? What then of your own attempts to manipulate me Marcus?'

'Rayna, you have inadvertently become a potent weapon in Freylarian politics, due to your rising popularity and demi-god status. You are a protector of the people, and they love you for it. Your actions have even enamoured you to the Knights Thranis, evidenced by Vorian's presence in our queen's chamber no less. Perhaps, next time, you will include me in such decision making.' he said with a hard stare. 'Regrettably, however, you have a difficult decision to make. Your choice – whatever the outcome – carries with it the weight of the people who follow in your wake. You must decide whether to trust me, knowing that I have never made an attempt to deceive you, or, to trust another, who clearly operates from the shadows.'

Before Rayna could respond, his attention was drawn to the distant sound of shouting below. He directed his gaze towards the vale once more, quickly spotting a tiny figure below, fleeing from the Tri-Spires towards the river. The hooded figure – whoever it was – ran clumsily at first, then, after realising the futility of their efforts, rapidly accelerated in speed after deploying their wraith wings, evidenced by the blur of light trailing in their wake. Two house guards shortly emerged from the base of the Tri-Spires, presumably looking to give chase, yet neither chose to do so, probably on account of their attire. He had debated the use of armour within the Tri-Spires repeatedly. Ragnar had held the opinion that armour was for those who lacked skill, and was completely unwarranted within the Tri-Spires. Whilst there was indeed some merit to the former Captain's blunt assessment, most of the house guards were not skilled – at least not compared to Nathaniel's stock. Therefore, he had taken the decision to have the guards wear armour whilst at their station, a decision that he now questioned. He raised his hand, ready to bring a swift halt to the Freylarkin's escape, courtesy of his ability, when suddenly Rayna interjected, placing a hand on his own.

'Better to let them run.' said Rayna curiously.

'What is your thinking?' he said, interested in what the light bringer had to say.

'I know those people across the way, and they trust me. Whoever it is down there will not get far. With the help of the forest dwellers I'll know exactly where to look.'

'Better to let them run, so that we can discover where, or who, they are running to?' he replied, offering Rayna a wry grin.

'Exactly.'

He turned his attention back to the light bringer and gave her an approving nod.

'I miss Ragnar very much. However, you will make a worthy successor when the time is right.'

Assuming the form of the whimpering female's mother had been challenging, but adopting the old scrier's countenance was even more so – albeit in other ways. Mimicking Aleska's age lines convincingly proved to be particularly difficult. Furthermore, he continued to struggle with impersonating voices, especially those of females. Given Aleska's advisory role to Freylar's queen, he needed, at the very least, to sound plausible in passing – feigning illness would only carry him so far. To make matters worse, Mirielle's guard was also up in the wake of his failed attempt to release the arrogant bitch. It was entirely likely that his disguise would fail him now that the inhabitants of the vale were on notice. However, with his options limited and no sign of Lileah, he had little choice but to accept the risks involved. Nevertheless, there were some positives: the old scrier's posture closely matched his own, and Aleska's venerable cracked voice masked his lack of vocal talent. Even so, it was a bore feigning frailty in light of the preternatural strength and dark desire coursing through him, imparted by his dark companion. With each passing cycle, he could feel his soul succumbing to twisted yearnings of the parasite leeching off his very being. Though he had always harboured a need to experiment with his ability, in particular with the flesh, the dark cravings emanating from the darkness spreading throughout his body now eclipsed his own. Having savoured the delights of inflicting pain and misery on others, it wanted more – so much more. He felt like a spectator now, no longer in control of his own body, as though their roles had now switched entirely. His dark companion now directed his attention, firmly fixing it on Freylar's queen despite the risks. Having sampled her flesh once already, the evil inside him wanted nothing more than to savagely violate Mirielle's marble-like flesh for a second time. The thrill of hunting prey that had escaped its captor was intoxicating. The thought of ravaging her flawless skin filled him with ecstasy, making it difficult to focus on anything other than the hunt. In his growing stupor, he had crashed noisily through the woodland, towards the heart of the vale, his raucous approach scattering the local fauna, rightly fearing his tread. What remained of himself still recalled the noise of the wildlife scuttling through the brush, desperate to evade his uncouth presence. Previously, he had had the sense to limit his movements until after dusk, but now he could feel the pull of the darkness inside him forcing him to press on. It cared not for the subtleties of stealth and a well thought out plan, consumed by a need for Mirielle's flesh – a need that was fast becoming his own. He licked his dry cracked lips at the thought of violating Freylar's queen once more, as he approached the river separating the inhabitants of the Tri-Spires from those of the forest. He offered his surroundings a cursory glance, ensuring that no one else was present. As luck would have it, he was upstream of the old bridge, well away from the eyes of the gossiping Freylarkai who took endless pleasure from blathering on about routine events filling their mundane existences. Satisfied that he was alone, he used his enhanced strength to propel himself across the water with one almighty jump. After landing cleanly on the opposite bank with a deep thump, he assumed his hunched stance once more, ready to press on, doing his utmost to maintain his faux visage. However, before he could set off, a young female emerged from behind a group of weather-beaten trees, holding a large bundle of cloth in her hands. The Freylarkin's timing was appalling – for her, at least. Had she seen him crossing the river he wondered, albeit briefly, before a leering smile rapidly spread across his face.

'Then again…who cares…' he said, licking his lips once more.

NINE
Resolve

'Darlia, we are not ready for this.' said Gaelin.

The look of concern on the farmstead leader's face had been evident since the moment Lothnar had insinuated that Gaelin and the others would be required to pick up arms. The farmstead leader worried a lot, but then it was probably his job to do so, she mused. Even so, the cautious leader had a lot to learn, such as masking his thoughts instead of inciting panic amongst the people.

'It will be fine.' she said, trying her best to ease his nerves.

'Darlia, we are not fighters. We work the land. We do not go around picking fights with strays.'

For two cycles, Lothnar had worked tirelessly with those able members of the community in an attempt to prepare them for the challenge ahead. Given the short amount of time available, it was impossible for the Paladin to upskill Gaelin and the others to a satisfactory level. However, *some* training, no matter how condensed, was better than none. Lothnar had done well to teach them basic moves and wields, which, they hoped, would be enough to keep them in the fight, at least for long enough to provide adequate distraction. It would be down to herself, Lothnar and Krisis to do the bulk of the heavy lifting, whilst Gaelin's lot held the perimeter. The community only needed to defend their flanks, buying them enough time to deal with the pack's Alpha.

'Try not to worry.' she said in a sympathetic voice.

'Darlia, do not coddle them.' said Lothnar brazenly, undoing her attempts to calm their audience. 'Not all of you will make it tonight, but what choice do you have?'

'We could keep doing what we have been so far!' cried a voice from the back of the crowd.

'Sure, you do that.' replied Lothnar tersely, without any sympathy. 'Hole up in your homes whilst *they* devour your livestock. Go cower behind locked doors and allow the wolves to take what is not theirs, leaving you – and all the other inhabitants of Freylar – to go hungry this winter. And, whilst you are at it, explain to the Queen your justification for this action.'

'This is her fault!' cried another. 'She's supposed to protect us. Where are The Blades?'

'The Blades are spent!' she said, taking a step towards the irritable crowd. 'They gave everything to hold back the Narlakai. As for the Queen, she does not care about your insignificant troubles; Mirielle's only concern is maintaining her rule. Now then, you either do this – with our help – or go find yourselves someplace else to raise your herds.'

'This is *our* home!'

'Then defend it!' said Lothnar sharply, moving to stand alongside her. 'We are the only ones here willing to aid you, but we cannot protect this place by ourselves. If you cannot find the courage to defend your homes, what purpose was there to the last two cycles of training?'

There was no immediate response from the crowd. Lothnar's blunt proclamation had seemingly stunned their audience into silence, allowing no room for further excuses. She had tried to lend a sympathetic ear to the people, but she could see now that the community's spirit had waned through erosion over the passes. They stood before her, defeated, before the fight had even begun. It was clear to her that, rather than the promise of a glorious battle, they need something to hold onto – they needed hope.

'Your fates are not fixed.' she said, raising her voice so that each of them could hear. 'Stand alongside us and you *will* be victorious.'

'*What are you doing?*' communed Lothnar telepathically. '*You cannot know that – scrier's have made it clear, time and again, that the outcome of any war is uncertain.*'

'Have you seen it, Darlia?' asked Gaelin eagerly.

'I see the smouldering anger in your hearts; direct that towards the enemy, and it will compensate for any lack of skill.'

She could sense her words resonating with the farmstead leader as she poked at the fire in his soul. Despite his lack of confidence, Gaelin and his people sought only one thing: hope. With it, they were easily emboldened, and would rise to face the challenges ahead. The wayward community reminded her of an angry mob – easily broken, but also a potent weapon if wielded correctly. Gaelin was its mouthpiece, but she would be the one to lead them.

'Stand with us, tonight, and we *will* be victorious!' she said, giving Gaelin the final nudge needed to set him, and the others, to task.

'Get back to your training!' said Gaelin suddenly.

Immediately the crowd dissipated. Fresh enthusiasm permeated their ranks, giving them renewed vigour. Each promptly resumed their training, emboldened by her carefully chosen words and Gaelin's reinvigorated command.

'Darlia, a word please.' said Lothnar with steely eyes.

They took a step back from the training and joined Krisis, curled on the ground next to a weather-beaten outhouse. The loyal dire wolf was content to waive politics in favour of a decent nap.

'You lied to them.' said Lothnar sternly.

'I said nothing about scrying their future.'

'Regardless of your careful choice of words, you still implied as much.'

'I gave them hope – they needed it.'

'Agreed, but that hope could be a false one. Have you considered this fact?'

'A false hope is better than no hope. With it, they will fight beside us, and they *will* win.' she replied vehemently. 'Hope inspires determination, and that is a potent weapon – look to The Guardian if you need reminding.'

The Paladin considered her words carefully, free of the emotion that had previously clouded his judgement.

'The numbers are favourable; packs typically number six or seven, although, I have seen larger. With that said, they will have speed and agility that we cannot hope to match.'

'Then I need you to find a way to mitigate their physical advantage in the event that you cannot deal with their Alpha. We must plan for the worst possible scenario.'

'Some of them know how to hunt – a necessary skill for survival out here – which means they can shoot. We need to arm those Freylarkai adequately and get them off the ground.'

'Will these outhouses do?'

'Yes, although we will need to lure the pack here – we cannot fight them in the fields.'

'I have no intention of even trying to outrun a pack of wolves – this, you see, does not lend itself to feats of agility.' she said, raising her prosthetic claw, reminding the Paladin of her glaring disability.

'I need you on top of one of those outhouses – I have seen first-hand your skill with a bow.' replied Lothnar, who offered her a weak smile whilst studying her claw.

'Then it is agreed. I will coordinate those up high, whilst you lure the enemy in. Krisis will defend the ground along with the others.'

Upon hearing his name, the slumberous dire wolf suddenly stood up. She was unsure whether the black animal intuitively understood his role in their plan, or whether his master had communicated the details telepathically.

'Indeed.' agreed Lothnar, 'However, we are still vulnerable; we need to prepare adequate defences around the perimeter to slow them down – without them, you and the others will find it difficult taking your shots.'

'Continue their training. I will round up those who cannot fight. Between us we will have them prepare for the impending assault.'

Lothnar nodded in agreement before turning to resume his training of Gaelin's hastily assembled militia. Krisis remained with her; the dire wolf sat on his hind legs, staring at her obediently, awaiting her beck and call.

'I suspect that the others will require a little motivation if we are to coax them out of their dwellings on the eve of battle. No doubt your presence will coerce their frayed nerves.'

Krisis barked at her loudly, signalling his loyal obedience. Staring into his intense yellow eyes, her mind started to drift. She recalled the events that had taken place since the moment she had willed herself to get up from the grubby floor of the Meldbeast's pen. Much had happened since then; the domain no longer hated her, instead, there were those who now relied on her aid, affirming just how fickle the Freylarkai truly were. In that moment she started to appreciate the difficulties involved in holding the people together, and how politics were a necessary tool when managing the people. Part of her sympathised with Freylar's queen, in particular the challenges Mirielle undoubtedly faced during her rule. However, the Queen had overstepped her mark, abusing the authority given to her – there was no room in her heart to forgive Mirielle for the path of exile sentenced upon her. The burden of rule had undone their queen, bringing with it the need for change.

'Come on then. Let us go make a difference.'

Krisis barked enthusiastically, and together they made their way towards the heart of the farmstead.

Heldran hit the ground first. The colossal Knight's massive feet crashed upon the dusty floor beneath them with a loud thump. As predicted, the lone Narlakin manoeuvred slowly to face its unexpected assailant. Gangrenous writhing tendrils flicked towards the Knight, but despite his hulking mass, Heldran was quick on his feet, evading the horror's initial reflexive strikes with ease. After reorienting its gaseous body, the Narlakin pressed its attack, lashing at the Knight ferociously, unrelenting in its assault, which rapidly gathered momentum. Heldran continued to evade the whip-like attacks, many of which struck the dry earthy wall adjacent, filling the air with dust and grit. The remaining blows struck the hessian sack that Heldran used as a shield of sorts to absorb his opponent's strikes. In his right hand, the Knight held his monstrous blade, but, even with his impressive strength, the weapon clearly needed wielding with both hands. Heldran had played his part perfectly, baiting their prey. Now for his part. He quickly dropped to the ground directly behind horror, expertly slicing off one of its tendrils during his rapid descent. His falchion severed the horror's limb with ease, causing the Narlakin to release a dreadful moan that echoed around the open cavern. The severed appendage made a wet thump as it hit the dusty ground, where it continued to writhe despite the loss of its host.

'Hurry up and subdue this thing!' cried Heldran, who continued to evade the creature's relentless attacks.

Despite the Knight's successful distraction, the Narlakin's flailing limbs recoiled with such ferocity that it might as well have been attacking them both. The enraged appendages seemed to elongate at the creature's behest. They violently flicked back and forth, gathering momentum, yet were somehow capable of avoiding a collision with one another. A storm of tendrils now whipped around their host frenetically, shielding the Narlakin from his follow-up attacks. The rapid momentum of the appendages deflected his cuts, causing them to glance harmlessly off the fleshy barrier.

'It is too fast!' he said, struggling to get to grips with their opponent.

'We do not have time for this.' boomed the Knight.

Heldran discarded the sack, casting it into the hurricane of writhing tendrils. The hessian material shot upwards, high above them, where it danced vigorously, manipulated by invisible hands, like a leaf blowing in a circle on the ground, caught by an unforgiving wind. Free now to wield his weapon as it was intended, Heldran grasped the pommel of his ardent sword with his left hand, using the leverage to bring the colossal blade around for a devastating lateral cut. The blade's cutting edge scythed through the Narlakin's tendril-shield, severing multiple appendages, before ultimately coming to a halt. Heldran tried to pull his weapon free from the writhing mass, but the remaining tendrils quickly coiled around the blade and along the length of the Knight's right arm.

'If you have nothing better to do!' cried Heldran, now entangled with the horror in a desperate tug of war.

Heldran's brazen attack had diminished the Narlakin's defence, causing gaps to form in its shield. Taking full advantage of the damage inflicted by the Knight, he rolled forwards, breaching the Narlakin's circle of defence. He drew his falchion upwards as he rose to his feet, slicing through another of the whip-like tendrils that promptly fell to the ground where it writhed uncontrollably, along with the others. Realising its compromised defence, the Narlakin relented its shield, extending several of its remaining tendrils towards Heldran's legs. Unable evade their attacker, the Knight watched helplessly as the appendages sped across the ground and coiled around his legs. The nightmare horror hoisted Heldran effortlessly off the ground before smashing the hapless Knight against the wall. Heldran let out an audible groan.

'Damn it Nathaniel, release it!' cried the dazed Knight.

Blood dripped from the left side of Heldran's head, where it had bounced violently off the wall. Content that the Knight no longer posed an immediate threat, the

Narlakin retracted its tendrils after tossing Heldran unceremoniously across the cavern floor, causing the Knight's limp body to roll along the dusty ground. Enraged by the sight of his fallen comrade, he slashed wildly at the creature, which slowly turned about to face him. More of its tendrils fell to the ground as his blade severed the horror's remaining appendages with renewed vigour, fuelled by his growing anger and hatred. In his rage, he neglected to pay adequate attention to his own footwork, allowing his opponent's final tendril to wrap around his leg. The Narlakin quickly retracted its sole appendage, dragging him to the floor, where it proceeded to roll him around on the ground violently, attempting to loosen his grip on his falchion. Coughing and spluttering, having had the wind knocked out of him, he tried to breathe in the dusty air swirling around him. Disorientated, he tried to slash at the Narlakin's last remaining tendril, but his weapon was out of measure, allowing the Narlakin to continue molesting him, showing zero remorse. He found little success trying to shield himself from the cuts and bruises forming across his body due to the abrasion against the hard floor, in the wake of the Narlakin's relentless savagery. His torment continued for some time, until finally, when he was on the cusp of losing consciousness, the torture abruptly stopped.

'Come on.' said a groggy voice, 'Let us finish this!'

He looked up and saw the foreboding silhouette of Heldran through the dust lingering in the air. The indomitable Knight stood over him, grasping his ardent sword with both hands. He jumped to his feet, ignoring the pain wracking his body, and saw the Narlakin's last tendril writhing by his feet, freshly severed from its host.

'*You* can get the sack this time. Oh, and be quick about it!' said Heldran, pointing his grossly oversized blade towards their opponent.

The limbless soul stealer hovered several paces before them, immobile, yet despite its paralysis a long vertical maw began to open up in the centre of its gaseous body.

'The next time I have a stupid idea, remind me of this moment.' he said whilst quickly surveying their surroundings for the elusive sack.

The hessian sack had landed several paces from the fighting, doing its best to blend in with the dry cracked earth, aided by a thick layer of dust kicked up by the frantic combat. He ran over to the sack, snatching it with his left hand before doubling back to assist the Knight. Despite the narrow cavern in which they fought, Heldran did his best to flank the horror to avoid its soul-hungry maw, whilst still hacking away at its remaining stumps, ensuring that only its gaseous body remained.

'Come on, sack it!' cried Heldran, whose unease increased at the sight of the grotesque amorphous mass writhing before them.

Fighting through the aches and pains tormenting his body, he brought the sack down quickly over the top of the horror using his wraith wings for assistance. As predicted, the gaseous mass condensed under pressure, allowing him to pull the sack downwards, forcing their quarry reluctantly into its hessian prison. The process of sacking the amputated Narlakin was clumsy and awkward – he was convinced that he heard Heldran laughing at him.

'I will put your poorly-timed amusement down to concussion.' he said, struggling to contain the last of the soul stealer.

'It was worth getting my head split open just for this.' replied the Knight heartily.

'Bugger off!' he replied, failing to conceal his own amusement at the ludicrous sight he presented.

Eventually – with Heldran's reluctant assistance – they managed to secure their defeated opponent, ready for transportation back to the vale. Part of him felt sorry for their captive prey, given that Krashnar's cruel ministrations would no doubt eclipse their own. Yet, he reminded himself that their actions were a necessary evil, without which The Blades would continue to foster a growing culture of distrust.

'It looked smaller from up there.' said Heldran, as he worked his ability to heal the Knight's wounds. 'Speaking of which – how do we get out?'

'This would go a lot faster if you kept still.'

'I am not going down those tunnels – there could be hundreds more of the bloody things lurking in there.'

'Afraid of the dark?' he said, mocking his giant companion.

'I would happily fight through a column of Ravnarkai if the opportunity presented itself, but those soul-sucking bastards, with their flailing tendrils – you can forget that!'

Admittedly, he had underestimated the difficulty in apprehending a soul stealer. They had been lucky; in hindsight, more planning and research was warranted, although time had been against them.

'Then our only way out is up there.' he said, looking towards the precipice overhanging them.

'I cannot fly up there – and neither can you for that matter.'

'Perhaps we cannot fly the entire distance, but I reckon you have the strength to catapult me high enough if I use my wings as well.'

'Maybe, but I would still need to climb out.' replied Heldran, who ran his large fingers across his weathered face, checking his handiwork.

If only they had brought another sack, he mused. It might have been possible to cut the material into lengths to fashion a rope. Perhaps it would be possible to use their clothes, he wondered, whilst staring absentmindedly at one of the severed tendrils lying on the ground.

'Got it – you can use the Narlakin to climb out.'

'What?' replied Heldran in bemusement, 'I would like to remind you of your recent sermon about stupid ideas.'

'We require long fibrous material in order to fashion rope.'

'Your point being?'

'Look down – we are surrounded by the stuff.'

Heldran studied the ground. The dusty floor of the narrow cavern was littered with the captive Narlakin's severed tendrils. Though a couple still writhed slowly where they had fallen, the majority now lay dormant, motionless testaments to their frantic battle.

'Tell me you are joking.' said the Knight, realising now the morbid solution to their problem.

'Either that or the tunnels my friend – take your pick.'

She tried to slow her breathing, but her increasing anxiety had other designs. She felt more anxious now than when the house guards had tried to apprehend her back at the Tri-Spires. Although the trees made it easier to conceal her presence, the woodland was teeming with forest dwellers going about their business; the Freylarkai around her seemed oblivious to the political goings on within the Tri-Spires, content to go about their routines in ignorant bliss. As she moved between the trees, she instinctively tugged at the heavy shawl over her head to better obscure her features. Having abandoned everything she knew, she had no place to go, yet despite feeling lost, she felt welcome amongst the woodland community. Children hid behind trees, giggling playfully, pretending that she had not seen them. Adults passed her by, smiling and wishing her good morning. She felt a raw honesty from those living north of the river, as opposed to the culture of subterfuge increasingly prevalent amongst the inhabitants of the Tri-Spires.

'Excuse me, do you know who I can speak to regarding Kirika?' she said to one of the passers-by, eventually finding the courage to ask for help.

'Of course my dear.' replied an older female who took a step towards her. 'You should go speak with Nathaniel. He lives north of here, in the heart of the forest. Follow that trail over there. There is not a Freylarkin amongst us who does not know where The Teacher lives – we will be able to assist you.'

'Thank you.' she replied. 'Your help is very much appreciated.'

'You are most welcome young lady.' replied the female. 'Though before you disappear into the wood, perhaps you will tell me your name?'

She immediately began to tremble, caught off guard by the sudden unexpected request. Once again, her nerves got the better of her, despite her efforts to remain calm.

'Do not be worried my dear.' said the female earnestly, before closing the gap between them and placing a reassuring hand on her own. 'We do not get many visitors from across the river; therefore, naturally, we are all curious to know who you are.'

'My name is Kayla,' she said, immediately wondering if she had done the right thing, 'And I need to speak with Nathaniel, urgently.'

'Clearly something, or *someone*, is troubling you. If it concerns Kirika, Nathaniel will be able to help you.'

'How can you be so sure?' she said pointedly, regretting her words the moment they had passed her lips.

'Because he watches over us – he always has done. That is why he brought The Guardian here.' replied the female candidly. 'He has a close relationship with Kirika, he will know the way – he will guide you. However, you must go quickly.'

'Why is that?' she asked, trembling once more.

'Because someone is following you.'

'What! Where?'

She tried to turn but the female Freylarkin grabbed her arms, fixing her in place.

'Do not concern yourself with it my dear; we will deal with the matter. Just ensure that you make haste to The Teacher, and stick to the trail.'

The female released her grasp. She offered her benefactor a nervous smile before hurriedly joining the trail heading north into the forest.

The temperature in the forest was warmer due to the partial protection provided by the trees. She diligently followed the winding mud trail through the heart of the forest, which branched off repeatedly towards nearby dwellings that looked like extensions of the forest itself. Remembering her benefactor's words, she stuck to the main path and pressed on, pausing only occasionally to ask those around her for information regarding the distance remaining to The Teacher's home. She had previously considered Nathaniel's decision to live amongst the forest dwellers strange, given The Teacher's lofty rank and venerable status within The Blades. In light of recent events, however, she now began to appreciate his decision, realising the merits of distancing oneself from the Tri-Spires. She dearly hoped that the female she had spoken with was true to her word, and that The Teacher would indeed aid her. In the event that Nathaniel chose to refuse her aid, there was nowhere else she could go, or at least nowhere safe. She could ill afford to return to the Tri-Spires, assuming that she was now an active fugitive, and there was no one else she could turn to for help. Despite the gloomy outlook occupying her thoughts, she forced herself to focus on the present, mindful of her alleged stalker.

Eventually, she arrived at her destination, courtesy of another of the forest dwellers who happily directed her to The Teacher's home. She observed the dwelling from a distance, cowering behind the relative safety of a large tree, trying to muster the courage to knock on The Teacher's door. Fear of the unknown stopped her from approaching any closer, though she was keenly aware of the danger incurred by remaining out in the open. She wished now that she was able to scry, despite Kirika repeatedly lamenting that the ability was both a blessing and a curse. Surely knowing *something* was better than not knowing anything at all, she mused, whilst continuing to stare at The Teacher's abode. Suddenly, something tapped her lightly on her left shoulder. Startled, she turned around, her muscles tensing as she pressed her back flat against the tree.

'Relax. I have no intention of harming you.'

She immediately panicked, paying no heed to the stranger's words. Her breathing became shallow. She frantically turned her head left and right, seeking a means by which to escape, though none presented itself.

'Calm down.' said the stranger pushing back her shawl, before holding her head gently between their hands.

'Stay away from me!' she said, closing her eyes tightly, trying to block out reality.

'Look at me.' said the voice calmly, albeit with a slight hint of amusement.

Gingerly, she opened one eye and saw The Guardian crouched before her.

'You can open the other one too, if you like.' said The Guardian, who had a wide grin stretched across her face.

'Guardian. I feel so stupid.' she said, immediately calming herself down. 'I thought for a moment that you were the person following me.'

'I was, in fact, I still am...'

'I do not understand.' she said, entirely confused by The Guardian's unexpected response. 'Are you here to escort me back to the Tri-Spires?'

'Before we get onto all that, I think that you and I need to have a little chat – with him.' said The Guardian, directing her gaze to a figure standing behind her.

The Guardian withdrew her hands, allowing her to turn her head freely. Standing a few paces from them was a tall slender figure with shoulder length white hair, silver eyes that glinted in the dull light, and scars that covered the length of his exposed arms.

'Hello Kayla. Please do not be alarmed. I have been informed that you have some urgent news me. Perhaps you and I could talk?'

TEN
Deception

With his new guise now firmly under his belt, he infiltrated the heart of Freylar once more with ease. Despite their abilities, the Freylarkai were easily fooled. However, his parlour tricks would not work against Mirielle due to her enhanced vision. He had already put his work to the test and found his skill lacking under her intense scrutiny. There was no reason to believe that a second encounter with Freylar's queen would yield different results, as such he could ill afford to chance a close public reunion with her. He needed to find another way of drawing Mirielle out, ensuring that they were alone together and beyond earshot. Nevertheless, there was still merit to his chosen method of subterfuge, assuming Aleska's identity would afford him unprecedented access to the Tri-Spires, in addition to control over its internal security – the house guards would know better than to question a former member of the ruling council, especially one of such venerable status. He thought back to the scrier's final moments. The secretive old Freylarkin had been most talkative during her final moments – probably due to his persuasive charm – furnishing him with all the information he needed to maintain his ruse. Ever the realist, he had expected a torrent of lies and deceit to drip from her tongue. However, the fear evident in her fading eyes had confirmed the legitimacy of her words, much to his surprise. As a sign of his appreciation, he had thanked her sincerely for cooperating, albeit after dropping her frail body to the cold hard ground and sealing her nose and mouth shut – better to welcome release on a truthful note. His dark companion had rejoiced at his 'no loose ends' policy, watching with delight as the scrier desperately clawed at her mouth in a futile attempt to breathe. Listening to Aleska's muffled screams and watching her scrabble around on her knees filled the ever-present darkness inside him with joy, temporarily sating its appetite once more. He hoped that the experience, in addition to the incident down by the river, would be enough to content the parasite until he had his hands wrapped firmly around Mirielle's neck. After that, he would care little for his ally's needs, and would instead revisit his attempts to contain the thing inside him, reclaiming what was rightfully his.

By the time that he reached Aleska's quarters in the heart of the Tri-Spires, it was well past noon. Though he did not know the way, one of the house guards happily escorted him, ensuring that he reached his destination safely.

'Please inform the Queen of my return and that I will write to her shortly; she is not to visit me directly, under any circumstances! Have a guard of the Queen's own choosing return to my quarters later this evening for further instructions. Now leave me.'

He knew that his voice was off, nevertheless, the guard accepted his orders and left. The authority wielded by the old scrier was absolute. No one would challenge him – including Mirielle, provided he kept her at arm's length, since she was now desperate for counsel. The rest of the Freylarkai were of little concern to him. Audible gossip was rife as he navigated the outskirts of the arena towards the Tri-Spires; most recognised Aleska, and were surprised to see the venerable scrier meandering alone through the streets. Yet none of them had the perception to see through his façade and discern his true identity. He played the role well, but without a flesh sacrifice his disguise was only temporary. Having held the form for some time now he was relieved to finally reach the scrier's quarters so that he could drop the pretence, albeit temporarily. After the guard left, he quickly relaxed his muscles, allowing his body to default to its natural state. Although he had become accustomed to it over the passes, the process of change was always painful – his dark companion enjoyed the torment, even if it was self-inflicted.

After resuming his own form, he searched Aleska's quarters looking for documents, letters, message scrolls, anything with the old scrier's handwriting on it. Though much of it was enciphered, he found enough material to allow him to study her writing, enabling him to create additional works in her name.

'My dearest, I am here for you now. I arrived shortly after noon, and am ensconced in my quarters, for reasons that I shall explain.

Firstly, I am ill. Nothing serious – bed rest will see me right. Old age and the cold are having their wicked way with me, though I would rather not chance infection. You need your strength; therefore, I ask that you keep your distance. Please, do not send a renewalist. I am comfortable. Bed rest is all that I require.

Secondly, and more importantly, I have officially retired, thus it will weaken your rule if I am seen to be offering you counsel. For this reason alone, I must remain hidden. Going forwards, we will communicate by written word only. In light of the pressing circumstances and the length of these communications, we will forgo the use of ciphers, hence I have instructed you to employ a courier of your choosing – one that you can trust.'

He ensured that the content of the letter was concise and to the point. Prior to his exile, Aleska had never struck him as the type to engage in unnecessary pleasantries. In time, assuming that Mirielle took the bait, his wordsmithing would get better, but for now, his factual tone would suffice. He thought about luring Mirielle to his quarters, but Aleska had resided in the heart of the Tri-Spires, in the thick of the people. Someone would hear the struggle, meaning escape would be impossible – there would be no windows to jump through this time. At odds with his evolving nature, he convinced himself to play the long game – his dark companion permitting – and wait for the opportune moment to strike from the shadows. Besides, the old scrier's scared, desperate final ramblings had piqued his interest; it was clear that Mirielle's rule was now waning. His brazen decision to impersonate one of Mirielle's closest allies meant that there would likely be an opportunity to discredit the Queen, before ushering in her inevitable end. The thought of twisting a knife into Mirielle's back so deeply amused not only himself, but also his symbiotic ally, affording him some control over the parasite. The last time he had paid the Queen a visit, he had invaded her private chambers before violating her flesh. This time, however, he would invade her life! He laughed to himself, unable to contain the wicked excitement rising inside of him. The prospect of undermining Mirielle's rule from the inside was intoxicating, far more so than ravaging her flesh for a second time. How delicious it would be to aid the Queen in dismantling her own rule, he mused. The notion of sabotaging Mirielle's reign now dominated his thoughts entirely – he could think of nothing else.

However, before I can counsel you, you must furnish me with all the details – omit nothing. Your message, although disheartening, was nonetheless insightful. I need to understand everything that has happened during my absence from the vale.

Aleska.'

A malicious grin stretched across his grubby face whilst he appended the additional paragraph to the letter, before signing it off and sealing the communication. Thoughts began to churn in his mind, no doubt tainted by the parasite's presence. Until now, his vendetta against Mirielle had been garish; a trail of disfigured corpses lay in his wake. However, fate had recently guided his partially fingered hand to a powerful victim, one whose stolen visage afforded him so many more opportunities – it was time to broaden his unique skill-set.

When the Queen's courier knocked on his door later that evening, he opened the door to Aleska's quarters only slightly, partially revealing his altered face. He slipped the letter between the gap, though refusing to let it slip from his grasp when tugged eagerly by the guard standing opposite, whose lower face appeared to be heavily bruised.

'You are?' he said, forgoing any pleasantries.

'Ralnor,' replied the Freylarkin promptly. 'House guard to Queen Mirielle. The Queen chose *me* to receive your instructions, as requested.'

'Good. Take this message and ensure that Mirielle receives it immediately. It is not to touch the hands of another. Return the broken seal to me along with the Queen's response, so that I can validate the secure delivery of this message, along with her own, with my second sight. Understood?'

'I understand.' replied the guard nervously.

'I expect a response at dawn. Now go.'

It had been a long cycle, to which the sun had finally said its farewell. He had spent most of it training Gaelin's militia, whilst Darlia coordinated battlefield preparations, ready for what lay ahead. Now, he stood alone, in a field amidst the community's primary herd of Karlak. The muscular quadruped mammals, each with their three curved horns, knelt down in the field seeking rest following another cycle of strenuous grazing. Despite their impressive physical stature, the dim-witted mammals were unable to defend themselves effectively when attacked by predators looking for an easy meal. Typically, the farmstead community ensured the safety of their herds. However, so far at least, Gaelin's lot had been unsuccessful in fending off their newest quarry. Now, the onerous task of safeguarding the community's livestock lay with himself, Darlia and Krisis, given that the others had precious little combat experience to draw upon.

He remained perfectly still whilst standing alone in the field, allowing his eyes to do all the work as they scanned the edge of the forest bordering the far end of the meadow. His night vision was good, thus he had no trouble scanning the horizon for signs of activity, which, so far at least, had been strangely lacking. According to Gaelin, the attacks typically took place earlier in the evenings; it was now well past midnight, with the moon high in the night sky. Maybe their quarry had no intention of coming, he mused, or perhaps they were out there, amidst the trees, biding their time whilst assessing the revised risk of attacking the herd. Although Gaelin's lot, along with Darlia and Krisis, remained hidden from sight, their lupine adversaries would have no doubt picked up their scent upon the crisp air. The wolves would realise the increased risk of attacking the herd, however, given their persistent nature, he had expected them to attack nonetheless. Instead, there was nothing to be seen in the perfectly still landscape, rendered by the moon, which was now at its zenith. The Karlak also remained eerily motionless whilst resting, despite his obvious presence. He began to wonder if perhaps his being there kept the wolves at bay – he was, after all, no stranger to the lupine community. Perhaps baiting the wolves using a telepathic Paladin was not one of his better ideas, he mused. After waiting for what seemed like an eternity, he was about to signal the others to call off the operation when suddenly a lone Karlak turned its head sharply towards the neighbouring woodland. Despite their stocky profile, the large mammals had excellent hearing, which, aside from their sheer bulk, was their only means of defence. He opened a conduit to the Karlak's mind, seeking to understand what ailed the creature. Although incapable of intelligent thought, communicating with one another through body language alone, the mammals did possess a rudimentary understanding of emotion. The Karlak's mind was loaded with fear – something was definitely out there.

'*They are here. The herd senses their presence. Get ready!*' he communicated telepathically to Darlia.

The herd abruptly stood up in unison, as if they too had access to the thoughts of others, specifically his own. Pre-empting their default reaction to run, he began sprinting back towards the outbuildings, knowing that the simple-minded creatures would quickly follow. As expected, the herd immediately bolted in his direction, rapidly overtaking him as they desperately sought safety from whatever lurked in the forest at their backs. He glanced over his shoulder, stealing a momentary glance – nothing – then, as he turned to look forward once more, tripped over something manifesting in his path. He went down hard, tumbling through wisps of grey smoke that rose out of the cold ground. After quickly regaining his footing, he stood up and watched in horror as the ephemeral form responsible for his fall solidified before him.

'Louperdu!' he cried as the last of the Karlak thundered past him, desperately trying to warn the others in hiding who were ready to spring their trap. 'Watch your flanks – they could be anywhere!'

'Darlia, we screwed up. They are not wolves; they are the Louperdu – spirit wolves – and they have no Alpha. They can dissolve and reform. Watch your backs. You are not saf--'

Before he could finish, the fully reformed wolf, which had eerily manifested before him, pounced abruptly, leaping directly towards his neck. With no time to draw his weapons, he brought his right hand up through his attacker's centreline, using the heel of his palm to violently uppercut the wolf. The Louperdu's head rocked backwards, causing it to yelp loudly in pain, but the momentum of his attacker crashing against him sent him tumbling along the ground once more. Again, he scrambled to his feet, this time reaching for the custom dirks attached to his belt. He drew the blades ready to face his attacker, but the disorientated wolf was already dissolving into wisps of smoke that spread outwards across the ground; the cursed lupine had robbed him of a chance to follow up his initial counterstrike. No doubt, the creature would return once it had recovered from his well-placed attack.

'Louperdu!' he cried again, louder this time, as he ran back towards the outhouses.

Despite his efforts to warn the others, it was already too late. Bodies fell from the distant rooftops, savagely thrown by spirit wolves brutally mauling Gaelin's militia. His hasty training had not prepared the farmstead community for their shape-shifting assailants. Using his strength of mind, he opened up multiple conduits simultaneously, attempting to touch the minds of as many Freylarkin as his ability would allow. The mental strain of communicating with so many at once burned his mind, causing him to groan in pain.

'In their transient form your weapons are useless. You need to shoot the moment they reform! Those of you with melee weapons, pair up; one will receive the charge, whilst the other counters.'

As he approached the nearest outhouse, another Freylarkin fell from its roof. They crashed loudly onto the lower roof section of an adjoining room, which sloped downwards, breaking the Freylarkin's inevitable impact upon the cold hard ground. One of the wolves immediately set upon the hapless Freylarkin whom he recognised from their training; in a single fluid motion, the Louperdu leapt down from the outbuilding's upper roof, instantly pinning its prey to the ground. The savage lupine growled, baring its sharp yellow-stained teeth, ready to tear out its victim's throat. He threw one of his dirks at the creature's head, denying the enemy its prize, embedding the blade firmly into its skull. The wolf immediately went limp and collapsed upon the dazed Freylarkin.

'Get up!' he shouted.

Grabbing the dirk's hilt, he drove his left boot into the released wolf, rolling the lupine onto the floor, wrestling his blade free in the process.

'Get up now, unless you wish to court release further!'

The dazed Freylarkin rose unsteadily to their feet. Seeing that they had lost their weapon during the struggle, he thrust one of his spare throwing knives into the palm of the stunned militiaman.

'Use this; receive the charge and counter by driving it into the neck.'

The Freylarkin stared at him vacantly in shock, with blank wide eyes, though quickly woke from their reverie when a Louperdu thumped loudly into the ground close by. The spirit wolf let out a loud yelp immediately following the heavy impact. He looked up and saw Darlia retracting her menacing claw, before grabbing her powerful recurve bow. Expertly nocking an arrow to her bow with her good hand, the infamous scrier drew back on her bowstring, releasing a shot that pierced the wolf's hide. The fatally injured lupine yelped again before making a futile attempt to stand, only to flop to the ground once more, where it remained, motionless.

'Lothnar, behind you!' cried Darlia, nocking another arrow to her bow.

He turned immediately to see five spirit wolves manifesting before him, little more than eight paces from where he stood. The bewildered Freylarkin who had fallen from the roof turned and fled, or rather they desperately limped away, seeking shelter from the disorganised fighting.

'Get back here!' he cried, hoping that his authority alone would rally the fleeing Freylarkin – though it did not.

Alone he stood, with only Darlia at his back. Twice now, he had fought alongside the defiant scrier, who refused to back down when faced with conflict. Howls, snarls and horrid screams pierced the still night air, yet despite the ugly distractions of battle around them, both remained focussed on the ephemeral shapes taking form before them.

'Go for the two on the left, I will take the others.' He said, trying to convince them both that they stood a chance.

She flinched at the sound of a loud knock at her doors that echoed ominously around the chamber. Since Krashnar's desecration of her stone tree, even the slightest noise made itself known to her, as though the room's remaining furnishings were incapable of softening any ambient noise. It was late and she was tired. Yet despite feeling exhausted and on edge, she welcomed the abrupt announcement.

'Come in.' she said, eagerly anticipating her first written communication from Aleska.

The doors opened and Ralnor gingerly took a step into her chamber.

'Do you have it?'

'Yes, my queen. I have it here.' he replied, raising his left hand, clutching a sealed letter.

'Here, give it to me at once.'

The guard approached her quickly, before handing her the sealed letter.

'Thank you. You are dismissed.' she said, after snatching the letter from him using her good hand.

She had hoped for the guard's prompt withdrawal, but instead he stood before her, undecided as to whether or not to take his leave as commanded.

'What is it?' she snapped, eager to see the guard leave.

Ralnor tried to respond, but instead nerves got the better of him, tying his tongue in knots. She glowered at the stammering guard, irked by his pointless timewasting.

'If you have nothing to say, please, leave me.'

'It is just that…why did you select *me* for this errand, my queen?'

'It is not obvious?' she said, surprised that her choice of courier required explanation.

Ralnor tried to respond, but again, nerves stayed his tongue, preventing the house guard from speaking his mind in her presence. Keen to usher in his dismissal, she gave the guard the answer he sought.

'You disappointed me in the arena, during the Trials. Furthermore, The Blade Lord informs me that you also failed to apprehend a suspect in an internal investigation this morning. That Freylarkin has since fled into the forest, eluding our efforts to bring them in for questioning. Two failures in close succession is unacceptable. Ergo, you have no more chances; if you fail to complete this latest assignment, I will have you stripped of your rank – are we clear on this matter?'

'Yes, my queen.' replied the guard nervously.

'Now go. Leave me to respond to this communication alone, and say nothing of your assignment to others.' she said sternly, coercing the guard into performing his duties correctly. 'I expect you to return shortly after dawn, ready to deliver my instructions to Aleska.'

The guard turned on his heels and promptly left. She disliked commanding her subjects in such a terse manner, however, she needed someone that she could trust, and fear was an exceptional motivator. Under no circumstances would the house guard risk incurring her wrath for a third time, as such she expected Ralnor to perform his duty with distinction.

Finally, with the room to herself at last, she hurriedly broke the wax seal on the letter and sat down upon the side of her bed to read Aleska's words. The tone of the letter was dry – there were no pleasantries – though it was not unlike Aleska to adopt a formal approach when dealing with complex matters of state. In any event, she had little time for idle conversation given the pressure bearing down on her due to the challenges she faced to her leadership. In fact, Aleska's pointed words were exactly what she needed. She did not require sycophants or appeasing aides. She needed someone who could provide concise definitive advice on how to navigate the political maelstrom that had ensnared her. Aleska would know exactly how to brace herself for the incoming storm lurking on the horizon. With the venerable scrier by her side once more, there was no doubt in her mind that order would be swiftly restored to her reign once more. Reading the words raised her spirits, lifting the weight bearing down on her soul; the tension in her neck and shoulders suddenly reduced. She released a deep breath before flopping back onto her bed. Though she had Marcus to lean on, his presence brought with it another form of stress. It was clear now that The Blade Lord held a deep affection for her, an infatuation that she could never fully reciprocate due to the sacrifices she had made during her ascension to power. When the cycle was right, she would find the time to explain her innermost thoughts to Marcus – he deserved to know the truth of her self-mutilation. Although the vile shaper Krashnar had left his physical mark on her body, disabling the use of her left arm, she had only herself to blame for her mental scars, coupled with her inability to conceive. Nevertheless, she took solace in the fact that Aleska was there for her, and that the venerable scrier would help her to overcome the challenges she faced. Together they would restore order to the vale and quell the insurrection of those seeking to usurp her reign. She considered responding to Aleska's message at dawn, but there were too many thoughts bouncing around in her head to silence, none of which intended to let her sleep. With renewed vigour, she leapt from her bed and wandered over to her bench where she began unloading her troubles onto fresh vellum, ready for Aleska to consume. She recalled in minutiae the events that had taken place since the scrier's departure for Scrier's Post, detailing everything that had transpired to the best of her knowledge. The words spilled from her mind onto the parchment with ease, as though composing a novel that wrote itself. With each transcribed word, she felt the weight upon her recede a little more, until eventually, after completing her opus, she felt liberated from the burden that had threatened to consume her. She exhaled deeply once more, allowing the last of her troubles to manifest as lingering moisture in the cold air. The vapour reminded her of how cold it was, now that winter was upon them. The snow had come early, meaning that, in all likelihood, they would be in for a harsh winter. Not all of the Freylarkai would survive, especially the elderly and infirm. She made a mental note to have Krasus shape a hearth in Aleska's quarters, and to provide the scrier with an adequate stock of Firestones. This was not a conventional arrangement for those living in the Tri-Spires, due to the ongoing maintenance required; the inhabitants had to make do with thick garments and blankets instead. On this occasion, however, she would make an exception. She needed Aleska to make a speedy recovery in order to deliver her valuable counsel. Furthermore, she could rely on the arrogant shaper to keep his mouth shut about the particulars of the assignment whilst carrying out the work; Krasus loved to gloat about himself, though he had little time for others. It was entirely likely that Aleska's pride would intervene, and that the venerable scrier would resist her aid, however, on this point she would not bend.

'Furthermore, I have asked Krasus to fashion a hearth for you, which you will accept. Allow him to carry out his work – on this point I will not give ground, my dearest Aleska. I will keep my distance as you ask, at least until everything is resolved and you are well again. In the meantime, I insist that you keep warm. Winter has come early; I fear that it will be a harsh one this pass.'

After signing off the message and sealing it, she tucked the letter under her pillow and turned in for the night. She sunk her head deep into her pillow, closed her heavy eyelids and relaxed, peacefully. Finally, at last, events were turning in her favour. Come dawn, they would begin work on setting her affairs in order; those who challenged her would quickly feel the full extent of her wrath, with no exceptions.

ELEVEN
Louperdu

'Stand down, or I will end you!'

The threat was a hollow one. Nevertheless, he needed to try. Even if Darlia released the two on the left flank, the three remaining wolves would tear him apart. He would take one, perhaps even two, but anything more was wishful thinking on his part. He had hoped that release would find him on a grand stage of his choosing, as had been the case for Ragnar. Instead, his time would come defending those living on the fringe of society. Perhaps it was fitting, he mused. After all, he had spent so little time in the vale, preferring to roam the wild at the sharp end of Freylar's defence. Drawing a throwing knife from the sheath strapped to the underside of his left arm, he took aim, waiting for the wolves to solidify. He considered putting more space between them, but there was not enough time, at least not without compromising his aim. In any event, the increased range would affect his accuracy; he needed the throw to count. He was committed – fate would decide the rest. As the Louperdu shed their ethereal forms, he released his knife. The lethal projectile embedded itself into the skull of the right-most attacker, immediately releasing its victim. On the left, one of Darlia's arrows skewered another of the lupines, violently staking it to the ground. The power delivered by Darlia's recurve bow at short range was impressive. Unperturbed, the three remaining spirit wolves bounded towards him at breakneck speed, their maws wide open baring yellow stained teeth that glinted in the moonlight. Instinctively, he reached for one of his dirks, ready to sink it into his attackers whilst using his left arm as a shield. He breathed in deeply, ready to receive the inevitable violent impact, however, fate, it seemed, had other plans for him. A large black shadow suddenly obscured his vision, blocking the path of his attackers. The shadow launched itself forwards, disrupting the inbound charge. Two of the wolves went tumbling laterally, whilst a giant maw clamped down hard on the third. Silver blood gushed from the hapless lupine onto the ground, before spraying across his face as the shadow shook its prey violently, left and right, snapping the animal's neck in the process. Satisfied that the Louperdu had been released, the dark shape released its victim, launching it high into the air. The mangled body crashed in a heap on the cold hard ground with a sickening wet thud. The bright moonlight caught the outline of the shape before him, rendering the familiar silhouette of a dire wolf.

'*Thank you, my friend!*'

Another of Darlia's lethal projectiles split one of the redirected wolves, causing more of their silvery blood to splatter upon the ground. Although, by saving them, she neglected the second Louperdu on their left flank, which leapt onto the upper roof of the adjacent outbuilding in a single jump, with preternatural agility. Startled by its presence, Darlia dropped her bow, instead favouring her bronze mechanical claw as a shield against her attacker.

'*Go! Protect her!*'

Krisis leapt onto the outbuilding's lower roof section, before ascending to the main roof itself. Despite the power generated by Krisis' hind legs, the loyal dire wolf weighed significantly more than the preternatural Louperdu. Releasing its bite on the scrier's prosthetic hand, the spirit wolf turned its attention towards Krisis. Though he wanted nothing more than to watch his lupine comrade tear their attacker to ribbons, he was compelled to turn his attention to the threat against his own being; the remaining Louperdu, previously sent reeling by Krisis' charge, had now recovered from its impact and was bounding towards him. The wolf leapt at him, savagely trying to wrap its jaws around his face. He dropped the dirk in his right hand and slid his left arm under the incoming wolf's neck. Bringing his hand up, he pushed away its stinking maw, then, twisting his body anti-clockwise, wrapped his right arm around the spirit wolf's head before driving it hard into the ground, wasting none of the lupine's momentum. By redirecting the spirit wolf's charge into a devastating counter-offensive, he managed to stun his attacker. Still controlling the animal's head, he reached for the remaining dirk attached to his belt with his left hand. He drove the blade up through the spirit wolf's lower jaw, into its head, spraying the ground, and himself, with more of the silvery blood. Releasing his hold, he rolled away from his assailant and quickly rose to his feet. The spirit wolf's body went into spasm – unsurprising, given the injury it had sustained. He approached the lupine's twitching corpse, paying little attention to its death throes, before wrenching his dirk mercilessly from the animal. After which, he stooped to snatch up its twin that he had dropped earlier during the encounter, in order to free up his right hand.

Around him, the fallen spirit wolves began to dissolve into fine smoke, returning to their transient state once more, permanently this time. He looked up, to where Darlia once stood. The scrier was absent from her post, though he took solace watching Krisis hurl another of the dogged wolves from up high. The dire wolf's latest victim smashed into the ground several paces from where he stood, amidst its fallen brethren where it would soon abandon its broken physical shell, just as the others had done. He was about to scale the outbuilding to search for Darlia when screams, not more than thirty paces away, pierced the night.

'*Brother, follow me!*' he said, communing telepathically once more with his brutal ally.

Krisis leapt to the ground then rapidly overtook him as he ran towards the rear of the second outhouse. The dire wolf bounded towards the structure, forcing him to use his wraith wings to keep pace. Upon rounding the rear of the building, they saw Gaelin and the others. Approximately eight spirit wolves circled the farmstead leader and his hastily assembled militia. Several of Gaelin's militiamen had already fallen, causing the remaining few to close ranks forming a circle – at least they had gotten that bit right, he mused. Now the Louperdu were testing Gaelin's defences, picking off those foolish enough to stray from the circle's relative safety. Even for lupines, the Louperdu were a cunning breed; the spirit wolves circled their prey, testing Gaelin's formation, looking for holes in his defence.

'*Charge!*' he commanded. '*Disrupt their attack.*'

His order was little more than confirmation of the dire wolf's pre-determined intent. Whether he commanded it or not, Krisis' fury would be unleashed, regardless. The enraged dire wolf sprinted down the right flank, taking out three Louperdu, running straight through them without any heed to his own wellbeing. Using their preternatural reflexes, the wolves evaded the worst of Krisis' charge, but were scattered in the process, with the exception of the third spirit wolf; the muscular dire wolf locked its powerful jaws around the unfortunate Louperdu, before rolling across the ground, instantly snapping the lupine's neck, a technique favoured by Krisis. Although no slouch in melee himself, he lacked the dire wolf's power, preferring instead to attack his enemies at short range. With terrifying alacrity, he slid three knives from his right sheath, throwing them towards the lupines with unparalleled accuracy. As one befitting his rank, he had trained in the use of knives for countless passes, thus the use of his left had no bearing on his devastating aim. The first two knives found their mark, burying themselves into the skulls of the attackers, causing immediate release. The third, however, impaled itself into its victim's hindquarters, robbing the Louperdu of its agility.

'Attack!' he screamed, as the injured wolf limped awkwardly towards him.

Gaelin's lot immediately broke formation and began slashing wildly at the remaining wolves. The sudden rush of adrenaline impeded their ability to fight correctly; the majority of their attacks lacked control and were out of measure, nonetheless, he was grateful for the additional strength of arms. Several of their chance strikes caught the flanks of the Louperdu as they pounced on the Freylarkai, biting ferociously with their jaws. More screams filled the air as they bit down hard, tearing flesh from their opponents. The wounded lupine heading towards him went to pounce, but was immediately skewered by a well-placed arrow that impaled the animal's right eye socket. He turned and saw Darlia running awkwardly towards the melee. The scrier discarded her recurve bow and readied her menacing claw; a wise choice he decided, given the chaos unfolding around them.

'Keep them off me whilst I save the others!' she cried, running straight towards the nearest downed Freylarkin.

Grasping the head of a Louperdu busy sinking its teeth into the shoulder of a fallen Freylarkin, Darlia pulped the animal's skull by closing her merciless claw around its head. Bits of bone, flesh, mashed brain and silver fluid oozed out between the gaps in her left fist, before flying in all directions when her mechanical digits violently retracted, ready for their next victim. Drawing his dirks once more, he used the blades to stave off the wolves' desperate attacks, allowing Darlia to pick her way through the carnage around them, dispatching the Louperdu with ease. Seeing their brethren crushed by the scrier's bronze mechanical claw broke the lupines' resolve; the spirit wolves promptly withdrew their attack, dissolving their forms once more in a bid to retreat. One of the wolves caught the sharp edge of Gaelin's falchion before giving up its solid form. The injured Louperdu flopped to the ground yelping in pain, whilst the others made good their escape.

'Find a renewalist, now!' cried Darlia, whose left hand dripped gore down the length of her dress. 'These people need help.'

He woke earlier than usual that morning, unable to silence the thoughts bouncing around inside his head. The unexpected arrival of Kayla had piqued his curiosity; the nervous Freylarkin had a tale to tell, and he was keen to listen. However, despite the allure of a good story, Rayna had insisted that it could wait until the morning. Kayla seemed shaken by her recent ordeal; Kirika's aide needed a good hearth, some food in her belly and a decent night's rest to calm her jangled nerves. Conceding Rayna's point, they did their best to make Kayla feel at ease, as well as insisting that she turn in early in an attempt to get a decent night's rest.

It was still dark outside as he thumbed through the pages of his books. He paid little attention to the words written in them. Instead, he attempted to recall the fading memories of his wife, desperately trying to hold onto them. Though he had long since come to terms with his wife's release, it irked him knowing that Alarielle had never known her mother. Perhaps they would make contact in the Everlife, he mused. However, The Guardian's presence threw into doubt everything that they had once thought to be true. Rayna was an enigma, wandering around in his daughter's body, yet despite the strangeness of it all, he had developed a close relationship with the light bringer, not unlike the relationship he had previously enjoyed with his daughter, prior to her capture.

A loud cough suddenly woke him from his reverie.

'I apologise. I did not mean to startle you.' said Kayla.

Kirika's aide waited patiently by the wooden stairs, respecting his personal space.

'Please, join me.' he said, setting his book down on top of the closest pile to his chair.

Kayla walked across the room slowly and sat down in the rocking chair opposite him. She tried to maintain eye contact with him, but he could see her wanting to inspect the books piled up around them, curious as to their content.

'You can borrow one if you wish.'

'I am sorry. I did not mean to be distracted.'

'You need not apologise. Books are amongst our finest creations – they deserve our attention.'

'We have many books in the study hall.' replied Kayla, who seemed more at ease now. 'I have read most of them.'

'A female of your age should be out there, enjoying the wonders the domain has to offer. Not ensconced within that cold dingy hall.'

She laughed at his comment, and in that moment, he realised how much like a lecturing parent he sounded.

'I am getting old; you should ignore me.' he said with a wry grin. 'If books give you pleasure, why not indulge?'

'And yourself, why do you read Nathaniel?' asked Kayla, easing back into her chair whilst lifting her feet off the floor, reminding him of Rayna.

'They too give me certain pleasure, but the real reason I read them is to remind me of my late wife. Her release seems like an eternity ago now. She loved to read – much like yourself. Reading them makes me feel connected to her, even though she has moved on. My memories of her are all that I have left – I would like to hold onto them.'

'You have Rayna too.'

'Yes, that is true, though we are both still trying to figure that one out.' he said, inadvertently allowing a small laugh to pass his lips.

'In any event, you did not come her to talk about dusty old books, young lady. Something terrible is preying on your mind; I can see it in your eyes, and it concerns me. You are far too young to be shouldering such burdens.'

'It is the Queen. She is not herself.'

'Please explain.'

'She has changed. Something has snapped inside her.'

There was a lull in their conversation, during which he could see Kayla's nervousness resurfacing once more.

'Fear is healthy; it protects us. However, it should not be allowed to govern us. You must learn to control your fear; know when to invite it in, but, more importantly, when to shut it out.' he said, trying to put Kayla at ease once more. 'You are amongst friends here Kayla – Mirielle cannot get to you here. With a single loud holler, we shall have ourselves a bleary-eyed Guardian to protect us – assuming she ever gets out of bed.'

Kayla laughed, causing the shaking in her fingers to abate.

'The gossips say that she never sleeps.'

'There was a time when that was indeed the case. Now one has to go tip a bucket of water over Rayna's head to get her out of bed – I think she might be playing catch up. In any event, do not let fear silence your tongue. Say what you have come to say. We *will* help you.'

Kayla stopped shaking once more after hearing his words, and promptly resumed her account.

'I overheard the Queen threatening Kirika; she has Larissa in custody and is going to charge her with the release of Hanarah, *if* Kirika does not leave the vale with her sister, Darlia.'

'Larissa would never intentionally harm another.'

'Nevertheless, that is the case Mirielle will present if Kirika does not cooperate and leave quietly.'

'Kayla, are you certain about all of this?'

'I heard it myself, Nathaniel – I was there. The Queen plans to have Larissa publicly lambasted prior to Kirika's own public trial.'

'Were you seen?'

'I do not know for certain – I do not think so.'

'Then it is possible that you were due to be questioned simply because of your affiliation with Kirika. We know that the Queen did not take kindly to what happened in the arena. She sees Kirika as a threat to her rule. Targeting Kirika's known associates, therefore, makes perfect sense, especially those of a more nervous disposition – no offence meant.'

'None taken.' replied Kayla with a weak smile.

Kirika's aide wanted to say more, but she seemed unable to get her words out; perhaps the strange environment stayed her tongue, or maybe it was him – due to his venerable status throughout the vale, there were some who found his presence intimidating. In any event, he was keen to learn everything she knew on the matter.

'Remember to control your fear, so that it does not control you. It is safe here…and please, do not feel intimidated by *me*.' he said with an honest smile.

'But *you* are The Teacher,' continued Kayla, managing to speak once more. 'Everyone knows and respects you; it is hard *not* to be intimidated by you.'

He laughed, amused by the innocence of Kayla's words. He forgot what it was like to be so inexperienced and young, constantly standing in the shadows of titans, seeking the approval of those who had done it all countless times before.

'You must not be intimidated by the likes of me or my generation. We all deserve the respect of our peers, and each of us has an important role to play. Right now, you are playing your part; just ensure that you find that voice of yours.'

Kayla eased herself further into her chair, doing her utmost to relax. The young Freylarkin closed her eyes and exhaled deeply, trying to breathe out all of her troubles. When she reopened her hazel eyes, they quickly dilated, adjusting to the dim light provided by the solitary candle atop one of the piles of books adjacent.

'There is growing unrest amongst those living in the Tri-Spires. There are still many who vehemently support the Queen, out of loyalty or due to the fear that you mentioned, however, a growing number now feel that Mirielle is no longer fit to rule over Freylar. Those questioning Mirielle's suitability to lead are troubled by the consequences of her actions, especially given the harm her decisions have wrought upon the vale. Confidence in the Queen's rule is waning. Furthermore – in light of recent events – my own faith has been rocked.'

He leant towards the light, allowing the candle to illuminate his face fully.

'Kayla, do you trust Mirielle?' he said, cutting to the heart of the matter.

'No – not now.'

'And what about me…do you trust me?'

Climbing out of the cavern had been a challenging and undignified affair. Together they had worked to create an ugly rope from the remains of the Narlakin's severed tendrils, previously littering the cavern floor. After squeezing the viscous liquid from the gangrenous appendages, they tied the rubbery lengths together to fashion a long fleshy cord. Working the tendrils together was vulgar, nonetheless, the theory had worked in practice. With the help of his wraith wings, and Heldran's impressive strength, he had managed to climb out of the cavern with the unsightly cord tied around his waist. Once out, Heldran had tied the other end of the skin rope to the sack containing their prey, successfully hauling the immobilised Narlakin to the surface, after which, it had been Heldran's turn to exit the cavern. At first, he had underestimated Heldran's weight, prompting several failed attempts to extract the Knight. But after digging his heels hard into the barren earth, he eventually managed to anchor his body sufficiently, enabling Heldran to climb back to the surface, albeit with supreme effort and no small amount of cursing all round.

'No one needs to know about this.' the Knight had said, after eventually reaching the summit.

'Agreed!'

Whilst engaged in another relentless march across the borderlands, sack in tow, Heldran came to an abrupt standstill partway through their journey.

'This is where we must part company old friend.' said the Knight in his habitual deep tone.

'What do you mean?' he replied, confused by Heldran's sudden refusal to accompany him any further. 'We have gone this far, surely you will see this endeavour through to its conclusion?'

'I will catch you up. But, for now at least, our paths must separate.'

'I do not understand. We need to return the Narlakin to Krashnar.'

'And we will.'

'How then, do you propose to keep pace if you go gallivanting off?'

'There is something I need to do before we revisit that ill-fated shaper.'

'Which is what exactly?'

'I cannot tell you, but suffice to say, we were asked to deliver two items. You carry one, and the other I promised to make good on.'

'The Waystones!'

'You should get going.'

He gave Heldran a sidelong glance. The Knights Thranis were a secretive lot. Despite enjoying a close relationship with Heldran, ultimately, he was not a Knight himself, and thus was not privy to certain information disclosed only to members of the Order.

'You have no intention of giving up your little secret, do you?'

'Who said it was little?' replied Heldran, before giving him a jovial wink with his right eye.

'How long have we known each other?' he said, trying to tease the information from Heldran's lips.

'Too long, and no, your tricks will not work on me – you cannot coerce me Nathaniel.'

'Yet I have looped you into my plans to manage Caleth.'

'If successful, that strategy is a mutually beneficial endeavour. Besides, that is *your* secret to share. I cannot share that which is not exclusively mine. I swore an oath to the Order, which included safeguarding its knowledge – you know this. The fewer people who know of its secrets, the better protected they are.'

They stared mutely at one another for some time, standing perfectly still as they listened to the distant cries of Sky-Skitters and other indigenous life struggling to survive in the barren wasteland. It was strange that creatures would choose such an inhospitable landscape as their habitat; perhaps it was a way of strengthening the species, by subjecting their kin to harsh conditions where only the strong survived. In any event, he had no desire to remain in the borderlands any longer than was required. The captive Narlakin continued to writhe in the sack that, until now, had been carried between them. He did not relish the thought of dragging their captive prey back to the vale alone, yet the sooner he got going, the sooner he could put the desolate wasteland behind him.

'You cannot blame an old Freylarkin for trying.' he said, finally breaking their silence.

'I would have been disappointed, had you not tried.' replied Heldran with a wide smile.

They dropped the sack before giving one another a firm pat on the back – a mutual sign of endearment and respect.

'Go, do whatever it is that you must. I will drag the soul stealer back to the vale and meet you at the shaper's hovel.'

'Very good.' boomed Heldran. 'Oh, and Nathaniel…do not turn that head of yours. Besides, you know that I will be walking in the opposite direction anyway.'

He was unable to discern if Heldran was bluffing. In any event, there was nothing around them, except for the occasional black and twisted tree or rocky outcropping. Whatever it was the Knight intended to seek out, he would likely never learn of it himself. Despite his hulking weathered appearance, Heldran had a sharp mind. When put to use, the Knight's ability to mislead others was impressive. Heldran was a keen student in the art of misdirection, though his true strength was information gathering. That, and an unbelievably strong sword arm.

'See you later old friend.'

He pulled on the sack containing the captive Narlakin and continued his march south, towards the vale. As he dragged the sack towards the horizon, incessant curiosity clawed at his mind, doing its utmost to cause him to steal a glance over his shoulder. Out of respect for Heldran's wishes, he defiantly locked his gaze on the distant horizon. He began reciting poetry from the dusty texts littering his home, knowing that the only thing capable of distracting him from the Knight's secret were the memories of his late wife.

TWELVE
Consequences

It had been a long night. They had convincingly seen off their attackers, but the price had been high. Despite the best efforts of the farmstead community's renewalist, there had been several casualties. Two members of the community had been released, and there were numerous injuries, including one of Gaelin's lot who had suffered a life-altering wound; one of the Louperdu had bitten through the Freylarkin's left arm, severing it entirely, and by the time the overworked renewalist attended the scene, it had been too late to reattach the severed limb. At first, the farmstead's residents had been in shock – it had been their first taste of raw combat. The savage attack had rocked Gaelin's people, leaving a sombre mood in its wake. However, as the cycle wore on, the community quickly came to terms with its losses, demonstrating remarkable resilience. Gaelin's own actions had been notably commendable; the farmstead leader had quickly gathered his people for an impromptu service to mourn their released, realising the importance of rapid closure.

It was noon. Having finished burying those released during the violent skirmish, all eyes now turned to her for their next move.

'Darlia, we have fought, and we have bled.'

'I am so sorry that this has happened.' she said.

Her soul felt heavy. Though she had only known the community for a short time, their losses felt like her own, reminding her of everything she herself had lost, especially her beloved Lileah.

'I should have seen this.' said Lothnar in a sombre voice.

'This is *not* your fault. If it were not for your actions, we would have lost our herds, the result of which would have been far worse. Though we have lost family and friends, their release had *worth* – they gave their lives valiantly so that we could survive the winter.'

'You are a credit to your people, Gaelin.' she said, placing her good hand gently on the farmstead leader's shoulder.

'And we are in your debt.' replied Gaelin, tipping his head towards Krisis, who barked enthusiastically in response. '*This* could have been prevented by Mirielle, however, she ignored our pleas for assistance. Had she sent The Blades to aid us, the Louperdu threat could have been dealt with expediently. Instead, the courage of strangers passing through has seen off our attackers.'

'They will not return.' said Lothnar confidently. 'Though you have suffered losses, theirs were significantly higher. It will take them many passes to rebuild their pack, after which, they will not risk coming back here. The Louperdu have no Alpha to lead them; they are opportunists operating as a pack. Furthermore, we have time to erect some proper defences and put procedures in place to help safeguard this place from other threats that may be out there.'

'You are all most welcome here.' said Gaelin, before giving Lothnar a firm handshake. 'We are keen to repay the debit that we owe you.'

'You owe us nothing.' she said firmly.

'On this point, we must disagree.' replied Gaelin, who glanced over his shoulder towards the other members of the community, all of whom nodded in agreement. 'These are unsettled times, and we need to band together if we are to survive the winter – we know all about harsh winters. We have corroborated the events that took place at the Trials, and have confirmed that the Queen has your sister in custody. This is an injustice. We would like to help you get her back!'

Whether it was the prospect of getting Kirika back, or the long-forgotten feeling of acceptance – she could not tell – her eyes began to water as tears threatened to spill from them. For too long, she had played the role of the outcast, unjustly exiled from Freylar having suffered Mirielle's wrath. No doubt she would incur the Queen's ire once more, in all likelihood courting release, if she attended her sister's trial. However, with the community behind her, Mirielle would have a tough time ejecting her from the public proceedings, let alone issuing reprisals of a more severe nature.

'Thank you.' she replied earnestly, 'Your support means a lot.'

Lothnar too acknowledged Gaelin's words with a respectful nod, as did Krisis, who chose to bark loudly once more. When first they had met, Gaelin had been extremely wary of Krisis' presence, but now, things were different. Gaelin smiled before kneeling down, offering to stroke the adolescent dire wolf with his hand. As expected, the affection-loving dire wolf promptly accepted the farmstead leader's offer, enjoying the spoils of his victory against the Louperdu.

'And you…I judged you poorly. Please accept my deepest apologies.' said Gaelin whilst rubbing Krisis' neck enthusiastically.

Krisis stretched his neck, making the most of Gaelin's affections. The dire wolf's eyes became heavy, suggesting that he was particularly pleased with the outcome of events.

'Regrettably, I must leave you all now. I intend to be at my sister's trial to help defend her actions, regardless of the consequences.'

'You cannot go there alone Darlia.' replied Gaelin, looking up from his crouched position on the ground. 'If you do, the Queen will have you taken into custody and tried alongside Kirika.'

'Nonetheless, I must go – she is my sister.'

'Then we will join you.' said Gaelin adamantly, glancing over his shoulder once more for affirmation.

'Thank you. I am eternally grateful for your support.'

'I will also join you Darlia,' said Lothnar, 'However, we must first apprise Nathaniel of what has happened here.'

'Gaelin, we will meet you and your people at the trial.' she said with renewed purpose. 'Provided he is willing, Krisis will remain here in the meantime for your protection.'

Lothnar communicated her request to Krisis. The dire wolf barked loudly again, almost knocking Gaelin off his feet in the process.

'Krisis is in agreement.' said Lothnar.

'Excellent. In that case, we will see one another very soon.'

'Very well.' replied Gaelin, who continued to stroke Krisis, who was now panting heavily. 'We will treat this one like a king.'

'See that you do – he loves the attention.'

They shared a moment of laughter at the dire wolf's expense, before parting company. With any luck, they would reach Nathaniel's tree by dawn. Though it was dangerous traveling without the cover of darkness, she felt reassured by Lothnar's presence. Besides, the cycles were shorter now due to winter's grasp, meaning that the light would soon begin to fade. She had heard many tales of the Paladin's prowess, and having witnessed his skill and courage first-hand, she was confident that they would reach their destination safely.

Two cycles had passed since her meeting with Kirika, yet there had been no word from the scrier regarding her offer. Prior to Aleska's return, she had been nervous about the prospect of revisiting Kirika's cell. However, with her venerable ally by her side once more, she no longer feared the inevitable confrontation. After dismissing the guard at the far end of the corridor, she approached the troublesome scrier's cell, ensuring that she kept her distance from the cell door's narrow slit to avoid being seen, thereby thwarting Kirika's ability to scry her person.

'Have you reached a decision?'

As with her previous visit, there was no response at first. She waited patiently for the scrier to respond, yet there was nothing.

'I am your queen – do not ignore me!'

'You are no longer my queen. You have lost your way Mirielle. Now, let me and the others out of here; you have no right to imprison us.'

'I have every right. Your actions were treasonous.'

'No. My actions were in the best interests of the vale, a notion that you have lost sight of.'

'So, you are insistent on this course of destruction, despite the harm it will cause to others?'

'As I said to you before, I will not be coerced by your threats.'

'I do not make threats, Kirika. Either you and your sister leave, or I will make an example of you both, including the dressmaker.'

'Your actions have created monsters from good people, and now those monsters wish to see you gone. But the worst monster of them all is the one staring back at you in the mirror.'

'Stupid girl! Your decision will lead to ruin for both yourself and the ones you love.'

'I have attempted to scry my fate many times Mirielle, and that outcome remains a possibility. However, if your scenario is to be my lot, I will accept responsibility for my actions, not cower from them – as you do!'

'Enough! You and the dressmaker *will* stand trial, three cycles from now. In the meantime, you can rot in here for all I care.'

She heard the impudent scrier mutter something in response as she hurried back down the corridor, seething with rage. It was clear that Kirika did not intend to leave the vale quietly, though it mattered not. Aleska had planned for this eventuality and she would now act accordingly. She followed the corridor to a junction at its end, before turning right towards the cell containing Hanarah's daughter and the dressmaker. The house guard she had posted stood vigilantly by the door to the cell.

'I want the daughter.' she barked, in no mood for pleasantries. 'I will personally escort her to my chamber.'

The guard carried out her order immediately, clearly not wanting to incur her ire. After ordering the young female to leave her cell, she tried her best to block out the incessant wailing from the chamber's remaining occupant.

'What are you doing Mirielle? Bring her back! Let me out of here!' cried Larissa vehemently.

The young, mute female was trembling badly, clearly frightened by her ordeal. She removed her heavy brown shawl and draped it across Cora's shoulders, doing her best to ease the Freylarkin's obvious distress.

'You must be scared.' she said, doing her utmost to mask her anger. 'Come with me and I will see that you are treated properly.'

Cora did not respond. Instead, the young Freylarkin tried to look back, and so she quickly ushered Hanarah's daughter back down the corridor and away from the raucous cries emanating from Larissa's cell.

'Curse you Mirielle!' she heard Larissa cry as they neared the junction.

'You must not concern yourself with the dressmaker – she is not herself. I should never have left you alone with her my child; please accept my deepest apologies.'

After ordering the house guards to remain behind at their posts, she guided Cora safely to the Waystone chamber and together they ascended the Tri-Spires. She guided the visibly shaken youngster to the double doors leading to her private chamber. Cora jumped as the guard on duty closed the thick wooden doors behind them, causing a loud thump to echo around the room.

'Apologies.' she said sincerely, hoping to ease the young female's nervousness. 'I forget how noisy this room can be without the crystals on my tree.'

Using her good arm, she pointed to the few remaining crystals, still desperately clinging to the polished granite tree in the corner of the chamber by their dainty silver chains.

'It was magnificent once. Sadly, however, the exiled shaper Krashnar defiled that magnificence – beauty does not last forever, so it would seem.'

As the words escaped her lips, she cast her gaze absentmindedly towards her left arm. Her personal wellbeing resonated with the tree's own plight; both had been majestic once, but had since been defiled and subsequently spoilt by the vile shaper's touch. Krashnar was a plague, bringing ruin to everything he met. It irked her knowing that the abhorrent Freylarkin was still at large; despite his best efforts, Marcus had yet to apprehend the rogue shaper. Whilst she appreciated the difficulties involved in tracking Krashnar down, nevertheless, The Blade Lord had given her his personal assurances regarding the shaper's capture, only to come up short. Her closest scriers had also been lacklustre in their aid, their second sight clouded for reasons unknown to them. Their lack of foresight suggested that The Guardian was somehow connected with future events concerning the shaper, calling into question Rayna's allegiance. In light of her close relationship with Nathaniel, it was difficult to get a read on The Guardian's direction. Rayna had the ear of the people; it was therefore unwise to dismiss The Guardian as a potential threat to their plans.

'Speaking of beauty, perhaps you would let me clean your face, so that the domain can get a better look at you?'

Again, the young Freylarkin said nothing. Cora seemed determined to keep her own counsel, content to allow others to deal with the awkward silences she cultivated. It was clear that Hanarah's daughter would not engage in conversation anytime soon, therefore she sat the Freylarkin down on the end of her bed, before going to find something with which to clean her youthful face. After returning with a bowl of water and some cloth, she sat down beside Cora and began to wipe the dirt from the young Freylarkin's face.

'I imagine that you have many questions.' she said in a soothing voice. 'I will do my best to answer them for you.'

'Thandor!' she cried, hoping that the aloof Paladin would hear her voice.

There was no response. The only sound came from the wind disturbing the leafless trees. Very little transpired without the aloof Paladin's knowledge; Thandor had mastered the art of remaining inconspicuous, thus he witnessed a great deal in person. Perhaps it was folly, therefore, trying to find someone who generally avoided being seen, she mused.

'Maybe he is not out here.' said Nathanar in a hushed voice. 'The Freylarkin we spoke to could have been mistaken.'

'Oh, he will be out here.' she replied with conviction. 'He is probably close by, watching us, thinking this is all rather amusing.'

'Why did Nathaniel not contact him directly, as he did with us?'

'It is likely that The Teacher did not know where to find him.' she said whilst carefully scanning their surroundings. 'In some ways, Thandor is very much like Lothnar; they both enjoy their own company.'

'And you enjoy his.' replied Nathanar, followed by a wry grin.

'Knock it off, before I knock *you* out!'

'Just an observation.' said Nathanar, who raised his hands in mock surrender.

'You know, you have become rather cocksure of yourself since that business with Rayna after the battle for Bleak Moor. Playing the role of the agitator has clearly bolstered your confidence.'

'I apologise if I have offended you.'

'No need. The old Nathanar was too stuffy and rigid for my taste – I rather like this new one.' she said, offering him a teasing smile.

'Natalya, you are a bad influence.' he said, fixing her with his piercing blue eyes.

She smiled again, before continuing to scan their surroundings. Less than eight paces away she spied a booted foot, protruding from behind a nearby evergreen bush. Recognising the footwear, she turned to Nathanar and playfully slapped the Paladin across his derriere.

'Come on – play time is over.'

Together they jogged towards the lone boot and its hidden occupant. They peered gingerly around the corner of the foliage to spy a Freylarkin lying peacefully on the ground. She kicked the exposed boot.

'Get up Thandor!' she said, irritated by his casual demeanour, knowing that the Paladin had overheard their conversation.

'Why? It is peaceful – at least it was until you two showed up.'

'You heard us looking for you, and yet you chose not to respond.' said Nathanar, clearly vexed by Thandor's unorthodox behaviour.'

'Do not waste your time Nath.' she said, kicking Thandor's boot irritably for a second time. 'He does not operate like the rest of us. He likes to keep people hanging.'

Thandor winked at her, acknowledging her brief character assessment. Yet no matter how much he frustrated her, she could not shrug off the feelings she had for the master duellist.

'I offered you my boot.' replied the Paladin lazily, feigning tiredness.

'Get up.' she said impatiently, irked by the continued pretence of the Paladin's feigned lethargy. 'There is something urgent that we must discuss.'

Sensing the seriousness of her words, Thandor swiftly leapt to his feet and directed them deeper into the forest.

'It is best that we stay clear of the river. I do not want the three of us being seen publicly together – not yet.' he said as they ventured further into the barren woodland.

'Then you know what it is that we wish to speak with you about?' asked Nathanar naively.

'Of course he does; he has been waiting for this moment ever since the three of us first discussed the matter.' she said flatly.

'The growing unrest in the vale has reached a tipping point; the erosion of The Blades, Kirika's custody and rumours of changed policy relating to the use of sanctioned scriers has made people nervous. Nervousness is a catalyst for change, and now we have an *icon* who can oversee that change.'

'You mean Rayna?' enquired Nathanar.

'Yes.'

'Thandor, Nathaniel has contacted us. The Teacher has asked for a private meeting. He has asked that you also attend.'

'Interesting.'

'How do you mean?' asked Nathanar curiously.

'Who do you think is behind all of this?'

'Mirielle, obviously.' replied Nathanar confidently. 'The Queen's own actions were the seed for the growing internal conflict throughout the vale.'

'Yes, but who has been nurturing that seed?'

'Kirika then; one would assume that she never forgave Mirielle for her sister's exile.'

'An interesting theory; her talents certainly lend themselves towards such action, though I do not believe it to be the case. Kirika lives in the public eye – she is too exposed to orchestrate an insurrection by herself.'

'So, you are suggesting that someone else is working the people?'

'Nathaniel!' she said, interjecting herself into the conversation.

'But Nathaniel is not a Paladin, he is not on the ruling council, nor does he engage in politics.' replied Nathanar.

'Correct, however, the fact that he is not shackled by any of those things means that he is well-placed to operate discretely from the shadows.' replied Thandor, who stopped to lean against a slender tree. 'He is also rather fond of Kirika – one of his favoured students. Furthermore, consider who lives with The Teacher.'

'The Guardian!' said Nathanar with wide eyes.

'Indeed.'

They each stood quietly contemplating Thandor's musings against the ambient sounds of the woodland fauna, shifting amongst the sparse flora still clinging to the windswept forest. The temperature had dropped noticeably and the blue sky above was now miserable and grey. Gentle flakes of snow started drifting down silently from the sky, resting on the leafless branches of the trees surrounding them. Autumn had said its final farewell, and now winter was upon them. She hated the cold, preferring instead the warm caress of the sun and the lighter cycles that came with it. The bland hues now bathing the vale did nothing to aid her mood, nor did their talk of an oppressive rule and potential insurrection. Things had –in her opinion – had become complicated. War had ravaged the people, leaving its usual bitter aftertaste. The inhabitants of the vale were struggling to come to terms with their recent losses, and desperately needed to apportion blame in order to achieve some semblance of closure. Some would lay the ills of the vale at Mirielle's feet, though there were others, specifically those coerced through fear, who would have no qualms watching the scrying sisters burn instead for Freylar's misfortunes. The community was divided. Like a powder keg, it was ready to explode, ushering in a bloody civil war.

'In any event, will you be joining us or not?' she said, fixing her gaze firmly on Thandor. 'Are you ready to get your hands dirty, or would you rather continue lying on the floor?'

'Rayna, I need you to do me a favour.'

'What kind of favour?' she said, regarding Nathaniel with a curious look from across the table.

It had been a long cycle. The sun had finally set and the sky was thick with clouds that seemingly absorbed the winter moonlight, blanketing the vale in darkness. They sat closely together around the table whilst they ate, trying in vain to keep their feet off the floor to prevent the cold from rising up their legs. They each wore thick cloaks, pulled tightly around their chests, in order to stave off the worst of winter's chill.

'Kayla and I will be leaving shortly.'

'What!' she said, after swallowing her food without adequately chewing it first. 'It's pitch black outside Nathaniel. Besides, where would you go?'

'I intend to use the cover of darkness to provide Kayla safe passage to the Cave of Wellbeing – she cannot remain here indefinitely, at least not whilst Mirielle still rules.'

'Then I will come with you both.' she said, before taking another bite from the meal Kayla had kindly prepared for them as a thank you for their hospitality.

'I expected as much, however, the favour I ask is that you remain here – at least temporarily.'

'I don't understand Nathaniel. If you feel the need to travel at night, then surely the offer of an additional escort is welcome?'

'In your case, no.' replied Nathaniel bluntly. 'You cannot see well in the dark, and the use of your ability would give away our position. Besides, you have a rare gift that will serve us better here.'

'Which is?'

'Your ability to disrupt scrying, as I said before.'

'Yes, but what good is that if I am here alone?'

'You will not be.' replied Nathaniel setting the remains of his meal down on his wooden plate. 'I have sent word to others, including Darlia and Lothnar who will be returning soon. I need you to redirect them all to the Cave of Wellbeing. By doing this, their trails will dead end here.'

'I see.' she said, raising an eyebrow. 'You realise of course that your actions may prompt Marcus to revisit this place?'

'I appreciate that this strategy will likely place you in danger. Mirielle will probably be tracking at least one of those whom I have sent word to. However, I do not believe that she wishes to cross swords with The Guardian – that would be bad for public perception.'

'Do you lay awake at night, Nathaniel, incessantly plotting and scheming?'

'Ha.' replied The Teacher, followed with a wry grin. 'Only when the situation demands it – which it does.'

'I have no desire to lie to him Nathaniel.' she said wearily. 'If Marcus comes knocking, what do you propose I say to him?'

'There is no need to lie; simply evade his dialogue as you would a blade.'

'That is your talent. For the rest of us, manoeuvring as such doesn't come naturally.'

'Get better at it.' replied Nathaniel flatly. 'I have no doubt that one cycle you will assume captaincy of The Blades, and when that time comes, you will need to know how to manage others effectively.'

She offered Kayla a sidelong glance, curious as to whether or not Kirika's aide had an opinion on Nathaniel's designs. Kayla seemed caught out by her sudden change in target audience; the nervous aide hunkered down whilst continuing to eat her meal.

'Are you OK with all of this Kayla?' she asked in a polite manner, trying her best not to agitate the Freylarkin's nervous disposition.

'Kirika trusts Nathaniel.'

'This isn't about Kirika, this is about you.'

'The darkness will cover our passage to the Cave of Wellbeing. I trust Nathaniel to deliver me there.'

'Kayla, I am not convinced that you understand what is required of you here.' she said, leaning in closer. 'When this thing goes to trial, you will be a key witness in Kirika's defence.'

Kayla gave her a nervous stare, before looking to turn her attention to Nathaniel, from whom she was likely expecting answers. It was clear to her that Nathaniel had smoothed over the cracks in order to leverage the cooperation of Kirika's most trusted aide. Although, in her mind at least, it was reckless of him to mislead the Freylarkin – Kayla needed to understand the risks involved.

'Don't look at him for answers.' she said, holding Kayla's attention. 'You need to look in here.' she said, leaning forward to tap Kayla lightly on her chest. 'You need to find the courage to stand up in open defiance of our queen, as your mentor did during the Trials.'

'Rayna tells it like it is – that is her way.' Nathaniel intervened, placing a reassuring hand on Kayla's own. 'However, we will be there to support you.'

Kayla's obvious stress rapidly dissipated in the wake of The Teacher's reassuring words. His ability to coerce and manipulate was impressive, a trait that, until now, she had sorely underestimated.

'Rayna.' said Nathaniel, now focusing his charisma on her. 'Please join us at the Cave of Wellbeing, one cycle from now. You and I need to have a discussion, one that is long overdue. There are many truths of which you are blissfully unaware. It is time that I gave you a lesson in history, though I cannot do it here – Kayla and I must get moving.'

'Very well.' she said with a sigh. 'I don't know what you're planning Nathaniel, but all this collusion better be worth it.'

'Rayna, I appreciate that you have misplaced your trust in others before, however…you can trust *me*.'

THIRTEEN
Revenant

The unfriendly shaper scoffed at his presence, after gingerly opening the door to the hovel. Krashnar peered through the narrow gap between the poorly constructed door and its frame. The shaper's face looked contorted, as though having smelt something bad.

'You survived then.' said the ill-disposed shaper, who seemed put out by his return.

Krashnar's beady eyes widened as they drifted towards the sack laying on the ground beside his feet.

'Is that it?'

'Yes, but you will not be getting your grubby hands on it out here.' he said, irritated by the shaper's complete lack of hospitality.

The door to Krashnar's abode shuddered open as it scraped across the forest floor.

'Why do you not fix that?'

'Bring the sack inside, now!' rasped Krashnar.

He sorely wanted to reprimand the inhospitable Freylarkin for his poor manners, though he immediately realised the futility of such action. Krashnar was a breed apart from the Freylarkai; the distasteful shaper cared not for pleasantries or the feelings of others. Krashnar was a self-absorbed individual, completely disinterested in both the domain and others around him, unless their involvement somehow furthered his own personal desires. Accepting the shaper's uncaring disposition, he followed Krashnar into the gloom, sack in tow. He was about to close the excuse for a door behind him, when suddenly a huge shadow stepped into the doorframe, obscuring what little light penetrated the hovel.

'Not going to leave me behind, were you?' boomed Heldran with a wry grin.

'How the--'

'The how does not matter.' replied the Knight, cutting him off mid-sentence, before pushing his immense bulk through the doorframe. 'What matters is that I have the other item requested by our wretch of a host.'

'You have the Waystones?'

'Indeed.' replied Heldran.

'Stop wasting my time and bring the items.' came the shaper's raspy voice from beyond the gloom.

'After he is done shaping these new blades of yours, I suggest that we test them…on him – just to be sure.'

He laughed heartily at the Knight's comment. The remark had been one made in jest, but even so, there was some merit to Heldran's light-hearted proposal. Although Krashnar had no knowledge of the details of their plan, specifically their intended use of the soon to be forged blades, nonetheless, the unorthodox shaper was a loose end. He trusted Heldran implicitly. Krashnar, however, was another matter entirely.

'Do not tempt me.' he said, feigning disinterest in the Knight's surprisingly practical suggestion.

'Hurry up.' said the shaper, scolding them once more.

Not wishing to antagonise their host any further, they moved along the short corridor into the grubby room where they had initially offered Krashnar the job of shaping the blades. The lonely wooden stool that had previously occupied the room was now gone, replaced with a grimy workbench, upon which lay numerous strange looking instruments, the likes of which he had never seen before.

'I see that you have been busy.' he said, curious as to what the shaper had been up to prior to their arrival.

'Show me the soul stealer.' said Krashnar impatiently, completely ignoring his remark.

It was clear that the shaper had no intention of engaging in small talk, therefore he dropped the sack onto the dirty floor, before opening it just enough to allow Krashnar a glimpse of its contents. The horrid looking shaper licked his cracked lips and his eyes appeared to bulge with excitement.

'Good, good. And the other item that I requested.'

'Here.' replied Heldran, who held out his large right hand, which contained two small objects wrapped in linen.

'Excellent.' said the shaper, rubbing his calloused hands together. 'Leave the items here. Come back in one cycle.'

'Unacceptable – what guarantee do we have that you will not up sticks and leave with the items?' he said, irked by the shaper's terse demeanour.

'Leave the items and bugger off, before I change my mind about your job offer.'

He could feel his choler rising, but his bargaining position was weak; he needed Krashnar's unique talents in order to carry out his plan. Heldran's off the cuff remark ran through his mind once more. Ordinarily, his nature prohibited him from such action, though in Krashnar's case he was prepared to make an exception.

'Come on old friend, there is little to be gained by attempting to negotiate with this wretch.' said Heldran, placing a firm hand on his shoulder. 'Besides, there is a pressing matter that you and I need to discuss – in private.'

They put the hovel behind them before setting up a camp close by in the surrounding woodland, with the intention of maintaining a watchful eye over the shaper from afar. After erecting a crudely built shelter, Heldran quickly got a fire going, the purpose of which was not only to keep them warm, but more importantly, to send a warning to Krashnar in the event the shaper decided to leave his abode. As they lay on the forest floor by the fire, quietly observing the Night's Lights, thoughts of his daughter occupied the fore of his mind. He had been away from Alarielle for too long; he desperately needed to return to their tree to relieve her of any worry due to his prolonged absence.

'Provided the shaper does what is expected of him, we need to get this done tomorrow, so that I can return to my daughter.'

'Agreed.' replied Heldran in his habitual deep rumbling tone.

'The sooner this is done, the better. Hopefully we can begin to undo some of the damage wrought by Caleth's incessant paranoia.'

'On that note.' said Heldran ominously. 'I have some regrettable news to report.'

'What is it?' he replied, sighing heavily.

'The Knight Lord recently decreed that the Order of the Knights Thranis will close its doors firmly on The Blades. My Order will continue to defend the domain's southern lands against the Ravnarkai, though it will have no further dealings with the inhabitants of the vale, particularly The Blades.'

'When did you learn of this?'

'I learned of the news shortly after we parted ways in the borderlands.'

'Did you verify the source of the Sky-Skitter's message?'

'The message was relayed to me in person – do not ask how – by Korlith *himself*. Furthermore, I was the one chosen to deliver this news to the vale. So, here we are, trying to unite our Orders, yet I am commanded to deliver the hammer blow that will divide us indefinitely. What sad irony.'

He signed heavily once more. His heart sank at the news, though it was far from unexpected. It was only a matter of time before the Knight Lord executed such a decision. The Knights Thranis were a close-knit community; they would not jeopardise their family by allowing Caleth's poison to spread to their ranks. Cutting themselves off from The Blades was an understandable reaction, if a heavy-handed one. He was convinced that there were smarter ways of managing the issue, though until Heldran assumed the mantle of Knight Lord, there was little he could do to influence the Order's decision-making.

'This news saddens me, greatly.' he said, in a forlorn tone.

'I assumed as much.'

'Did you *try* to sway his opinion?'

'No. There was no point, Nathaniel. The Order supports Korlith's decision. Though despite this turn of events, you have my word, that when the time is right, I will reverse this decision. However, you *need* to find the right candidate to facilitate this – *devotion* is no good to me.

As amusing as it was pulling Mirielle's strings, he was bored, cooped up alone in Aleska's quarters. His dark companion was growing restless, rattling against its cage; he could feel the urge to do something heinous manifesting inside him. The desire, perpetuated by his symbiotic ally, was growing exponentially. Soon, his companion's needs would dominate his thoughts entirely, making it impossible for him to think about anything else. Though he normally welcomed the urges spurred on by the parasite, now was not the time. He needed to remain level-headed in light of his chosen strategy – there was no room for error. The trial would soon be upon them. There, he would see Mirielle fall into ruin, her reign dismantled due to infighting, the flames of which he now fanned incessantly. Manipulating Freylar's queen, driving her down a path to civil war, was delicious. However, the stage had been set, and all that he needed to do now was wait – the hardest part.

Again, the parasite tugged at his urges, trying its best to steer him towards reckless action. He thought about luring one of the civilians to Aleska's chamber, but that would draw unwanted attention, and then there was the issue of disposing of the body. Dumping his playthings into a river was one thing, but hiding his victims within the Tri-Spires would be a challenge. He tried to distract himself with thoughts beyond those of violating the flesh of his neighbours, but the thing inside him was entirely disinterested. Realising the truth of it, that it was not himself that needed distracting, he turned his thoughts to the ill-fated moment when he had first encountered the evil soulmancer.

'Leave the items and bugger off, before I change my mind about your job offer.' he said, having quickly grown tired of their presence.

The two Freylarkai promptly left his workshop, after which he quickly got started on the task assigned to him. He unravelled the linen parcel first. Inside were two stone fragments, presumably taken from two separate Waystones, each supposedly attuned to the other, as he had instructed. Preferring not to leave anything to chance, he placed the stone fragments at different points in the room, careful not to touch them, using the linen to prevent contact with the alleged Waystones. Crouching down, he pressed his hand against the smooth surface of the stone closest to the door and watched as the room began to slip from view. His stomached lurched and he felt lightheaded, but before his mind could consider what was happening, he was already crouched in the opposite corner of the room. He looked down and saw that his hand now touched the other stone fragment. He stood up unsteadily on his feet, and stumbled towards the workbench to support himself. It had been many passes since last he had used a Waystone – he hated them then, and equally so now.

'Wretched things.' he said aloud, venting his annoyance.

Having glimpsed the captured Narlakin already, confirming its authenticity, he decided to commence with the Waystones – it made sense to shape the less troublesome blade first. Whilst his irksome employers had been dallying around in the borderlands, he had procured two identical falchions, which he laid on the workbench. The blades were nothing special, indeed the quality of their manufacture was questionable; Krasus, the arrogant shaper responsible for their creation, had been showing off in the streets, giving the weapons away freely, claiming that he could fashion a blade faster than anyone else in the vale. In all likelihood, the overconfident Freylarkin had been massaging his bruised ego, trying to reinstate his superiority following the strange news that an enigmatic shaper had arrived in the vale and was erecting something spectacular south of the arena. The mysterious shaper was a female, one who was rapidly gathering a cult following in awe of her work. Frankly, he cared little for the achievements of others, but there were those, Krasus included, who were jealous of such works.

'This will not do.' he muttered to himself, scolding Krasus' shoddy workmanship. 'That excuse for a shaper needs knocking down a peg or two.'

He opened a concealed drawer in the workbench, and removed two Dawnstones from his private collection. The stones were silky-smooth to the touch and light as a feather. Both were light grey and had a slight pearlescent look about them. In order to fashion anything of note, one had to use the right materials, just as any cook would require the right ingredients. Krasus overlooked the obvious and, in all likelihood, the same was true of the unknown shaper camped out by the arena. The details mattered. Anyone with the ability could fashion a blade from steel, but Dawnstone…that was another matter entirely.

'You will do nicely.' he said, licking his dry cracked lips with excitement.

It took some time to work the Dawnstone into the blades, creating a silvery-grey alloy that shimmered in the dull light. Though he had no use for melee weapons himself, nonetheless, he was able to appreciate the quality of their workmanship when he saw it. The blades laid out on the workbench before him, although uninspiring in their design, were masterpieces. Both were extremely light, making them effortless to wield. Furthermore, their pearlescent finish enhanced the blades' splendour, giving them an understated beauty, unlike the ostentatious works of others who sought to mask the inferior raw materials they habitually used. Those other shapers were fools. All were underachievers, afraid to experiment, thus stunting their ability and limiting their imagination. Pleased with his efforts, he selected one of the newly-shaped weapons and began working the Waystone fragments into the tip of the blade and below the falchion's cross-guard, along the top of its grip, melding them seamlessly with the sleek Dawnstone. He was careful not to touch the Waystones directly, having only recently settled his stomach, though indirectly shaping the fragments was far trickier than he had anticipated. Eventually though, his work was done, and the magnificent weapon was complete.

After a short break to regain his strength, his attention turned to the captive Narlakin. The soul stealer continued to writhe inside its hessian prison, trying desperately to escape the confines of the sack. Wisps of grey smoke permeated the sides of the hessian, as though the creature inside intended to push itself through the porous gaps in the material. How would it manage, trapped inside the other Dawnstone blade, he mused. Wrenching the sack off the floor, he dumped his prisoner onto the workbench. Opening the sack ever so slightly, he created a gap large enough to allow him to insert the length of the blade, less its hilt. Then, using his ability, he gripped the falchion's hilt and began manipulating the surface of the weapon, drawing in its immediate surroundings, specifically the Narlakin now in direct contact with the blade. The soul stealer released a hideous moan, whilst being drawn helplessly, against its will, into the weapon. The awful moaning sound grew louder and louder as his victim writhed ferociously, desperately trying, in vain, to avoid its doom. The sack expanded and contracted violently, as the thing inside tried to escape its destiny, but it was then that something entirely unexpected occurred. Strange translucent, ephemeral shapes began permeating through the hessian sack, some of which assumed rough forms, like small animals and insects. Others grew much larger, lingering in the air above his workbench, causing him to recoil from their presence. The bizarre forms loitered for a moment, before rising upwards, passing through tiny gaps in the roof. One by one, the shapes disappeared as they drifted upwards and out of sight, with the exception of one. A single form hovered in the air before him, seemingly reluctant to ascend along with the others. Slowly, the form began to assume a recognisable shape, eventually taking on the guise of a bony skeletal being, not unlike an emaciated Freylarkin. A colossal set of wings protruded from the apparition's back, although only their skeletal frame was visible – the membrane being entirely absent – giving the spectre a sinister look. The strange incorporeal being wore a tattered cloak full of holes, which was unsecured around the waist, allowing him to see the spirit's ugly body. The apparition tried to speak, evidenced by its moving jaw, but there was no sound. Unable to communicate, the spectre circled the room, trying in vain to interact with the various objects it contacted. Realising its inability to touch as well as speak, the spectre quickly became angry. It thrashed violently in the air, its large wings passing through the walls and roof of his workshop whilst it seemingly struggled to contain its rage. He backed away cautiously, releasing his hand from the possessed blade in exchange for its twin. The hessian sack lay flat on the workbench, suggesting that the Narlakin had now been fully absorbed into the weapon. Moving slowly, he backed towards the door whilst the apparition continued to thrash in the air. He reached behind with his free hand, fumbling the door's release catch, all the while maintaining a tight grip on the other Dawnstone blade. The sound of his failed attempts to open the door attracted the spectre's attention. The frenzied apparition fixed him with its soulless gaze; where once there had been eyes, now there were only obsidian orbs, loaded with malice.

'Leave this place!' he rasped, still struggling with the door's latch in his frightened state.

The apparition suddenly gathered itself, as though ready to strike. Panicked, he spun around and drove the Dawnstone blade into the rickety door, splintering the cracked wood. He passed his thumb over the Waystone fragment fused into the top of the weapon's grip, below the cross-guard. In his peripheral vision, he saw the apparition stretch into a thin vertical line, before slipping from view entirely. After his vision returned, it became clear to him that he was staring at the same door, but from its opposite side! Panicked by what he had inadvertently unleashed, he turned and ran along the narrow corridor towards the exit. Hurriedly closing the entrance to his hide behind him, he caught a further glimpse of the ghastly apparition as it passed through the jammed inner door, its incorporeal form meeting no resistance. Before he could seal the door shut, the apparition raced towards him, passing effortlessly through the outer door of his abode and penetrating his body. Everything froze, and a stream of harrowing visions violently assaulted him. Images of the apparition's past ripped through his mind, each one depicting its deplorable acts in graphic detail. Without any regard to his consent, the monster filled his soul with its ghastly experiences, immediately corrupting what little good remained at his core. The *thing* was not of Freylar, originating instead from some other distant domain. It offered him no clue as to the reason for its presence in the borderlands, though it did reveal the final moments of its original sinister form, prior to the capture of its soul by the trapped Narlakin. It was clear now that shaping the blade had forced out those souls previously bound by the soul stealer. The images continued to violate his mind, each more graphic than the last and seemingly in no logical order. Some depicted the thing with large ugly scars, which then disappeared in subsequent imagery, only to then reappear. Far more disturbingly, however, where those scenes that depicted the being drawing down souls from the Everlife, and reinserting them into half-decayed corpses of the released, exhumed from their graves. He was in awe, watching the deplorable art in stunned amazement, expertly performed by the enigmatic being.

'Who are you?' he rasped, disorientated, before losing his balance and crashing hard to the ground.

'*I am T'mohr – now get up!*'

The images suddenly abated, allowing his sense of balance to return. He scrambled back to his feet and pressed his back firmly against the shelter, keenly aware of his heavy breathing and the thumping in his chest.

'Where are you?' he asked, snapping his head from left to right.

It was dark, and the temperature had dropped. Moisture from his breath lingered in the air, forming strange shapes, not unlike the one from which he had just fled. T'mohr laughed, an ugly sinister laugh, one that reverberated throughout his entire body.

'*I am here – inside you!*'

'What! Get out!' he rasped, instinctively touching his own body, trying to discern the apparition's point of entry.

'*You fool. Physical boundaries mean nothing to me, at least not in this form. My soul now rides your own.*' said T'mohr, in a deep foreboding voice.

'Get out!' he rasped again.

'*No – you get out.*'

'This is *my* body!'

'*And a wretched one it is too. Still, it will do, at least until my strength returns.*'

'Then what?'

'*Then perhaps you might have this decrepit body of yours exclusively to yourself once more.*' said T'mohr, laughing again.

'How are you doing this?'

'*I am a soulmancer.*'

Like all young Freylarkin, he had heard the dark accounts of the soulmancers; sinister tales told to the young, in order to coerce fledgling minds.

"Go to bed, or the soulmancers will get you!"

He remembered the words well, nevertheless, they were nothing more than stories, old wives' tales, designed to scare the young – no one had actually *seen* a soulmancer.

'You lie!'

'Ha, you think I care what you do or do not believe?' said T'mohr, before releasing another of his hideous laughs. *'You are a weak, pathetic wretch, despite your curious talent for manipulating trinkets. But, there is still hope for you; under my guidance you will become so much more.'*

He could feel the soulmancer trying to exert his will over his own, trying to push him out. Whilst it was true that his body was old before its time, T'mohr had severely underestimated his innate talent. Using his ability, he began to modify his own body, shaping it in a manner that would allow him to confine the evil that he had unwittingly allowed to enter his body. Since he did not possess the means to expel the soulmancer, containment seemed like the next logical solution. He could hear T'mohr screaming in his mind as he reworked his internal systems, attempting to contain the parasite. With supreme effort, he reworked his own flesh, trying to shield his soul from T'mohr's incorporeal touch. Such changes, however, needed to be permanent; he required a flesh sacrifice to cement his work. With no other relevant sources of material available to him, he was forced to use a parts of *himself* to effect the changes permanently. He grunted painfully, his eyes full of hate, as he watched his left hand deform. Both his ring and little fingers reduced in length, until both ceased to exist. The recycled flesh bolstered his ability, allowing him to shore up the internal cage around the parasite's soul.

'Stay there and rot!'

'Irrelevant! I will break free o--'

A loud crack echoed across the wood, shortly after silencing the soulmancer. The sudden noise was the unmistakable sound of a fallen branch, snapping beneath the heavy tread of an unwanted visitor. Clutching his deformed limb due to the pain, he tried to retreat into his abode. Instead, a heavy hand slammed the door shut to his hide, denying him access.

'What are you up to, *little* shaper?' boomed Heldran in a thunderous tone. 'And what is the matter with your hand?'

'Not just his hand.' said Nathaniel, startling him, having crept up from behind. 'Look at his eyes!'

The giant Freylarkin pressed him against his shelter, before moving his head closer for inspection.

'What have you done to yourself?' said Heldran.

'Irrelevant!' he replied, evading the question. 'Do you want to see the swords you commissioned or not?'

FOURTEEN
Misdirection

Almost three cycles had passed since the Sky-Skitter's arrival. Since then, she had used the time to process her grief, moreover, the range of emotions that had assaulted her in the wake of the news. She was heartbroken, after learning of her brother's release. For a time, she had been completely inconsolable, but her sorrow had since evolved into sadness and depression, followed by anger and hatred. Only now was she able to think more clearly, having endured the worst of it. Alone, in her room, she pulled the message scroll out and read the words once more.

'Keshar, I hope you receive this message, and that you are keeping well. I write to you because something awful has happened. Your brother, Riknar, was found released, down by the river. A rogue shaper, Krashnar, was responsible for the deplorable act. To my knowledge, a Sky-Skitter was sent to you regarding this news. However, ten cycles have passed, yet you remain strangely absent from the vale, ergo, I believe that you have not received word of this terrible news. Your family needs you – please return to the vale, with haste. Nathaniel.'

'You lied to me!' she said aloud, her eyes watering as tears spilled from them. 'I trusted you, and you lied!'

She grabbed a wooden carving from the table by her bed and hurled it against the wall, venting her anger. The wooden figurine crashed into the wall, splintering apart, then fell to the ground with a dull thud. Standing in the middle of her room, she started to shake with rage, unable to keep the emotions she felt in check.

'You deceived me!'

Nathaniel had been right. Aleska wanted her to remain at Scrier's Post purely for personal gain. It was clear now that her tutor had no interest in her personal wellbeing, unless it furthered her own agenda. Realising the truth of it, she felt hurt and betrayed. Until now, she had never felt the sting of being used. Aleska's betrayal felt intensely personal; withholding news of her brother's release was unforgivable.

'Keshar, are you OK?'

'I am fine.' she said, blatantly lying to the new students who were clearly eavesdropping from behind her door.

'We heard the noise. Do you require any assistance?'

'*Trust* me, I am fine.'

The word felt bitter in her mouth – never before had she encountered something so distasteful. Acting on impulse, she abruptly opened her door. Had she not been so full of anger, it might have been amusing to see Aleska's students stumble forward into her room. The pair quickly stood up, then made their apologies for invading her private space.

'Keshar, you have been crying.' said the most perceptive of the pair.

'Yes…I have some regrettable news to report.'

'What is it?' asked the other.

'I regret to inform you that the sanctuary will be closing its doors. I will be leaving for the vale shortly, to return to my family, and ask that you both do the same by accompanying me.'

'But what about Aleska and our studies?'

'Aleska is attending to other, more pressing, business in the vale. I do not believe that she will be returning to this place anytime soon.'

'What will happen to the sanctuary?'

'I do not know. The fate of Scrier's Post will be determined by others.' she said. 'In any event, you must both pack your personal effects and say your goodbyes. I intend to leave shortly.'

She could see their visible shock, nonetheless, as the senior student stationed at the sanctuary, both eagerly followed her orders without further question, hurriedly returning to their quarters to pack their belongings. She felt bad cutting their education short, but without her presence, Scrier's Post would cease to operate in Aleska's absence. The parallels between her own actions and those of Aleska were not lost on her. Aleska had deceived her so that she would remain at Scrier's Post, and now, she coerced the remaining students to leave, effectively shutting down the site. She tried to look past her anger, but the wound caused by Aleska's deception refused to heal. Forcing the closure of Scrier's Post, therefore, was the least her mentor deserved. In any event, the remaining students needed to be protected, since Aleska's interests were not necessarily aligned with their own.

'You will *not* use them, as you have me.'

She hurriedly packed the few belongings that she had accrued during her time at Scrier's Post, before extinguishing the single candle in her room. Lingering for a moment, watching the smoke from the candle evaporate into the gloom, she thought back over her time spent at the sanctuary, and the lessons imparted by her former mentor. It saddened her that her time at Scrier's Post had ended, especially given the abrupt manner of its ending. She wished dearly that things had played out differently, but Aleska's selfish manipulations had put paid to her aspirations. There would be no further instruction from the venerable scrier, who had irrevocably broken her trust. Supressing information was one thing, but withholding information about the wellbeing of loved ones was unforgivable. If Aleska was prepared to sink to such depths to maintain her agenda, there was no telling what else their former mentor was capable of. She would cherish her time spent at the sanctuary, in particular the knowledge she had acquired, however, it was time now to move on.

'We have packed our belongings.' a voice said softly from behind her.

'Very well,' she said, turning to face her former students, 'Let us depart this place. If we leave now, we should make the vale before nightfall.'

'Do you think that we will ever return?' asked one of the students expectantly.

Using her newly acquired discipline, she had tried to scry their mentor's fate, but for reasons beyond her understanding, Aleska's future remained shrouded. The interference of another clouded the venerable scrier's fate, masking it from her second sight. Yet despite her inability to scry their mentor's future, and her personal feelings towards Aleska, she considered the question objectively. Although wronged by Aleska, she still believed in the work they had been doing. It was possible that under fresh direction there would be renewed hope for the twice-abandoned sanctuary.

'In time…perhaps.'

'Let me sleeeeeeep!'

She pulled her bedsheets over her head, pretending for a moment that the world around her did not exist. Despite the drop in temperature, her bed was warm and comfortable – she did not wish to leave. Ironically, there was a time when she feared the thought of going to sleep, due to the suppressed memories of her past returning to torment her. With Alarielle's help, however, she had learned to accept the transgressions of her former life, using her ugly experiences to forge a more meaningful path in her new one. Her time in Freylar had been relatively short, but in that brief time, so much had transpired, and now, the promise of change was more prevalent than ever. The Freylarkai were growing restless under Mirielle's rule. The Queen's leadership was being called into question, and it would not be long before the backroom discussions spilled into the public forum. In both her lives, she had endured her fair share of conflict – too much in fact – thus the thought of remaining in bed called to her, like a siren of the sea. The muffled banging sounded once more – it was not a dream. She leapt out of bed, grabbing one of the sheets to conceal her modesty, and stumbled down the wooden stairs whilst wiping encrusted rheum from her bleary eyes.

'I'm coming!' she blurted out, her voice cracked and dry.

Without giving her actions any thought, she flung open the door to Nathaniel's tree. Standing before her, with mixed expressions, were Nathanar, Thandor and Natalya.

'I like your new look, Rayna.' said Natalya playfully.

'Catch you at a bad time?' asked Nathanar, who had an amused look about him.

She rolled her eyes, signalling her lack of appreciation for their supposedly witty quips, although, her unamused expression failed to have its desired effect, with Thandor also taking the opportunity to garner further amusement at her expense.

'I see now why Lothnar had a thing for her.' said Thandor, giving the others a sidelong glance.

'Shut up and get inside, the lot of you.'

Stepping aside, allowing them to enter the tree, she laughed as Nathanar banged his head against the top of the doorframe, despite stooping as he entered.

'It's good to see that karma is a thing, here in Freylar.' she said, laughing at the Paladin's misfortune.

'I have no idea what you are talking about.' replied Nathanar, who grimaced whilst rubbing his forehead.

'Take a seat, and I will fix us something to eat.'

'Thank you,' replied Thandor, 'However, it might be prudent to fix your *attire* first.'

She gave the master duellist a good-natured smirk, before withdrawing up the stairs to her room, where she deliberately took her time getting ready. Having forced them to wait long enough, she returned to the living area where she found all three engaged in a lively debate, the subject of which was Nathaniel, specifically, the reason for their summons.

'Look, I know what you're going to ask me, and the answer is that I do not know what *he* is up to, nor is he here.'

'Then why ask us to come here?' asked Natalya, who was clearly uninterested in chasing ghosts.

'Because of me.'

'Then it is you who wishes to speak with us?' asked Nathanar with a confused look about him.

'Nathaniel has asked me to relay his whereabouts to you all in person.'

'He could have done that himself.' replied Natalya, the sound of annoyance detectable in the tone of her voice.

'True enough, though he did not want anyone else to learn of your destination.'

'Rayna, are you *trying* to be evasive?' asked Thandor, who gave her a hard stare.

'No, not intentionally – let me explain.' she said as she took up position, choosing to lean against the nearest wall. 'My presence confounds scriers; they have a difficult time discerning my fate, and that of those entwined with it. Kirika believes that my presence in the body of another is, in part at least, responsible for this bizarre phenomenon.'

'Are you saying that, by you being *here*, that scriers will be unable to learn of this meeting?' ask Nathanar inquisitively.

'It is possible that you could be tracked here by one of Mirielle's sanctioned scriers, however, the details of this meeting will be beyond their second sight. Furthermore, your trail ends here.'

'For that to be true, you would need to accompany us to Nathaniel's location.' said Thandor with renewed interest.

'I will accompany you part way through the forest to conceal your departure. However, you must then each tread separate paths to your common destination.'

'Why do you choose not to travel with us?' asked Nathanar.

'The choice is not mine.' she replied, casting her gaze towards the empty rocking chairs by the piles of dusty books. 'Nathaniel wishes to speak with you all privately.'

'When *will* you be joining us?' asked Thandor with obvious interest. 'Surely The Teacher will not be absent his star pupil, she who holds favour with the people.'

'You are assuming that I am his fulcrum in all this.' she said, turning her attention to Thandor. 'I am not as close to Nathaniel as you may think. He has something else planned, besides manipulating me.'

'I see.' replied Thandor flatly.

'I will meet with you all later.' she continued. 'Your absence from the vale will not go unnoticed; others will likely be coming here, whom I will be required to deal with in person.'

'Then why warrant the attention – why not meet somewhere within the vale instead?' asked Natalya.

'You will need to ask Nathaniel that question, the answer to which I am still owed myself.'

'Do you trust him?' asked Thandor abruptly.

All three looked towards her, eager to hear her response to Thandor's pointed line of enquiry. The more she learned of Nathaniel's past, the muddier the water appeared in which he sailed. Nathaniel had an agenda – that much was obvious to her – though she could not tell whether his interests aligned with those of the people. It was clear now that The Teacher played his cards close to his chest.

'Kirika trusts him – that's good enough for me. But, perhaps you should ask me again tomorrow.' she said, offering them all a playful wink.

'OK,' said Natalya, 'So where does The Teacher propose that we meet, for real this time?'

'At the Cave of Wellbeing. You will find him there.'

'She has been busy – this changes things.'

'We cannot back out now.' he said, giving the Knight a hard stare. 'He *is* in there.'

'I do not doubt that.' replied Heldran, whose voice sounded akin to a deep rumble. 'However, we have no map of the internal structure.'

'Follow your nose brother.'

'Nathaniel, that *spire* up there is new – it was not there before!'

'And that is where Caleth will be – I am certain of it.'

'I am not climbing up that thing!'

'Afraid of heights?'

The weathered Knight glared at him. He understood well the reason for Heldran's reluctance to infiltrate the ephemeral structure, given the uncertainty of its internal layout. Admittedly, he had failed to appreciate the alacrity of the mysterious female shaper furiously working on the imposing structure. Though he had seen other shapers create wonders with impressive speed, the rapid pace with which this new Freylarkin forged her unique vision was unprecedented. With each passing cycle, more and more Freylarkai had gathered to watch; they stood in awe as they witnessed the lone shaper give birth to her opus, without the aid of others. The rumour touted by the people was that Caleth had commissioned the unknown Freylarkin to erect the unorthodox structure in his name. In all likelihood, the paranoid Blade Lord intended to ensconce himself within the citadel indefinitely, thus avoiding direct contact with those in his dominion.

'I have obviously underestimated her talent. However, this is our best chance to get the job done. Once that thing is complete, The Blade Lord will likely double the guards stationed throughout the warren at its base – we will never have a better opportunity to make this work for us.'

The imposing Knight released a heavy sigh.

'You are right of course, but going in blind does not sit well with me.'

'I appreciate your concern, but what alternative is there?' he asked candidly, eager to learn whether the well-informed Knight had any tricks up his long sleeves.

Heldran craned his neck back to better observe the tall spire that rose defiantly from the base of the citadel, flouting the laws of nature. Its immense height was impressive, a testament to its shaper's skill.

'We will return before dawn. The guards on the night watch will be tired; their eyes will play tricks on them, giving us an edge.'

'Agreed.'

'In the meantime, see if you can learn anything of the citadel's layout. After all, your Order stands guard over the thing, does it not?'

He spent the remainder of the cycle gleaning what information he could about the enigmatic structure, agreeing to reconvene with Heldran shortly after dusk. As he had expected, the guards on duty were reluctant to discuss the matter of the citadel's internal layout; no doubt, Caleth had ordered them to remain tight-lipped on the subject. Despite the setback, however, those off duty were more carefree with their speech, especially after a few drinks in the local taverns close to the arena. Given his respected position within the Order, and his good standing with the people, he encountered little difficulty loosening the tongues of several of his Blade brothers and sisters. He quickly discovered that Caleth had brought guards in from outside the Order, all of whom remained obstinately tight-lipped when questioned. Despite this, he managed to obtain some useful information from his fellow Blades, seconded to help guard the citadel.

'Pretty soon, *he* will not need us!' said the Freylarkin slumped across the table beside him.

'Why is that?' he asked, feigning merriment.

'Because, dear Nathaniel, we are not cut from the same cloth as that *other* lot.'

'The ones outside the Order you mean?'

'Mercenaries, all of them.' said another, from across the table.

'Where is he recruiting them from?'

'Why so interested?' replied his intoxicated drinking companion.

'I like to know who my allies are.' he said, quickly dismissing the question.

'Ha, I very much doubt you would want them fighting at your back. The Blade Lord recruits them from the outer fringes. They have no loyalty to the Order; he pays them to guard the citadel and to keep quiet – that is how he likes it. He has us fill the gaps in his private security, but that will not last.'

'You get all the glamorous assignments.' he said, baiting his companion in an attempt to keep the disgruntled Blade talking.

'Hardly! We are not permitted to enter the chambers, he has us stationed in the corridors instead.'

'But you must see The Blade Lord wandering the corridors.'

'Not likely. He sits up in that new tower of his. Rumour has it that you need to use a Waystone to get up there!'

It was getting late; he was losing the light and his patience had worn thin. Deciding that it was unlikely that he would leverage any further useful information from the locals, he chose to leave the tavern and wandered back to the meeting point with Heldran. When he arrived, the Knight was already present, slouched against a tree, sharpening his ardent sword with a whetstone.

'Any luck?' asked the Knight, whose attention remained focused on the cutting edge of his blade.

'Some.' he replied, as he sat down on the ground beside Heldran. 'Would you like the good news, or--'

'Good news – do not ruin my mood.'

He watched for a while as the Knight continued to sharpen his blade, occasionally dipping the whetstone into a murky bucket of water beside them, renewing the stone's effectiveness as he ran it along the blade's cutting edge. It was rare that The Blades engaged in such work; watching the Knight sharpening the blade reminded him of the hands-on approach adopted by the Knights Thranis. The Knights numbered few compared to The Blades, and the Order lacked any civilian support; there were few with the desire to make their home in Freylar's southern lands given the incessant conflict with the neighbouring Ravnarkai, therefore the Knights learned quickly to fend for themselves.

'Caleth does not trust The Blades.'

'Ha, so his paranoia is worse than you supposed.'

'Yes, however, this is to our advantage.'

'How so?' replied Heldran, dipping the stone into the water once more.

'The Blades assigned to guard the citadel have been stationed exclusively in the corridors. Caleth's personal guard secures the internal chambers.'

Heldran paused for a moment to consider his words. He imagined a network of gears and leavers turning inside Heldran's mind as the Knight processed the information, using it to formulate a strategy that would best serve them.

'What level of influence do you hold over The Blades assigned to guard the citadel?'

'They trust me.'

'Good – we can use that.' replied Heldran, before continuing to work his blade. 'I propose that you relieve them of their shift, early, enabling us to quietly clear a path to the target.'

'That could work. Like you say, they will be tired, plus their support for The Blade Lord wanes the more Caleth distances himself from them.'

'Good. So, what is this bad news to which you allude?'

'So…you recall that spire we talked about…'

It was late evening when the knock at the door finally came. She had spent the cycle cooped up in Nathaniel's tree, waiting for the inevitable visit. In hindsight, it had made perfect sense to keep her hanging, affording her the time she needed to become nervous and irritable. The Blade Lord excelled at mind games, and knew best how to manipulate others, although The Teacher's schooling had prepared her for the eventuality. She took a deep breath, before slowly exhaling, attempting to calm the last of her jangled nerves. Although she was now accustomed to conflict and attention, she had a great deal of respect for The Blade Lord, making what she was about to do even more difficult. After setting down the book that she had been reading for most of the cycle, she rose from her rocking chair and stretched her arms and back, before opening the door.

'Marcus, I have been expecting you. Please, come in.'
'Thank you.'

Marcus stepped confidentially into the centre of the room, deliberately making his presence known, flaunting his authority. She had seen The Blade Lord act in such a manner many times before, typically when addressing The Blades, though it had been a while since he had done so for her personal benefit.

'The last time we spoke to one another, I said that you had a choice to make.' said Marcus, getting straight to the point of his visit. 'I also said that the outcome of that choice would affect others who look to you for guidance.'

'Please, sit with me Marcus.' she said, gesturing towards the rocking chairs adjacent to the small window.

'This is not a social call, Rayna.' replied Marcus sternly.

'I understand that. Nevertheless, I am your friend, and I would feel more comfortable if we could sit together.'

Marcus sighed heavily, before taking a seat in the chair nearest to the door. The Blade Lord's growing impatience, evidenced by the increased number of lines across his forehead, increased her unease, causing her muscles to tighten. She could feel the palpable tension between them, so much so, that it made her feel sad.

'I do not want this *thing* to come between us.' she said, trying to melt The Blade Lord's cold exterior.

'Where is Kayla?'
'With Nathaniel.'

'Then where is Nathaniel?' asked Marcus tersely.

'I cannot tell you.'

'Why?'

'Because I have yet to make my choice.'

'Rayna, by shielding *him*, you have already chosen a side.'

'That is not the case. I have not yet spoken to him about the truths you alluded to.'

'Is this another of your tricks, Rayna? A means, perhaps, to play for time?'

'It is not a trick of my making.'

'Then it is *his*, and you are his obedient student.'

'You are well aware that I share an unshakable bond with Nathaniel – I inadvertently stole his daughter's body! However, that bond does not mean that I, by default, trust him. I am not blind to his machinations.'

'Did you even try to sway his thinking, as I requested?'

'No, his course is set – it cannot be altered.'

'Then you realise what this means?' replied Marcus, whose expression became grim.

'I have a pretty good idea.'

'You must realise by now, that Nathaniel is a political agitator. If his sedition--'

'It is *not* sedition.'

'I do not care what you call it!' replied Marcus tersely. 'Rayna, my Paladins and Valkyries are *all* absent, and Darlia is still missing – this is not a coincidence.'

'No, it is not.'

'If this is allowed to continue, he could incite civil war amongst the Freylarkai. Surely, you cannot want this.'

Marcus fixed her with slate grey eyes, keenly watching her body language for involuntary signs that might contradict her words. Yet despite her nerves, she remained unconcerned; she spoke the truth, and her body would tell the same story.

'I do not want civil war.' she replied. 'Nothing good can come of that. A victory gained through war sows the seeds of another war.'

'Then help me stop it, Rayna.' said Marcus sincerely. 'Get him to end this – whatever *this* is.'

'I cannot alter his course, any more so than you can Mirielle's. Nathaniel's will is bent on his intent.'

'If that is truly the case, there will be further bloodshed in the vale – the people have already had their fill.'

'Marcus, you are looking at all this too linearly.'

Clearly taken aback by her words, The Blade Lord suddenly regarded her with a stony expression.

'And how else am I supposed to look at *this*?'

Concerned that she had crossed a line, she took a moment to consider her next words carefully; having clearly tested the limits of her friendship with Marcus, she was reticent to push The Blade Lord any further.

'This whole situation is like a coin – it has two sides. But when flipped, there are more than two possible outcomes.'

'How so?' asked Marcus, whose previously stern expression now softened to one of interest.

'Because sometimes, that coin will land on its edge.'

Marcus relaxed into his chair, before releasing another heavy sigh.

'I am afraid that I cannot see that edge.'

'Maybe not now, but when the time comes, you will, I am certain of it. I have faith in you.' she said sincerely. 'In any event, I must leave here and speak with Nathaniel prior to making my *choice*. Please…do not follow me Marcus.'

FIFTEEN
Fallen

'Damn it!' she cried, swiping her good arm across the workbench, sending the intricate ornaments that littered her desk clattering across the granite floor.

The malformed object responsible for her outburst remained intact, defiantly opposing her will to see it laid to ruin. The misshapen trinket glinted in the dim light, taunting her with its continued existence.

'My queen, are you all right?' called a voice from behind the door to her chamber, which then opened abruptly. 'We heard a noise and--'

'It is nothing.'

'But the floor...' replied Ralnor lowering his gaze towards the polished granite surface.

'There was an accident. However, there is no cause for alarm.' she said, regaining her composure.

'Do you require assistance?'

'No…thank you. I am fine.' she said, doing her best to deter the guard from entering her room any further. 'I will see to the mess myself. You may leave.'

'My queen, there is something else.'

'What is it?'

'Another communication, from Aleska.'

'Why am I only hearing of this now?'

'I thought that you were still asleep. I did not wish to wake you.'

'Here, give it to me.'

The obedient guard quickly crossed the room, hand delivering Aleska's latest correspondence.

'You may leave.' she said, dismissing Ralnor with a quick wave of her hand.

Ralnor promptly left, closing the door firmly behind him. Alone once more, she slowly began gathering up the ornaments – most of which were now broken – and placed the pieces haphazardly upon her workbench. She sat down, glowering across the room at the object responsible for her frustration. The trinket alone had not been the sole reason for her outburst, although its taxing design had ultimately pushed her over the edge mentally. She felt tired from all the stress and worry that had denied her any meaningful sleep, which in turn had made her even more irritable. Aleska's return had been of great comfort to her, giving her renewed focus and alleviating some of her concerns. However, a late report received from The Blade Lord painted a grim picture. Marcus' analysis was far less optimistic than Aleska's own, suggesting that opposition to her rule was increasing due to an emerging insurrection lead by The Teacher. According to Marcus, Nathaniel was gathering influential Freylarkai to an undisclosed location, the purpose of which was officially unknown. Reading between the lines, however, it was clear that The Teacher intended to drive a wedge between her and the people, in an attempt to force her to step down. Aleska had warned her in the past about Nathaniel's talent for subterfuge, furthermore Marcus had, albeit more recently, alluded to the same. She began to understand why Kirika had put up little resistance when escorted back to the Tri-Spires. It was obvious to her now that both had colluded with one another, in all likelihood orchestrating the manoeuvre since their return to the vale following the battle for Bleak Moor. Kirika must have foreseen that she would reprimand the scrier for her actions in the arena, and had therefore enlisted Nathaniel's aid, working with the renewalist to subvert her fate. Upon assembling the pieces of the jigsaw, she had immediately written to Aleska advising the venerable scrier of the latest developments. Breaking the seal on Aleska's correspondence, she unfolded the message, eager to read the scrier's latest thoughts.

'I am glad that you have brought this matter to my attention. In light of this development, I propose that we advance our schedule. We should bring forward the trial, commencing at noon, starting with the dressmaker. An example needs to be made, quickly and effectively, one that will shock the people and rein them back into submission. The Freylarkai need to understand that everything you do is for their own protection. Call out Larissa and have her answer for her heinous crime, the price of which must be public release. This will reaffirm your authority, and in doing so will disadvantage Kirika, who will be emotionally compromised when called to account for her own transgressions. I realise that what I ask of you will be difficult. However, it has become apparent that the threat of exile is not sufficient to ensure compliance from those whom you have selflessly chosen to protect.

In other news, I am feeling much better following my prolonged bed rest. Although you already have my signed written statement for the case against Larissa, nonetheless, I shall attend the trial to show my support. Irrespective of my presence, we should continue to maintain our distance so that I do not weaken your authority. It is important that the Freylarkai witness first-hand your strength of character and unwavering leadership.

Aleska.'

The venerable scrier's latest message was a sobering read. She agreed that Larissa's actions warranted punishment; releasing Hanarah and coercing her into separating Cora from her released mother were both unforgivable acts. Even so, the sentence proposed by Aleska was high – though it was nothing the dressmaker had not merited due to her actions. She was no stranger to passing judgement on those guilty of crimes against the domain. She had sentenced several Freylarkai to exile, including Krashnar and Darlia, and had even ordered The Blade Lord to sever the notorious scrier's left hand. Yet despite these acts, she had never once ordered the release of another. She knew that Aleska was capable of cold and ruthless acts when the situation demanded it, but even so, the thought of ordering the release of another made her feel uneasy. Furthermore, there was the matter of Hanarah's daughter to consider. Cora remained traumatised in the wake of her mother's release, moreover the manner in which it had occurred. Thus far, the young Freylarkin had remained silent and was clearly struggling to process her loss. With the trial imminent, she needed to ensure that Cora was onside, or at the very least continued to remain silent.

'Ralnor.' she said loudly, certain that the jittery guard would hear her summons from beyond the door.

As expected, the door to her chamber opened promptly.

'I wish to spend some more time with Cora. Please have her brought to me at once.'

She closed the door to Nathaniel's tree, uncertain as to whether or not either of them would return. Since her arrival in Freylar, Nathaniel's unconventional – to her at least – abode had been home. Though she had spent much of her time living in the Wild prior to her encounter with the alien entity, nonetheless, taking up residence inside a giant tree had been an odd experience. Despite the cramped living space, she felt safe within the tree's hollow, unlike in her many bolt-holes scattered throughout the artificial wilderness in the heart of the metropolis. Her mind drifted back to her time in the metropolis where each day had been spent scavenging for survival, uncertain where her next meal would come from. What had become of the shelters that had ultimately kept her alive, hidden from the authorities, and what path had her socially awkward ally, Trix, ultimately taken, she mused. Was Mr L. Cameron's lifeless corpse still decomposing unceremoniously in hab one-seven-one, or had the Peacekeepers found the body hidden in the storage cupboard and initiated an investigation into the murder, she wondered. The debris of her past actions littered her former life, though she knew now that angsting over her previous mistakes achieved nothing. There was little point in revisiting her past – she was not going that way. Perhaps the butterflies in her stomach were responsible for her momentary relapse. Having finally dealt with her own demons and made peace with them, the thought of exposing herself to Nathaniel's own did not appeal to her. Despite her reticence to learn of any potential new horrors, she owed it to Nathaniel to hear him out, as Heldran had requested during her time spent with the Knights Thranis.

After offering the tree one final regard, she set off on a north-westerly route through the woodland, careful to avoid the forest's commonly used paths to minimise contact with other Freylarkai. Though she had explicitly asked Marcus not to follow her, it was possible that Mirielle's orders – whatever the Queen's instructions were – conflicted with her request, therefore testing the value of their friendship. Unwilling to accept the risk, she chose a convoluted route to the Cave of Wellbeing, making frequent use of her wraith wings in order to throw off those potentially following her. She took one last look over her shoulder when finally nearing her destination, before beginning the final leg of her journey, travelling back to the location of her rebirth where her adventures in Freylar had begun. It felt strange returning to the place of her genesis. When last she had spoken with Nathaniel at the site, The Teacher was but a shadow of himself, ruined by grief and sorrow following the untimely release of his daughter, Alarielle. If not for Kirika and her own revenant-like resurrection, The Teacher would, in all likelihood, have succumbed to his despair, his will to continue entirely snuffed out. Thinking back once more, had she declined the abrupt offer put to her by the alien entity things would have played out very differently. She would be dead, her ruined corpse still rotting on the ground in the Wild trapping her soul within it. Furthermore, Mirielle would not have an uprising on her hands. Although it could be argued that the Narlakai would have successfully invaded Freylar, putting an end to Mirielle's reign regardless. What would that alternate future have looked like, she wondered, as the black entrance to the cave grew ominously larger, threatening to engulf her – much like the darkness inside her once had. As the distance to the cave grew shorter, she struggled to shake a growing sense of dread suggesting that her time in Freylar had come full circle, perhaps signalling an end to everything that she had come to know. No doubt, the feeling was a manifestation of her own lingering insecurities, the final remnants of her internal battle, like shrapnel from a bullet or the many scars covering Nathaniel's body – reminders of trauma or events that could never be erased and forgotten.

Less than ten paces from the cave's entrance, a lone figure stepped out from the gloom. The silhouette belonged to Darlia, immediately recognisable by her mechanical claw. Darlia offered her a curious smile, which she found surprising given the history between them. The infamous scrier surveyed the landscape, presumably checking to see if she had been followed – which she had not.

'I came alone.' she said, trying to allay the scrier's concerns.

'Forgive me, but I have it on good authority that your sight is not the best.'

'Ha, that is true enough. Did Natalya tell you that?'

'She says that you are late.' replied Darlia, taking a step closer.

'She likes to berate me, and I let her – it makes her feel like she's in control.'

'I do not suppose that anyone could control your actions, Rayna. I think that perhaps you and I have that character trait in common.'

'There are some that might try. For instance, The Blade Lord, or even The Teacher, perhaps...'

'He is waiting for you. Apparently, you and he have a lot to discuss.'

'I believe that we do. Did he send you to escort me to him?' she asked with a wry grin.

'No. I was just curious to see if you are ready.'

'Ready for what exactly?'

'To get my sister back.'

It was dark when they returned, although dawn was already chasing their heels. It would not be long before the sleepy inhabitants of Freylar rose with the morning sun.

'We do this now, or not at all.'

Heldran grunted his approval before pulling the cowl of his cloak over his head, in a poor attempt to conceal his identity – it would be a challenge to find another with the Knight's imposing stature. Once he had relieved the guards by the entrance, he too would follow suit in order to help mask his identity.

Together they silently worked their way towards the base of the citadel, advancing as a column to hide their numbers in the unlikely event that the night watch spotted them. They made their approach quickly, using whatever means of cover presented itself, doing their utmost to become extensions of the night. Following their agreed strategy, he entered the citadel first to relieve the guards, leaving Heldran to seek cover. He slowed his breathing following their sprint to the base of the citadel, then strode confidentially inside, playing the necessary role as they had discussed.

'Nathaniel, what are you doing here?' asked one of the guards who instantly recognised him.

'I could not sleep, so I am doing you two a favour: go take a break, and report back ready for the next shift change.'

'But we are on duty until dawn.' replied the other guard naively.

'If you are *not* interested in my offer, I can always find some other way to amuse myself.' he said before turning about, signalling his immediate intention to leave.

'Wait!' called the veteran of the pair. 'He is new to this, and he is an idiot.'

'Fine.' he said, turning to face the guards once more. 'Just ensure that both of you are back here before the next shift arrives. Now get gone, the pair of you, before I change my mind.'

The guards promptly left, eager to find a quiet spot to enjoy a moment's rest. Getting involved in a scuffle by the main entrance would have ended their infiltration – fortune, it seemed, smiled upon them.

'Your instincts are sharp as ever.' he said when Heldran eventually crossed the entrance to the Citadel, having allowed the tired guards sufficient time to vacate their post.

'We still have a long way to go.'

'Follow me.' he said as he hurried along the wide passage leading away from the entrance, paying little attention to the numerous side passages that branched off in various directions.

'Are you sure this is the way?' asked Heldran, trying to whisper whilst keeping pace.

'I picked up a few landmarks earlier today, and besides, it is like I said – follow your nose.'

'Your nose will likely get--'

'Hush.' he replied, raising his right hand abruptly, signalling the Knight to stop.

The passage ahead banked away to the left, presenting the challenge of a blind corner. The structure's warren-like aesthetics were a visual mess, but not without their tactical merit. No doubt, The Blade Lord had influenced the mysterious scrier's design of the citadel's internal layout.

He looked over his shoulder towards his companion, and quietly communicated his intent.

'One guard for sure. We go round as one, column formation. Your silhouette will mask my presence. Once we are round, break step and feign a ranged attack. The guard will raise his shield. I will use the distraction to close rapidly, disarm the guard and promptly silence him.'

The Knight nodded his approval. As one, they moved swiftly around the corner ahead, before quickening their pace as a bleary-eyed guard ahead of them stared back in mute confusion. Heldran stepped right into his periphery, giving him the signal to break into a low sprint towards their opponent. As anticipated, the guard immediately raised his shield, instinctively defending himself against Heldran's feigned attack. He dived forwards towards his opponent, curling his outstretched right arm around the guard's legs. The hapless sentry toppled forwards, crashing hard upon the ground and landing flat on his face. Kicking his right foot backwards, he displaced the helmet from the head of his dazed opponent. Using the hilt of the curious smoke-wreathed blade given to him by Krashnar, he pushed himself backwards, bringing the pommel of the weapon down upon the back of the fallen sentry's skull. The prone body of the guard suddenly went limp, causing the sentry to release the grip on his weapon.

'Did you release him?' asked Heldran, who knelt down to touch his victim's neck.

'No. He is sleeping.'

'He will wake up with an *almighty* headache.'

'Yes…but he *will* wake up.'

'Even so, we cannot leave him here.'

He looked down the corridor, beyond the fallen guard. Up ahead there was a large wooden door blocking the entire passageway, and with it their way forward.

'Agreed. We will need to stash him behind that door up ahead, assuming that we can get past it.'

They carried the unconscious guard between them, including his weapon and shield, careful to ensure that no trace of the brief confrontation remained. Heldran held the sentry's legs with ease in one hand, leaving him to struggle with the opposite end.

'Feeling the weight there, brother?' asked Heldran with a wry grin.

'Just open the bloody door.' he replied in a strained voice whilst trying to manhandle the guard's heavy torso.

Heldran reached for the door's large metal handle with his free hand, quietly turned it and gently pushed. Nothing. The door remained steadfast, refusing to give any ground.

'Damn it!' he said, still struggling with the guard's mass. 'OK, let's put him down quietly and check for a key.'

Together they searched the body of the unconscious guard, mindful that time was against them and that the light of dawn would soon put an end to their risky endeavour.

'He does not have it.' said Heldran flatly, clearly frustrated by their lack of reward. 'He calls himself The Blade Lord, yet he denies The Blades access to his own stronghold. Does he trust no one?'

'Caleth trusts *himself*.'

'Evidently. So, what do we do about this door? Breaking through will draw attention, followed swiftly by our release.'

'Your weapon – I suggest that we use it.'

Heldran regarded him with a hard stare. He could sense the Knight's unease, having reluctantly agreed to carry the blade twined with his own. Accepting that the end justified the means, the Knight drew the blade from its sheath before thrusting it backwards into the door above his head. The blade's tip pierced the door, digging deep into the thick wood that splintered upon impact.

'Ensure that you hold onto the guard brother, else I will be leaving you behind.'

Heldran grabbed the guard's legs once more before sliding his large callused thumb across the Waystone fragment fused into the top of the weapon's hilt, just below its cross-guard. His stomach lurched as the passage slipped from view, replaced instead by a small antechamber on the opposite side of the door. The abrupt displacement made him feel queasy.

'Behind you!' boomed Heldran suddenly.

He immediately spun around, dropping the prone guard's torso. Any thoughts of securing the unsettled contents of his stomach were quickly dispelled; two guards about ten paces away sprinted headlong towards them, each armed with a shield and falchion.

'Damn it!' he cursed, reaching to unsheathe the alien blade attached to his belt.

He moved with purpose, engaging the guard to their right with unprecedented speed, leaving Heldran to deal with their remaining opponent.

'End this quickly.' boomed Heldran, forgoing the use of the weapon responsible for their predicament, which he left embedded in the door.

Unarmed, the colossal Knight feinted a grapple towards his opponent. The guard moved to counter, but was quickly out-manoeuvred by Heldran's masterful footwork, allowing the Knight to wrap his thick arms around his opponent's neck. The guard dropped his weapons, instinctively reaching for the arms around his neck. The trapped sentry tried desperately to loosen Heldran's grip, but the act was futile, with the Knight's immensely powerful arms refusing to shift. Heldran's victim rapidly lost consciousness, eventually passing out from the vicious blood choke. Whilst the veteran Knight dealt with the hapless guard, he continued to spar enthusiastically with his opponent, one clearly competent with a blade. However, time was against them, meaning that he could ill afford to wait for a natural opening in his opponent's defence. He pressed his assault by repeatedly cutting to the guard's head, causing his opponent to raise their shield. He then dropped his weapon and grabbed the guard's exposed right leg. Locking his fingers firmly around the target, he pulled the leg towards his chest whilst simultaneously driving his right shoulder into the guard's torso, forcing his opponent down onto the floor. The guard relaxed the grip on his falchion upon impact with the floor, causing the weapon to slide across the smooth granite surface. He tore off his opponent's helmet, instantly recognising the Freylarkin from the tavern the previous cycle.

'Sorry friend.' he said as he struck the sentry hard upon the head, using the palm of his right hand.

'Here!' cried Heldran.

The Knight grabbed the smoke wreathed alien blade that he had discarded in order to press his advantage, before expertly tossing it towards him. He caught the weapon around its hilt, bringing the pommel down hard upon the dazed guard's forehead.

'Eventually, you will thank me.' he said as he rose to his feet.

'We need to move!' said Heldran in a thunderous tone. 'All and sundry will have heard that raucous. We have lost our advantage Nathaniel.'

'No, we have not.' he replied, directing the Knight's attention towards the adjoining chamber.

They stared in awe towards a large chamber beyond the bodies of the unconscious guards. Ensconced within the chamber were a number of waist-high pedestals, spaced evenly around the room in a crescent formation. Half buried within the top of each pedestal was a colourless crystal, larger versions of the fragments worked into the blade still protruding from the door behind them, responsible for transporting them into the antechamber.

'Waystones!' said Heldran, whose anger quickly gave way to curiosity.

'Yes, lots of them. It would appear that Caleth has been busy.'

Heldran's expression suddenly became grim once more, as though bathed in a dark shadow that had rapidly swept across the Knight's weathered features.

'Nathaniel, we cannot follow your nose on this one. We have no clue as to where these will take us.'

'One of them *will* lead us to Caleth – I am sure of it!'

'Of that I have no doubt.' replied Heldran, who turned to face him. 'But we cannot afford to investigate each one. We could wind up in a barracks – what then?'

'Nevertheless, we must take the chance.'

'No, not this time old friend. I am not playing those odds – not again.'

The Knight's comment was curious. Regardless, there was little time to debate the matter.

'But we have come so far; we cannot turn back now.'

'I know how badly your Order needs this – the Knights Thranis need this – but we cannot go charging blind into the unknown. We have been fortunate to get this far, but you press your luck beyond reasonable chance.'

'I have faith.'

'Yes, but I do not.' said Heldran flatly. 'I am afraid that this is where you and I must part company old friend. You said it yourself: one cycle I will ascend to the rank of Knight Lord. As such, I have to consider the future of our Order. I cannot lead the Knights Thranis if I am released or incarcerated.'

'Heldran, I cannot do this alone.'

'And I cannot take the leap of faith that you require of me – the risk is too great.'

They stood opposite one another, each regarding the other in silence, unable to resolve the impasse presented by the current situation. Although too polite to admit it, Heldran viewed his intent as reckless. A part of him sympathised with the Knight's logical analysis of the current situation, though he could not bring himself to forsake The Blades, especially when they were so close to realising their goal. It was painfully obvious that neither of them possessed a solution. Then Heldran's opponent started to come around. The fallen guard groaned in discomfort, trying in vain to move his limbs, the act of which quickly drew their attention.

'What do you think?' he said, as a solution to their problem began to present itself.

'That armour will not fit me, but do not let that stop you should you decide to scout ahead.'

'Actually, I had something else in mind.' he said rather ominously.

'Such as?' asked Heldran who turned to face him once more.

'We could coerce the information from him.'

'He is a Blade, a young one at that, indoctrinated by *your* Order. He will not give us the information we seek, even if you decide to argue your case. Moreover, I just assaulted him – he will not aid us.'

'There are *ways*.'

'You mean intimidation, or worse still, torture.' replied Heldran, who lowered his gaze, offering the alien blade in his hand a cold hard stare.

'We do not have time for a charm offensive. We need that information, now!'

'Then I should be the one to do it.' said Heldran grimly.

'I cannot ask that of you.'

'You are not asking.' replied the Knight, who took a foreboding step towards the semi-conscious guard. 'Korlith has ended our ties to The Blades, and The Blades do not trust us. The relationship between our Orders has ended. If that wretch shaper is to be believed, that weapon in your hand will clean up your future mess, but do you really want to add this one – an innocent – to your conscience?'

'Heldran, they have already seen our faces, albeit only partially.'

'The one out there saw nothing and these two will not challenge your authority, especially with Caleth gone. However, if you make this personal, that scenario goes away. You cannot be the one who gets their hands dirty sorting out the loose ends. Let me do this brother.'

'And what of your honour?'

'Nathaniel, I try so very hard to sit on the right side of the fence, but I am far from perfect.'

Heldran stooped down and grabbed the dazed guard with both hands, before lifting his victim up and slamming them firmly against the wall.

'See if you can conceal the other one behind a plinth, and pull that wretched blade out of the door.'

Heldran had made it clear that he did not wish for an audience. As such, he immediately busied himself as per the Knight's instructions, affording Heldran the privacy to go about his business.

'Now then.' boomed the colossal Knight in a foreboding tone, 'Answer my question, and – provided I am satisfied – you will get to *walk* out of here. Otherwise, I will be forced to ask you again. Now, before we begin, there is one important thing that I must tell you: I do not like repeating myself.'

SIXTEEN
Arbiter

Upon her arrival, Darlia had asked her to wait inside by the cave's entrance whilst the scrier informed Nathaniel of her presence. She leant against the cave wall, casting her gaze south-east across the wintery landscape. Snow fell from the sky, settling on the leafless branches of the woodland through which she had travelled, contrasting against the brown hues denoting its mass. Winter had come early, forcing its native fauna to either emigrate or go to ground. Now, the woodland was silent, giving it an eerie, abandoned feel. She turned her attention back to the interior of the gloomy cave, lit by the numerous Moonstones that studded its walls radiating their soft violet and sapphire hues. Time and again, she wished that she had been gifted with better vision, but the sphere of light that had brought her to Freylar had set her upon a path that cared little for her quality of vision. Using her inner light, she illuminated the cave's interior. Light spilled across the cavern, casting long shadows where the cave's plinths intercepted its path. She saw the familiar stone plinth upon which she had lain when first she had arrived in Freylar. Seeing the raised stone bed sent a shiver down her spine; she imagined the experience was akin to staring at one's own grave. The ominous sight dredged up mixed emotions, reminding her of the life she had previously led and her achievements since then. After a long moment of quiet reflection, her gaze drifted towards the floor. The narrow stream that cut diagonally across the exposed bedrock floor was now silent. The spring water that traversed the uneven channel had frozen, confirming the biting presence of winter. Whilst absentmindedly studying the frozen liquid, fresh shadows emerged from the gloom at the far end of the cavern. Darlia had returned, accompanied by Lothnar, Nathanar, Natalya, Thandor and Nathaniel. Additional faces loomed in the background, including that of Kayla, although she failed to recognise the others.

'It's about time. I've been freezing my arse off up here.'

'Well at least you are awake.' said Natalya, followed by a playful wink.

'I thought the Sky-Walkers were supposed to *control* the weather.' said Nathanar with a childish grin.

'You two should be separated – she is a bad influence.' she replied, unable to adequately counter the Paladin's quip.

'You are here – that is what matters.' said Nathaniel taking a step closer.

'Just what is all this Nathaniel? Your actions of late have been nothing if not clandestine.'

'Yes, that is true, and I owe you an explanation.' replied Nathaniel sympathetically. 'I would very much appreciate it if you would all kindly leave us; I need some time with Rayna, alone.'

One by one, Nathaniel's entourage disappeared back into the gloom, except for Thandor, who curiously remained. The aloof Paladin was steadfast, content to remain where he stood partially obscured by the shadows. She turned to face the Paladin, acknowledging his defiance. Nathaniel noted her distraction, though he refrained from turning around.

'Do you have any advice to offer, Thandor?'

'I believe so.' replied the Paladin casually, who took a moment to consider his words before elaborating.

'Whichever path you ultimately decide to take, ensure that the decision is made by you alone. You have made a name for yourself by following your heart and defying the impossible – do not compromise your ethics now, for they are what define you.'

She nodded respectfully to the Paladin, who then took his leave. Alone now with Nathaniel, she offered The Teacher a flinty stare.

'So--'

'We need to talk.'

He had heard such screams before on the field of battle, but never before when extracting information from sealed lips. Now, the sound would forever haunt him, a permanent reminder of the lengths they were prepared to go to in order to achieve their goal. It pained him that the young Blade had been so stubborn – fear of The Blade Lord's wrath was clearly a strong motivator. Even so, Heldran apparently possessed the tools to break any Freylarkin's resolve.

'Do not dwell on it brother. Set your mind to purpose, ready for the task ahead.' said Heldran sternly.

'You are right of course. I just…did not know that you had that in you.'

'We are all capable of such acts when the situation demands it. Most of us choose to believe otherwise, but that is simply a lie that we tell ourselves.'

'It angers me, seeing The Blades *fear* their leader. Caleth should command respect, not dread!'

'That is why we are doing this – do not forget that fact! In any event, the Freylarkin's wound will heal – see to it yourself if you must. Either way, we need to press on with the information that we have learned.'

He took a deep breath, steeling himself for what was about to come.

'When we go up, there can be no quarter given.' he said, trying to prepare himself mentally. 'Caleth's mercenaries will *not* fall in line after the deed is done. They value only coin and I fear that we do not possess enough to purchase their allegiance.'

'Agreed.' Heldran affirmed. 'They cannot be allowed to speak of what comes next.'

He nodded in agreement and together they approached the stone plinth bearing the Waystone that promised to take them to The Blade Lord. They each drew their Dawnstone falchion, shaped and given to them by Krashnar, then readied themselves to charge the enemy. He had half-expected Heldran to unsheathe his ardent blade instead, but the Knight remained true to his word, using the twinned Dawnstone blade they had arduously commissioned for the task ahead. According to the guard interrogated by Heldran, at least three mercenaries guarded the door to The Blade Lord's chamber. Unable to sneak past the soldiers of fortune, the promise of a fight would soon be upon them.

'Ready?' he said, waiting to give the signal.

'Let us get this done!'

'Three, two, one--'

They touched the Waystone simultaneously. The surrounding stone plinths stretched and elongated, fading from sight, replaced instead by four heavily armoured guards standing less than five paces before them. Together they charged towards their opponents, catching the guards by surprise. Heldran drove his shoulder into the closest member of the group, who had yet to unsheathe their blade, knocking the guard violently backwards sending them crashing to the floor. The Knight then executed an upwards false edge cut, expertly knocking aside the blade from a fresh opponent, before short cutting deep into their exposed neck. Blood from the wound sprayed vigorously across the chamber, decorating the smooth granite floor with spots of crimson. Overtaking the Knight, he quickly engaged the next guard in line standing between them and the door to Caleth's chamber. His blade clashed violently against that of his opponent, but the force of the impact was not enough to disarm the guard. Again their weapons clashed, the Dawnstone blade gliding effortlessly through the air, leaving an arc of wispy grey smoke in its wake. Whilst he continued to fight his opponent, Heldran moved up quickly to engage the final guard, however, the first was already recovering from the Knight's ferocious impact – he needed to dispatch his opponent quickly. Their weapons clashed once more, but this time he chose to bind his opponent's blade, trapping it beneath his own. He drove the pommel of his weapon hard into the guard's helmet, stunning his opponent before wielding his blade around, cutting the mercenary deep inside their right leg. He then immediately withdrew to parry an attack from the first guard, who had since regained their feet and was now upon him. The third guard, whom he had cut, staggered backwards grabbing their leg as blood spilled onto the floor from the artery severed by his blade. Focusing his attention on his newest opponent, he thwarted left and right landing several cuts against the guard's armour. His opponent quickly backed up desperately trying to break measure, but he continued to press his attack aggressively, raining cuts down on his opponent who began to falter under the pressure of his relentless assault. His penultimate cut knocked the guard's weapon aside, allowing him to step in and draw the edge of his falchion across his opponent's throat. The slice cut deep into the guard's neck spraying more blood onto the polished floor, now slick with claret fluid. The guard fell to their knees, dropping their weapon, gargling and coughing blood whilst clutching their throat, desperately trying to prevent further blood loss. He spun around and saw his previous opponent; the guard lay perfectly still on the floor in an expanding pool of their own blood. He looked towards Heldran who garishly pulled his blade from the face of the last remaining guard.

'We are done here.' he said, wiping the blood of his opponents from his face.

'Let us finish this.' said Heldran, whose long dark brown hair was slick with blood.

As expected, the door to Caleth's chamber was locked. Rather than waste time searching the fallen guards for a key that, in all likelihood, they did not possess, they chose instead to call upon the aid of Heldran's blade once more. He grabbed Heldran's wrist. Using the same trick that they had employed back in the passageway, they passed effortlessly through the door, immediately appearing on the other side, albeit facing the wrong way.

They turned around. Standing before them was Caleth. The Blade Lord was wide-eyed, no doubt surprised by their sudden appearance. Caleth was only partially armoured, having presumably heard the fighting outside his chamber. Two female Freylarkai stood either side of The Blade Lord. Both were children, their heads barely above waist height, and each had violet coloured eyes and purple hair, though one's was considerably darker than the other's. The dark-haired female, obviously the older of the two, held a set of leather vambraces with linked silver plating, whilst her counterpart finished tending to The Blade Lord's fitted silver muscle cuirass. Although Caleth rarely engaged in actual combat since attaining his lofty rank, nevertheless, tales of his martial prowess were well known. To assume that Caleth no longer mastered the use of a blade was folly. Though he had distanced himself from frontline engagements, The Blade Lord was an opponent not to be underestimated. Irrespective of his poisonous flawed disposition, Caleth had attained his station due to his physical and mental skill. Although his actions dishonoured The Blades, his talent did not.

'Get out!' cried Caleth, whose face was loaded with venom.

'*You* sent our brothers and sisters to the borderlands for an early release.' he cried, as he advanced menacingly towards The Blade Lord, lowering his cowl. 'Furthermore, you poisoned the relationship between us and the Knight Thranis.'

'Lies! You have no proof Nathaniel. Now get out before I have you released for your treacherous behaviour.'

'No. I will not allow another Freylarkin to follow you into madness. This ends now!'

Caleth violently struck the child holding the vambraces across the face, sending her reeling to the floor. He then circled backwards pulling the remaining child – previously attending to his cuirass – close to his chest. The Blade Lord unsheathed his bastard sword and held it against the young female's throat.

'You have *no* honour!' thundered Heldran, whose face was loaded with rage.

'No!' cried the young female on the floor who held a hand to her bloodied face.

'You speak to *me* of honour, after you mercilessly butchered my guards? I heard the screams!'

'Let my sister go!'

'Be quiet! Had you done your job properly, we would not be in this position. What use is a scrier who cannot accurately foretell the future? You are of no value to me. However, *this* one may yet serve a purpose.'

'If you are truly our Blade Lord, fight me, one-on-one!' he said, trying to goad Caleth into releasing his hostage.

'And give up my tactical advantage? You take me for a fool Nathaniel.'

'*He* will not get involved.'

'You of course refer to Korlith's pet.'

He could hear the Knight behind him growling in response to The Blade Lord's derogatory remark. For Caleth at least, the fight had already begun. It was clear that The Blade Lord sought to gain an advantage by disrupting their focus.

'Let her go!' the young female with the dark violet hair cried once more.

'If you do not remain silent, your sister will have one less limb to concern herself with.'

'Let her go *now*, she is an innocent in all this.' he said whilst slowly closing the gap between them.

'Stay back Nathaniel!' replied Caleth, pressing his blade against the young female's throat.

'Nathaniel!' cried Heldran.

He turned and instinctively caught the Knight's weapon as it passed through the air, then immediately cut towards his opponent, instantly teleporting around the tip of the blade. Now in measure, he cut to The Blade Lord's head using the blade's twin, catching Caleth off guard, who instinctively moved to parry the sudden attack with his sword. Their blades clashed, allowing the young Freylarkin to drop to her knees and scurry away, thus escaping her captor. He pressed his attack, giving Heldran time to aid the sisters; the Knight quickly guided them away from the fighting ensuring their safety.

'How dare you cross blades with me!' cried Caleth, whose face was now one of rage.

'Your actions demanded it!' he said, evading another of The Blade Lord's vicious attacks before countering with one of his own.

Repeatedly, they cut back and forth, each looking for an opening that would allow them to gain an advantage over the other. The increased range afforded by Caleth's bastard sword served The Blade Lord well. However, the twin blades in his possession were faster to wield and provided more attacking options. Caleth began using their surroundings to his advantage as they moved deftly around the chamber, trying to break volume in order to land a cut against their opponent. The Blade Lord grabbed a wooden cup from one of the tables and hurled it towards his head. He instinctively raised his weapons to block the projectile, immediately realising the error. Using the distraction, Caleth caught his left leg, slicing through the skin. His opponent's blade glistened red as Caleth drew the weapon back into a fresh guard. Cursing his carelessness, he pushed forwards again only to encounter more of The Blade Lord's trickery. Caleth was a dirty fighter, but he played the game well and knew exactly how to win. Caleth's skill with a blade matched his own, though his opponent had the edge by maximising the use of their surroundings.

'Swallow your pride Nathaniel!' boomed Heldran, who continued to guide the young females away from the fighting as it spilled across the room.

Heldran's words stung, but they told the truth of it. The Blade Lord had no honour; there was nothing honourable about their fight. Inevitably, the victor would write history and he intended to be the one to dictate its course. He lunged forwards, overextending his reach into a forward stance, cutting towards The Blade Lord's torso. Caleth evaded the cut and moved quickly to counter, taking advantage of his apparent mistake. Caleth's blade came down fast, with the intention of severing his outstretched arm. Before his opponent could rob him of his limb, he swiped his left thumb across the Waystone fragment embedded into the weapon's hilt, teleporting once more around the tip of the blade. Caleth stumbled as the end of his blade struck the ground, missing its absent target. Before Caleth could react to the changed landscape, he sliced across the back of The Blade Lord's legs, forcing his opponent to drop to his knees, no longer able to stand.

'You will be released for your *treachery*, Nathaniel!' spat The Blade Lord, who winced in pain, trying to mask his agony.

He kicked Caleth's right hand hard, denying The Blade Lord his weapon, then moved to stand resolutely before his defeated opponent. Dropping to his knees, he executed a spiteful headbutt to the bridge of Caleth's nose, causing The Blade Lord to cry out in pain.

'Do not play with him, Nathaniel – finish this!' boomed Heldran who tried to avert the gaze of the two sisters standing beside him.

'Few will know of this, and those who do *will not* care. Now go, and take your poison with you!'

He drove the blade in his right hand up through Caleth's abdomen, just beneath the cuirass, before pulling his weapon up, rocking The Blade Lord onto his back. Caleth cried out in pain. Blood seeped from the wound around the side of the blade. Putting his full weight behind the weapon, he pushed the blade hard again, sinking it deeper into his opponent, until its tip pressed against the granite floor. Caleth's eyes roll back into his head and the wisps of smoke that wreathed the edge of the blade began to react vigorously, as though stimulated by its victim's intimate presence. Holding the blade firmly in place, he watched in horror as Caleth's body began to shudder violently, before entering into full spasm. He continued to maintain the grip on the strange weapon as he watched the grim spectacle, unable to tear his sight from the horrible events unfolding before him. The Blade Lord's body continued to spasm and watery pink fluid began trickling from the corners of Caleth's mouth. The horrified gasps of the sisters cowering beside Heldran filled his ears, all the while The Blade Lord's body continued to judder violently as though possessed by an invisible force. He was about to withdraw the blade when suddenly Caleth's skin darkened in colour, before fading to a greyish-white as though devoid of its pigment. Sections of Caleth's skin rapidly desiccated, and before long The Blade Lord's corpse resembled little more than an empty dried up husk.

'What is happening to him?' whispered the dark haired Freylarkin, her face heavily bruised by Caleth's hand.

'That evil weapon exacts a heavy price from its victims, when given the opportunity.' said Heldran in a foreboding tone. 'You should avert your gaze.'

Yet despite the Knight's wise counsel, neither of them was able to look away from the horrid sight. Eventually the dried husk folded in on itself, until little remained save for a pile of ash-covered clothes and armour.

'It is done.' he said, finally sheathing the ravenous weapon. 'We need to get out of here.'

'The guards will be changing shortly, plus there is the bloody mess outside to consider.'

'None of that matters. We just need to ensure that *we* are not here.' he said resolutely, trying to remain optimistic about their chances of escape.

'It matters not, Nathaniel.' replied Heldran. 'The young females here witnessed the entire barbaric act. Furthermore, they are scriers! We did not consider that fact. Even if we do somehow manage to make it out of the citadel, they will know it was us; they *will* investigate and they *will* learn the truth of it.'

'No, they will not.' replied the other sister, who until now had remained silent. 'We will tell them a *version* of what transpired here. There will be no cause for investigation.'

'Why would you do this?' he said, fixing his gaze on the young Freylarkin.

'The Blade Lord treated us…poorly. Because of your selfless actions, Caleth is no more – you have liberated us.'

Tears collected in the young female's eyes, but they were not tears of sadness. It was clear from the weak smile on her face that cycles of torment had finally ended, for which they would both be forever grateful. He nodded respectfully to the sisters, acknowledging their aid.

'But we still need to escape, and I fear that we cannot go back the way we came.'

'I may have a solution.' replied Heldran unexpectedly.

'What do you have in mind old friend?'

'It is unlikely that we can make a clean exit via the main entrance, however, this chamber has another.' explained the Knight, pointing his large right index finger towards the chamber's window.

'Our wraith wings will not adequately slow our descent. We will crater upon impact.'

'There is another way.' replied Heldran cryptically. 'Give me the blade with the Waystones and wait here. I will return shortly.'

The Knight quickly left the room, unlocking the doors from the inside, leaving him with the two young females and The Blade Lord's dusty remains. The purple-haired sisters began swiftly cleaning the room, setting right any signs of a struggle. He watched as they diligently restored the chamber to order whilst he attended to the deep cut across his leg, using his ability to heal the wound.

'What are your names?' he said, curious as to whom he now owed a debt.

'My name is Darlia.' replied the elder of the two, 'My sister, who you rescued, is called Kirika.'

'Well met.' he said, offering them both a warm smile. 'How do you intend to frame this scenario?'

'We will raise the alarm ourselves to detract any suspicion.' replied Kirika, the quieter, albeit more astute, of the pair. 'We shall inform the guards that we found the bodies outside, and that upon entering Caleth's chamber The Blade Lord was nowhere to be found. Then, after scrying the chamber, we will report that Caleth left the room and that he had been the one to release the guards prior to his departure.'

'Thank you. I owe you both a debt.'

'You owe us nothing.' said Darlia. 'His release is payment enough.'

'However, you *must* take Caleth's blade and armour with you – he would not have left without them.' explained Kirika.

'Agreed.'

The doors to the chamber flung open upon the Knight's swift return. Heldran cradled two stone fragments in a piece of cloth, presumably cut from one of the guards outside.

'Are those what I think they are?' he asked, as the gears in his mind began to turn.

'Yes, I cut them from a Waystone in the chamber below – this is our exit strategy.'

'But how did you attune them to one another?' he questioned, curious as to how the stones would facilitate their escape.

'Secrets Nathaniel – you cannot have them all.'

He gave the Knight a wry grin of approval, then turned to bid both Kirika and Darlia farewell before gathering up Caleth's personal arms. Heldran too said his goodbyes, before walking over to the window where he hurled one of the stone fragments through the archway, careful to avoid its direct touch. Using his impressive strength, the Knight ensured that the Waystone fragment came to rest away from the base of the citadel. The Knight watched with keen interest as the fragment plummeted to the ground, rapidly disappearing into the gloom.

'We need to leave.' said Heldran, satisfied with their means of escape.

'Let us go brother.' he said, before turning his attention to the sister for one final farewell. 'Once we have left, I need you both to do me one additional favour.'

'What is it?' asked Darlia with interest.

'I need you both to secure the other Waystone fragment for me. Should anything go wrong with the ruse, use it to return to me – I will keep you both safe.'

The sisters nodded in unison, after which both he and Heldran left the chamber using the Waystone, taking Caleth's former arms with them. They appeared on the ground some thirty paces away from the base of the citadel.

'You have a good arm.' he said, wrapping the fragment in a fresh piece of cloth that he cut from his cloak.

'And you have an unwavering resolve old friend.'

'What will you do now?'

'I will formally deliver my message to The Blades as ordered, after which I will return to the Ardent Gate. The Ravnarkai menace continues to erode our ranks – I am needed to bolster them.'

'I will miss you brother.'

'This was but another chapter – there will be plenty more.'

'Keep the blade. It is best that they are separated.'

'Nathaniel, the weapons are evil. We lack the honesty of heart necessary to wield them without succumbing to their corruption.'

'Perhaps you are correct in your assessment, however, until one such individual makes themselves known to us, they must be safeguarded.'

'Very well.' replied Heldran reluctantly. 'And what of Caleth's former arms?'

'They will be reworked for another. It is my hope that said individual will make better use of them.'

'I wish you all the best brother.' said Heldran before giving him an almighty slap across the back, nearly causing him to stumble.

'May good fortune always find you old friend. Until next we meet…'

SEVENTEEN
Insurrection

There was a long pause between them, after Nathaniel finished the recounting of his grim tale. She released a deep breath before standing up to stretch her back, after which she wandered over to the cave's entrance. It was dark outside and a thick layer of snow now covered the ground. So engrossed was she in Nathaniel's story that she had completely neglected the world around them. Snow fell heavily from the dark sky and the temperature had taken a noticeable drop.

'We should descend to the caverns below and join the others, where it is warm.' said Nathaniel, who approached quietly to stand by her side. 'Of course, if you wish to leave, I will respect your decision.'

'You released innocents, Nathaniel.' she said, struggling to come to terms with the revelations that had surfaced during The Teacher's ugly account. 'You colluded with Heldran, causing him to tarnish his honour, you deceived The Blades, and you sought aid from Krashnar!'

'Yes...I have committed many sins. However, they were all for one singular purpose: to protect the Freylarkai and my daughter. I sincerely hope that the result of my actions atones for at least some of my transgressions.'

'I am not your judge, Nathaniel. I have enough blood on my hands due to my own indiscretions. I am hardly qualified, therefore, to pass judgement over others.'

'You were coerced into that business with L. Cameron. I *chose* to release Caleth, knowing that doing so would likely lead to the release of others. My actions cannot be excused by ignorance or naivety on my part.'

'Nor can Heldran's own actions.' she replied whilst descending into a trance as she watched the snow continue to fall.

'Do not think poorly of Heldran. He sought only to protect his Order.'

She laughed at the remark.

'It's funny – he said something similar to me about you.'

'Then he and I are both fools.'

'No…you both protect the ones that you love, and love is the most powerful motivator of them all. It causes those in its thrall to commit extraordinary acts when required.'

There was another pause in their conversation whilst they each considered her words, despite the cold doing its best to drive them underground.

'I stand once more upon a fulcrum, Rayna, ready to commit such acts yet again.'

'And you would have knowledge of where I stand?'

'You are not a pawn to be manoeuvred, Rayna; your soul is far too strong to be manipulated by others. You will do whatever you feel is right – you do not need Thandor to tell you that.'

'And *you* do not need to gauge my allegiance.' she said, offering him a warm smile. 'I owe both you and your daughter a debt that cannot be repaid.'

'I would never ask you to do anything that might go against your ethics. I respect you too much for that. If you desire no part in this, I will understand.'

'Who would you have supplant Mirielle?'

'I have no *one* Freylarkin in mind for the task, Rayna. We have been governed by the pretence of a ruling council for too long now. The Freylarkai have accepted this arrangement. The notion is a good one, but its execution has been poor thus far. The ruling council has become little more than a façade for the will of a single individual. It is a sham – I will not allow that to continue. Therefore, I intend to rebuild the ruling council, ensuring that its new guise adheres to its founding principles. However, I do not wish to be a part of it myself, regardless of what form it takes.'

'Mirielle's reign has run its course – that much is painfully clear. But before casting my lot in with you, I needed to be certain that your motive is not tainted by the allure of power.'

'I desire only to protect the people, Rayna.'

'Yes, I see that – despite your questionable actions.' she replied. 'Although what of Mirielle and Marcus, who continues to remain loyal to her reign?'

'Mirielle will need to forge a new path, of her own choosing. Marcus, however, is a concern. His devotion to the Queen is a problem, one that I had hoped to avoid. I understand your respect for him Rayna. It pains me that my friendship with Marcus will likely not survive this.'

'I will do what I can.' she said, wishing there was some way of convincing The Blade Lord to take a back seat, albeit temporarily. 'Although I fear he will not be moved from her side.'

'Then, knowing all of this, will you aid us?'

She sighed heavily.

'First, there is something that I must tell you.' she said, before turning to look The Teacher directly in the eye. 'It concerns Alarielle.'

'What is it?' asked Nathaniel, who suddenly became very anxious.

'Perhaps first we should sit back down.'

'Just tell me!' replied The Teacher abruptly.

'Nathaniel, you have been candid with me. I owe you the same courtesy, although, I have been hesitant to bring you this news.'

'What is it Rayna, is my daughter safe?'

'No...she is not.' she said, her voice broken, unable to hold back the sudden wave of emotion that assaulted her.

'What has happened?' asked Nathaniel, gripping her arms tightly. 'Please, tell me!'

'It was *my* fault.' she explained as tears rapidly filled her eyes. 'There was nothing I could do to win her back.'

'Tell me!' said Nathaniel once more, whose calm demeanour had now completely dissolved.

'It happened during the battle for Bleak Moor, when the Narlakin tried to devour my soul.'

'But you released it, along with the others.' replied Nathaniel, whose voice was now trembling.

'I was too late. The soul stealer had already had its fill, Nathaniel.'

'What do you mean? Rayna, I *saw* you get back up. You denied the Narlakin its prize.'

'No, I didn't! It never took my soul. I got back up because it stole that of another; your daughter sacrificed *her* soul so that I did not have to!'

Nathaniel released the grip on her arms and staggered backwards, his mind drowning in the revelation. Similar to one intoxicated by drink, Nathaniel fumbled his movement, carelessly bumping into the archway opposite that formed the other half of the cave's main entrance. The Teacher sunk to the floor, overcome with the sudden weight of grief and anguish crashing down upon him.

'I am so sorry.' she said, wiping away the tears running down her cheeks. 'The Narlakin had my soul in its grasp – I was its prey. Alarielle selflessly interjected, offering the soul stealer a willing alternative. It consumed *her* soul instead of mine. In my rage, I lost control of my ability – as I did at Scrier's Post. My need for vengeance was so great that it consumed me. I vanquished the nightmare, and the others, obliterating them with my fury. After venting my rage, I implored Alarielle to return, but…she refused! Your daughter would not yield to my request. Her soul had become detached from Freylar, no longer a part of the fabric of this world. Thus she chose to move on, and I could do nothing to prevent it, Nathaniel.'

The Teacher drew his knees up, burying his face in them. His straight long white hair hung down, almost covering his thighs, doing its best to obscure his grief.

'Alarielle was like a sister to me. In fact, she was more than a cherished sibling. Her guiding presence helped me to make peace with the horrors of my past. It was Alarielle who aided me in defeating Lothnar – she helped to accelerate my training – and it was your daughter who assisted me in coming to terms with who I am now.'

Nathaniel suddenly looked up to meet her sad gaze, his face a picture of sorrow.

'As a single parent, you did your best to steer your daughter along an honourable path. Alarielle became your greatest student, Nathaniel. Even in release, the title of Teacher now belongs to her – your teachings made it so. She was proud to have you as her father. You meant everything to her. Your every action enriched her time in this world. However, your work is not done; you swore to yourself to make Freylar a better place for your daughter.

Though Alarielle now survives with us in memory alone, we, Kirika and I, are still here. We are your daughters now. Finish what you started. Get up, make this world a better place, and in doing so honour your daughter's memory.'

Nathaniel gave her a teary-eyed smile and laughed, though his laughter was full of anguish.

'I invited you here in the hope that I would motivate you to join my cause. But instead, it is you who emboldens me.'

Nathaniel stood up and wiped the tears from his eyes, pushing his hair away from his face.

'The last time I lost my daughter, it was Kirika who prevented me from drowning in my own sorrow. Now, my daughter is lost to me for a second time. However, on this occasion it is you who stands before me, steadying my course. So much has happened to me Rayna. I have repeatedly loved and lost; I gained a wife and a daughter, only to lose both. Yet despite my personal tragedies, I still have people around me who love me and care for my wellbeing. I *need* to look to the future and stop dwelling on the past – as my daughter taught you. You are right. I have lost, but I have also gained. It fills me with joy knowing that you and Kirika look to me as a father figure. I promise you both, Darlia too, that I will be there for you all. We will face our hardships together.'

Nathaniel stepped forwards and gave her a heartfelt embrace, which she received in kind. They stood by the entrance to the cave silently holding onto one another, enjoying their shared melancholia. It had been a long time since last she had felt the embrace of another. Her mind strayed towards thoughts of Kaitlin and the precious time they had spent together playing house within the metropolis.

There had been very few times in her life when she truly recalled feeling safe. Her time with Kaitlin had been one such occasion, albeit for a brief period only. Now, as Nathaniel held her tightly, she recalled that same feeling once more, which she had enjoyed so rarely in her life.

Despite the warmth of the body heat they shared, the temperature continued to drop as the snow outside came down thickly. They had overstayed their welcome in the mouth of the cave. It was time to go down and join the others, to descend below the surface where winter's chill could not reach them.

'Come. It truly is freezing up here. Let us join the others.'

Together they strode towards the rear of the cave before entering a network of winding passages that descended ever downwards. The sprawling tunnels spiralled down through the bedrock, connecting to a network of living spaces, personal quarters, food stores and meditation chambers.

'Do you know where all of these tunnels lead to?' she asked as Nathaniel led her this way and that, further down into the underground warren.

'For the most part. I have spent many cycles exploring the cave's root structure.'

'Who built it?' she asked, in awe of the cave's subterranean construction.

'Telekinetics, shapers, from generations well before my own. Alas, we no longer know for certain who excavated all of this.'

'Have you ever become lost down here?' she continued, unable to suppress her curiosity.

'I know that all is well when your curiosity runs rampant.' replied Nathaniel who had a wide grin on his face, bringing about an end to his sorrowful visage.

She laughed, acknowledging the defining characteristic.

'But to answer your question: once or twice,' replied Nathaniel, before turning left into a large chamber, 'Though it was mostly during my youth, prior to learning how to better observe my surroundings – something that you need to work on.'

She smiled back, before looking up to see the others gathered by a large hearth excavated into the rear of the chamber wall. Standing by the hearth with her good arm outstretched was Darlia, adjacent to whom stood Lothnar. Nathanar, Natalya and Thandor were also present, in addition to Kayla who stood apart from the others.

'Rayna, you know everyone here.' said Nathaniel outstretching his arms, motioning everyone to gather closer to the lit hearth. 'Thank you all for coming. You all know the reason why I have gathered you here, but what you do not know is *how* I intend for this to all play out.'

'And what is *this*?' asked Thandor candidly.

'A good question. It is time that we called it what it is. *This*, is treason, and each of us is about to commit an insurrection, assuming that you all still wish to follow me. I cannot guarantee the outcome we desire, nor can I promise that you will not be released for opposing our queen. If you do not have the stomach for such things, now is the time to leave. Should that be the case, I will harbour no ill will towards any of you. All that I ask is that you stay out of my way – let me finish what I started.'

'Thank you for coming so late in the evening.' she said, inviting The Blade Lord to sit beside her on her bed.

'You are our queen; your title grants you the right to summon those who serve you.' replied Marcus who gently sat down beside her.

'Even so, it is appreciated.'

'What troubles you?' asked Marcus softly.

'Tomorrow's trial, specifically security arrangements for the affair. Plus the need to execute certain means of punishment if sentencing demands such.'

Colour drained from The Blade Lord's face, which quickly became one of stone. It was obvious that Marcus did not welcome the forthcoming proceedings, nevertheless, The Blade Lord had pledged his support and would see her will executed. It then suddenly dawned on her: given the time and location of their ad hoc meeting, she wondered in hindsight whether she had summoned The Blade Lord under a false pretence.

'I am sorry if perhaps you thought--'

'An apology is not necessary.' replied Marcus abruptly. 'What security arrangements did you have in mind?'

It was clear now that she had indeed given Marcus the wrong impression. She felt awful knowing that The Blade Lord harboured such strong feelings towards her, yet she was powerless to reciprocate his affections in the manner that he desired.

'I fear that Nathaniel, and those whom you suspect are in league with him, will attempt to interfere with tomorrow's trial. For this reason, I intend to bring the trial forward to noon. Furthermore, I would like you to set up a cordon south of the river, to prevent the forest dwellers from entering the arena.'

'My queen--'

'Please, you need not be so formal with me Marcus.'

'Mirielle, the forest dwellers have every right to attend the trial, as do Nathaniel and those who follow him. Both Kirika and Larissa are well known to the people. Denying access to the trial to those who have fallen from your favour could have undesirable consequences.'

As was typically the case, The Blade Lord's words warranted consideration, though she could ill afford for events at the trial to unfold in a fashion dictated by another. Allowing Nathaniel access to the proceedings was too great a risk – one she was not prepared to take. She placed her hands upon Marcus' right thigh and stared deeply into his eyes.

'I acknowledge the civil unrest my decision may cause. However, the trial must be conducted in both a fair and just manner – that cannot happen if The Teacher is allowed to play his political games. Nathaniel cannot be present at the trial, and the only way to ensure that outcome is to deny those outside the Tri-Spires access to the proceedings.'

Marcus sighed heavily, before placing his hands on top of her own.

'Are you certain this is wise?' asked Marcus, his expression imploring her to reconsider.

'Please, Marcus, I need you to support me in this.'

'And you shall have my support, if this is truly *your* decision.'

'It is.' she said resolutely, doing her best to convince Marcus that the decision to take the chosen path ahead was indeed hers alone.

Although Marcus seemingly harboured no ill will towards Aleska, since the venerable scrier's retirement his guard was habitually up whenever Aleska involved herself in matters of state, be it directly or indirectly. The Blade Lord was no fool; he knew that Aleska had played a part in her decision. Even so, the decision to instigate the cordon was hers – not Aleska's.

'Then you shall have my full support. I will order the house guards to setup a cordon at first light.'

'Thank you. Also, there is one other matter that we need to discuss.'

'You wish me to mete out the aforementioned punishment.'

'Yes.' she replied flatly.

'You realise of course that the punishment for treason is release. If Kirika is convicted of such, you would ask me to do this?'

'If Kirika *is* convicted of treason, she will have brought the appropriate response on herself.'

'Even so, the repercussions of meting out such punishment will far eclipse the fallout from any cordon. Please reconsider your stance on this matter. Kirika is well liked throughout the vale. She has served the people for many passes during her time with The Blades and her former role on the council. Her release could incite martyrdom, thus potentially fuelling Nathaniel's cause.'

'What would *you* have me do? Exile?'

'No. There has to be a better solution. In the meantime, I recommend incarceration, at least until a better option presents itself. If Kirika *is* convicted, it may be possible to negotiate a more suitable arrangement for both parties.'

'You would have me negotiate with insurgents?'

'I only ask that you demonstrate restraint before the people.'

'And why should I entertain such a notion, Marcus?'

'May I speak candidly?'

'Of course – speak your mind.'

'To be frank, your actions of late have caused you to lose favour with the people. That relationship needs to be managed very carefully going forwards, else it could fracture entirely. Kirika enjoys a level of protection due to her good standing with the people. It would be wise to respect the position she has attained.'

'I appreciate that fact Marcus. However, the Freylarkai must accept that severe crimes warrant punished in a manner that befits their severity. If I do not act accordingly, such behaviour could escalate.'

'That is of course a possibility, but the Freylarkai are not inherently unruly. They gossip incessantly and they lie, but they are not revolutionaries by nature.'

'The events instigated by Nathaniel and Kirika suggest otherwise.'

'They are isolated cases – you cannot paint all of the Freylarkai with the same brush.'

'Let us consider a compromise then: *if* found guilty, Larissa will be punished to the *full* extent of Freylarian law, which you will administer, and Kirika will be detained, indefinitely if needs be.'

Marcus' expression was stoic whilst he considered her proposal. The compromise she had outlined would still weigh heavily upon The Blade Lord's soul, though he would find it difficult to argue a case for the dressmaker. Larissa's release would serve as a stark reminder to those intending to subvert her rule, and would likely subdue

Kirika's spirit. After the trial, she would resume her talk with Fate Weaver. Sentenced with incarceration, it was likely that Kirika would reconsider her proposal of exile alongside her sister, in exchange for their freedom. Although Darlia remained in the wild, she felt sure that the notorious scrier would turn herself in of her own volition if sufficient motivation presented itself.

'Are you in agreement?' she asked, trying to push Marcus on the matter.

'I do not like your proposal. Release should not be the result of a compromise, and neither you nor I should decide whose time has come to an end. However, Freylarian law is clear and exists for a purpose, one that cannot be undermined. All Freylarkai know the consequences of flouting our laws.'

She chose not to push the matter any further. Though he was clearly against the notion of release as a form of punishment, nevertheless, Marcus understood the need to reaffirm her reign and the strict adherence to Freylarian law.

'What of your position on scrying?' asked Marcus, shifting the conversation to a less distasteful subject. 'Freylarian law is clear on that matter also, yet you yourself have challenged our policy.'

'That is different.'

'How so?' asked Marcus boldly.

'That initiative is in the interests of domain security. Furthermore, I am drafting new policy on scrying – as is my prerogative.'

An awkward silence passed between them. Marcus worried too much about public perception, in particular how the people would judge her actions. The Freylarkai, awed by her ability, had nominated her as their queen. She would be the one to dictate policy, not those in her charge, a fact The Blade Lord had lost sight of. Yet despite his caution Marcus remained loyal to her reign and would ultimately see her will done.

'Forgive me. I do not seek to sour the mood.' said Marcus, whose stony expression softened. 'I meant no offence.'

'And none was received.' she replied, contrary to the truth. 'I understand your concerns, and in part I am to blame, having spent much of my time isolated within the walls of my own creation. For too long I have remained ensconced within my chamber, attempting to learn all that I can about the thing above us that ensnares us all. In my distraction, the people have pushed me to the back of their minds. They have forgotten my rule, the things I have done and the protection I afford them. With the exception of those closest to me, the Freylarkai *have* become unruly and dissident. Yet despite the discord that has seeped into our ranks, I *will* restore order. Though in order to do this, I need your support.'

She leant forward and pressed her lips to Marcus' right cheek, kissing his smooth skin. Then after slowly pulling away, she offered The Blade Lord an affectionate smile, coercing the response that she sought.

'And you shall have it.'

EIGHTEEN
Cordon

'Are you all clear as to your purpose?'

'Teacher, we are ready.' replied Nathanar. 'However, if we do not leave for the Tri-Spires promptly our show of strength will be for nothing.'

'We have plenty of time; the trial is scheduled for this evening.' he replied.

'Perhaps, but winter's caress has turned the landscape white. It would therefore be wise to journey to the Tri-Spires ahead of schedule.'

'Nathanar gives voice to reason.' replied Thandor. 'We should make ready to depart.'

It was late morning, or thereabouts. The gloomy sky masked the weak sun's presence, making it difficult to track its passage above. Experience cautioned him to be patient and remain at the Cave of Wellbeing a while longer, but he could sense their apprehension rising, which would only diminish their focus. Deciding it unwise to keep them waiting any longer, he gestured towards a small chamber adjacent to the one they currently occupied.

'Come, follow me. I want to show you all something.'

He led the way into the small round chamber, in the middle of which was a pedestal with a small stone fragment embedded in the top. One by one they entered the room and gathered around the artefact, their expressions perplexed, with the notable exception of Rayna's own.

'You have a Waystone fragment here, hidden in the Cave of Wellbeing.' explained Rayna observantly.

He smiled at the light bringer who had clearly paid attention to his recounting during the night.

'I had hoped to keep this secret for a little while longer, but your restless state hastens my intent.'

'How did you come by this?' asked Natalya, who wasted little time in her search for answers. 'It is only a fragment – does it still work?'

He glanced towards Rayna who offered him a raised eyebrow. Whatever her feelings concerning the way in which he disseminated information, the light bringer remained fortuitously tight-lipped.

'It is a long story. Suffice to say, we will have no need to suffer the harsh embrace of winter.'

'Where does it lead to?' asked Thandor curiously.

'The last place anyone will be.' he replied, raising his hand to touch the fragment. 'We are committed; there can be no turning back.'

He touched the stone fragment with his right hand and felt the familiar lurch of his stomach as the chamber and those in it slipped from view, promptly replaced by fresh surroundings. He took a step back from the fragment's twin, which had been set into the top of an ancient staff positioned vertically in a display stand. The gnarled long wooden staff stood upright at least a pace from the corner of the familiar chamber in which he now stood. Appearing next was Rayna. The light bringer grinned widely as she moved to join him, creating space for the others to appear.

'Ha, this is more cunning than any of my trickery, Nathaniel.' said Rayna, sweeping her gaze across the room.

He smiled, acknowledging her compliment. Gradually their numbers grew, until the entire party stood present and accounted for. Although there were very few known incidents related to Waystone use, the unconventional means of travel had claimed its share of casualties over the passes. Frivolous use of the stones was ill advised, for one never truly knew where they would appear. There were known incidents of Waystone use that had seen those using them disappear from existence. As such, he tried to limit his use of the arcane devices, preferring to travel by foot or wraith wing instead.

'Hopefully this answers your question satisfactorily, Thandor?' he said, offering the Paladin a wry grin.

'Clearly you have another tale to tell, Nathaniel, but for the moment at least, I am content in the knowledge that we stand here, in Fate Weaver's chamber. As you say, our arrival here will go entirely unnoticed, at least until we choose to announce our presence.'

'We need to ensure that the route to the arena is clear before we start piling into the passageways.' said Natalya. 'Most of us have been absent from the Tri-Spires for some time now, and will therefore draw attention when sighted.'

'Agreed.' said Nathanar. 'Someone needs to scout ahead before we make our move.'

'I could go.' replied Kayla softly. 'I know this structure better than any of you.'

'No.' he replied quickly. 'You are a witness to Mirielle's offences. We cannot afford to lose you.'

'I will go.' said Lothnar, who immediately began walking towards the chamber door.

'Why you?' asked Kayla, who was clearly eager to prove her worth amidst the presence of legends.

'Because I am a ghost; my absence is not missed, nor my presence felt. I come and go as I please, without notice. In the unlikely event that I am questioned, I will feign disinterest in the trial. There are few who will care whether I am in attendance or not during the proceedings.'

'I care.' said Rayna unexpectedly. 'Make sure that you haul your arse back here, promptly, else you will have me to contend with – I already embarrassed you once.'

Lothnar smiled before taking his leave. Like a shadow, the nomadic Paladin slipped silently past the door, bent on completing his mission.

'How long should we wait?' asked Natalya, turning to face him.

'As long as it takes – I see no immediate rush. You may as well all get comfortable whilst we await his return.'

The passageways were strangely absent of guards, as was the Waystone chamber, which he had never before seen unattended. Indeed, there appeared to be very few Freylarkai present at all within the Tri-Spires. He had expected to see the Queen's puppets stationed at all the major choke points throughout the structure, yet they were completely unguarded. It was clear to him now that the house guards had been reassigned elsewhere, to perform other duties of note. Nonetheless, even by Mirielle's standards, the apparent decision to empty the structure, leaving it entirely undefended, was negligent. There was little chance Marcus would have sanctioned such action. It was likely, therefore, that Mirielle was pulling the strings in order to satisfy her own agenda.

'Where are you?' he muttered to himself, whilst continuing to work his way down through the structure.

What game would possibly prompt such disregard of public security, he mused, as he quickly moved through the sprawl of interconnecting passageways and chambers, virtually all of which were eerily vacant. The trial was not until late afternoon, and there were no other events scheduled prior to the spectacle, or rather none to his knowledge. In light of the unexpected circumstances, he decided to backtrack and approach one of the few civilians he had passed earlier still present within the structure.

'Where is everyone?' he asked, dispensing with unnecessary pleasantries.

'Lothnar, honoured Paladin, it is--'

He waved his hand, cutting the Freylarkin short.

'Where are the house guards?'

'Where you not informed?' asked the Freylarkin with a concerned look.

'Clearly not.' he replied tersely.

'The Queen has reassigned them.'

'I realise that, but to where?' he asked agitatedly, rapidly growing impatient with the Freylarkin's inadvertent evasiveness.

'Some of the guards have been commanded to oversee the trial, however, the remainder have been ordered to establish a cordon south of the river, to ensure that the arena does not breach capacity. For reasons of public safety, our queen has deemed this course of action necessary.'

'How did you come to learn of all this?'

'I overheard the guards grumbling about their assignments.'

'As I understand it, the trial is not until late afternoon.'

'I am afraid that your information is out of date – the trial has already started.'

'What?'

'The announcement was made at first light. Perhaps you were absent when--'

'How many guards maintain the cordon?'

'I am not certain. I only heard bits of conver--'

'How many?' he asked abruptly again.

'Perhaps twenty or so.'

'Thank you for your assistance.'

He ran back the way he had come, leaving the confused Freylarkin behind, who loitered in the passageway looking perplexed. When eventually he returned to Kirika's chamber, he burst into the room causing all those present to draw their arms.

'Good, bring them, we need to go – now!'

'What is it Lothnar, what's going on?' asked Rayna brandishing her exotic blades, one in each hand.

'We have been outmanoeuvred: the trial is already under way. Furthermore, a cordon has been setup, south of the river, to prevent those beyond the Tri-Spires from attending the proceedings. We have to leave *now*!'

'Lothnar, you and Nathanar disband that cordon. The rest of us will head to the arena.' said Nathaniel, whose expression quickly darkened.

The press of Freylarkai gathered around the arena was unlike anything she had seen before. Even her much anticipated duel with Lothnar had failed to draw such an audience. If not for their status, carving a path through the crowd would have been impossible; their lofty positions meant that the Freylarkai were more amenable to moving aside. Even so, pushing their way to the front of the chaos was time consuming. As they snaked their way through the throng of people, she could sense Nathaniel's growing agitation, The Teacher's voice becoming ever shorter as he asked the Freylarkai to step aside. Eventually they made their way to the front of the rabble by the west gate, only to find their path blocked by a handful of the Queen's house guards.

'Let us pass.' said Nathaniel with authority to the group of guards standing before them.

'We cannot allow anyone else into the arena – it is at capacity.'

'Let us pass, now!' demanded Nathaniel sternly.

'I am afraid that we cannot permit that. We have our orders.'

'You *know* who I am.'

'Of course, honoured Teacher, but with respect, you are not permitted to enter the arena at this time.'

'On what grounds?' she asked, finally involving herself in the terse exchange of words.

'Public safety – as ordered by the Queen.'

'I have had enough of this.' muttered Nathaniel under his breath, before offering her a quick glance.

She winked in return, acknowledging his intention. They watched in awe as Nathaniel disarmed the guard standing before them with unparalleled alacrity, before striking his dumbfounded opponent across the side of the face using the pommel of their own weapon. Nathaniel stepped through the newly created gap, after promptly taking down another of the guards who foolishly tried to block The Teacher's path. Three more house guards closed in rapidly. However, each was quickly turned away by a brilliant flash of light from her left hand. The sudden burst of white light sent the guards reeling, clutching at their eyes whilst struggling to regain their sight. Realising the futility of their actions, the remainder of the house guards gave way allowing them to enter into the arena without further challenge.

Two guards stood in the centre of the arena, with Larissa between them. She knew the famed dressmaker well; after her arrival in Freylar, Kirika had taken her to see Larissa, who had played a significant role in her reimaging. She recalled the first time she met the fearless seamstress, remembering how confident and outspoken her tailor was, perhaps even a little too wilful. Now, Larissa looked gaunt and pale, her posture was demure and her arms were bound together with thick rope. The renowned dressmaker stood before the people on full display, a broken version of her former glorious self.

'Look what they have *done* to her!' she said, appalled by Larissa's subjugated appearance.

'Keep your emotions in check, both of you.' said Thandor who moved to stand immediately behind them. 'We need to gauge the situation before making our move.'

'Agreed.' replied Nathaniel through gritted teeth.

To their right was Mirielle, who sat in the front row of the amphitheatre, flanked by The Blade Lord and a young Freylarkin female, beside whom was an entourage of personal aides. Kirika sat adjacent to Marcus, her arms also bound tightly, and beside the Fate Weaver was a house guard whom Kayla quickly identified.

'Ralnor is the one who assisted me when I fled the Tri-Spires – he is not like the others.'

'Is she OK? I cannot see her clearly with these wretched eyes of mine Nathaniel.'

'She looks to be unharmed.' said Natalya, quickly allaying her fears.

Before they could assess the situation any further, Mirielle rose from her place upon the tiered stone seating, raising her good arm to silence the raucous din of the crowd. The Queen turned her gaze towards them, specifically Nathaniel, to whom she offered a venomous glare before turning her attention back to Larissa in the centre of the arena.

'You have all heard in detail the accusations put to the accused. In particular, you have heard how Larissa brutally released this one's mother, Hanarah, leaving Cora alone without parents to care for her.' proclaimed the Queen with conviction, whilst turning towards the young female beside her. 'This act of *evil* cannot be met with impunity. The severity of this crime warrants the full extent of punishment as set out by Freylarian law. However, before the ruling council is required to pass judgement over the accused, the accused herself is permitted to defend her actions so that perhaps we might better understand the reason for this atrocity.'

Mirielle took her place once more, sitting back down upon the tiered stone seating. Once more, the lively members of the packed amphitheatre began to chat amongst themselves, rendering it impossible for Larissa to make her voice heard above the noise.

'Nathaniel, we need to do something.' she said, looking to The Teacher for a solution. 'If Larissa cannot offer a compelling defence, Mirielle will have her released!'

'Would she?' asked Thandor, playing devil's advocate. 'This whole charade is nothing more than a starter, designed to wet our appetites early in order to draw us out.'

'Thandor is right.' said Nathaniel, who bore a grim expression. 'We cannot use our resources this early to engage in this skirmish.'

'I understand the position we are in.' she said, acknowledging their words, 'Nonetheless, this cannot go unchallenged. Larissa is spirited, she is confident and brash, but she would never release an innocent!'

'I know.' replied Nathaniel, 'However, we did not anticipate this move. None of us believed that Mirielle could be so…base.'

'Regrettably, Larissa has become a pawn, Rayna.' said Natalya angrily, 'Sometimes they must be sacrificed in war – you know this from your own experiences.'

'I know. It's just that I spent most of my former life tolerating injustice, and now you ask that I stand by and watch this farce, one that will likely result in a huge miscarriage of justice.'

'Save your anger, Rayna.' replied Nathaniel. 'We will have one chance to save Kirika, and with it bring an end to Mirielle's tainted rule. Act now, and we jeopardise that opportunity.'

She could feel the familiar anger and hatred festering inside her once more, desperate to escape the shackles of her mind. Twice now, she had lost control of her darker emotions with devastating consequences. With so many civilian Freylarkai present, she could ill afford to lose control for a third time. Mirielle's war was one of words and politicking – her wraith blade would do her no good.

'That bitch!' she said, failing to form words that might spill from a more educated tongue. 'When the time comes, I will be the one to end her.'

'No!' said Darlia, who until now had remained silent on the matter. 'You must remain a child of the light. If it comes to it, my hands are already dripping with blood – a little more will make no difference. And besides, I owe it to Lileah.'

'You have done enough already.' said Nathaniel, who turned to face the infamous scrier. 'I started this, for reasons that you will eventually come to understand – I must be the one to finish it.'

They sped north using their wraith wings, away from the Tri-Spires and the turmoil surrounding the arena. Nathanar flew closely behind him, but the exceptionally tall Freylarkin's weight hindered his flight, causing the Paladin's left leg to trace a line in the fresh snow. In the distance, they could see the Queen's house guards, who occupied a makeshift barricade that stood between them and the people. The Queen's private army was busy trying to quell a large group of Freylarkai amassing on the opposite side of the blockade. As they made their speedy approach, he began to recognise some of the distant faces, in particular a large black-furred dire wolf accompanying the growing rabble.

'It is Gaelin and his people. We must lend aid and get the guards to stand down, before the situation turns ugly.'

'Go on ahead!' cried Nathanar, 'I will join you presently.'

Channelling all the strength he could muster, he increased his speed, determined to arrive at the scene of the growing confrontation before things turned nasty. Gaelin's mob had grown considerably since last they had spoken, suggesting that the farmstead leader had succeeded in rallying others from the outlying communities to their cause. Furthermore, it became apparent that the sight of Gaelin's militia had drawn in support from those living north of the river, prompting a steady stream of Freylarkai to cross the old bridge, swelling the farmstead leader's disorderly ranks. The disciplined guards held their position, refusing to give any ground to the growing mob bearing down on them.

Amidst the growing chaos, one of Gaelin's lot suddenly hurled what looked like a large stone, catching one of the guards flush against the side of their head. The unruly behaviour agitated the house guards, prompting one of them to forego their training and strike back. The undisciplined guard landed a cut against the nearest opponent standing on the opposite side of the barricade, causing the injured Freylarkin to cry out in pain. There was a momentary reprieve as the astonished mob took stock of their injured comrade, before directing their hatred towards the Freylarkin responsible using blunt instruments, rocks and detritus torn from the snow-covered barricade to hurt the assailant. Predictably, the house guards retaliated, injuring several of Gaelin's lot with their falchions, causing tensions to escalate beyond reprieve. Fighting immediately broke out on both sides, followed by the inevitable wailing sounds of those injured during the sudden violent clash that ensued. Spots of crimson began to appear on the pristine white snow, a prelude to worse acts to come.

'Cease this madness at once!' he cried out as he approached the scene, hoping in vain to end the fighting before release inevitably ensued.

Fear and anger had already gripped those involved, the result of which was chaos as the civilian Freylarkai began jumping the barricade, aided by the use of their wraith wings. Several members of the unruly mob dragged one of the guards down to the ground, before trampling them underfoot. He could see Gaelin at the centre of the maelstrom, desperately trying to get the situation under control. Irrespective of the farmstead leader's failing endeavour, it was clear that tensions could no longer be dispelled by words alone. He needed a way to end the fighting quickly, with minimal casualties.

'Krisis, I need you! Take down the house guards, but do not release them!'

The obedient dire wolf responded immediately to his command. Krisis leapt cleanly over the barricade and began dragging the guards in turn to the ground by locking his fierce jaws around their legs before pulling them down. The dire wolf's victims tried in vain to repel the lupine's attacks, but Krisis' speed and agility thwarted their attempts with ease.

'Gaelin! Restrain the guards!'

Nathanar, who by now had caught up, waded into the confrontation and began promptly disarming the guards by knocking aside their falchions with his double-handed sword. The Paladin's impressive power and reach saw the guards relieved of their weapons in short order, allowing the mob to subdue their opponents with relative ease. Absent their arms and footing, the house guards were helplessly overrun, bested by skill and numbers. Realising the futility of their actions, three of the guards broke rank and retreated towards the Tri-Spires.

'Krisis, take them down!' he communicated telepathically, before expertly throwing one of his knives towards the closest fleeing guard.

The knife struck the house guard's right thigh, causing the leg to give out. The wounded guard fell to the ground with a thump, half burying himself in the thick snow. Krisis bounded up the incline towards the Tri-Spires with preternatural speed, the harsh climate seemingly having no effect on the powerful lupine. The dire wolf bounded past the first guard, choosing instead to pounce upon the other one leading the retreat. Seeing the fate of his companions, the remaining guard panicked, dropped their weapon and fell to their knees in surrender.

'Stay here, and do not let them leave.'

Leaving Krisis to maintain watch over the subdued house guards, he turned his attention back towards the fighting south of the river. Streaks of crimson criss-crossed the white snow, with a number of Freylarkai clutching at wounds – the ugly result of the regrettable infighting. Yet despite the casualties, the bloody confrontation had now burnt itself out, with Gaelin's militia presiding over their defeated opponents.

'Tend to the wounded.' he cried, fearing the worst as he quickly assessed the injured Freylarkai.

'Even the Queen's guards?' asked Gaelin, who applied pressure to a cut across his shoulder.

'Gaelin, these people need assistance – all of them.' he said, fixing his gaze firmly upon the farmstead leader. 'They were following orders; this was not *their* intent.'

Gaelin took a moment to consider his words before nodding in agreement. Realising his error, the farmstead leader promptly set those around him to purpose.

'Nathanar.' he said, marching directly towards the Paladin. 'We need to head back to the arena.'

'Agreed.' replied Nathanar, who sought to compose himself by regaining his breath. 'Let us make haste.'

'We are coming too.' said Gaelin, interjecting himself into their conversation.

'Very well. Krisis will remain here with a handful of your people whilst your renewalist tends to the wounded.

The remainder of your group will accompany us to the arena, where the trial is already under way.'

'You mean they have already started?' asked Gaelin with a surprised look.

'Mirielle brought the proceedings forward.' replied Nathanar, having since caught his breath. 'We do not have much time.'

'We are coming too.' cried a voice from those quickly gathering around them.

A tall young female with violet coloured hair approached them, along with her entourage; a sizeable group of forest dwellers flanked her, all of whom bore an angry look.

'And you are?' he said, failing to place the young female.

'A friend of Kirika and Nathaniel.'

'Why do you wish to accompany us?' he asked, intrigued by the young female's words.

'He is up there in the arena, The Teacher, is he not?'

'Yes. He intends to argue Kirika's case.'

'Then take me to him, immediately. I can help, I am certain of it.'

'How can you know that?' he asked suspiciously, whilst gazing deeply into her violet eyes.

'Because I have *seen* things which you have not.'

NINETEEN
Trial

She gave The Blade Lord a hard stare, looking to him to restore order. Marcus promptly rose from his place beside her and raised his right fist to silence the wagging tongues of the crowd.

'Larissa, you have heard in detail the accusations laid against you.' said Marcus with commanding authority. 'How do you respond?'

The browbeaten seamstress raised her head slowly, before fixing her gaze intently upon her. She could feel Larissa's hatred burning like the heat of a roaring hearth. She could see the anger boiling over inside the famed dressmaker, whose seething expression told all. Ordinarily she took pity on the falsely accused, but in light of Larissa's coercion – forcing her to separate Hanarah and Cora – she had little time or compassion for the unruly seamstress.

'You lie!' cried Larissa in a broken voice. 'It was *your* lack of ability that forced Hanarah to accept release in place of her daughter, Cora. A loving mother chose her end, so that her daughter could endure the horror of your rule.'

'Enough!' replied Marcus. 'It is not our queen who stands trial and I command that you show decorum in her presence. Now, is there anything of note that you wish to say, notwithstanding base accusations?'

'I released Hanarah because she asked as much from me, so that her daughter would be saved.' said Larissa defiantly.

'We have two witnesses, including our queen no less, who saw you release Hanarah. You yourself admit to committing the heinous crime, yet you ask that we suspend disbelief and place our trust in you, believing that this is truly what the mother wanted?'

'For what other reason would I do such a thing?'

'You were scared of the *thing* that they had become, as were many of us, ergo, your fear drove you to such end.'

'That is a lie!'

'Where is your evidence to the contrary?'

There was long uneasy pause as all those in the arena collectively held their breath, waiting for the accused to bolster her claim. Part of her admired Larissa's conviction. Had she been an ally, the dressmaker's headstrong nature would have been a valuable asset. Instead, the once famed Freylarkin now served as a means to strengthen her rule, casting aside any doubt regarding her ability to lead the people when challenged with both confrontation and ugly decisions.

'Liar!' said Larissa once more, this time spitting upon the snow-covered floor of the arena, causing a loud gasp from the audience.

Ultimately, there was no evidence to support the dressmaker's unrealistic claim, only base insult, prompting The Blade Lord to turn to her in order to move the proceedings forward. She rose slowly from her seat, pushing herself upright with her good arm, and turned to face the shocked audience.

'This abhorrent act has been confirmed by our most venerable scrier, Aleska, whose sworn written testimony I have here, confirming that which she saw using her second sight.' she announced, pulling a written scroll from the thick folds of her brown dress before turning towards Aleska, acknowledging the scrier's presence in the crowd.

Aleska nodded, affirming the validity of the testimony that she carried, which she raised high above her head allowing her captive audience to bear witness.

'This testimony, plus the witnesses who saw the crime first-hand, corroborate the *actual* events that took place.'

'THAT IS A LIE!' cried a female voice suddenly from the direction of the west gate.

They watched expectantly, hoping that Larissa would convincingly counter the accusations heaped upon her, but instead the dressmaker glowered at Mirielle as if to bring about the queen's release through eye contact alone. Whilst the two females stared coldly at one another, an unexpected commotion arose from behind them. He spun around and saw a tall slender Freylarkin nursing a cut across his shoulder. The Freylarkin stood at the front of a growing throng of working-class Freylarkai. Lothnar and Nathanar flanked him, joined by another who he quickly recognised.

'Keshar!' he said, moving to embrace the eager young Freylarkin. 'I take it that you received my message?'

'Yes, am I too late?'

'No. The ruling council is about to pass judgement over Larissa, shortly after which Kirika will stand trial.'

Keshar watched keenly as Mirielle lamented about a written testimonial that she had acquired, citing Aleska as its author.

'I did not realise that Aleska offered the Queen counsel at this time.' he muttered under his breath. 'This could compli--'

'THAT IS A LIE!' cried Keshar suddenly, her voice piercing the cold air of the arena.

All eyes abruptly turned towards them, drawing unwanted attention from across the entire arena. A sense of dread swept over him as his carefully crafted plan began to unravel.

'Who speaks out of turn?' cried Mirielle angrily, turning to face them from across the arena.

'I do, on behalf of an innocent!' replied Keshar boldly, who pushed her way forward from the mouth of the west gate, allowing the audience to see her fully.

'You dare interrupt me, and with false claim!'

'I speak the truth, as does Larissa.'

'Give me your name petulant child!' demanded Mirielle tersely.

'I am Keshar. Riknar was my brother. And Aleska is a liar! The scroll in your hand was written by one who manipulates all those around her, to further her own agenda; her testimonial carries no weight in these proceedings.'

The audience gasped once more before rapidly falling silent, dumbstruck by the allegations given voice by the fearless young Freylarkin.

'How dare you insult the credibility of our most revered scrier!'

'I dare with good reason: Aleska concealed the truth of my brother's release from me in order to preserve the unsanctioned reinstatement of Scrier's Post – endorsed by *you* – to which I was seconded for training. Aleska feared the unravelling of the fledgling clandestine endeavour in the event I chose to leave the sanctuary. As such she withheld news of my brother's release, so that I would remain at Scrier's Post furthering *your* agenda!'

'Guards!' cried Mirielle angrily, 'Take this female into custody immediately!'

The crowd came alive with chatter as the Freylarkai gossiped amongst themselves in light of Keshar's scolding revelations.

'Nathaniel, our plan must be brought forward.' said Thandor with an uncharacteristically concerned look.

'No, it cannot. You said yourselves that Larissa is a pawn in all this.' he replied quickly. 'The timing is all wrong, and besides, we still have Kayla.'

'Agreed, but we no longer have a say in any of this. You called Keshar here, deliberately, to discredit the Queen and her counsel, thus destabilising her rule. Keshar is our fulcrum – we either stand with her now or lose this opportunity, which you have worked so hard to set in motion.'

The aloof Paladin spoke the truth of it. Events were unfolding faster than he had anticipated, throwing his carefully orchestrated timeline into freefall. Yet despite the chaos playing out before them, Freylar's queen was now vulnerable. Buried truths had surfaced in a public forum, which in turn would force Mirielle to change her tactics, no doubt resorting to the application of fear and intimidation to subdue the people.

A large group of house guards started to cross the arena towards their position at the behest of their queen, intent on removing Keshar from the public eye. The house guards securing Larissa moved closer to the crowd, giving way to the Queen's private army that slowly marched towards them. The young scrier held her ground defiantly, refusing to be intimidated by Mirielle's guards bearing down upon her. Gathering up her long dress, the fearless scrier drew a long knife from a concealed sheath strapped to her right thigh. Keshar held the blade out before her in the manner of one lacking discipline and training, albeit brimming with heart and conviction.

'Nathaniel!' said Thandor once more, 'Do not let this come to pass.'

He turned towards Kayla, fixing his gaze firmly upon Kirika's loyal aide.

'You wanted to help. Are you sure that you are ready for this?'

'We cannot let her stand alone, Nathaniel. It is as you said – we are committed. The timing is poor, but we will not be found lacking in conviction.'

'Then let us move forward and face this challenge together, as one.' he said ardently.

Together, they advanced into the arena to stand beside the young female brandishing her knife. The crowd ignited once more, descending in to frenzied chatter that filled the space with noise, akin to that of the Trials. Keshar turned her head towards him, offering him a nervous smile.

'Thank you.'

'You owe me no thanks.' he said, placing a reassuring hand on her right shoulder.

'I was wrong to part with your company at Scrier's Post – please forgive me.'

'No, you were right! Your actions have ignited my cause, giving it the spark it sorely required.'

More of the Queen's house guards quickly took to the arena, joining those who opposed them, bolstering their ranks. As he surveyed the crowd, he spied a number of Blades dotted throughout the auditorium, yet none chose to involve themselves in the growing confrontation. Given the conflict of interests, no doubt they were waiting to see how events would play out between The Blade Lord and The Guardian.

'SILENCE!' cried Marcus, rising abruptly from his seat, raising both arms to quiet the crowd.

The arena immediately fell silent as everyone present looked to The Blades' commander, who, since early in his appointment, had commanded the respect of Freylar's military might.

'What is the meaning of this?' asked The Blade Lord pointedly.

'In addition to Keshar's testimony, calling into question Aleska's written account, and the information we have all heard regarding our queen's decision to renege on Freylarian law concerning the sanctioned use of scrying, I--'

'You overstep your mark, Nathaniel!' interjected Marcus, 'Larissa is on trial, *not* our queen.'

'Marcus, this trial is a sham!' he cried, focusing his glare on Mirielle whose face was now loaded with venom.

'Stand down!' barked The Blade Lord.

'We have further evidence supporting Keshar's claim. I myself was at Scrier's Post, and have witnessed the site's rebirth first-hand.' he said, careful not to mention how he had tracked Aleska to the sanctuary. 'Aleska instructed Krasus to reimage the ill-gotten sanctuary at our queen's behest, *without* first consulting the ruling council, which at the time Kirika held a seat upon. How convenient then, that Fate Weaver now faces public trial following Larissa's.'

'I will not ask you again, Nathaniel. Cease this insurrection at once!'

'And if I chose not to do so, what will happen then, Marcus? Will I be tried, alongside those accused of an offence where none exists? Power and isolation have clouded Mirielle's judgement. Kayla, who stands with us now, overheard our queen threatening Kirika when remanded in custody. Mirielle offered to spare Larissa from release, *if* both Kirika and her sister, Darlia, left the vale quietly, never to return. Are these the actions of one fit to pass judgement over another, let alone lead the people?'

'ENOUGH!' cried Mirielle. 'Larissa released Hanarah, the punishment for which is release itself; a regrettable, but necessary sentence, one that The Blade Lord will now execute as per my command.'

'You are not fit to make such decisions, nor do we recognise your authority to do so!' he said vehemently.

'Guards, detain them!' ordered Mirielle, 'They are to be remanded into custody on grounds of treason.'

The house guards standing opposite resumed their cautious advance, understandably wary of whom they opposed. Mirielle turned to Marcus, commanding The Blade Lord with a single look to carry out his duty. He could see the conflict in his former protégé's eyes, courtesy of his keen vision. Yet regardless, The Blade Lord remained devoted to Freylar's queen and thus vaulted on to the floor of the arena, before advancing towards Larissa. Kirika rose from her seat, her arms still bound, begging The Blade Lord to stop.

'Marcus, please, do not do this – I beg of you!' cried Kirika, 'You *know* this is wrong.'

He watched with sadness as The Blade Lord paid little attention to Kirika's words, continuing his approach towards the bound seamstress, bent on executing the will of the Queen. Removing his bastard sword from its scabbard, Marcus held the imposing blade before him, as Caleth had once done, high up in the Tri-Spires.

'Marcus, please, stop this! Do not let your love for the queen blind you!' begged Kirika, whose face now streamed with tears.

The house guards continued to edge towards their position, drawing ever closer. He could sense the apprehension of those standing alongside him, few of whom were veterans of war, hardened through repeated conflict, yet such experiences did little to prepare a warrior when asked to fight against one's own kin.

'Nathaniel, if we do this, it will ignite a civil war.' said Thandor anxiously. 'There has to be another way.'

'Natalya,' he said, turning his head towards the Valkyrie. 'Hold them back using your ability.'

'There are too many!'

'Try!' he replied abruptly, before shifting his attention to Rayna. 'Our numbers are not sufficient to quash Mirielle's forces without confrontation. You command the respect of The Blades – you must use it!'

'Nathaniel, they follow The Blade Lord.'

'Marcus is lost to us right now; he cannot see past his blind devotion to the Queen. They respect me, but they will *follow* you, if you so wish it. Please, Rayna, help us finish this without the need for bloodshed.'

He could see the indecision etched across the light bringer's face. Rayna had sworn an oath to the Order, as had they all. No doubt, the thought of undermining The Blade Lord's command spat in the face of that oath.

'Do not see this as a betrayal. I realise that I am asking a lot of you, though I only do so in the best interests of the people. If Mirielle is allowed to continue along the path upon which she now treads, it will mean ruin for us all.

Please, do not allow Caleth's legacy to drag us down with it.'

Rayna sheathed Shadow Caster, then, using The Ardent Blade, cut along the open palm of her left hand, tracing a line of claret in its wake. She clenched her hand, causing blood to flow from her balled fist, before raising her left arm high above her head. Opening her fist, The Guardian presented her splayed crimson fingers to the audience, allowing the excess blood to trickle down her left arm onto the snow. The encroaching guards hesitated in their ponderous advance, having heard the stories told by those surviving the battle for Bleak Moor. They recognised well the symbol presented by The Guardian, and the intent it carried. One by one, the off-duty Blades within the crowd began filtering their way down to the arena floor where they quickly moved to stand by Rayna's side. Marcus watched with obvious disappointment as a handful of Blades descended from their high perches within the auditorium, ultimately choosing to stand alongside them. Witnessing their brothers and sisters publicly affirm their allegiance to The Guardian encouraged more and more Blades to rise from their seats, until a steady stream began descending towards the arena floor, notably bolstering their show of strength. Their numbers swelled, further strengthened by more forest dwellers now pushing their way into the arena through the west gate. Seeing this, the house guards quickly ceased their advance, clearly intimidated by the overwhelming show of force now gathering rapidly opposite them. The queen's private army redirected its gaze towards The Blade Lord, seeking confirmation of their orders in light of the changed circumstances. In turn,

Marcus directed his gaze towards Mirielle, offering the queen a sombre look.

'Release her!' said Mirielle sternly, her pupil-less eyes offered no comfort or remorse.

'My queen?' replied The Blade Lord respectfully, seeking confirmation of Mirielle's will.

'RELEASE HER!'

The crowd had reached a fever pitch, with tensions in the arena running high. She could feel herself suddenly trembling in the wake of the queen's irrefutable command. The Blade Lord's face hardened as he turned to face Larissa once more, before slowly raising his bastard sword ready to deliver its coup de grâce. Her heart pounded rapidly behind her breast, thumping increasingly faster as tensions continued to rise. Since the ill-fated moment of her mother's release, she had wanted only one thing: to erase the abhorrent memory from her thoughts. Yet despite her best efforts to bury the ordeal, the mental anguish continued to assault her with each passing cycle, determined to drown her, pushing her down to the lowest possible depths of despair. With her mother gone, she was all alone. She had no siblings of which to speak and her father had long since been released in service to The Blades. She had no one else. There was no longer anyone left to care for her. Although the Queen had provided her with hospitality and shelter within the Tri-Spires, that act of kindness had felt cold and contrived, offering her no solace. Freylar's queen could not provide her the reassurance she sought. Her mother was gone, and with it any feelings of love and security.

'I am alone.' she said in a broken voice inadvertently, weeping tears upon the fresh snow falling around her feet.

'No, you are not!' said Kirika, clearly overhearing her remark.

'Silence!' said Mirielle tersely, who gave the rebellious scrier an evil scowl.

'Cora, you will *never* be alone.' Kirika continued persistently. 'Each of us is here for you, moreover, Larissa, who stands before you right now, honours your mother's memory by upholding the choice that she made so that you could--'

The Queen abruptly cut Kirika's heartfelt words short, striking the scrier hard across the face using her good hand, turning Kirika's left cheek a vivid shade of pink from the sudden impact. The audience gasped at the Queen's unexpected violent outburst, shocked that their ruler would assault a former member of the ruling council, no matter the cause.

'She wanted *you* to survive Cora.' said Kirika defiantly, raising her voice so that the crowd could better hear her words. 'Larissa tells the truth; I have just witnessed it with my second sight, courtesy of our queen's vicious right hand!'

'Stay your tongue, else I will have it removed!' screamed Mirielle, losing all sense of decorum.

The awful memory of her mother's release surfaced once more, this time in more detail than previously recalled. She remembered, now, the final words spoken by her mother with unerring accuracy:

"*Release me! Save my daughter and release me!*"

'No.' she whispered to herself, quietly under her breath.

"Larissa, you promised me! Please – save my daughter!"

'No!' she said again, louder this time, tears trickling down her face.

"You promised me, no matter the cost – do it for my daughter!"

'NO!' she screamed, no longer able to suppress her emotions, the act of which had previously rendered her mute. 'Stop it! Let Larissa go! She did only as my mother begged of her – get away from her, now!'

Silence immediately fell across the arena, save for the shuffles of all those present turning to face her. She turned to the Queen with ruddy tear-filled eyes. Mirielle's face was hideously contorted with rage, revealing an ugly side to Freylar's queen previously unknown to her.

'Let her go.' she said, her voice now trembling as the consequences of her actions began to crystallise. 'Larissa is innocent; she did only as my mother requested in order to save me. Her actions do not warrant such punishment. You must let her go!'

All eyes were fixed on Mirielle and Cora. The young female's sudden heartfelt outburst had stunned all those present, rendering them mute. Now they watched, anxious to see how Freylar's queen would react to the unforeseen change of events. When first they had entered the arena, they had done so expecting a war of words, or worse still, the bloody clash of arms against their kin. Kayla was to be his weapon of choice, with Keshar secreted away in reserve. Yet despite their lengthy preparations, none of them had anticipated such a young female standing before their queen, rendering Freylar's ruler speechless. There was no salvaging the situation for Mirielle now. Freylar's queen had played a dangerous game, using fear and deceit to shore up her waning rule in the wake of a torrent of unfortunate events that had hit the people hard, denying many their loved ones. Now that fear was crumbling as it evolved into something else: loathing perhaps, or maybe pity.

He shifted his gaze towards The Blade Lord, who maintain the grip on his bastard sword, awaiting further confirmation from the Queen in light of Cora's outburst. He smiled to himself – perhaps there was hope for Marcus after all, he mused. Turning his attention once more towards Cora and the Queen, he noticed the young Freylarkin trembling badly. Clearly, she had suffered enough torment already, and as such, it was time to put an end to the stalemate between them. He started walking slowly towards The Blade Lord, defiantly closing the distance between them despite the flinty looks from the house guards, until only a single pace remained.

'Lower you weapon brother.' he said quietly, assured that Marcus would welcome the opportunity to capitulate. 'Find another one; that blade is cursed.'

Slowly, The Blade Lord lowered his weapon, allowing its tip to disappear into the snow that continued to fall from the murky sky.

'Thank you.' said Marcus softly, before offering him a curious smile. 'You can inform Rayna that her coin did indeed land on its edge.'

'What coin?' he said, confused by Marcus' cryptic choice of words.

'Never mind.' replied Marcus, before directing his solemn gaze towards their queen. 'Nathaniel, you need to end this. The young Freylarkin has suffered enough. Indeed, we have all suffered.'

'Agreed.'

Turning to address their queen, he began slowly walking towards Mirielle, Cora and Kirika, who remained standing in the front row of the auditorium's tiered stone seating. He offered Cora a gentle smile, attempting to allay some of the young female's fears. Following his lead, Kirika bent down and extended her hand in front of the Queen, signalling for the young female to take it. Cora quickly accepted the invitation, and together they stepped aside allowing him to face Freylar's ruler alone before the people.

'Mirielle, you have served the people well during your reign, and for that each of us owes you a debt that cannot be repaid. Regretfully, however, it is clear now that the burden of leadership has taken its toll on you over the passes, especially that which has passed most recently. You have guided us safely through many a dark moment, however, it is time now for you to step down. On behalf of the people, I ask that you take a well-deserved break with which to enjoy the remainder of your passes – something that many of us lose sight of.'

He could see from the confusion on the Queen's face that she had expected him to choose his words more aggressively. It was clear to him that Mirielle's defence had been prepared to counter such an approach, and that his alternate approach had disabled the weapons at her disposal. The Queen had no further room left in which to manoeuvre. In light of his audacious public offer of a dignified withdrawal from power, Mirielle had little choice but to accept his proposed exit strategy. Refusing his offer would court a dangerous game of chance, plunging the Freylarkai into civil war. Even if Mirielle eventually won that potential conflict, the devastation caused would be far greater than any Narlakai invasion. The silence in the arena was palpable as everyone regarded their queen with interest, eager to see whether Mirielle would accept his proposal, or instead reject it, plunging the domain into chaos. The eerie calm become uncomfortable as they waited torturously for their queen to make her decision. Eventually, after what felt like an eternity, Mirielle awkwardly climbed over the low wall separating them, her fused arm making the simple task far more challenging than it should have been. Having overcome the obstacle, despite her disability, the Queen walked straight past him towards The Blade Lord. She stood less than a pace from Marcus and held out her good arm, inviting him to accept it.

'I am tired now. Will you come with me?'

TWENTY
Nemesis

It was the first time he had held Aleska's shape for so long. Without a sufficient flesh sacrifice to shore up his new form, maintaining the pretence of the venerable scrier for such length required a tremendous amount of effort on his part. To compound the issue, his symbiotic dark companion was restless again. Despite the promise of Mirielle's emotional torture, the parasite continued to demand more from him. His dark companion rattled against the cage that he had hastily constructed so many passes ago, when first the soulmancer had invaded his body. In hindsight, it had been a mistake imprisoning the Narlakin, which had previously trapped the miserable soulmancer within itself. Had he known of the cruel joke fate had in store for him, he would have rejected The Teacher's alluring offer. Now *he* had taken over the role of jailer. Yet even now, despite the setbacks he had suffered, his lust for questionable new experiences continued to lead him inexorably to his doom. Like a moth, he would always be drawn to the flames, despite the disastrous inevitable consequences.

'Be quiet T'mohr.' he muttered under his breath.

He grew tired of the soulmancer's ceaseless attempts to escape its prison. He wondered if perhaps liberating T'mohr's soul would free him of his dark companion, who might seek alternative accommodation, perhaps even the body of an actual female. On the other hand, there was every chance that the sadistic parasite would worm its way throughout his entire body. Given the chance, T'mohr would likely consume the remainder of his body, of which he currently still maintained control. Over the passes, T'mohr's cage had grown as the parasite relentlessly pushed against its confinement, desperate to escape. On a number of desperate occasions, he had actively sought the parasite's preternatural strength, the price of which had always been the same: relaxing his dark companion's confinement, therefore allowing T'mohr's cage to expand. It was only a matter of time before the soulmancer ultimately broke free of its bonds, at which point there would be no telling how the vile entity would react. Even now, despite its chastisement, T'mohr continued to rage inside him, testing the boundaries of its confinement.

'Be quiet!' he rasped once more, this time failing to even make attempt at mimicking the old scrier's voice.

'Are you OK?' whispered a male Freylarkin sat beside him in the packed auditorium.

He nodded awkwardly in response, deciding it best to remain silent, lest the nosey Freylarkin discover his actual identity.

Doing his best to block out T'mohr's distractions, he turned his attention back towards the centre of the arena. Watching Mirielle squirm whilst those who openly opposed her rule amassed defiantly before the Queen was a delicious sight. He licked his parched lips, taking great please in the fact that he had played a significant role in orchestrating the chaos unfolding before them. He had played Freylar's queen for a fool, whispering in her ear, tricking her into hastening her own inevitable downfall. All it took was the abused trust of one held dear to the Queen. He chided himself for not attempting the strategy sooner. Had he done so, there would have been no need to give into the demands of the parasite festering inside him. His self-flagellation quickly ended, however, as the loathsome Guardian, of whom he had heard much talk, again involved herself in the affairs of others. The idolised light bringer raised her left hand, which appeared to be dripping with blood. Though he had no recollection as to its symbolism, there were clearly those who did as a handful of Freylarkai began descending from the tiered stone seating towards the arena floor. They moved to stand beside The Guardian, swelling the ranks of those who opposed Freylar's queen.

'How wonderful.' he said before releasing a wicked laugh, unable to contain his sociopathic enjoyment of the events taking shape below. 'I revel in the glory of your demise, you bitch!'

The male sat adjacent to him suddenly got up and quietly moved away, whilst the remainder of the audience focused their attention on Freylar's increasingly hysterical queen. It was then that he realised that his carefully constructed veil had begun to slip, courtesy of his own amusement no less. He tried hard to regain control of his body, but when his formerly mutilated pastime – abandoned in the streets outside of the arena – suddenly rose to confront the Queen, it was all he could do to stop himself from howling with ecstatic laughter. His mouth began to salivate uncontrollably and drool started to collect at the corners of his overstretched grin. Even the wicked soulmancer within abated its cage rattling, albeit temporarily, preferring instead to soak up the delicious irony of Freylar's queen dismantling her own rule. All eyes were now firmly fixed on Mirielle, meaning that few around him paid attention to his increasingly odd behaviour. He had lost track of the number of passes he had spent in exile. For so long now, he had pondered what his revenge would look like and how it would take form. At last, playing out on a grand stage before them was his opus, rendered in all its ironic splendour. However, before his ecstasy could reach its anticipated climax, Nathaniel approached the Queen. The meddling Teacher unexpectedly offered Freylar's queen a dignified exit strategy as opposed to the bloody massacre he had planned.

'No!' he shouted abruptly as The Teacher threatened to deny him his long-awaited prize.

He could feel his anger suddenly rising, and with it, his body started to twitch uncontrollably. He could feel the soulmancer's desire for chaos and altercation swelling within him, all the while the mounting pressure from their unfulfilled desires continued to grow exponentially. Mirielle and Nathaniel fixed their gaze upon one another, whilst all those present eagerly awaited their queen's response. Would she accept the olive branch offered by The Teacher, or instead, condemn the Freylarkai to civil war? The promise of elation was almost too much for him to bear; it was palpable, like an overripe fruit fit to burst. The thought of its sweet sticky juice drove him to stupor, intoxicated by the anticipation of the Freylarkai turning on themselves with their queen at the centre of the primal bloodletting. Then, only moments from the climax of his orgasm, Freylar's queen did something that he did not expect. After awkwardly stepping down onto the snow-covered floor of the arena, Mirielle strode past Nathaniel, paying The Teacher little regard. Closing to within a single pace of The Blade Lord, she immediately offered him her hand, which he readily accepted, and together they made their way towards the arena's east gate.

'NO! Order them to fight you bitch!' he cried, leaping from his seat in anger.

Consumed by uncontrollable rage, he unfurled his flesh-coloured wings once more. They tore through the back of Aleska's garment, extending abruptly to reveal their colossal magnificence. His jaw dropped, much lower than should have been physically possible, and from his mouth flopped a thick forked tongue dripping with saliva. The remainder of his fingers fell to the floor, giving way to vicious sharp claws that extended from his raw knuckles, leaving only his thumbs remaining as grim reminders of the hands he once had. He felt his eyes bulge, and with it his peripheral vision expanded enormously, allowing him to bear witness to the host of screaming Freylarkai around him running from his ghastly presence. His body grew rapidly in size, almost doubling, and his muscles expanded, ripping apart his ridiculous attire and leaving naught but a pile of torn fabric around his bulging feet. He retched suddenly, belching forth viscous black liquid that splattered across the stone seating before him. More of the black substance streamed from his eyes and ears as well as running down the inside of his legs, dripping forth from his mutated body's every orifice. The evil substance quickly expanded outwards, slithering rapidly across rock and snow in search of fresh hosts. The delicious screams of those around him filled him with carnal delight, causing him to slide his forked tongue across his elongated teeth, of which there were now two sets.

'Irrelevant!' he rasped, watching with amusement as the black substance contacted with victim after victim, hunting down those unable to escape beyond the press of the fleeing crowd.

The viscous black liquid slid up their legs and violated their bodies, riding up through their lower cracks.

'Join me, my puppets!'

One by one, the evil liquid conscripted the panicking civilians who were unable to escape, turning them to his cause until he had a shambling flock at his command. Each had obsidian eyes, similar to his own, and all stood motionless ready to act on his whim.

'Release them!' he hissed, pointing his left claw towards the dumbfounded Freylarkai on the arena floor.

Without hesitation, his puppet army launched itself towards the centre of the arena. Following suit, he leapt high into the air with his muscular legs, before using his wings to glide swiftly towards his prey. As his shadow swept over both Mirielle and Marcus, he gathered in his colossal wings, quickly dropping to the arena floor with a loud thump. Drawing back his right arm, he then thrust it forwards towards the Queen. His razor-sharp claws elongated rapidly, like long spears extending from his swollen knuckles. The claws sped towards Mirielle, thirsting for their prey. Yet again his prize was denied, as another intercepted their flight, taking the devastating hit intended for Freylar's queen.

She watched in horror as the *thing* that was Aleska leapt into the air, its giant wingspan casting an ominous shadow across the arena. The civilian Freylarkai who had stood close by the aberration – screaming at first, though now rendered mute – promptly followed suit. They leapt towards the centre of the arena, some using their wraith wings to slow their descent whilst others chose to crash hard into the ground, cratering upon impact, twisting limbs and snapping necks. The brutalised civilians immediately righted themselves, seemingly unfazed by their horrible injuries, and began shambling towards her guards. Their eyes were like black orbs, similar to those of the abhorrent shaper who had violated her in her chamber.

'He is here, that *thing* is Krashnar!' she screamed as the grotesquely mutilated shaper landed beside them, impacting hard upon the arena floor.

She tried to run, but in her blind panic she slipped on the snow-covered floor, falling awkwardly to the ground. She scrambled to her feet only to watch in horror as the beast's claws suddenly elongated, speeding towards her, intent on impaling her flesh. She screamed, expecting no less than the pain of her body being impaled by the savage attack, but instead, it was Marcus who suffered the blow in her stead, selflessly placing himself between her and the abhorrent shaper.

'NO!!!!' she cried, watching in dismay as the mutant's claws speared through Marcus' body, causing him to judder violently from the impact.

Irritated by The Blade Lord, who had successfully blocked its attack, the hulking mass retracted it claws and stepped forwards, before batting Marcus aside, who had dropped to his knees defenceless. The Blade Lord's ruined body rolled five or six paces across the snow towards the northern edge of the arena overlooking the vale blow.

'You bastard!' she screamed, rising to stand before the beast whilst clutching her fused arm.

Her eyes burned white hot with fury as she channelled her anger into the ground. Shards of rock akin to stalagmites grew from the floor of the arena around the shaper, savagely impaling its torso from every conceivable angle. Trapped in place, Krashnar howled in pain whilst black ichor gushed from his wounds spilling across the rock piercing his mutilated body. The evil-looking substance began rapidly eating through the rock restraining the shaper. It released a foul acrid stench into the air as it quickly eroded the beast's shackles.

'You are weak, Mirielle!' hissed Krashnar whilst the rock piercing his deformed body continued to smoulder. 'And to think, it required this much effort to end you.'

'You shit! I should have had you released!' she screamed, unable to keep her emotions in check. 'Exile was a kindness I should never have afforded you!'

'A kindness! You delusional bitch. You have learned nothing from your transgressions. And now you are alone, with no one to stand by your side – that is the ugly truth of your *kindness*!' he spat, before flashing his ugly teeth as he raked his calloused tongue across them.

She looked past the vile creature and saw Nathaniel and the others fighting tirelessly against the shaper's shambling hoard. Despite their wounds and the relentless cuts landed by those fighting against them, the civilian Freylarkai, held under Krashnar's sway, continued to press their assault. Their possessed bodies were seemingly immune to any form of injury or pain, allowing them to shrug off the damage inflicted upon them.

'They will not help you, even if they could. You have lost their respect. You are no longer Freylar's queen.'

She glared angrily at the wretched shaper, using her ability once more to shore up the stalagmite piercing the front of the mutant's torso. Krashnar howled again in pain as the rock lanced through his body, splitting bone and organs before exiting via his back. Raising his clawed fists high above his head, he brought them down hard upon the smouldering rock, splintering it into countless shards that fell to the ground. He hissed menacingly at her as he pried his body from the stone entrapment. Once free of the snare, the hideous mutant commenced a thunderous charge towards her.

'RAYNA!' she screamed whilst running towards the fighting, forcing Krashnar to correct his charge.

She caught the light bringer's eye, who had just knocked back one of the shaper's unfeeling puppets.

'Help me!' she cried, desperate for The Guardian's aid.

The Guardian immediately sprinted towards her. Her regal attire and fused limb hindered her flight as she ran headlong towards the light bringer. She could feel the shaper's hulking mass bearing down upon her whilst she tried desperately to evade his grasp. Sensing Krashnar was about to strike, she dived forwards. Expecting to crash hard into the ground, she was met by Rayna's embrace instead. As they collided with one another, The Guardian held out her left blade in a seemingly futile attempt to parry the creature's attack.

Before the screams could pass her lips, they appeared behind the hulking beast as though it had passed straight through them. She turned around and saw The Guardian's blade slice through the rear of the creature's right arm, severing the limb cleanly, which fell to the floor showering the snow with more of the evil black ichor.

'Leave!' cried Rayna, abruptly pushing her aside. 'This one's mine – I have unfinished business with this wretch!'

The thing standing before her was no longer the shaper that had violated her. In his place was something far worse: an abhorrent aberration, a spawn of the darkness that had once touched her soul. She pitied the ill-fated shaper for what he had ultimately become. If not for the kindness and friendship of others, she too would have been destined for such an end. Krashnar, however, had no one to guide him towards the light – salvation was now beyond the twisted shaper's reach. The evil darkness festering within him had consumed the shaper entirely now, rendering him little more than a puppet. Acknowledging their true nature, she offered her Dawnstone falchions a momentary glance. How ironic she mused, that such evil weapons be used to release their maker.

She rolled towards the creature, before executing a rising cut towards her opponent. The mutated shaper leapt backwards, evading her cut, then lunged forwards looking to strike her down with his left claw. She stepped right, evading the blow, and delivered a slice to the creatures left flank, using Shadow Caster to trace a line of black ichor across the side of the mutant's torso. Krashnar swept his overextended arm towards her, again seeking to knock her down. She dived over the sweeping limb, quickly regained her footing and drove the Ardent Blade deep into the thing's torso. Krashnar brought his right knee up, intending to catch her flush under the chin. She read the move well, using the blade's Waystone to evade the attack and counter with one of her own. Unable to fathom how the thing remained standing, she tried to pull the falchion from the creature's back. The Ardent Blade remained steadfast, buried deep within the beast's torso. The enraged shaper spread his colossal wings, this time catching her as originally intended. The force of the impact sent her tumbling backwards through the snow dazed by the jarring blow. Krashnar spun around before launching his claws towards her, expectantly looking to spear his second victim of the cycle. She tried desperately to evade the attack but one of the creature's claws found its mark, tearing through the flesh of her right shoulder. She cried out in pain before involuntarily releasing her grip on Shadow Caster as her right arm went numb. The hulking creature stepped towards her, forcing her down onto her back and spearing her to the cold floor of the arena.

'Pathetic!' rasped the abhorrent wretch, 'Again you disappoint me.'

The mutant beast moved closer, shortening the length of his claw as he drew nearer. The creature's shadow swept across her body, instilling a sense of dread within her, reminding her of the time Krashnar had last paid her a visit. Unable to move, the twisted shaper savoured his prize. Krashnar bent down slowly, flopping his forked tongue onto her right leg, before dragging it up the length of her body. Fear clawed at her with its familiar paralysing grasp, threatening to send her back to the abyss, but this time without Alarielle's presence to tether her to reality. Thoughts of her previous life began to assault her mind once more, reminding her of the atrocities she had previously committed.

'No!' she cried, 'I will not go back there!'

Using her left arm, she grabbed hold of the rough salivating tongue, wrapped it around her wrist and pulled the creature's head towards her. The abhorrent creature released a hideous laugh, finding sadistic pleasure in her seemingly futile defiance. She closed her eyes, then, channelling her light energy, she unleashed a massive burst of searing light that exploded out of her body setting the creature instantly ablaze. Krashnar recoiled in pain, ripping his claw from her ruined shoulder before dropping to the ground attempting to douse the flames in the snow. The aberration rolled around, desperately trying to extinguish that which seared its flesh. She scrambled to her feet and quickly recovered Shadow Caster, before driving the evil blade into the creature's neck using her good arm. Krashnar howled in pain once more whilst trying to bat her aside with his remaining arm. Releasing her grip on the weapon, she tumbled away, narrowly avoiding the desperate attack. Lunging forwards, she wrapped her fingers around the hilt of the sunken blade once more, putting her body weight into the thrust. Shadow Caster sank deeper into the shaper's neck, severing nerves and rendering the creature's remaining arm inoperable. Flames continued to lick at Krashnar's mutated body, causing the black liquid dripping from his wounds to fizzle and pop. She stepped back, leaving the evil blade to do its thing and directed another searing bolt of light into the creature's smouldering corpse. The shaper let out an awful scream whilst its flesh tightened and split, before turning black and withered, unable to cope with the searing temperature of the flames and the Dawnstone blade desiccating it. The mutant shaper's body went into spasm, eventually flopping onto its back, forcing the Ardent Blade through the centre of the charred cadaver.

The vicious flames eventually receded, allowing Shadow Caster to complete its gruesome task. However, before the Dawnstone blade could trap yet another victim, a soul – unlike any other she had previously borne witness to – slowly emerged from the burnt flesh. With no small amount of effort, a bony skeletal figure sprouting a colossal set of wings defiantly wrenched itself free of the charred cadaver. The spectre wore a tattered cloak riddled with holes, allowing her to regard its poorly concealed emaciated body. It struggled to tear itself free from the smouldering pile of burnt flesh, fighting desperately against the pull of the Narlakin trapped within the Dawnstone blade.

'Who are you?' she said, pushing away the hair matted to her face with blood and sweat.

The apparition paid her no regard. Eventually working itself free of its bonds, the unusual soul sped towards the tail of the fleeing crowd still pushing its way through the west gate. It promptly disappeared into the throng of panicked Freylarkai who were desperately fleeing the arena. Having lost the opportunity to question the spectre further, she retrieved her blades from the remains of the mutant shaper's corpse before focusing her attention on Krashnar's puppets. The released shaper's wretched offspring continued to fight tirelessly, their numbers holding as they spread their infection to those opponents of weaker prowess.

'Blades, protect and guide the civilians to safety. Natalya, hold back what you can. The rest of you, to arms!' he cried, paying little heed to the hulking creature bearing down on the Queen.

The broken reanimated bodies of those propelled from the auditorium's stone seating advanced towards them, their movement little more than fits and starts, but enough to pose a threat. Those puppets with sufficient intelligence to avert self-injury had already closed on the Queen's guards, vomiting black liquid at their quarry in an attempt to upgrade their hosts. Together with Lothnar, Nathanar and

Thandor, he charged the infected civilians currently assaulting the house guards, leaving Rayna, Darlia and the farmstead lot to aid Natalya against the deformed shamblers.

'Cut them down, quickly, lest their ranks bear armour and weapons!' cried Thandor who moved to engage the closest infected.

Nathanar's double-handed sword cut through several of the possessed Freylarkai with ease, cleaving them in two. Yet even absent legs, the severed torsos continued to drag themselves around through the snow, using their arms to propel them. His own efforts to drive back the invaders were equally ineffective; the infected cared little for the absence of limbs, finding creative ways to push themselves along the ground. Even Lothnar's precision headshots bore little fruit, the Paladin's knives seemingly having no effect on the possessed.

'Nathaniel, this is hopeless!' cried Lothnar, 'They feel nothing!'

'Then we must find another way!' he said watching in horror as the fallen corpses vomited black liquid upon the snow, which slithered away in search of more susceptible hosts.

'Stay away from the ichor!' cried Thandor, moving swiftly to evade contact with the vile substance gliding across the snow-covered floor of the arena.

'Use the torches!' he cried, directing their gaze towards those that still burned, fixed to the inner walls of the arena. 'Burn them – it is the only way!'

Light on their feet, both Lothnar and Thandor sprinted towards the burning torches, leaving himself, Nathanar and the remaining house guards to hold the line against the unfeeling puppets. From the corner of his eye, he saw Rayna sprinting away from the fighting; the light bringer ran towards Mirielle, seemingly attempting to lend aid to Freylar's queen.

'Should we assist?' asked Nathanar whilst cleaving another of the possessed in two.

'No, we must buy time to allow The Blades to evacuate the civilians. Rayna will deal with whatever that *thing* is.'

Nathanar nodded in agreement before continuing his fruitless massacre. More of the puppets fell beneath their blades, but those felled were quickly replaced by armoured kin no longer in control of their bodies.

'Nathaniel, there must be a way to save them.' cried Nathanar, whose blade now clashed against metal as opposed to linen and flesh.

'Only release will save them now brother!'

'May they find better fortunes in the Everlife.' replied the Paladin tirelessly wielding his weapon, landing cut after cut against the enemy.

'Nathaniel!' cried Lothnar running headlong towards him, before handing him a burning torch.

'Keep it brother. Our weapons are more effective than your own. Nathanar and I will clear a path. You and Thandor send them to the Everlife.'

'Agreed.'

They pushed forwards with renewed purpose, setting alight all those who fell in their wake, ensuring that the evil liquid had nowhere to turn by burning the flammable black ichor, casting it into oblivion. The viscous liquid crackled and fizzed releasing an acrid stench, made more prominent by the crisp winter air. Meanwhile, behind them, the others struggled to contain the infected civilians. Natalya did her best to corral the shamblers using the power of her mind, though it was inevitable that the Valkyrie would tire. Darlia and the farmstead lot worked hard to drive the infected Freylarkai back; they attempted to ring-fence the enemy, and in doing so allow Natalya to constrict them with reduced effort.

'The torches will not last.' cried Thandor who moved with impressive speed, burning all traces of the black liquid in his path.

'Nathaniel, use this!' cried Rayna, handing off one of her Dawnstone blades as she tore past him, seeking to aid Natalya and the others.

He grasped the familiar weapon, knowing full well what its insatiable thirst would seek from its victims. He drove Shadow Caster into the neck of the nearest infected Freylarkin, dropping his mundane weapon to free up his other hand, which he clamped over his opponent's mouth. The ichor within tried to make its escape through the victim's remaining orifices, but the ravenous blade's renewed thirst drew the liquid back in, devouring it in a futile attempt to sate its endless appetite. His opponent twisted and withered before him, the ugly sight reminding him of a memory best left forgotten.

'Fall back and close your eyes!' she cried, drawing upon the same strength that she had used to end the mutated shaper's miserable existence. Channelling her light energy once more, she released a searing white-hot blast into the pack constricted by Natalya's mind. The horrid puppets instantly burst into flames, their close proximity to one another causing the blaze to spread rapidly, giving rise to a conflagration that quickly consumed the reanimated corpses. Exhausted, Natalya released her hold on the wretches allowing the burning cadavers to stumble forwards a few paces before crumpling to the ground. More of the acrid stench filled the air, causing their eyes to water. All around them, the fallen puppets burned ferociously. Lothnar and Thandor made short work of the few still remaining, aided by Ralnor who had since taken up a torch in order to assist them. The once glorious arena was now a demonic graveyard, marred by the smouldering remains of things that never should have been, with a singular notable exception – The Blade Lord. Quickly sheathing the Ardent Blade, she ran towards Marcus' ruined body laid out on the floor by the northern edge of the arena.

'Nathaniel, you must help him!'

TWENTY ONE
Genesis

'Please, you must help him.' sobbed Mirielle uncontrollably, who knelt down in the snow gently cradling Marcus' head with her good arm.

He knelt beside Rayna and Mirielle, before gently rolling The Blade Lord onto his back so that he could better inspect the damage to Marcus' torso. Blood seeped through the puncture holes in Marcus' armour, many of which were large enough for him to press his fingers in to. The dark red liquid pooled beneath The Blade Lord, who faded in and out of consciousness, despite the snow's best efforts to absorb the claret lifeblood. Marcus' wounds were significant, a match for even his skill.

'Marcus, your wounds are grievous.'

'I know.' whispered The Blade Lord, short of breath, before using the last of his strength to lay a reassuring hand upon his own.

'I shall do what I can.'

'No...save your strength old friend.'

'Marcus, even with my assistance, you may not survive this.'

'It is time.' croaked Marcus, coughing blood from his mouth.

'But there is a chance that you can still lead the life that you seek!'

'No. She cannot love...another...even me.'

'What do you mean?' he said, looking to Mirielle for answers. 'Is this true? Can you not find it in your heart to forget about notions of power, or the *thing* above our head, and instead enjoy the warmth of another to whom you mean everything?'

Tears collected along the bottom of Mirielle's pupil-less eyes, betraying her cold vacant stare.

'I am tired.' said Marcus, whose eyes rolled back in his head.

'Stay with us brother – let me help you.' he implored.

'No…this needs…to end. Look to the futu…'

Lacking the strength to finish his words, Marcus' body went limp, signalling The Blade Lord's release.

There was a long period of silence following The Blade Lord's passing. Lothnar, Darlia, Nathanar, Thandor and Natalya all gathered round the fallen hero, each paying their respects. Kirika also wandered over, eager to say farewell to The Blades' much respected lord commander. The vindicated scrier held Cora's hand tightly, the young female standing close to Fate Weaver's side. There was no malice or animosity between Kirika and Mirielle. Instead, a moment of quiet reflection was shared, each offering silent tribute to one who had stood as a legend beside them.

'I did not love him, but it was not through choice Nathaniel.' said Mirielle quietly, finally ending the long period of silence.

'What *was* the reason?' he asked, watching as a tear rolled down the Queen's cheek.

'As Freylar's queen, I was duty-bound to protect the people, which drove me to the pursuit of knowledge – a thing Darlia understands all too well. Knowledge is power; it enables us to protect ourselves, and those who we love. However, the pursuit of knowledge is an ugly thing, causing many who seek it to perform unspeakable acts. My sin was my enhanced sight, more specifically, that which I sacrificed in order to make the change permanent. At the time, I had not believed it to be of importance given my lofty position and the commitment demanded of it.'

'What did you sacrifice?' he asked, absentmindedly casting his gaze back towards his fallen brother.

'It was love, Nathaniel…I sacrificed the ability to love.'

'Then I pity you. Not for your loss – we have all lost – but instead for that which you will never know.'

He looked up, turning to Kirika, Darlia and Rayna, offering them each a tearful smile. The loss of his family had been devastating, but Marcus' final words told the truth of it. All that mattered to him now was the future – one that was not preordained.

'I pity myself – I do not need yours.'

Mirielle gently laid Marcus' head upon the snow before righting herself. She cradled her fused arm and gazed up at the murky wintery sky, offering the entity above them a mournful stare.

'I tried my best to protect the people, but there is no longer anything here for me. Marcus and Aleska have gone, and those who I sought to protect have since turned their backs on me.'

She reached for the intricate wreath-like crown upon her head, which now exuded delicate silver thorns that grew upwards from its rear. She pulled the symbol of her regal status slowly from her head, allowing it to fall to the ground by her feet. The crown made a dull thump as it landed on the ground, half burying itself in the fresh snow that still fell from the murky sky.

'Take it. I wish to rid myself of its burden. Perhaps its next wearer will have better luck.'

'There will not be one.' he said, rising to meet her vacant gaze. 'The leadership we require cannot originate from a single individual – that is the ruling council's raison d'être. My actions are attributed to the sole purpose of restoring the notion that you lost sight of.'

'A noble idea, but democracy has its own inherent flaws. Whilst you squabble amongst yourselves, that *thing* up there will continue to have its way with us.'

'That is where you and I differ. I put stock in the worth of others, and in the belief that many can work together towards a common cause, setting aside their differences for the benefit of the greater good – you do not.'

'An admirable notion, Nathaniel, one that is easily undone by self-interest.'

'I fear that you will always be destined to wander alone, taking solace in your own company.'

'And I fear that you are right.' she replied, before taking her leave.

'Where will you go?' he asked, as Mirielle walked slowly towards the arena's east gate.

'Scrier's Post now stands empty. I will ride out the winter there. Aleska would have left the sanctuary well stocked. Come spring, I will move on. As to where, I cannot say – perhaps I will let fate decide.'

'Your self-imposed sentence sounds much like exile.'

'The irony is not lost on me.'

'Thank you all for coming.' she said, sweeping her gaze slowly across all those present, offering each of them a warm smile. 'I appreciate that this meeting comes at short notice, however, the people desperately need leadership and it falls to us to decide now what that looks like going forwards.'

Her decision to hold the emergency council meeting beneath the arena seemed appropriate given their loss. Marcus had often tabled discussions of a more sensitive nature within the subterranean chamber, away from the prying eyes and wagging tongues of their gossiping kin. In light of the recent hardships endured by the Freylarkai, they needed to act quickly to restore some sense of structure and stability in order to quell the understandable concerns of the people.

'Now that we are all gathered, I would like to propose that Rayna assumes the title of Blade Lord.' said Lothnar unexpectedly, abruptly commencing their meeting.

'Well said.' proclaimed Nathanar, bringing his right fist down hard upon the thick wooden oval table around which they all sat.

'Are you looking to ease your defeat in the arena?' asked Thandor with a wry grin.

'The Guardian commands the respect of The Blades, holds favour with the Knights Thranis, has good standing amongst the people and can now conjure fire! Furthermore, her appointment *would* ease my bruised ego.' he said, returning Thandor's smile. 'Given that Nathaniel will *never* accept the charge, I vote Rayna in his stead.'

'As do I.' said Thandor, quickly supporting Lothnar's proposal.

'I admire your enthusiasm.' she said, offering the three of them a warm smile. 'Is there anyone else who would like to speak on the matter, or are you all in agreement?'

There was a respectful pause in their discussion, allowing ample chance for those present to give voice to any concerns with the suggested appointment in addition to alternative proposals, yet none came. After allowing sufficient time to pass, she worked her way around the large oval table canvassing each vote in turn, discerning those present to be unanimously in favour of the Paladin's proposition.

'Your proposal, Lothnar, clearly has the overwhelming support of all those present, however, there are two points that we must consider: the first being Rayna's own thoughts on the appointment.' she said, turning to the famed light bringer. 'What are your thoughts, Rayna? Will you lead The Blades into the future?'

'I do not seek the title of Blade Lord, nor do I want it.' replied Rayna, garnering the immediate attention of all those present.

'Go on.' she said, entirely unsurprised, by now familiar with the light bringer's unconventional ways.

'I am not Marcus, nor would I make attempt to replace him. He was the best of us, loyal to a fault. The title of Blade Lord should remain forever his. Besides, the people have already given me a title, one that I have come to reluctantly accept – I have no desire to collect any more.'

She could sense the acceptance of Rayna's words amongst all those present. Marcus had done much to restore honour to the once tainted title, and it seemed inappropriate now to pass on his achievements.

'Well said, however, will you *lead* The Blades into the future, Guardian?'

'Very well, yes, but I would like this one to be my captain.' said Rayna, pointing her left index finger towards

Nathanar, offering the surprised Paladin a playful wink. 'I fear that Natalya's feminine wiles have led this one astray – he needs discipline.'

'Then it is done!' proclaimed Lothnar, striking his fist energetically upon the table, reminding her of the passion exuberated by Ragnar, former Captain of The Blades.

There was a loud cheer from all those present, affirming their approval of The Guardian's appointment. Enthusiastic chatter and merriment quickly ensued as they discussed the new appointments and congratulated those deserving of them. She was about to bring their discussions back to the table when suddenly Darlia gave voice, assisting her in the matter.

'If I could please have your attention, there was a second point that my sister wished to discuss concerning the recent decision – we should hear her thoughts.'

'Agreed.' said Nathaniel, aiding Darlia to quiet the chamber once more.

'Thank you both.' she said, returning to the matter. 'We cannot have a Blade Adept leading The Blades. In light of her new position and her tireless efforts to protect the domain, I propose that Rayna be promoted to the rank of Valkyrie, effective immediately.'

'I agree.' said Natalya, eager to usher in the appointment of a new Valkyrie.

'As do I.' said Lothnar, followed shortly by Thandor and the others, all echoing his thoughts.

'Good.' said Nathaniel, who rose from his seat and began pacing around the subterranean chamber. 'As each of you know, I have – for the most part at least – been the driving force directing us all to *this* very moment. Whilst I do not wish to be a part of whatever ruling body forms here this cycle, nevertheless, I do have strong views as to who should represent Freylar's new ruling council. If you would kindly all indulge me, I would therefore like to propose a number of candidates for the task.'

'Who do you have in mind?' she asked, keen to learn of The Teacher's thoughts.

'Yourself foremost, and I propose that you continue to chair these meetings. Lothnar--'

'Nathaniel, I am not one for councils and matters of state.' said the Paladin, vehemently interjecting.

'*You* are our eyes! When your emotions do not cloud your judgement, you are capable of keen logical analysis and decision making – I can think of very few more deserving of a place on the council.'

'You give me too much credit Nathaniel.'

'Come home Lothnar. Spend time with your kin. Freylar has been ravaged by war and dissention; the domain needs to heal and the council will look to you for guidance in this. You have spent countless passes scouting the way ahead for The Blades. Now it is time for you to find a new path for the people.'

Lothnar considered Nathaniel's words carefully. There was a time when such a thing was unthinkable, when both had harboured a deep-seated hatred towards one another. Indeed, she recalled the Paladin's cutting words when Nathaniel had introduced Rayna to him.

"*That...body thief dishonours your daughter's memory Nathaniel!*"

Even Marcus had been unable to mend the rift between them. Yet so much had happened since then, and during that time their common enemy had inadvertently brought them closer, reaffirming their bonds of brotherhood. Their goals were now aligned. Yet despite this changed state of affairs, it remained to be seen whether Lothnar would give up his nomadic ways for the betterment of the people as proposed by The Teacher.

'I have never taken instruction from you Nathaniel – perhaps now is the time to start.'

'You speak your mind brother and you challenge those who would blindly take the path laid out before them – both are qualities that I admire. I look to you now to keep this council honest and guide its way.' said Nathaniel approaching the Paladin with his hand outstretched.

'I will see it done brother!' replied Lothnar earnestly, who rose from his seat to grasp Nathaniel's hand in a firm shake.

'Good. Moving on then, I also propose that Thandor takes a seat on the council, in addition to two others of the council's own choosing.'

The aloof Paladin barely reacted to The Teacher's recommendation. As always, the master duellist maintained his relaxed demeanour. Appointing Thandor made sense. The Paladin's sharp mind and ability to assess the larger picture would be a welcomed asset to any ruling body. It was clear that The Teacher had given his proposal a great deal of thought prior to making his intentions known.

'Why five members?' she asked, curious as to the number's significance.

'Too many and the council will fracture through inevitable division. However, with too few we run the risk of history repeating itself.' said Nathaniel before retaking his seat. 'The council should be formed from those with differing perspectives. Furthermore, its members must have the courage to give voice to their concerns whilst accepting those of others, in order to reach valued compromise.'

'Agreed.' said Natalya, nodding in favour of The Teacher's wise counsel.

'And what of yourself, Natalya? You are not one to sit idly by without airing your thoughts.' she said, extending an invitation to the Valkyrie.

'No.' replied Natalya, shaking her head. 'There should be no further appointments from our rank; the people need to be better represented in such matters. Besides, my place is beside Nathanar and Rayna – someone needs to ensure that the bringer of fire gets out of bed before noon.'

There was a moment of shared joviality at Rayna's expense, before her sister unexpectedly rose from her seat promptly commanding their attention.

'You would recommend yourself, sister?' she said, intrigued by the notion.

'No. I must first atone for my actions before being eligible for such a position. However, I would like to offer counsel in this instance, if permitted.'

'Go on.' said Lothnar, keen to learn of her sister's thoughts on the matter.

'Gaelin and Larissa. Both represent the working classes and both will provide a much-valued perspective, one that I feel would strongly benefit the council in its decision making.'

'Interesting.' said Thandor, at last stirring from his casual position at the table. 'I approve. Larissa is no shrinking violet and Gaelin has demonstrated considerable resolve, leading his people here to fight for their beliefs. In my opinion both would be excellent appointments.'

'I agree.' she said, quickly seeing the merit in her sister's unconventional proposal.

'As do I.' said Lothnar, 'Both will ground this council, ensuring that it does not stray from its raison d'être.'

'Fine appointments, both!' said Nathaniel, who gave Darlia a warm smile. 'Then, if there are no objections, I would see this council ratified so that I can resume training in the arena.'

'You would resume your training of the Aspirants and Novices?' she asked, reassured by The Teacher's words.

'Indeed. The Order has suffered badly due to the recent conflict. However, embers still burn within its hearth, begging to be stoked – I am keen to see them ignite once more.'

'Very well. Who here objects to any or all of the proposals that we have discussed here this cycle?'

She swept her gaze across the oval table once more, searching for signs of doubt within the eyes of all those present, yet she could discern none.

'Then I ask that you raise your hand now if you are in favour of these proposals.'

All those present raised a hand in perfect unison, giving their approval to the reformed council. It lifted her soul to see so many unique personalities working together towards a common goal: the betterment of their kin. With the reformed council's guidance, she felt assured that the Freylarkai would recover from the recent conflict, rising again to stand tall in the face of fresh challenges that would inevitably confront them. Pleased with the outcome they had achieved, she too raised her hand, before hammering her fist down hard upon the thick wooden table.

'It is done. I will speak with Gaelin and Larissa, offering them both a position on this council.'

'Excellent. Then, if there is no further business requiring my involvement, I shall return to what remains of my arena. There is a foul stench which yet lingers there – I would see it removed.' said Nathaniel, rising from his chair once more.

'We will join you.' said Rayna, tipping her head towards both Nathanar and Natalya.

'May I also accompany you?' asked Darlia, who continued to stand.

'Of course. I am in need of good archers to instruct the Aspirants.'

It warmed her seeing her sister smile again, having now found a place amongst their kin who had once shunned her for overreaching. In time, she hoped that the dark events that had plagued the people would recede from their minds, fading into distant memory, or perhaps becoming legend. The Freylarkai had endured their share of conflict. Now was the time for something better.

'Do you not wish to involve yourselves in the arrangements for Marcus' pyre?' she said, not wishing to deny Nathaniel the opportunity to shape The Blade Lord's parting ceremony.

'Not necessary; such things are now in good hands.' replied The Teacher before taking his leave with Rayna and the others.

'Thank you for your help in the arena.' said Nathaniel, who sat down in the rocking chair opposite her.

'You're welcome, though I suspect it will be some time before it returns to its former splendour.'

'Yes, but it is a start at least, and an important step. Seeing things return to normal will help to reassure the people. It is critical that their routines are not disrupted, therefore I would see The Blades resume their training as soon as possible.'

'As I would have you do it.'

Nathaniel smiled, no doubt content that they were of the same opinion.

'How do you feel about your new position, now that you have had a moment to reflect upon it?'

'I am trying not to let it go to my head; I do not wish to let the appointment change me. However, I am now charged with the responsibility of protecting the vale, a duty that weighs heavily upon me.'

'As it should, lest the person charged with such fail to appreciate its true responsibility.'

'True. However, I fear that Natalya will no longer have need to stir me from slumber.' she said whilst easing into her chair, removing her feet from the cold floor.

'Then she will need to find a new job.' replied Nathaniel with a wry grin. 'In light of the Order's reduced numbers, it may be prudent to prioritise the training of more archers.'

'The Tri-Spires *are* easily defended at range, but the forest is not – I shall give it some thought.'

'Whatever you decide, know that my faith in you will never be misplaced.'

'Now it is me to whom you give too much credit.' she said as she ran her fingers through the dust gathered on top of the pile of books closest to her.

'Do you know *why* those books still linger?' asked Nathaniel curiously.

'Because you're messy?'

'No.' replied The Teacher, laughing heartily. 'Because they remind me of my wife.'

'And do I still remind you of your daughter?' she asked, immediately chiding herself for not properly considering her words before allowing them to escape her lips. 'Sorry, that was insensitive of me.'

'No… You speak the truth of it, as is your way, a disposition that I admire. Sadly, however, I am ashamed of the answer to your question.'

Without warning, Nathaniel leapt from his chair and began immediately tidying the piles of books around them. He placed them back onto their shelves or threw them into the trunks from which they had spilled.

'What are you doing?' she asked, her eyes widening as she watched Nathaniel work fervently, like one possessed by a singular purpose. 'It's late – surely that can wait?'

'No, it cannot. I have let my past weigh heavily upon me for too long now – it is time that I moved on.'

'What do you mean?'

'When Marcus left us, his parting words told me to look to the future – he was right. I will remember both my wife and daughter for as long as I am able, but it is time now that I escaped the shadow of their release. For too long I have clung to its familiar embrace, fearing the light of discovery and what it might bring.'

'I'm glad.' she said with a beaming smile. 'It makes me happy to see you this…animated!'

'Rayna, you are my future now.'

Allowing the books to fall from his grasp, Nathaniel held his arms outstretched towards her, insisting that she take his hands – which she did.

'What *is* up with you?' she asked as he pulled her vigorously from the rocking chair, almost sending it careening backwards to the floor. 'Nathaniel, are you feeling OK?'

'I should have done this sooner – one who instructs is not necessarily the quickest of study.' he said, followed with a playful smile.

'I don't understand, but do not let my confusion spoil this moment.'

'Rayna, *you* are the reason for this moment. I...'

'What is it?' she asked, keen to discern the cause of The Teacher's new found happiness.

'I would like... I... I would have you call me father, and I you daughter – if you would allow it, of course.'

'Wha... You wish to adopt me as your daughter?'

'Very much so! Provided you are willing.'

'I... Yes.' she stammered, unable to hold back the wave of emotion that abruptly assaulted her, causing tears to stream from her eyes.

The Teacher – his own eyes full of emotion – pulled her close, embracing her tightly. Together they stood quietly enjoying the warmth of each other's embrace in their shared moment of happiness, anxious about their future yet welcoming it with open arms. Irrespective of her thoughts towards The Deceiver and its selfish reason for bringing her to Freylar, despite furthering its own agenda the alien entity had given her life meaning. The waif known as Callum – who she had once been – was now little more than a stain on her soul, one that would continue to fade in time. The Freylarkai had accepted her as one of their own, even appointing her as The Guardian of their domain. Yet these achievements paled in comparison when measured against the one gifted to her by Nathaniel: the promise of a family – an experience unknown to her, yet one that she desired with all her heart.

EPILOGUE

The welcome return of spring swept across the domain, bringing with it the verdant foliage that typically covered the vale in the absence of winter. The Sky-Skitters returned to their nests amidst the thick canopy that protected the forest dwellings, announcing their presence with their familiar chorus that echoed through the forest. The sound of fauna scrabbling through the woodland also returned, signalling an end to the prolonged winter, which had long overstayed its welcome with its harsh caress. Not all the Freylarkai survived the winter's unforgiving embrace, mainly those of a more venerable status who had struggled due to lack of heat and nourishment. However, despite the arduous climate, the Freylarkai made it through the winter, with the promise of a fresh start now upon them.

Thoughts quickly turned to rebuilding that which had been lost during the ravages of war. In particular, vigorous recruitment was encouraged to help bolster The Blades' eroded ranks. In addition to strengthening the Order, the people worked the fields with renewed enthusiasm, commencing preparations early, ready for the following harvest. The outlying communities no longer feared the Louperdu; both scriers and Blades vigilantly watched over the farmsteads, working together for the greater good of the people. In order to facilitate the innovative endeavour, The Guardian garrisoned the Blade Adepts amongst the outlying communities. There, they trained alongside their senior Masters and Mistresses, who also took up residence. This radical shakeup of the Order's deployment allowed those already experienced in melee to develop their skill with a bow, away from the confines and artificial training facilities of the arena. The unorthodox strategy allowed the Adepts and Novices to train under Nathaniel's watchful eye without the distraction of their seniors' spirited quips. Furthermore, seeing The Blades carry out their duties amongst the people reassured the Freylarkai, encouraging many of the young to enlist in the Order, inspired by tales of The Guardian's heroics and those of her allies. In addition, the presence of scriers employing their second sight in a clearly defined role helped to erode the stigma associated with the ability. It was a busy time for the people, now with their minds firmly set to task, an endeavour she herself continued to aid in.

Advancing silently through the forest, she could feel the warmth of the sun on her cowl as its rays speared down through the gaps in the canopy above. It felt good to bathe in the light once more, having endured the prolonged chill of winter for so long. Moving with purpose, she glided swiftly along her intended path, taking care to minimise the sound of her approach. Having gone to great lengths to learn of her quarry's whereabouts, failure now was out of the question. The beating of her heart quickened as she neared her destination, one that had eluded her sight for so long. Breathing in deeply, down into the pit of her stomach, she tried hard to slow the thumping behind her breast, fearing that the ferocious sound of its beating would betray her presence. As she continued to advance towards her target, the dwelling in her mind's eye took shape before her, slowly revealing itself nestled within the woodland ahead. There she would find them, each in a drunken stupor, as was their unwavering routine. When finally she draw near to the dwelling's entrance, she lingered for a moment, ensuring that there was no mistake in her intent.

Satisfied that she had indeed located her quarry, she grasped the dwelling's door handle firmly with her left hand, forcing the poorly constructed lock to break within her vice-like grip. It splintered into tiny pieces, allowing its host to swing open revealing a gloomy room beyond. Embracing the darkness, she promptly entered the dwelling. Her keen eyes quickly picked out that which she sought; laying asleep, each on separate beds, were three Freylarkin, all sparsely clothed and reeking with the stench of drink. Another room connected to the main chamber, from which appeared a startled young female clothed in a grubby linen dress. The alarmed Freylarkin pressed a finger to her lips then directed her gaze towards one of the drunken males.

'Leave this place.' she whispered as one of the males stirred, no doubt drawn from their slumber by the sound of her forced entrance. 'Go, now!'

'I cannot.' replied the female.

'Yes, you *can*!'

'They *will* find me.' whispered the young female, clearly fearful of waking the sleeping males.

'No, they will not.'

'You cannot know that.'

'Yes, I can – I have *seen* it.'

'You are a *scrier*!' said the female loudly, inadvertently raising her voice.

One of the sleeping revellers rolled over in their cot, cradling a ceramic jug, the vessel that was likely the cause of their inebriation. The jug fell from its owner's grasp, breaking noisily upon the floor.

'Go, NOW!' she said as the intoxicated Freylarkin started to come around.

'What about you?'

'Do not concern yourself about me. Now go! Find another who would take you in.'

The young female quickly fled the room, leaving her alone with the three males. She closed the door behind her, before dragging a small table nearby across its entrance, barricading the broken door firmly shut. Turning her attention back to the room's occupants, the male who had dropped the shattered jug now stood by the side of his cot, struggling to make sense of the situation.

'Who are you?' he said, 'What are you doing here?'

'I am here to balance the scales.' she replied, dropping her cowl, allowing him to see her face in the gloom.

The bleary-eyed male rubbed encrusted rheum from his eyes, allowing him to see her more clearly.

'You are that scrier! The one who--'

'My chequered past is of no concern to you. What is of concern, however, is the manner in which you will leave this room.' she intervened, revealing her left hand, or rather her bronze mechanical claw – no longer a thing of flesh and bone.

'WAKE UP!' screamed the alarmed male, who by now was sober enough to discern the intent behind her words. 'Get up you fools!'

She strode towards the panicked male, who raised his arms in a pathetic attempt to block her attack. She grabbed one of his arms using her claw, clamping down on it hard with her vicious talon. The bone in his arm snapped under the pressure of her grip, causing him to cry out in pain. She forced him back, causing his bare feet to tread agonizingly upon the broken pieces of ceramic littering the floor. He cried out again in pain, his feet cruelly cut to ribbons by the shards of ceramic slicing into both of his feet.

'Please, have mercy on me.'

'As you showed *her*?'

'We have not touched her!'

'Lies, and in any event, the young female who I have liberated from your cruel *hospitality* is not the one of whom I speak.'

She violently pushed the male back onto his cot, before swinging her claw backwards, easily foreseeing the attack to her rear courtesy of her second sight. She caught one of the male's inebriated companions flush, sending them reeling back in pain. Her fresh opponent's face caved in under the force of the impact, the nose and left cheekbone crushed by the violent backhanded strike. The injured male staggered backwards, clutching his ruined face whilst howling in pain. The third male immediately juddered towards her with a jug raised in his right hand. He hurled the ceramic container towards her head, causing it to smash across the back of her claw, which she hastily raised to shield her face. Liquid and shattered pieces of ceramic sprayed across the room, covering the floor with further detritus. Her newest assailant advanced menacingly towards her, only to receive her right foot to his groin. The drunk Freylarkin doubled over in pain, courtesy of the low blow, allowing her to bring her bronze claw up under his chin. The male's head snapped backwards with a loud crack, immediately after which his body crumpled to the floor in a heap, his lower jaw no longer attached to his head. The second male, whose face she had ruined, stumbled towards her brandishing a ceramic shard hurriedly snatched from the floor. The other male, now to her back, leapt up, sliding his good arm around her throat in a foolish attempt to restrain her. Bringing her right knee forward slightly, she violently kicked her heel back and up, delivering the same paralysing blow that had allowed her to send his comrade to the Everlife. Once again, the unfortunate male fell back down onto his cot, affording her time to deal with the incoming ceramic blade. She grabbed her opponent's hand as it struck, crushing his fingers around the sharp object in his grasp, forcing him to cry out in agony whilst he dropped to his knees.

'What do you want?' cried the miserable wretch, struggling to pronounce his words properly due to his ruined face.

'Justice!'

She swung her left arm once more towards the male's head, annihilating the little that remained. The force of the brutal impact sent his bloodied corpse rolling across the floor, leaving a trail of scarlet in its wake.

Two of her three assailants had been released, allowing her to focus her attention on the one yet remaining. The surviving male cowered on his cot, shaking, his legs drawn close to his chest in a fetal position. Blood trickled from his ruined feet, cut to ribbons by the sharp ceramic littering the floor. His right arm was clearly broken, evidenced by the horrid angle in which it lay.

'What *justice* is worth this?' whispered the male, whilst sobbing miserably.

'Do not beg for my forgiveness – you will find none. You and your abhorrent companions have committed unforgivable acts, ones that left scars on your victims that would never heal.'

'We offered shelter to those without it.'

'At what price? You forced yourselves on the vulnerable, preying upon their insecurities!'

'Name one!' whimpered the male, giving her a spiteful glare. 'Where is your proof?'

'She was petite, with raven black hair.'

Her broken victim took a moment to consider her words, searching his frightened mind for the one whom she described.

'She was nothing.' the male eventually replied, 'Unlike the ones who you just released! That runt was just another stray, a waif with no place to go. What concern is she to you?'

'She *was* my lover!'

'Then go be with the wretch and leave me be.'

'I cannot – you took her away from me! Your deplorable actions poisoned her mind. The trauma you subjected her to caused her to hate our kin, irrevocably. It was that hatred that fuelled her need for vengeance; she was unable to let it go.'

'Is one so insignificant worth the release of three Freylarkai?'

'The entire vale felt her wrath! She released hundreds because of *your* actions, moreover given that our former queen did nothing to balance the scales – an oversight I now intend to correct.'

'She was just a waif! There is no evidence to support your allegations!' replied the scared male, who began to shake uncontrollably.

'You are wrong – I have *seen* it!'

'You cannot lay this at my feet. I am not responsible for her actions.' the frightened male continued, pulling his knees in tighter as she approached. 'I do not even know her name!'

'I will refresh your memory, for her name will be the last word that you ever hear.' she said, raising her bronze mechanical claw, now steeped in gore. 'Her name was Lileah.'

– www.thechroniclesoffreylar.com –

If you enjoyed volume four of The Chronicles of Freylar, I would greatly appreciate an online review from you on the Amazon store. You can also 'Become a Blade Aspirant' on the website and join the ranks of The Blades.

DRAMATIS PERSONAE

Ruling Council of Freylar
Kirika 'Fate Weaver', Valkyrie
Marcus 'The Blade Lord', Paladin –
Commander of The Blades
Mirielle, Queen

The Blades
Dumar, Blade Novice –
The Vengeful Tears
Lothnar, Paladin
Natalya, Valkyrie
Nathanar, Paladin
Nathaniel 'The Teacher', Blade Master
Rayna 'The Guardian', Blade Adept
Thandor, Paladin

Knights Thranis
Anika, Knight
Falkai, Knight
Gedrick, Knight Captain
Heldran, Knight Lord
Loredan, Knight Restorant
Vorian, Knight
Xenia, Knight
Zephir, Knight

House Guard
Ralnor, Guard

Deceased Freylarkai
Alarielle, Blade Adept
Caleth, Blade Lord
Hanarah, Store Proprietor
Katrin, Knight
Korlith, Knight Lord
Kryshar, Blade Aspirant
Morin, Knight
Ragnar, Paladin –
Captain of The Blades
Riknar, Fisherman

Civilian Freylarkai
Aleska, Retired Valkyrie
Cora, Store Proprietor
Gaelin, Farmstead Leader
Galadrick,
Kayla, Administrative Aide
Keshar,
Krasus,
Larissa, Dressmaker

Exiled Freylarkai
Darlia
Krashnar
Lileah

Soulmancers
T'mohr

Dire Wolves
Krisis

Orders
Knights Thranis
The Blades

Races
Freylarkai
Narlakai
Ravnarkai
Soulmancers

Humans
Austin 'Trix'
Callum 'Fox'
Kaitlin Delarouse